THE MINDMAGE'S WRATH

A BOOK OF UNDERREALM

GARRETT ROBINSON

THE MINDMAGE'S WRATH
Garrett Robinson

The author greatly appreciates you taking the time to read his work. Please leave a review wherever you bought the book or on Goodreads.com.

Interior Design: Legacy Books, Inc.
Publisher: Legacy Books, Inc.
Editors: Karen Conlin, Cassie Dean
Cover Artist: Sarayu Ruangvesh

1. Fantasy - Epic 2. Fantasy - Dark 3. Fantasy - New Adult

Second Edition

Published by Legacy Books

LEGACY

To my family
Who make everything I do better

To Johnny, Sean and Dave
Who told me to write

To Amy
Who is endlessly patient (though I don't deserve it)

And to everyone who followed me
from the Birchwood to the Academy

You have made my life epic.

I hope I can enrich yours.

GET MORE

Legacy Books is home to the very best that fantasy has to offer.

Join our email alerts list, and we'll send word whenever we release a new book. You'll receive exclusive updates and see behind the scenes as we create them.

(You'll also learn the secrets that make great fantasy books, *great*.)

Interested? Visit this link:

Underrealm.net/Join

For maps of the locations in this book, visit:

Underrealm.net/maps

THE BOOKS OF UNDERREALM

THE NIGHTBLADE EPIC
NIGHTBLADE
MYSTIC
DARKFIRE
SHADEBORN
WEREMAGE
YERRIN

THE ACADEMY JOURNALS
THE ALCHEMIST'S TOUCH
THE MINDMAGE'S WRATH
THE FIREMAGE'S VENGEANCE

CHRONOLOGICAL ORDER
NIGHTBLADE
MYSTIC
DARKFIRE
SHADEBORN
THE ALCHEMIST'S TOUCH
THE MINDMAGE'S WRATH
WEREMAGE
THE FIREMAGE'S VENGEANCE
YERRIN

THE MINDMAGE'S WRATH

A BOOK OF UNDERREALM

GARRETT ROBINSON

ONE

ONCE, A NEW INSTRUCTOR AT THE ACADEMY WOULD have been the talk of the school for days, but now the count of corpses made her unremarkable.

Indeed, Ebon only knew about Perrin, of the family Arkus, because he was to be her pupil. A woman named Lupa had once taught second-year alchemists, but she had perished in the attack upon the High King's Seat, falling beneath the blades of the grey-and-blue-clad warriors who had struck from the west, who some said were called Shades.

In the weeks since that battle, Ebon was surprised

to see how quickly the Academy had resumed its routine. But repetition could not entirely wipe away the memories. Meals were now muted affairs, and students whispered to each other beneath nervous eyes. Too often, instructors mistakenly called upon students whose seats were empty, and classrooms fell to mournful silence. Too often, Ebon passed other students in the common room, tucked into a corner chair, weeping beyond comfort at the loss of a friend.

Too often, Ebon's thoughts drifted back to the day of the attack, and he saw flesh turn to stone beneath his fingers.

The High King had tripled the guard upon the Seat, and watchfires never ceased their burning in the towers that looked west and east across the Great Bay. The larger part of the Selvan army was now stationed upon the island. Once that would have filled it to bursting, but now there were many empty buildings to house them. Droves of students had been called home despite the increased guard, their parents no longer confident in the strength of the Academy's granite walls. This despite the fact that the Academy had largely been untouched in the fighting. Only one other structure had stood so firm: the High King's palace, bloodstained but unbroken.

"I heard that the High King slipped through the Shades like a thief in the night and led the escape to Selvan's shores," Kalem murmured. He, Ebon, and Theren sat in the nearly-silent dining hall, eyeing their food without eating it. The boy's copper hair stuck out in all directions, for he had roused late that morning.

"And the Lord Prince with her, thank the sky," said Ebon. He had heard the same tale. These days, rumors flew like wind through the Academy halls. It had begun to weary him. He picked at a stain on the table, causing grime to collect beneath his fingernail.

"Thank the sky," echoed Kalem, who seemed not to notice Ebon's mood.

"If you say so," said Theren. She rolled her shoulder and slowly moved her arm in a wide circle. It had been injured in the attack and was only recently free from its sling. Sometimes it still pained her. "Yet she could not stop the sacking of the island, and still she has not struck back against Dulmun. Her flight could be taken for cowardice."

Kalem's hand tightened to a fist, and he glared at her. "You would rather she had fallen in the palace? Then Dulmun would have won, and there would be no rebuilding now. The nine kingdoms would be in chaos."

Theren tossed her short bob of hair. She had not renewed its dye in some time, and her dark roots were beginning to show. "Dulmun *did* win. And do you mean to say that the kingdoms are not already in chaos? Half seem to waver on the brink of joining the rebellion."

"If the other kings have no wish for war, that does not make them cowards, nor traitors." Kalem lifted his chin, freckled nose twitching. "And besides, we from Hedgemond have pledged our strength to the High King."

"Your kingdom sits a half-world away. It could not be farther from the war," said Theren. "Not for nothing is Dulmun's army so feared. If your king shared a border with them, he might not be so eager. I fear the others will join Dulmun before taking up arms against them."

"Hist now," said Ebon, stabbing a spoon into his porridge. "I grow weary of war talk."

But that was not the truth. Ebon hated any reminder of the Shades' attack. Not because of the carnage they had wrought, but because of his own battle, alone save for Adara, on a cliff at the Seat's southern shore. Again his mind showed him flesh turning to stone. The porridge soured in his mouth.

He had not told his friends the truth of that day. Instead, with Adara's help, he had concocted a well-crafted lie. For how could he tell them that the day the Shades attacked the Seat, he had killed the dean—*former* dean, he reminded himself—and his own kin besides?

That truth would not go over well with the King's law or the Academy's faculty. Neither, Ebon suspected, would his friends find it easy to forgive.

"What else would you discuss?" said Theren. "War is all about us."

"Yet it need not consume our lives," Ebon said.

"We still have our studies. Today I shall finally leave Credell's class behind."

"And you have my congratulations," said Kalem. "Almost any instructor would be better than he has been to you. If Lupa were still alive, I should say you would be lucky to fall under her tutelage."

The boy fell silent at the mention of Lupa, his eyes cast down. Theren put a hand on his shoulder, but furtively, as though it were an inconvenience. "Try not to dwell on such thoughts. Let us be grateful for those of us still here."

"As long as we *are* here," Kalem muttered. He froze and darted a quick look at them, as though the words had been an accident.

"What do you mean?" said Ebon, frowning.

"Nothing," said Kalem, staring very hard at his breakfast.

Theren narrowed her eyes and then reached over to pinch the back of Kalem's neck, as though she were a mother cat and he her kitten. "Kalem. What troubles you? Tell me now."

"Ow!" Kalem cried out, batting at her hand. "Leave me be, witch."

Ebon leaned forwards. "Tell us, Kalem."

Kalem sighed and looked at them uneasily. "It is nothing. I will make sure it is nothing. It is only . . . my parents wish to bring me home. Back to Hedgemond."

"What?" said Ebon, eyes widening. "You cannot leave!"

"That is what I have told them," said Kalem. "And so far they have listened. It is only that . . . well, after the attack on the Seat . . . they no longer consider it safe."

"But only the parents of the smallest children are withdrawing them," said Theren scornfully. Then she gave Kalem a sidelong glance. "Although, now that I think of it, your size—"

Kalem swung a fist, which she easily blocked. Ebon gave her a dirty look. "Stop it."

She grinned. "I am sorry. The temptation was too great."

"In any case," Kalem continued, still glaring at her, "thus far I have managed to convince them I am safe here. Indeed, I feel safer at the Academy than I would in my family's own home, what with the war brewing."

"And does your family agree?"

"For now, at least," said Kalem softly. "I am not leaving just yet."

"I wish others' parents would pull them from the school," muttered Ebon. Across the dining hall, Lilith's malicious gaze had caught his eye.

Something had changed in Lilith since the attack on the Seat. Before she had seemed to take Ebon for a joke and had mocked him with open scorn. But now she seemed truly hateful. He knew not why she despised him so, nor what he could do to mitigate it— and he feared what might come of it if he did nothing.

Theren followed his gaze to Lilith, and her countenance grew hard. Turning back, she leaned in close to speak in a low voice. "That reminds me. Have you heard about the vaults?"

Ebon frowned, but Kalem leaned in closer. "I have heard only a rumor."

"It seems something was stolen from them," said Theren. "Though we are not yet certain if it was taken during the attack, or some time after the students returned to the citadel."

"That is like what I heard," said Kalem. "But why do you say *we?*"

"Did you not know? I conduct my servitude in the vaults."

Kalem's eyes widened. But Ebon raised a hand to stay them both. "A moment. As far as I am concerned, you are both speaking in tongues. What servitude? And what are these vaults you speak of?"

"Every student in their sixth year embarks upon servitude in the Academy," said Kalem. "It is meant to teach us the value of simple work in the service of others. Also we are paired with advanced wizards with many years of experience, so that we may learn from them."

"And what are the vaults?"

"They are rooms buried deep within the Academy's bowels," said Theren. "Within them are contained magical artifacts of thousands of years of history. Some predate the Academy itself."

Ebon opened his mouth to ask another question,

but Kalem spoke first, and eagerly. "What was it that the thief stole?"

"An artifact, but which one, we do not know," said Theren. "I have spent the last several days trying to find out. But I cannot find the records for the room where the theft occurred."

"What are these artifacts?" said Ebon. "What do they do?"

"Wizards of great power can imbue objects with magical qualities," said Kalem. "These can perform some small bits of magic even without a wizard's power. Some are little more than baubles. But others, especially older ones, often carry the power of the Wizard Kings."

"And that is what made me think of the theft when you were staring your daggers at Lilith," said Theren. "You see, she—"

But just then, the bell tolled, signaling the start of morning classes. Theren looked across the dining hall, where Lilith was collecting her dishes for the kitchen.

"Damn. We should speak more of this, for there is much to tell. This afternoon, in the library." She shot to her feet and scooped up her plates with a simple mindspell, suspending them in the air as she weaved her way through the dining hall.

"The library? But . . ." Kalem's voice trailed away, for she was already gone. He and Ebon rose more slowly, scooping their dishes up with their hands. But as Ebon found his feet and turned, he ran hard into another student, and all their dishes fell to the stone floor together.

"Sky," spat Ebon, trying to brush remnants of egg and porridge from his sleeve. Then he looked up and blanched. He stared into the dark eyes of a girl he had met before. He had seen her in his common room on his first day in the Academy. When he had tried to befriend her, she had crushed an iron goblet before his eyes.

"I am sorry," stammered Ebon.

"Why should you be?" said the girl, her voice an apathetic monotone. "It was an accident. I was behind you anyway."

Her eyes glowed, and Ebon braced himself for a blow. But instead, his dishes sprang up from the floor and into his hands, while the girl's flew into her own. She sauntered off without a word. Ebon let out a sigh.

Kalem snickered beside him. "I was afraid you would soil your underclothes. Why are you so afraid of that one?"

"I met her the day I arrived. She was . . . much less friendly, then. She crushed a goblet of iron like it was parchment, and I thought I saw ill will in her eyes."

Kalem shrugged. "Well, she is a powerful mind-mage, and no mistake. Isra, I believe her name is. But she is not so fearsome as you make her out to be. And after the attack on the Seat, I think any ill will between students has fled the Academy's halls."

"Not so with Lilith."

"No, I suppose not."

They shuffled with the other students towards the kitchens to discard their bowls, and then the assembly passed muted and mournful into the halls. Theren joined them outside the dining hall, and just before Ebon left for the first-years' classroom, he gave his friends a wan smile.

"Wish me good fortune," he said.

"You do not need it," said Theren. "Or if you do, then you should not be graduating in the first place."

"That is not helpful," Kalem said, scowling at Theren. "Good fortune, Ebon."

TWO

OLDER STUDENTS PEELED AWAY AS EBON MADE HIS way towards Credell's class, and the crowd around him grew ever younger. He quite looked forwards to having older classmates soon. Credell's students were all first-years, children of ten or eleven. The next class would bring only one year's improvement, but Ebon hoped he would look a little less out of place.

He reached Credell's classroom and stepped through the door. The instructor had not yet arrived, but many students had, and in the front row he saw little wild-haired Astrea—the only student in his class to befriend him. She brightened at the sight of him and waved eagerly. He gave her a small smile and waved back, ruffling her hair and making her giggle as he made his way to the back row of benches.

More first- and second-years had been withdrawn from the Academy than from among the older children. Astrea was one of only six left in the class, besides Ebon himself. It made him wonder why they did not combine this class and the next into one. But then he realized Credell would teach him for two years if that were the case, and he shuddered.

Credell arrived at last. He gave the room a quick look, his eyes lingering for a moment upon Ebon. Since the attack on the Seat, Credell's fear seemed to have lessened somewhat. Yet still the instructor jumped when Ebon spoke too loudly or moved too quickly.

"Well, ah, class. Ahem," said Credell. "Normally I would have you all resume your lessons. But today we have a matter of ceremony we must attend to first. Ah, er . . . Ebon, would you please approach the front of the classroom?"

Ebon slid down his bench and went forwards, acutely aware of the other students staring at him. Many of them had been there months longer than Ebon, and he could feel their awe that he had graduated so swiftly. He wondered if he would have been ready for this first test so quickly, if it had not been for Cyrus.

Credell held forth a wooden rod, careful not to

brush Ebon's fingers with his own as he handed it over. Ebon turned to the class, holding the rod high. He felt the grain of it beneath his fingers, the tiny ridges and valleys of its form. In his mind's eye, he peered *into* the wood itself, seeing its true nature, the countless tiny parts that composed it—

—*his hand wrapped around Cyrus' ankle, the spark of power within him, flesh turning to stone*—

—he squeezed his eyes shut, shaking his head to banish the images. They faded, but reluctantly. The rod was still wooden. Now Credell and the students were staring at him expectantly.

Ebon drew a deep breath through his nose and released it slowly from his lips. He focused on the wood again.

And then the room grew brighter—or at least it appeared to, for Ebon's eyes were glowing. He saw the wood for what it was. And then he changed it.

Pure, simple stone, grey and lifeless and solid, rippled from his fingers. In a moment it was done, and the rod had been turned. Around the room, children reached up to scratch at their necks, or shook their heads as though repulsing a fly. Ebon knew they could sense his magic, though many of them had not yet learned to use it themselves. Wizards could always detect spells from their own branch, or from the mirror branch.

"Well done," said Credell, his relief plain. Clearly he was as eager to be rid of Ebon as Ebon was to leave the class. He reached out and awkwardly patted the boy on his shoulder. Ebon returned the rod. With a flourish of his fingers, Credell turned it back into wood.

"Class, you have borne witness. Ebon has mastered the first test of the transmuter, and has moved beyond us. Rise now, and let us escort him to his new instructor."

The children rose silent and solemn, filing into a line in the room's center. Credell led them into the halls. They passed several doors—the first-year classes of the other branches of magic—before reaching one where Credell stopped. He tapped out a trio of soft knocks.

"Come in!" commanded a woman's voice, thick and rich and full of power. Credell nearly dropped the rod in fright, so sudden was her call. But he swallowed hard and opened the door. Ebon followed him inside.

This room had a window overlooking the training grounds, and for a moment the morning's light made Ebon blink and shield his eyes. Once they adjusted, he looked about. The room was much the same as Credell's: two files of benches stretching from the front to the back, every one with its own desk, and a handful of students scattered among them. But many bookshelves were lined against the wall with the door, filled with thick leather tomes of every description. Ebon was surprised. He had not seen any other classrooms with bookshelves. He had thought the Academy's books were all harbored in its vast library. The thought of yet more things to read set his head spinning.

Then Ebon looked to the front of the room, and his heart skipped a beat. There behind the lectern was, quite simply, the most massive woman he had ever seen. Her shoulders seemed to stretch as wide as Ebon's arm span, and though the ceiling was at least a pace above her head, her stature made it seem that she might bump against it. Huge hands gripped the lectern's edges and nearly enveloped it, and her dark grey instructor's robes strained mightily to contain her frame. Her eyes seemed small compared to the rest of her ruddy features, yet they sparkled with interest even when the sunlight missed them. Ebon thought this woman looked nothing like a wizard, but rather a mighty warrior of campfire legend, stripped of armor and shrouded instead in cloth, against which her body tried to rebel.

"This is the new one, then? Well, come in, boy. I am Perrin, of the family Arkus. Let us get your test seen to, for I was just introducing myself to the other students."

"Erm . . . ah . . . yes," said Credell, quaking as hard as he ever had when confronting Cyrus, the former dean. "E-E-Ebon, here you are. T-take it."

Ebon took the wooden rod, which Credell had extended in trembling fingers. He brought it to Perrin and waited.

"Well? Go on. You have done it once already—or should have, before you were brought here."

Ebon nodded, at a loss for words. He turned to the class and held the rod aloft. This time, shock at Perrin's appearance kept his thoughts from drifting to Cyrus. His eyes glowed, and stone rippled along the rod.

"Good!" said Perrin. She clapped her hands, and the sound was like thunder. "And can you change it back?"

The blood drained from Ebon's face. "I—what? No, I only—"

"Oh, calm yourself," said Perrin, waving him off. "I only asked from curiosity—it is not a requirement. Now, be seated quickly. Or, no, that is not right. Remain here. There is the ceremony, is there not?"

She stepped out from behind the lectern—revealing boots that Ebon could have fit both feet into—and approached Credell. The craven little instructor quailed as Perrin thrust the rod towards him.

"Do you vow that you have instructed this pupil to the best of your ability, in judgement as well as in skill?"

"I . . . I so vow," whimpered Credell, taking the rod. He made a brave, but ultimately futile attempt to straighten his shoulders. "Do you vow that you will continue his instruction, in judgement as well as in skill, to the best of your ability?"

"I so vow. Now, as I said, I have scarcely been able to speak to my new students. If you do not mind."

Perrin reached out and threw the door open. Then, quickly—but not unkindly—she ushered Credell's class through it. Ebon caught one last glimpse of Astrea waving him a happy good-bye before the door shut between them.

"Well, then. Find yourself a seat. There are many open benches—too many, it is a tragedy to say. Sit near the front, for I shall have to work with you first, or else you will no doubt wander like a hatchling without its mother."

Ebon nodded and made for a seat. One bench in the second row was entirely unoccupied, and he slid onto it. Perrin returned to the lectern and cleared her throat into a meaty fist.

"Now, then. Welcome, ah . . . hrm. What was your name?"

"Ebon, of the family—" He stopped short. He had not meant to mention his family name. But now Perrin was peering at him, and he could feel the other students' curiosity at his pause. He gritted his teeth. "Of the family Drayden."

If Perrin thought anything of it, she gave no sign, though Ebon thought he felt several students stiffen. "Well then, welcome, Ebon. I will say to you what I told the class before your arrival: I do not know you, and you do not know me. Yet I knew something of your former instructor, Lupa, for she was only a few years behind me when I myself studied here. A good woman. But you are left with me, for which I apologize. You deserve someone wiser, more powerful in transmutation, and certainly a good deal more patient. Those things I cannot promise you. But this I can vow: I will do my best to make of you what I can, and help you along your road to knowledge. And I can promise you what the High King Enalyn, sky bless her name, has promised us all: I will keep you safe with my every breath. I will serve you to the limits of my power. And I will—"

A sharp rapping came at the door, and Perrin stopped short. She glowered, hands gripping the lectern tighter for a moment. "Come in, and be quick!" The bark in her voice made every student in the room jump.

The door swung open, and in swept the Academy's new dean, Xain of the family Forredar. He was a lank man and sun-pale under his dark skin, with thin black hair hanging down to his shoulders. His dark grey robes bore no ornamentation as the former dean's had, and yet somehow Xain looked far more impressive in them. It was something in his eyes, Ebon decided. They were haunted, yes, and yet they bore also a steely resolve. Though his frame was slight, and could have appeared frail, there was a set to his shoulders that spoke of grim determination.

It was a moment before Ebon realized that Xain was not alone. Beside him was a boy who could not have been more than ten years of age. Ebon wondered if he was a new student at the Academy—until he saw the boy's dark eyes and pinched nose. They were the same as Xain's. He had to be a relation, mayhap even his son.

Though Perrin had answered gruffly at Xain's knock, she now beamed a warm smile. "Good morn, Dean Forredar. We are honored by your presence."

"No more than the Academy is honored by yours, Perrin. Instructor Arkus, I mean. Forgive me—my tongue has nearly forgotten the Academy's courtesies."

He stepped forwards and extended a hand. Perrin clasped his wrist firmly. "And mine the same. Though no great surprise, considering the years."

Xain nodded and turned to the class. His tone grew brisk, though not entirely unfriendly. "Greetings, students. You know who I am, or something of me, at least. But I would wager you have had little chance to know your new instructor, and thus you cannot understand the honor you have been granted. Perrin of the family Arkus is as good a woman as I have ever met. I hope you will afford her your utmost attention and your most earnest effort."

"The dean is far too kind," replied Perrin, stifling a smile. "Though I will not deny you should heed his advice, if ever you wish to pass this class. And who have you brought with you? This cannot be little Erin."

"It is, though not so little anymore." Xain beckoned the boy forwards. Erin came timidly, balking at the instructor's great size. But Perrin stooped until she was nearly at eye level with the boy and gravely reached for his hand.

"It is my pleasure to meet you, young sir. And my heart is gladdened to see you by your father's side again."

Erin smiled bashfully. "Thank you, madam." His voice was so soft, Ebon could hardly hear it from where he sat.

"I did not mean to distract you all," said Xain, his eyes roving the room. "I am only showing him about the Academy and could not pass without stopping to see you. I expect you—"

Xain's glance fell upon Ebon, and there it stopped. He grew rigid as a board, hands tightening to fists by his sides. Ebon felt hot blood flooding his cheeks, though he knew not why.

"You there," said Xain, nearly spitting the words. "What is your name?"

"E-Ebon, Dean Forredar."

"Your family name," he snapped.

The color that had flooded Ebon's face drained away at once. "I am of the family Drayden, Dean."

Xain gave no answer. But his hand went to Erin's shoulder and drew him close, as if to shield him. A moment longer he stared, and Ebon could not mistake the look in his eye: hatred, fiery and pure, more so even than Lilith had shown. Then at last Xain turned away.

"Good day," he said tersely, and swept from the room with his son in tow.

Slowly, every eye turned to Ebon in wonder. Even Perrin gave him a hard look. Ebon's gaze fell to his desk, and he stewed in a shame that he did not understand.

THREE

THE REST OF THE MORNING CLASS PASSED QUICKLY, IF uncomfortably. Ebon tried to pay attention as Perrin laid out the studies he would need to complete, and he retrieved a book from the shelves at the instructor's commands. But though he sat for hours staring at the first page, the words had become a blur before his eyes. He could see only Xain's dark gaze, gleaming with unknown malice.

When at last the bell rang for midday meal, Ebon shot from his bench. But just as he reached the door, Perrin bellowed to stop him.

"Ebon! Return your book to its place on the shelf."

Ebon turned sheepishly to do as he was bid. Several other students had been about to leave their books out as well, but quickly they scrambled to return them. Though he might have imagined it, Ebon thought he felt Perrin's careful eye upon him as he returned the book and fled the room. Only then did he break into a run, flying through the citadel towards the dining hall.

He found Kalem and Theren standing in the food line and fell into place beside them. He had little desire to eat, but neither did he want to be alone. Something of his mood must have shown in his face, for Kalem frowned in concern.

"What is wrong? You look as though you woke this morning to find yourself a wizard no longer."

"Oh, it is no great matter," said Ebon bitterly. "Only that the new dean seems to despise me even more than the old one, and just as with Cyrus, I have no faintest idea why."

"What?" said Theren, arching an eyebrow. "What do you mean?"

Ebon told them all that had happened, doing his best to convey in words the hatred he had felt in Xain's eyes. Kalem shook his head mournfully.

"That seems ill fortune. I wonder what it is all about?"

But Theren rolled her eyes. "I think you may be imagining things, Ebon. It seems far-fetched that he could so quickly detest you. Though I have no doubt he will learn to, once he knows you better."

"This is no jest," said Ebon irritably. "You doubted me when I told you of Dean Cyrus' treatment. Do you recall how that turned out?" His body still bore the fading bruises from when Cyrus attacked him.

As Theren's eyes fell in shame, Ebon's guilt grew in response. She felt remorse that she had let Cyrus strike Ebon with his mindmagic. But she did not know what Ebon had done to the dean on the day of the attack. That secret was his alone—and Adara's, of course. His mood softened at that thought.

"I apologize," Theren said quietly. "If you say that is what happened, I believe you."

"Think nothing of it," Ebon muttered, unable to meet her eyes.

"If Xain indeed has animosity towards you, there must be some reason," said Kalem. "I will see if anyone knows what it might be. In truth, I know little of the man, beyond the fact he is favored by the High King herself."

"I shall ask about as well," said Theren. "Though I do not have many friends."

At the front of the line, they fetched their food and sat to eat without speaking further. But Ebon's appetite had gone from little to nothing, and he could not force himself to eat much of the soup. He gnawed at his bread instead, chewing until it was a soggy mess in his mouth.

Theren scooped up the last of her soup, slurping it

noisily, and then shoved the bowl away. "A fair meal today. I think they have started cooking better since we returned to the Academy. No doubt in an attempt to raise our spirits."

"Or they are more liberal with their spices, since they have fewer mouths to feed," muttered Kalem.

Theren snorted and punched his shoulder. "Still such dark words! That sounds like something I might say. Here is something that might cheer you: I have changed my schedule. Hereafter, I shall spend my afternoons in the library with you."

Kalem grinned. "So that is why you said we would speak in the library this afternoon. I had wondered."

Ebon, too, found his mood lifted. But then a thought struck him, and he frowned. "I thought you were no fan of book learning."

"Of course not," said Theren, pursing her lips. "I am not joining you because I wish to study with you, but because I do not want my afternoons to be so incredibly dull."

Ebon and Kalem stifled groans as they looked sidelong at each other. Ebon would be glad for Theren's company, but he enjoyed the peace of his time in the library. Many hours had he and Kalem whiled away, tucked into their armchairs with books of ancient lands and Wizard Kings.

"Well, we will certainly enjoy your presence," said Kalem. But Ebon could hear that his heart was not in the words.

"Of course you will," said Theren. "And that reminds me. This morning we were speaking of Lilith, and of the theft in the vaults. I meant to tell you that—"

Someone stopped behind Ebon, abruptly enough that their shoes squeaked upon the stone.

"The vaults."

Ebon turned. Behind him stood Credell. The thin-faced, wheedling instructor wore a vacant look. He turned to them all, his eyes fixed on Theren. "The vaults," he repeated.

"Yes, Instructor?" She raised her eyebrows. "My servitude is in the vaults. What of it?"

"I had almost forgotten." Credell's voice was absent its customary shake, and his nervous tics had disappeared. "I must enter the vaults. Give me your key."

Kalem looked uncertainly at Theren. She met the boy's eyes and gave a barely perceptible shrug. "Instructor, I have no key. It is only given to me during my servitude, and only when I must enter the vaults themselves."

"The vaults," he said, more urgent this time. "I must enter them. Give me your key."

Now Theren was growing exasperated. "I do not have one," she said, very nearly snapping at him. "Besides, you are an Instructor. If you have Academy business within the vaults, you can enter them yourself. Egil will admit you. But I do not have the key."

Her last words crackled, and Credell jumped at

last. He blinked twice, and then looked down as if noticing Ebon at his elbow for the first time. He drew back as if from a viper, wringing his hands just under his chin.

"Ah, yes, of course," he stuttered. "Of course you have no key. Silly of me. I had forgotten. I do not know why . . . why I thought you . . . er, I am sorry. Good day."

He turned and left, winding away through the tables. All three of them kept their eyes fixed upon his back until he was out of sight.

"That was most odd," said Kalem.

"Bizarre," agreed Theren. "I wonder if he is all right. After the attack upon the Seat, I mean. War can break one's mind, they say."

"He seemed well enough the past few days in class," said Ebon quietly. "That was unlike I have ever seen him . . . and yet, not worse. He was less frightened. More sure."

"Mayhap he is finally growing a spine." Theren shrugged and seemed to dismiss the matter. "In any case, I was speaking of the theft."

"Of course," said Ebon. "What news have you?"

"Well, few students perform their servitude in the vaults. But Lilith is another."

"The both of you?" said Kalem. "I am amazed the Academy is still standing, if the two of you have been in such close quarters so long."

Theren glared at him. "I can control myself when

I wish to. And besides, we are rarely present together. The caretaker, Egil, almost never requires two students at once."

"Yes, well and good about all of that," said Ebon, waving her words aside. "But what of Lilith? What does she have to do with it?"

"I have had a thought brewing," said Theren. "Mayhap it was some member of the Academy's faculty who carried out the theft. But it could also have been a student. And if it were a student, who better than one who performs their servitude in the vaults? Such a one would know better than any other how to do it."

Kalem looked at Ebon, his brow creased with doubt. "That seems a far reach, Theren. What student would dare risk such a thing? Even Academy faculty might think twice about trying to breach the vault's defenses."

"Yet many of us are more powerful than our instructors," said Theren. "I am stronger than any mind-mage here, especially now that Cyrus has vanished. Lilith is at least as great as any firemage on the faculty—though, I say that without knowing the new dean's measure. He may be a great firemage, for all I know."

Talk of Cyrus had begun to make Ebon uncomfortable, so he steered the topic away. "I hear little evidence beyond 'It could be so,' Theren. And I do not know if even that is true, for Lilith was far away when the attack occurred. How could she have carried out such a theft from another kingdom?"

"She said she left the Academy, yes," said Theren. "But what if she lied? What better alibi?"

"Ebon is right," Kalem said. "If that is your only proof, it is flimsy indeed."

Theren frowned. "It is at least a place to start."

"To start what?" said Ebon.

She looked at him with wide eyes, as though the answer was obvious. "Why, to find the thief, of course."

Kalem gawked. "No. No, we are not engaging in another mad scheme, Theren. If the theft is indeed a matter of great worry, then let us—"

But just then the bell rang, and the dining hall filled with the sound of scraping benches as students stood from their meals. Almost chipper, Theren jumped up to bring her dishes to the kitchen. Kalem growled and followed her.

Ebon went with them, but he stopped and looked over his shoulder one final time. Credell stood in the doorway of the dining hall, looking about with a far-away gaze. One hand stole up to scratch at the skin beneath his collar. He shivered as though cold and then vanished into the hallways.

It is no matter, thought Ebon. *You have left his class, and he is no longer your concern.*

Yet a chill crept up his spine as he followed his friends to the kitchen.

FOUR

Later, in the library, Kalem and Ebon introduced Theren to their nook on the third level. Predictably, she seemed to think it boring. She dragged another chair over to join them and draped her feet across the table in their midst. Kalem snatched books from beneath her shoes with a scandalized expression, and soon both he and Ebon were grinding their teeth as they tried to read, for Theren seemed far more interested in talking. Though they tried to give her only short, one-word replies, and thus dissuade her from speaking, Theren refused to take the hint.

Soon Ebon felt himself at the breaking point. He leapt to his feet and scuttled away towards the bookshelves, muttering something about finding another reference book for a report he was writing for Instructor Jia.

Once safely ensconced in the bookshelves and out of earshot of Theren's endless chatter, Ebon sighed in relief. Leaning around the shelf's edge, he saw Theren still going on animatedly to Kalem, while the poor boy shoved his nose very nearly into the spine of his book. Ebon chuckled and ducked out of sight.

"How heartwarming to see the three of you united in your pursuit of wisdom."

The words made Ebon jump, but then he recognized Mako's voice. He softly chuckled and turned to find the bodyguard behind him, leaning against one of the shelves. Mako was clad all in black, black shirt beneath an even darker leather vest, and tight leggings that paraded his wiry muscles. Black, too, were the scabbards at his waist, where his long and cruel daggers rested.

"Mako. It has been some time since last you visited me."

"Well, war blazes across Underrealm." Mako waved an airy hand. "I have been here and there and most places in between."

"And now you return. To what do I owe the honor?"

"To this," said Mako, reaching within his vest and producing a letter.

Ebon shook his head and took it. He had never

fully understood Mako's role within the Drayden family's business, and it still confounded him every time he saw the bodyguard running messages like a simple courier. The letter bore his family's seal, and Ebon's heart skipped at the thought that it might be from his father. But no, Shay Drayden had a personal seal. Ebon peeled the letter open.

Dearest Brother,

There are not words in all the tongues of the nine lands to describe how angry I am with you. Why is it that the first letter I received from you did not come until the High King's enemies had invaded the Seat? Two months you had to write me a letter, and yet you did nothing. You are an inconsiderate lout and a brute besides.
That said, I am, of course, so very glad to hear you were not harmed in the fighting. But only one way may you retain my good humor towards you! If you write me back, at once and without delay! I know <u>nothing</u> of your time at the Academy so far and it is <u>unbearable</u>.
Of course, your letter may very well find me upon the road, rather than at home. For yes, we are traveling, dear brother! Even now, we make ready to travel to the

Seat to visit you. (Well, we do not come only to visit you, but of course we will visit you while we are there.) Are you not excited? It will be wonderful to see your face again, inconsiderate and selfish as you might be.

Write me at once, dear Ebon. Send it back with Mako if you can, but send it quickly in any case. And be ready to visit me on the Seat, for I have a thousand and one questions.

With love,
Albi

Ebon was weeping almost from the moment he recognized his sister's frenetic scrawl upon the parchment, and he laughed with every insult, for he could almost hear the way she would deliver them. Her nose would be scrunched up tight, as it was when she grew angry or excited, and her brow would be furrowed, and she would plant her fists on her hips just so, moving them only to brandish them before his nose as if ready to strike him.

But though his heart sang at the thought of seeing Albi again, it darkened, too, at the thought of his family. If the Draydens were returning to the Seat, his father would be there as well. Shay had been against Ebon's coming to the Academy from the first. Might he use the attack as an excuse to withdraw him?

Ebon turned to Mako. "Albi says they are coming to the Seat. Do you know when they will arrive?"

"Some time before Yearsend, certainly," said Mako.

"But that is just around the corner."

"Of course it is." Cruelty lurked in Mako's grin, buried behind an indifference that Ebon thought must be feigned. "That means they will be able to celebrate the holiday in your company. Mayhap they can even meet your little Academy friends—though no doubt there are some other, more private friends you would rather keep hidden." His grin widened.

Adara sprang to mind, and Ebon felt color in his cheeks. "I . . . am surprised they would wish to visit the Seat so soon," he said, changing the subject for his own benefit as much as Mako's distraction. "Many think it dangerous here. Some parents are even bringing their children home."

"The attack upon the Seat was a tragedy, no doubt."

"As you say. But that begs a question: how did you learn of it in time to warn me?"

Mako shifted on his feet, uncrossing and recrossing his arms through a moment of silence. "How do you think I learned of it, little Ebon?"

Ebon felt his pulse quicken and his breath came shallow. "Did you hear of it from someone in our family?"

Mako snorted. "A Drayden? No. This may shock you, Ebon, but I have friends outside our clan. Well, I say 'friends,' of course, though they might not agree.

But in any case, brigands and ne'er-do-wells are of a kind, and through us news may travel from one end of Underrealm to the other, faster than a bird's flight."

That was not quite an answer, Ebon realized. "Did the family Drayden have aught to do with the attack?" he pressed. "I . . . just before that day, Cyrus confronted me in a rage. He seemed to think Halab was plotting—"

"If he spoke those words, then he was a fool in truth," said Mako vehemently. "For years I called him scum, and untrustworthy. Halab would not listen. She tried so hard to see the good in him, when I knew there was only pettiness and selfishness and greed. Mayhap even a touch of madness."

Ebon thought of when Cyrus attacked him in the garden, and a phantom pain flared into his ribs. Then his thoughts went to their battle on the cliffs, and he shuddered. "You may be right about that," he murmured.

"To accuse Halab was to prove his ignorance. There are reasons for that, which I cannot explain now, though mayhap the day approaches when I shall. Your father, on the other hand . . ."

He trailed off, and when Ebon looked up he saw the man regarding him with a keen glint in his eye. "What of him? He was the one who had me deliver the parcel to that inn upon the Seat. Are you saying that played some role in the assault?"

Mako laughed, but softly, for they were still in the

library. "Your question is absurd. Not because of its premise, but because you think I would tell you if you were correct."

"That is no answer."

"It is not meant to be." Mako pursed his lips at Ebon's scowl. "Oh, very well. Enough games. You wish for more certainty? Then think upon what you know. Cyrus was a madman. Quite useful to the family, yes—yet prone to baseless fears of being undermined."

"Then he was lying."

"The family Drayden had an agent at the height of power within the Academy. The dean has the ear of the High King herself, and a place upon her council. Would your father leave such a resource upon the Seat to die?" His dark grin returned. "You, mayhap, he would allow to perish. But not Cyrus."

"Very well," Ebon muttered. "I believe that—not for your words, but for the truth you speak of my father."

Mako gave a mocking bow. "You are too gracious, little lord goldbag."

Ebon felt as though a great weight had lifted from his shoulders. If the Draydens had no hand in the attack, then he had played no part by delivering that parcel for his father. But with that worry removed, Ebon's thoughts ran to a more pressing concern.

"I must ask you something else," said Ebon. "What do you know of the Academy's new dean? The replacement for Cyrus?"

The bodyguard's countenance darkened, his upper lip curling in a snarl. "That meddlesome fool. You would do well to stay away from him."

"That choice may not be mine. He has seen me already, and from the moment our eyes met, I felt that he hated me. His malice was like a physical thing, reaching out to grip my throat."

Mako snorted. "How poetic. Yet if I were there, I might not doubt your words. Xain of the family Forredar has much cause to hate the family Drayden. And as it happens, your woes with this dean stem from his troubles with the former."

Ebon blinked. "With Cyrus? What has he to do with this?"

"Everything. You know the dean spends much time within the High King's court. Upon a time, Xain was often in that court as well, along with another mindmage of our clan: a man named Drystan, who you would never have met. Always Drystan and Xain were at odds, for both were powerful wizards of mirror branches, and Xain always gave counsel against Drystan's advice. They had been rivals even from their Academy days, yet it was not until they were both grown that their rivalry blossomed into violence, invited by Xain's own arrogance. There was a duel—a wizard's battle. Drystan received aid from Cyrus, and another, still more powerful wizard. When the duel was finished, someone lay badly hurt, but it was neither of the contestants. Xain's magic spun out of control, striking a bystander with no stake in the fight. The victim was a distant kin of the High King herself."

The blood drained from Ebon's face. "That is no small crime."

"No indeed. Constables and Mystics pursued Xain from the Seat and across all the nine lands. But now, for reasons beyond understanding, the High King herself has pardoned him. Something to do with this war that now engulfs Underrealm, though I have not learned any details. And now that he is ensconced in power again, he hates the family Drayden. He blames us for his own failures, his own weakness. Thus if you have earned his ire, I warn you: hide. He is an eagle, and you are a mouse. Do not provoke him. Do not even speak with him if you can help it."

"I have no wish to spend any more time with him than I must," said Ebon, shivering. But he was thinking of Xain and Cyrus and their duel. What might Xain think if he knew Ebon had killed Cyrus in the end? But now Mako was looking at him keenly, and he forced himself into a steady calm. "But this is an unreasoning cause for hate. I am not Cyrus. What happened to Xain had nothing to do with me."

Mako shrugged. "You are a Drayden, even if not by your choice. Every great family has some dark deeds to their name. And your best intentions do not pardon the actions of your kin."

Ebon sagged against the bookshelf, his head lolling back to strike the leather spines. Another dean whose hatred of him he could neither explain nor hope to alleviate. His life seemed a sad mockery, a jester's play. His hands clenched at his sides.

Mako, for his part, seemed to be reveling in Ebon's discomfort. He smiled again and then straightened. "Well, I came only to deliver a letter. Now I must be on my way. Unless you wish to reply to Albi?"

"It would take me time. I will send it by regular courier. I am grateful for the letter—and for the truth about Xain."

"It was my pleasure, truly," said Mako with a flash of his teeth. But then his eyes drifted past Ebon, and he grew somber. "As for your other question—about the attack on the Seat. You know the Draydens are not the only wealthy family in Underrealm."

He nodded, his gaze still fixed on something over Ebon's shoulder. Ebon turned. There, a few shelves away, was Lilith, half-hidden by gaps in the books.

Ebon turned quickly to Mako. "Are you saying Yerrin was behind the attack?"

Mako shrugged. "I know nothing for certain. Only it seems unlikely that Dulmun and the Shades could have staged such an invasion without the coin of a great merchant house. I will say this: if Halab commanded me to investigate the attack, that is where I would start my search."

And Theren had believed that Lilith might be behind the theft in the vaults.

Mako turned as if to leave, but Ebon reached out

and gripped his arm. It felt like iron. Mako glanced down at Ebon's hand. Ebon gulped, trying to hide a tremor of fear.

"Thank you. I have not had the chance to say that since you saved my life. I may owe you the very beating of my heart, along with the lives of my friends. I have not always thought highly of you, but I see now that that was my mistake."

Mako looked almost startled, which in turn surprised Ebon; the bodyguard rarely showed anything other than contempt and condescension. But his wide grin slid back into place after only a moment, and he flicked two fingers in dismissal. "That is no mistake on your part. Few think highly of me, especially among the wise. And if I saved the lives of some within the Academy, well, then, it was an accident. I had only hoped that you would be around a bit longer, at least. You are so amusing, after all."

He stepped around the corner of the bookshelf and vanished.

FIVE

Ebon returned to Kalem and Theren in their alcove against the wall. Kalem appeared to have given up trying to read. He leaned back with his chin in his hand, listening to Theren as she went on about some new spell she was trying to master. They both looked up at his approach.

"Thank the sky," said Kalem. "It is my turn to go and look for a book."

"What do you mean?" said Theren, frowning. "You cannot tell me the two of you do not enjoy my company. I have changed my entire class schedule for you."

"Theren, I come here to *read,* not to *speak,*" said Kalem.

She seemed about to reply, until she looked up and saw the concern in Ebon's face. "Ebon? What is it?"

Ebon glanced up at her, and then over his shoulder where he had been speaking with Mako. He shifted on his feet, the letter from Albi crinkling in his hand. "Er . . . my family is coming to the Seat," he said, holding the parchment aloft.

Both his friends grew solemn. "Well. That is a pleasant surprise," Kalem said, with visible effort.

"Oh, do not be an idiot, Kalem," said Theren. "When will they come?"

"Some time before Yearsend. But in fact, that is not what troubles me." He sank into a chair between them, his mind racing at how he might tell them without revealing Mako's involvement. "I have been thinking on what you said before. About Lilith being the thief who robbed the Academy vaults."

"Yes?" said Theren, sitting straighter. "Do you believe me now?"

"Let us say that I did," said Ebon. "What would we do about it? What do you know of Lilith?"

Theren frowned. "What makes you think I know anything of her? She is a goldbag, like any other. Well, besides the two of you, mayhap."

Ebon rolled his eyes. "I mean, how might she have done it? Where might she have hidden what she stole?"

Kalem spoke before Theren could answer. "I do not understand, Ebon. Why have you changed your mind so suddenly? Just this morning you agreed with me that there was little evidence pointing to Lilith."

"I have been considering the possibility," Ebon said, hearing Mako in his mind. "And I think it is unlikely that Dulmun would risk open war against the High King, even with the alliance of these Shades—whoever they are—unless they also had the support of one of the great families. A royal family, for your strength of arms, or of a merchant family, for the depth of our purses."

"But there are dozens of merchant families across Underrealm," said Kalem.

"Few have purses deep enough for a civil war," said Theren, leaning forwards in excitement. "Only Drayden or Yerrin could do it. And Yerrin removed their children from the Seat during the attack, while you and Cyrus stayed here. I think I see your mind, Ebon."

Kalem shook his head. "All of this is still only conjecture. And I ask you both again: even if you are right, what do you mean to do about it?"

"To expose her," said Ebon, leaning forwards. "Think of it. If we can prove the Yerrins had something to do with the attack—and the theft within the vaults—they would face the High King's justice. Dulmun would lose a powerful ally and be forced to surrender before this war has truly begun. Does your loyalty towards the High King not demand this of you?"

He thought he might have convinced Kalem, for the boy paused with a frown. But when he finally answered, he was angrier still. "No. This is a mad scheme. Where do you even get such thoughts, Ebon? And do not tell me they came from that letter."

"I have been thinking on this, as I said," Ebon muttered.

"I can see the lie in your eyes, Ebon. I have seen it there before. Can you not even trust me with the truth?"

Now even Theren was looking at Ebon askance. So he sighed and looked away uneasily. "Very well. When I went to fetch a book just now, I was visited by Mako, my family's bodyguard, of whom I have spoken before."

"Here?" said Kalem, his voice shrill. "In the library? In the *Academy?* How did he enter?"

"I do not know. He seems to come and go as he wishes."

"He has been here before?" said Kalem, nearly shouting.

Now Ebon was growing angry. "Yes, and somewhat often. What of it? Mayhap Cyrus permitted it, and he has heard no different from Xain. Or mayhap he knows a way in and out of these walls that no one else is privy to. What matters is not how he came to tell me, but *what* he said."

Theren seized Ebon's knee, gripping it tight enough to make him wince. "Did he tell you Lilith had something to do with the attack upon the Seat?"

Ebon looked away uncomfortably. "He . . . not exactly. It is rarely so plain with him. But he did say that if he were to investigate the attack and the theft in the vaults, he would begin his search with the family Yerrin."

She released his knee, but only to slap his leg. Ebon grunted and rubbed at the spot. "I knew it!" Theren hissed, her voice shaking. "She must have used her time in the vaults to scour the records for the artifact her family wanted. In exchange for helping Dulmun in their assault, they would have access to any artifact they desired within the vaults. Her family must be putting her up to it."

"Understand that Mako did not *say* any of this," said Ebon. "It is only a theory, for now, and we must carefully consider our steps before taking them."

"Only a theory, you say? But I am certain of it. It was a Yerrin plot, set in motion months ago."

"Yet what would they earn from this?" Ebon asked. "Do we believe they would risk the fall of an entire kingdom for a handful of magical trinkets?"

"Some of those 'trinkets' hold power beyond reckoning," said Theren. "And what does Yerrin care if the kingdom of Dulmun should stand or fall? They are not royalty. Their business will go on, and their wealth will accumulate as it has for countless generations."

"Very well," said Ebon. "If we consider ourselves correct, and that Lilith was the thief, what now? How can we prove it and expose the Yerrins?"

"We could follow her."

Ebon and Theren went still, staring at Kalem in amazement. He met their wondering looks with tight-pressed lips and eyes smoldering in anger.

"I am surprised to hear that from you, Kalem," Ebon said carefully.

"Are you?" said Kalem. "If it is true—and if your family's spy says it might be, mayhap we should listen—then Lilith must pay. All the Yerrins must. How many empty chairs are in the Academy? How many lecterns require new instructors? And if the invasion was a tragedy, the coming war will be far, far worse. If blame for that may be laid at Yerrin's feet, then let it be laid, and let them pay the price."

Theren snorted, but Ebon could see admiration in her eyes. "You sound like one of the kings you scorned earlier, eager for war."

Kalem shook his head. "I have no wish to fight," he said, more quietly now. "I only want proof. If we can get it, then let us do so—but in secret, and without recklessly endangering ourselves, or I will not help you. Then we can take what we have learned to the Academy's faculty, or mayhap to the constables. Let them deal with the criminals. If we can do that . . . well, then mayhap my parents will no longer wish to bring me home."

They all fell silent. Then Ebon rested a comforting hand on Kalem's shoulder. "No doubt you are right. If we are all of us resolved, we should start immediately.

We shall follow Lilith's steps outside of class, as close as her shadow. If Yerrin should plot against the Academy again, we three will be first to know."

They spent the rest of their afternoon in studious silence. Theren even stopped trying to speak to Ebon and Kalem while they read. But when the day's final bell tolled, they stacked their books upon the table and made quickly for the halls. Ebon tried to spot Lilith on their way out, but either she left as soon as the bell rang, or she was lost somewhere in the crowd.

Only moments passed, however, before Theren summoned them with a sharp whistle. There was Lilith, heading towards the dormitories. Her lackeys, Oren and Nella, had joined her from their classes, and the three of them walked in step. Ebon and Kalem moved to close the gap between them, but Theren gripped their arms.

"Not too close," she said, bringing her mouth to their ears to be heard above the crowd. "We do not want them to think we are following."

Once Lilith reached the stairs, she led the others up. The older students' dormitories were nearest the bottom, so they left the staircase almost at once to enter the common room. While Lilith went into her dormitory, Oren and Nella remained behind to keep watch.

"What do you suppose she is doing in there?" whispered Theren.

"Nothing good, I feel," said Ebon. "If she does not emerge in a moment or two, one of us should sneak—"

But then Lilith reappeared in the doorway, and the words died on his tongue. She had changed from her plain black student's cloak to a finer one trimmed in dark green brocade. He had never before seen her in specially tailored student robes—indeed, he would have thought it was against the rules.

Lilith swept past Nella and Oren, who hastened to fall into step behind her. Ebon and his friends followed all the way back to the library, where she swept in through the wide doors.

"I have never thought that Lilith was the studious type," said Ebon. "And if she is studying, why should she go to change her cloak?"

"Do you wish to wait here and wonder? Only one thing will reveal the truth." And so saying, Theren pushed through the library doors. Ebon and Kalem traded a final worried look before running behind her.

Inside it was silent. Only a handful of students were in view, puttering about the shelves with candles or lanterns now that the sun was fading from the skylight above.

"There." Kalem pointed, and Ebon's gaze followed. He saw a number of students sitting near the library's rear, and Lilith was among them.

"Let us get closer," said Theren.

They stole off to the right so they could wend their way through the shelves towards the gathering without being seen. As they drew near, they slowed their pace until they were moving little faster than a crawl. At last they stopped behind a thick shelf and leaned around the corner to watch.

About a dozen students had gathered to meet with Lilith. They had arranged armchairs into a circle with some tables set about for refreshments—cheese and bread, and many flagons of wine. They spoke lightly and laughed often, drinking freely; Ebon noted that some already had ruddy cheeks and noses. He could catch snatches of conversation, of lessons learned and spells mastered, of which instructors were kind and which cruel. But Lilith was silent and cold, positioned as if at the head of an invisible table, and her eyes were grave as they stared into nothing.

"What is she brooding on?" wondered Ebon.

"More to the point, what is this gathering all about?" said Kalem. "Why would they meet in the library if not to study?"

"Not everyone enjoys books as much as you and Ebon, Kalem," said Theren.

Ebon looked about the room with a frown. "No, he is right. If they do not wish to study, they could meet in the city. There are inns and taverns aplenty with better refreshments than they have here. So why the library?"

Theren's brow furrowed. But after a moment, Kalem snapped his fingers. "What else might they find in a tavern?"

Ebon blinked. "I know not what you mean. Noise? Distraction?"

"Near enough to the point. Other people. Whatever they are discussing, they do not wish to be overheard."

"But that is silly," said Theren. "There are other students here, in the library. Sky above, *we* are here, and can hear them."

"*We* came looking for them, and can only hear their words because we are eavesdropping. Who else would be here now, except students who enjoy learning more than an evening spent with friends? Bookish children, as you might call us, Theren. And look: none of those will draw within a stone's throw of this gathering of merchant children and nobles who bully them."

Ebon looked and saw that Kalem was right. Some students there were indeed, pulling tomes from the shelves to study by candlelight. But they all steered well clear of Lilith's party. If he had happened to be here for other, more innocent purposes, he would have done the same.

As if in answer to Kalem's words, Lilith stood abruptly from her chair. The other students went silent after a moment, looking up at her expectantly.

"We must invite more to this gathering," she said. "The goldbag society must grow. We will reach out to every merchant's child. Every royal son and daughter."

"Hear hear," said one of the students, raising her goblet with a prim smile. "Though I am nearly scandalized to hear you use that uncouth term. Goldbag. Honestly. Such a weak word, if truly they mean it as an insult."

"Surely you do not mean everyone, Lilith," said Oren with a nasty grin. "Not that Drayden whelp, at least." He gave a laugh and looked around. The other students tittered in approval. But Lilith fixed him with a steely gaze.

"Every merchant's child. Every royal son and daughter."

Oren's face fell. "Even Ebon?"

"*Every merchant's child.* The goldbag society must grow. We must invite more students to this gathering."

"All right, Lilith, we have heard you," said Nella. She shook her head with a weak smile. "Sit and drink. You are drawn tight as a Calentin bow."

Lilith shuddered, shaking her head as she placed a hand to her brow. "Yes. Yes, very well. Only do not forget."

She took her seat again and gratefully accepted the wine that Nella pressed to her before leaning back into her cushions.

Ebon turned to the others. Kalem's face was scrunched up as he peered at the gathering. But Theren had gone stony, her hands balled into white-knuckled fists.

"Every child of merchants and royalty, is it?" said Theren. "Such petty, small-minded revenge. How very like her."

"What do you mean?" said Ebon.

Theren tossed her head. "Do you not see, Ebon? She is forming this little gathering of children with wealth and power. Sky above, she is even willing to mend her bridges with you. And why?"

"I do not know," said Ebon, frowning. "I myself have no wish for such a mending."

"Of course not. Yet she aims to beguile you. Because one day you will rule over your family and its deep reserves of coin, as Lilith will rule hers. What an alliance that could be. And if she sat at the head of your group of Academy friends . . . well, think how amenable you might be to any favor she might ask."

"I would never do her any favors, nor would I join this little cabal," Ebon insisted.

"As I have said already, I *know* you would not," said Theren. "I am angry at Lilith, not you. *Think*. She knows we three dislike her. We have confronted her in the past. And what does she think of to solve this problem? Division. Seducing the two of you while she leaves me out in the cold."

"You may overestimate our importance," mumbled Kalem, eyes at his feet. "I would be surprised to know that Lilith thinks much of us at all, let alone enough to concoct such a scheme as that."

"Neither of you has known her as long as I," said Theren darkly.

"Look!" said Ebon, pointing. "Where is she going?"

Lilith had stood and begun to move away, but when Oren and Nella made to rise with her, she waved them down. "I must use the privy," she said, and swept off, drawing her black cloak tight. Her steps were brisk and clipped, and she stopped only once, to look back over her shoulder when she reached the library doors.

Ebon shared a look with his friends. "The privy, she says?"

"I doubt it," said Theren. "Let us go."

"But do you not think—oh, never mind," grumbled Kalem, for they had started off without him.

By the time they reached the hallway, Lilith had almost vanished, but they spied her just before she turned a corner. They hastened to follow down another two halls—but when Lilith reached the turn to the privies, she passed it by. Again Ebon, Kalem, and Theren shared a silent look before running behind her. She reached one of the white cedar doors that led out, and then again glanced down the hallway in both directions. Ebon and his friends were only saved because Lilith looked the other way first, for they dove into an alcove before she could turn back to see them. Once they heard the door swing shut, they ran after her again.

The night air outside was wonderfully cold upon their cheeks, for inside the citadel Ebon had begun to sweat beneath his cloak. Snow had yet to fall, and so they could keep their steps silent upon the soft grass as they followed Lilith deep into the Academy's training grounds. She took an odd path, weaving through bushes and hedges first one way, and then another.

"Has she seen us following her?" said Kalem.

"I do not think so, for still she moves slowly," said Theren. "She could be lost, but more likely she is taking precautions."

But even as she spoke, Lilith turned the corner of a great hedge and broke into a run, her steps fading towards silence.

"Go!" said Ebon. They sprinted for the end of the hedge and came into the open. Lilith was nowhere to be seen.

"Split up!" hissed Theren. She ran off.

"Theren!" said Ebon. He could follow her, but it would be a waste. He ran straight, and Kalem scampered to stay at his heels.

"How do you know she went this way?" said Kalem.

"I do not," growled Ebon. "I am hoping."

The hedges formed into a sort of maze in this part of the garden, but they could see a fair distance in every direction. Ebon thought he could hear running footsteps around every corner. Whenever he wondered if they were only in his mind, they came again, and Kalem would seize the sleeve of his robe. Then they would run pell-mell to catch up, only to hear the steps fade and vanish again.

"Darkness take her," said Ebon. "She must know we are here."

"Hold!" said Kalem, gripping his arm.

They went deathly still. Footsteps on the other side of the hedge continued for a moment before petering to nothing.

Kalem met Ebon's eyes in the moonslight. The boy's were wide and frightened, but then, Ebon guessed that he must look much the same.

They crept along, Ebon's steps slow and soft as a field mouse. He heard one sharp step on the other side of the hedge. It sounded like a stumble. He looked at Kalem again and received a nod. Lilith was sneaking along beside them.

Then they heard murmuring voices from the other direction.

Ebon whirled. Kalem barely stifled a cry. From the other side of the hedge came the sound of running. Lilith was trying to flee, taking advantage of the distraction.

"Catch her!" Ebon whispered.

"I think I can—" Kalem's eyes began to glow. He stepped towards the hedge and held forth his hands. Where he touched the shrub, it hissed and vanished into steam. Leaping forwards, he cleared a tunnel through the plants—only for Ebon to hear him give a muffled cry from the other side.

"Kalem!" Ebon barely kept his voice muted as he bounded forwards through the bush. On the other side were two dark figures. He flung himself at the taller one, tackling it to the ground.

"Get off me, you idiot goldshitter!" hissed a familiar voice.

"Theren?" said Ebon, for indeed it was her. He pushed up and away, holding out his hands. "I . . . I am sorry, I did not know—"

"Leave it," she growled. "And help me up."

He hastened to take Theren's hand and pull her to standing. "We heard you and thought it was Lilith."

"I heard you and thought *you* were Lilith. When I heard those voices, I thought she was trying to escape."

The voices. Ebon waved at his friends for silence. Together they crept towards the gap in the hedges that Kalem had cleared. The voices were still there. Two of them, both hushed.

"That must be Lilith," whispered Kalem.

"Aye, and one other," said Theren.

"It is a good thing they did not hear us," said Ebon. "Now, if we can see who—"

But there came rustling steps on the grass, and the trio threw themselves behind a rosebush. Lilith emerged from the garden into the moonslight. Her eyes were fixed straight ahead, and her steps were steady. Had she glanced to her left she might have seen Ebon, but she did not waver on her way back to the citadel.

"After her," said Theren.

"In a moment," said Ebon. "First I would like to know who she spoke to."

"Her accomplice means nothing. We are following Lilith."

"It will be but a moment." Ebon did not wait for an answer, but slipped around the rosebush and into the hedges. Here the plants formed a sort of fence around a small yard with two stone benches. Ebon had come here on occasion, when he wished to be alone with his thoughts. He reached a narrow gap in the hedge, pressing himself up against it to peer inside.

He could see no one.

Ebon turned to find Theren and Kalem eyeing him expectantly. He frowned, shaking his head. Theren pushed past him to see for herself.

"Theren, wait!" Ebon grabbed for her sleeve, but she cast him off. Ebon flinched as she stepped into the open. But nothing happened. Slowly, he straightened and joined her.

No one was there. The benches were empty.

"Who was she talking to?" Kalem asked.

"They must have slipped away," muttered Theren.

"Our eyes were upon the exit the whole time," said Ebon. "They could not have left without us seeing it."

Theren snorted. "This is the Academy, Ebon. A weremage could have turned to a snake and slithered away, a mindmage could leap over the hedge. A firemage—"

A child's piercing scream rang out from the citadel, cutting her words short.

Shock froze them. Then Ebon cried "Lilith," and ran, while the others hastened to follow. Together they burst through the white cedar door and flew through the halls, towards the screams that grew louder and more terrified the closer they drew.

"We make for the vaults," said Theren as they ran. "Something has happened. Lilith must—"

They rounded the final corner and froze, struck dumb at the sight before them. In front of a great iron door lay Instructor Credell. His eyes were no longer anxious and shifting, but vacant and staring up at the ceiling, as blood spilled from his slit throat to pool around his body.

SIX

FOR A MOMENT EBON COULD SEE NOTHING BUT THE body. Credell's face was Elf-white, marked only by the dark blood that had spattered his skin as it spurted forth. That blood ran thick and slow now, soaking into his hair and robes. Ebon thought of the day the Seat was attacked, and that Credell had been bloodstained then, too, fighting to defend his students from the Shades in an uncommon display of courage.

His students. Astrea. *Darkness take me,* thought Ebon. For there she was: little Astrea, cowering against the wall. She was screaming, still screaming, and he realized it had been her voice they had heard from the garden. Her feet scraped the floor and her hands dragged at the stone wall as though she wished to burrow into it and away, but she could not remove her eyes from Credell sprawled on the floor.

Another student stood beside her, holding her in a tight embrace—Isra, the girl he had run into in the dining hall that morning. She held Astrea tight, her face held to the girl's, whispering comfort into her ear. Some other students stood about as well, drawn by the commotion just as Ebon and his friends had been— but all, like Ebon, were frozen in fear.

He forced himself to move, crossing the hallway towards Astrea. He knelt before her, placing his face in between her and Credell's corpse.

"Astrea. Astrea!"

She stopped her screaming long enough for her wild eyes to find his. It took a moment for her to recognize him, but when she did she flung herself forwards, wrapping her arms around his neck. He turned so her face was pointed away from Credell. But then, to his surprise, Isra reached out to drag Astrea backwards. She knelt to hold the girl as Ebon had done. Her eyes were wide, her face even more gaunt and pinched than usual. Astrea gripped her hard, tears soaking the older girl's robes.

"What happened?" said Theren.

For a moment Isra seemed unable to speak, only looking up and blinking. At last she shook her head and stuttered, "We—we were walking. Together—the two of us. We found him here, like this."

"Who else was here?" said Theren. "Was it Lilith? Did you see her?"

Ebon frowned. "Theren."

Isra only blinked, still in shock, and her hands tightened on Astrea's shoulders.

"What is going on here? Stand aside, all of—oh, sky above. Back. *Back!*"

They turned to find Jia. Her light skin had grown paler still, and she stood before the students, waving them back from the body. Instructor Dasko arrived a moment later. He stared at the body a bit longer than Jia had, but then he joined her in ushering the students away.

"Sky above, Ebon, get that child out of sight of him!"

Jia's sharp rebuke jarred him from his thoughts. Crimson blush crept into his cheeks that he had not thought of it. Quickly he went to Astrea, guiding her down the hallway. Isra kept a tight grip on the girl's shoulder, but she did not stop him. They halted around the corner as Astrea collapsed to the stone floor. Isra sat beside her, one arm still wrapped protectively about the girl's shoulders.

Heavy, thudding footsteps sounded down the hall, and Perrin came into view a moment later. She caught Ebon's eye and tossed her head. "What is all this commotion for?"

Ebon pointed down the hall. "It . . . Instructor Credell, he is . . . they found him . . ."

Perrin's face grew solemn, and she broke into a heavy jog. Though she vanished around the corner, Ebon could still hear the sharp hiss of her breath when she saw Credell. Then her booming commands rang forth, ordering students to draw away from the body so the instructors could do their work.

"Are you all right?" Ebon winced at once, hearing how foolish the question sounded. "Would you like some water? Or anything else from the kitchens? I could fetch something . . ." But Astrea only shook her head, eyes fixed sightlessly upon her feet.

Theren drew close, and pulled Kalem in as well. "It was Lilith," she murmured. "It must have been. She slipped away from us so she could do this. I knew we should have followed her."

"Murdering an instructor?" said Kalem. "That is madness. She could not. And besides, why would she?"

"The vaults, of course," said Theren, frowning. "Did you not see the door where Credell lay? That is the entrance."

Kalem balked, sharing an uncertain look with Ebon. But sharp, clipped footsteps down the hallway distracted them, and they all turned to see Jia approaching. She swept her gaze across them, lips pursed.

"Did anyone see what happened?"

"No, Instructor," said Ebon. Astrea shook her head.

"Who arrived first?"

"Them—Astrea and Isra, I mean, or at least they came before we did," said Theren. "But Instructor, in the garden we saw—"

Jia silenced her with a raised finger, and then went to kneel before Astrea and Isra. She took the younger girl's hands in her own, pressing them gently together. "Astrea," she said softly. "It pains me greatly that you saw that. I am sorry to ask, but it may help us—did you see anything? Anything at all that might help?"

Astrea shook her head, eyes still saucer-wide. Isra gripped her tighter. "We were together, Instructor, walking through the hall. We found him just as you saw him."

"Is that true, Astrea?" The girl nodded. Jia sighed and stood. "Thank you both. Isra, please see Astrea to her dormitory, and wait with her in the common room until I can visit you. Do you understand?"

Isra nodded and stood. But before she could leave, Theren sprang forwards to take Jia's sleeve.

"Instructor. We may have seen something that could help. Moments before we heard Astrea scream, we were following Lilith in the gardens. She spoke with someone out there, though we could not see who. Then she eluded us, vanishing from sight. It was only moments later that they found Credell's body."

Jia frowned. "Why were you following her? What do you mean, she *eluded* you?"

"She snuck away. She stepped out of sight so that we could not follow her."

Ebon had grown more uncomfortable with Theren's every word, and now he took her by the arm. "Theren, that is not exactly what happened. Instructor, we were following Lilith, but she did not know it, and she did not try to evade us. She went into the Academy while we stayed behind."

Theren's eyes upon him were full of fury and hurt. "But it *was* before Credell was killed," she insisted.

Jia glared, folding her arms across her chest. "Theren, I know something of the feud between you and Lilith, but accusing her of murder is far beyond reason, even for you. Unless you have something more substantial than this—"

"I have not accused her!" cried Theren. "I have only told you what I saw. Is it not at least worth questioning her?"

"Little more than any other soul at the Academy," said Jia. "Many were surely alone when—"

Abruptly she stopped talking and drew up straight, folding her hands together before her. Ebon *felt* a presence behind him and turned. There stood Dean Forredar, imposing in his robes of office, his dark eyes fixed on Ebon.

"Son of Drayden," he said, his voice dripping with scorn. "I am not surprised to find you present in such a commotion."

"Dean," said Jia gravely. "Instructor Credell has been found dead. I will show you the body. Dasko and Perrin have cleared the students out of the hall."

That gave Xain pause, but only for the space of a breath. "Did any witness what happened?" he said, never taking his gaze from Ebon. "Were you there, son of Drayden?"

Fear mixed with anger in Ebon's breast—fear of Xain's reckless malice, and anger at the injustice of it. "No, Dean. I was in the garden with Theren and Kalem."

Xain looked to Ebon's friends. Theren nodded, and Kalem said, "It is true, Dean."

"Several other students reached the body before Ebon and his friends, Dean," Jia added. "We had just begun to question the students when you arrived."

Xain looked from her to Isra, who met his gaze with one of equal steel. He shrugged and pushed past Ebon, who was forced to step aside. Jia followed him around the corner. Ebon had almost decided to go with them when he heard many footsteps coming down the hall from the opposite direction. In a moment, Lilith appeared. Behind her were the students she had gathered in the library.

"Lilith!" Theren's voice rose to a furious shout. "What have you done?"

The students stopped, and Lilith glared back. "What are you talking about, Theren? We heard a tumult and came to see what it was."

"You lie." Theren stepped forwards. Ebon gripped her arm, and Kalem took the other. "We know what you did, Lilith."

"And what exactly is that?" Xain's voice rolled through the hallway, freezing them like mindmagic. The dean swept forwards, Jia at his side, and both came to a stop between the two groups.

Jia spoke first. "Lilith, can you account for your whereabouts this evening?"

Lilith blinked, brow furrowing with doubt. "I . . . I was in the library with my friends."

"We saw you!" cried Theren. "We saw you in the garden, Lilith. And then you came back into the citadel, just before Credell was killed."

Beneath her dark skin, Lilith went grey as ash. "Killed? I . . ." She swallowed, looking at the others beside her. "I only stepped out to get some air, and then I went straight back to the others. They were there, and know I am telling the truth."

"She is," said Oren immediately. But on Lilith's other side, Nella hesitated. It was only a moment before she nodded in assent, but Ebon noted it.

"Very well," said Jia. "Then we are done here. All of you, return to your rooms. Ebon, if you would, look in upon Astrea in her dormitory. I will be there as soon as I can, but I want to ensure she has friends about her. She is far too young to have witnessed something so wretched."

"I will, Instructor." Ebon noted that Xain had fixed him with a dark look, and did not seem pleased to see them go. But again he turned without speaking, and Ebon hastened away before they could be recalled.

The students with Lilith were silent. Theren gave them all dirty looks as they went, and once the hallway branched off, she dragged Ebon and Kalem in another direction. Out of earshot, she pressed them both into an alcove.

"Lilith *must* have had something to do with this. I know it."

Kalem frowned and looked down at his feet. "I am not so certain."

Theren opened her mouth, but Ebon jumped in before she could speak. "He is right, Theren. We cannot know anything for certain. We only lost sight of her for a moment. How could she have killed him and then returned to the library so quickly?"

"It was not such a long distance," said Theren. "I think that, after she lost us, she made for the vaults. But she came upon Credell, killed him, and then ran for the library as quickly as she could before anyone could see what she had done."

"But why?" said Kalem. "For what purpose?"

"For no purpose," said Theren. "He must have surprised her. Do you remember this morning, when he asked for my key to the vaults? Credell never enters the vaults, but some business must have called him there. Lilith did not expect that, and so when he saw her, she panicked."

Ebon looked down the hall, towards where Lilith and the others had vanished. He gritted his teeth and shook his head. "I do not know, Theren. Lilith has been cruel to me since the day I arrived. But a murderer?"

Theren scowled. "I do not think she is some vile killer who sits about plotting the slow, torturous deaths of others. But I know she is ruthless, and ambitious, and tied closely to the dark dealings of her family. The Yerrins may hold no candle to the family Drayden, yet it is known that they, too, will kill any who stand in their way."

"But Lilith is scarcely more than a girl," said Kalem. "We all are."

"You mean *you* are," said Theren. "She is on the cusp of her eighteenth year. More than old enough to act as an agent of her house—and indeed, I believe she may be. She might not have wished for Credell's death, but she had a hand in it nonetheless."

"If what you say is true, I am more fearful than before," said Kalem. "I want to prove the guilt of those who had a hand in the attack. But if the Yerrins will kill to protect the secret, might we not die ourselves? And our new dean is out for Ebon's blood. If we try to investigate, we may land ourselves in even greater danger, or be expelled. And from outside the Academy, we can do nothing."

"If we remain, but do nothing, then what does it matter if we are expelled or not?" said Theren. "Underrealm itself is in danger. Do you think we can attend our studies for the next few years and hope the war will pass us by?"

Kalem fixed her with a hard look. "I think it is easier for you to say that than for us. You have completed your studies, and everyone knows it. If you left now, you would be a full-fledged wizard, whether or not you had the Academy's blessing to practice. Ebon and I have not that luxury. You ask us to risk all our learning, many years more of education, trying to prove guilt that may or may not exist."

Theren had no answer for that, and looked uneasily away from them both. "Do you feel the same, Ebon?"

But Ebon scarcely heard her. His thoughts were far away, upon the southern cliffs of the Seat, where Cyrus' flesh had turned to stone under his hand. He felt as though he stood upon those cliffs again. He could step forwards, plunging himself into the abyss with no hope of return. If he joined Theren in her hunt for Lilith, he could be expelled, or die—or be forced to kill again. But if he stayed his hand? If he shut his eyes and feigned ignorance of the dark clouds swirling about the Academy? Then others might perish, and if Ebon did not kill them, still he would bear the guilt of it.

"Ebon?" said Theren.

"I do not know. I do not know. I have no wish to be killed or expelled in a hunt for the truth. But neither do I wish to sit and do nothing, when it may lead to the deaths of others like Credell. I know not what to do."

"That is hardly helpful," said Theren, snorting. "Choosing to do nothing is still a choice."

"I do not wish to do nothing," said Ebon. "Yet I fear to do *anything*. I . . . how can I explain it, when I do not understand it myself?"

"Ebon, stop being a coward and—"

"Leave off, Theren." He pushed her away and strode down the hallway without looking back, for he knew he would find her glaring at him in anger. Cyrus' face flashed before his eyes again, and then again, and the former dean's dry, crusted lips whispered the word *murderer.*

He shivered, hating himself for his indecision. Yet how could he ease his mind? To whom could he speak?

The answer came in a flash. Only one person would understand. Only one soul could hear him freely.

Adara.

SEVEN

İꜱ ᴡᴀꜱ ꜰᴀʀ ᴛᴏᴏ ʟᴀᴛᴇ ᴛᴏ ᴄᴏɴꜱɪᴅᴇʀ ʟᴇᴀᴠɪɴɢ ᴛʜᴇ Academy to see her, and the instructors were all on high alert after Credell's murder. So Ebon did as he had promised and went to Astrea's dormitory to visit her. But he found Isra sitting in the common room instead. She looked up as he entered. Her eyes were vacant.

"Is Astrea here?" Ebon said, keeping his voice hushed. The common room was empty save for the two of them.

"She has gone to bed," said Isra.

Ebon nodded. "I should do the same, then. As should you, I suppose. Do you . . . do you wish me to walk you back to the dormitories?"

Isra scowled.

He raised his hands at once. "I only mean . . . it must have been terrible. To find . . . to find him."

She seemed to consider that for a moment. "I suppose it was terrible," she murmured. Lifting a hand, she showed Ebon her fingers. He could see them twitching. "See? My hands are shaking."

"Who could blame you? I can only imagine what it has done to Astrea."

Isra lowered her hand and looked at the dormitory door mournfully. "I wish she had not seen him," she said, voice scarcely above a whisper. "She has always been so fragile."

"You have known her long, then?" said Ebon.

Her eyes flashed. "I am not here to swap tales with you, goldbag."

Ebon ducked his head. "I am sorry," he muttered. "Good eve."

He returned to his dormitory and went to bed at once, hoping his thoughts would be clearer in the morning. Instead he lay awake for hours, wrestling with thoughts of Cyrus and Credell. Both had made his first few months at the Academy terrible, though for very different reasons. And now both were dead. He fell asleep seeing their faces, their lifeless eyes staring into his own.

A dark mood had settled over the Academy the next morning, like a funeral pall thrown over all who dwelt within. The dining hall was somber, and no one dared speak above a whisper. Ebon found Kalem and sat with him, neither saying a word. Theren arrived soon after, and though she sat with them both, she did not meet Ebon's eyes.

"I did some asking last night, after . . . well, after," she muttered. "Nothing was taken from the vaults. Credell must have happened upon Lilith as she was trying to get in, not out."

If she did not wish to discuss their argument from last night, Ebon was happy enough to oblige. "That is good, I suppose."

"Not good for Credell," said Kalem.

Ebon looked away. Then his eye caught on something strange: a white tabard amid the sea of black robes. He looked about the room to find more of them; soldiers in white and gold, and all bearing swords and shields.

"Who are they?" he said, pointing.

Theren and Kalem raised their eyes, and Kalem's mouth fell open. "The High King's guards. What are they doing here?"

"No doubt they were sent to aid the Academy's defenses after the murder," said Theren.

Despite himself, Ebon laughed. "What do they

hope to do? Have they forgotten this is a school of wizards? Their blades and armor will help them little against all but the youngest of students."

"Mayhap they think the murderer was no wizard," said Kalem. "After all, Credell was not killed with magic, but by a dagger to the throat."

They fell silent at that. Credell's sightless eyes danced in Ebon's vision again, and then his face turned into Cyrus'. Ebon's breath came harsh and shallow, and lights danced at the edge of his eyes.

"Ebon, what is wrong?" said Theren. "Your face is pale."

"I need . . . I need to walk. I need air." He stood, and they made to follow, but he waved them back down. "No, thank you. I would rather be alone. I will find you later. In the library, mayhap."

His friends settled back into their seats, though Kalem clearly wanted to come. Ebon left the dining hall, nearly stumbling against the door on his way. The hall was cold, colder than he remembered—or mayhap it was just that the dining hall had grown too warm. He pressed his hand against the frigid stone to steady himself.

He must see Adara.

Now? he thought.

Yes. He could not attend his studies like this. Half of him wanted to vomit, and the other wanted to return to bed, to curl in a ball and never rise again. If he could not unburden himself, he feared his heart might fail him.

His mind made up, he went quickly to the Academy's wide front hall. His heart crashed in vicious thunder at his temples as he entered the open space with its vaulted ceiling—but then he sighed in relief. The sharp old caretaker, Mellie, was not standing guard at the front door as he had feared she might be. It was a bald man instead, with a crooked back and rheumy eyes, who Ebon had heard was named Cratchett—some old wizard called back to duty long after his prime to fill one of the many sudden vacancies in the Academy's staff. He wandered about his post, eyes seeming to catch nothing at all. Ebon waited until he had rounded the corner before running out the front door into the street.

He gave silent thanks for the well-oiled hinges as he swung the door shut behind him. Sticking his hands into either sleeve against autumn's chill, he set off into the streets. The air bit briskly into his skin, even through his thick robe, and he hurried his pace to get the blood moving. He thanked the sky that it had not yet snowed, though clouds crowded above, making him anxious. Quickly he turned his steps west and north, winding his way through the city to where he knew a blue door was waiting.

All about him, the Seat was bustling. Soldiers patrolled the streets, wearing different colors: the white and gold of the High King, the blue and white of Selvan, and the Mystics' red and silver. But, too, there were masons and carpenters aplenty, for buildings across the island were in need of repair. Dulmun had wreaked terrible havoc across the city, as had their allies, the Shades. Houses and shops and taverns alike had been torn asunder, and now, if the owners were still alive, those structures were being rebuilt. The air rang with hammer beats, and the songs of saws, and choirs of shouting builders. After the tragedy, the new activity joined into a chorus that lifted the heart, and yet it held also an undertone of urgency. War was upon Underrealm now, and if it had not yet blossomed to its full fury, not a soul upon the Seat doubted that it would, given time.

When at last he reached his destination, Ebon ducked into an alley and looked furtively about. Most upon the Seat knew that Academy students were not allowed out until evening, and he had no wish for word to be sent back about where he had gone. But no one seemed to pay him any mind. So he slipped from the alley and across to the blue door, entering as quickly as he could.

There were not so many people lounging about the front room as when Ebon had first come. No doubt some had fallen in the fighting, while others had left the Seat. But Ebon guessed that the blue door saw its fair share of customers these days; not only would many seek comfort after the attack, but the Seat now housed soldiers from across the nine kingdoms. His stomach twisted at the thought that Adara might be occupied already—but then he saw her in the corner playing her harp. She flashed him a wide smile, and he returned it. Then the matron swept forwards to greet him.

"Good day, sir. Do you wish to visit Adara?"

"If she will see me." Ebon reached for his coin purse, but the matron waved it off.

"I do not doubt that she will. But you have not yet used up all your last payment."

Her gaze slid past him. Adara stood at once and approached, leading Ebon to her room by the hand. Inside, she gripped his robes and pulled him close for a deep kiss.

"I have sorely missed you," he said, holding her out by the shoulders to look at her.

"And I you. But what are you doing here now? It is the middle of the day."

"I had to come. My heart is in turmoil, and my mind will offer no rest."

Her hands slid down his chest, her smile coquettish. "Then it will be my pleasure to soothe you."

"I . . . that is not what I came for."

She cocked her head, though her smile did not wilt. "I never thought to have you refuse me."

That made him chuckle. "Nor did I ever expect to. But I came because there are things I must speak of. And they are . . . they are things I can say to no one else."

The smile faded, and her eyes grew solemn. "I think I see your mind. Come, then. Sit and speak. Will you take wine?"

"Please."

She fetched him a cup and poured one for herself as well. He took a deep drink and then stared at his hands in silence. Adara said nothing, only waited patiently, soft eyes never leaving his face. He wanted badly to tell her of the thoughts that plagued him, but now that he was here, his tongue felt thick and limp in his mouth.

"My family is coming to the Seat," he said, because that, at least, was easy to say.

"And are you pleased?" she said, her tone very careful.

Ebon shrugged. "Mayhap. I shall see my sister again, and that is a joy. But my reunion with my father shall be . . . not quite so happy, I fear."

She placed a hand on his knee. "If he should trouble you, I will always be here to help you forget."

"That would be most unwise," Ebon said quickly. "I would be foolish to visit you while my father resides upon the Seat. No doubt he will have me watched. He might scorn me if he learns I am visiting a house of lovers, and that I could bear. But then he might go further, seeking to visit some sort of harm upon you."

Adara's eyes hardened, and her lips drew tight. "He would not dare raise a hand against a lover. The King's law protects us."

"Nothing so brazen." Ebon shook his head. "He is a snake, and could devise any manner of trouble for you."

Some of the fire left her. "I will take you at your word. Worry not—if you cannot see me while your family is upon the Seat, I will still be here when they leave. And yet . . . forgive me for saying so, Ebon, but this is not why you have come to see me today, and you are only wasting time by not speaking of it."

He dropped his gaze, staring at his hands where they fidgeted in his lap. When he spoke, his voice was far smaller than he had meant it to be. "No, it is not. I . . . I cannot stop seeing . . . that is, remembering what happened."

"I understand," she murmured. "It was no happy memory."

"That was the first day I saw someone killed—and then in the same day I, too, struck a death blow."

"You are blameless. Had you not . . . done what you did, he would have murdered you instead."

He winced. "And yet."

She nodded slowly. "And yet. It may be the truth, but I know that makes it no easier to bear."

His throat grew dry, and so he drained the cup. She went for the pitcher, but he shook his head. "No more. At least not yet. There is something else . . . something I have thought of often since the attack. Had I not seen the two of you slipping away through the city, you would have gone with him."

Adara's eyes grew sharper. "Ebon, I have told you—"

"No, forgive me," he said hastily. "I did not mean

that as it sounded. I understand that you are a lover. And you had no knowledge of Cyrus other than his custom, I imagine. What I mean is . . . had I not come after you, he would have taken you from the Seat in safety. He only hurt you after I attacked him. Without me, you would not have been harmed."

"Oh, Ebon," she said, softening. "Does that truly worry you? I am glad you came when you did. I knew Cyrus for a snake, but not the extent of his treachery. I thought he could remove me from the Seat in safety, and so I went with him, planning to leave his company in the first town we reached. But if I had known he ever laid a hand upon you, I would not have taken a single step by his side." She cupped his cheek with her hand, and brushed her fingers to push a lock of hair behind his ear.

Lover's words, he thought. And yet, when she had learned the truth, she *had* rejected Cyrus. It sent his mind reeling, but he could not waste thought on this now. He had come here to speak, not to wrestle with his feelings for Adara—though already he suspected that they were stronger than might be wise.

"I think of him often," said Ebon. "I see his face, frozen in that death scream, and I hear him as he plunges into the Great Bay. In my dreams he visits me, and in my waking hours his wail is like a far-off thing, drifting to my ears through the windows, and I can neither escape it nor speak of my troubles. How could I look Kalem or Theren in the eye if they knew what I had done? Yet sometimes I wish to tell them, if only so I need not bear the burden alone."

"You cannot tell them. You must not."

Ebon raised an eyebrow. "Why so adamant? They are my friends. They would not betray me to the constables."

Adara pursed her lips and took another sip of her wine. "The King's law would justify what we did, were the constables or the Mystics to know. It is not the King's law we must fear. It is your family. No matter the justification, how do you think your father would react if it were known that you killed a scion of the family Drayden?"

Ebon's hands trembled at the thought. "My friends would *never* tell my family."

Her eyes grew mournful, and she put a hand on his. "I know Theren well enough. She would understand. I know she had no love for Cyrus. But Kalem . . . understand that I have not met him. Yet he is a royal, and thus holds a greater regard for the King's law. He would not tell your kin. But he might tell the constables, and then word of it would reach your family regardless. I cannot believe a royal would be satisfied until the matter was brought before the law."

Ebon's brow furrowed. He wished to deny Adara's words. And yet, it *did* sound like something Kalem would do. The boy would wish the matter resolved to the satisfaction of himself, the King's law, and likely some within the Academy. Then word would surely reach his father. The thought made him cringe. Ebon could only imagine what might happen to him then.

Some of his worry must have shown in his eyes, for Adara gripped his hands tighter. "I see your fear. Do not let your heart be troubled. We need fear nothing, for your family will never learn the truth."

"But then what am I to do? I may keep the secret from my family and the King's law, and even my friends, but I cannot keep it from myself. And it is my own mind that plagues me."

"Then take comfort in me." Adara gently pulled him close, planting a kiss on one cheek, and then the other. "Tell me of your worries and your fears, and let me dispel them." Her kisses fell to his neck as her hand slid across his chest.

Ebon gulped. "That is an attractive prospect, to be certain." He drew back and met her eyes. "It will be as you say, at least for now. But you might not feel the same if you could only get to know them better—or Kalem, at least, since you know something of Theren. What if we spent time together, all of us, beyond the blue door?"

Adara frowned, and in her eyes there was a worry Ebon could not place. "Are you certain that is wise? If your father is having you watched . . ."

"He would not do so yet. Not until he reaches the Seat. And it would gladden my heart to have you all together—you three, who I love most in this world."

He blushed and looked away, for that seemed a

foolish thing to say. *She is a lover,* he reminded him-self. He had known that when first he came to see her, and every time since. Why, then, was it so hard not to think of Adara as something more? He did not see her as *his,* certainly . . . and yet, whenever he thought of her, it seemed to him that each belonged to the other.

Then, to his surprise, Adara's hand was on his cheek, and she turned him to face her. Softly, she said, "If it would ease your mind, then gladly will I meet them." Her hands fell to push him onto the bed, and then she was atop him. "After all, it is my duty to ease your burdens."

His only reply was to kiss her.

EIGHT

SOME HOURS LATER, EBON SAT DRINKING IN A TAVERN a few streets over from the Academy. Soon the bells would ring for the midday meal, and he might slip in through the front door unnoticed. It was not uncommon for students to take their meal in the city, and he could merge with the crowd without drawing much attention. Some gave him odd looks as he waited—his Academy student robes were out of place in the tavern before the midday—but after his visit to Adara, he was unable to summon much concern.

"You must learn to wash the smell off, little goldbag."

Mako's growling voice nearly made Ebon choke on his wine. The bodyguard had appeared at his elbow without warning. Now he pushed Ebon aside and slid onto the bench beside him. Ebon was glad to see the man, but he could not stop a nagging thought, warning him that Mako had blocked his exit.

"Mayhap I shall bathe instead of eating."

"You had better. You smell more like your lover than yourself." Mako's teeth appeared in a cruel smile—though Ebon did not find it quite so frightening as he once had.

"How did you know to find me here?"

"I did not. I had planned on visiting you in the library this afternoon, and was waiting for my chance to slip inside the citadel. Only by chance did I enter this place to find you waiting for me instead."

"Waiting for you?" said Ebon, chuckling. "I knew not that you sought me."

Mako's smirk widened, and he motioned to a barman for ale. But then his face grew solemn. "You should have guessed it after what happened in the Academy last night. I had to come to see that you are all right."

Credell's corpse flashed in his mind, and Ebon shook the thought away. "I am whole. It is kind of you to worry, but I was nowhere near the murder."

"That is not what I have heard. It seems you were one of the first to arrive after the body was discovered."

"One of the first, but not *the* first. Credell was already cooling and beyond any help when I got there."

"Do you know aught of what happened? Have you learned anything since?" said Mako. Ebon looked around with discomfort, but the bodyguard set a steady hand on his shoulder and grinned. "No one gets close enough to listen in on me, boy. Not without my knowing it. Speak."

Still Ebon hesitated a moment before answering. "We were following Lilith just before it happened. She was sharing wine with friends, and then she went out into the gardens. We thought she was alone, but then we heard her speaking to someone."

"Who?"

"We do not know. We tried to find out, but Lilith left, and her friend disappeared. That is when the screaming started, and Credell's body was found."

Mako drummed his fingers on the table but never took his gaze from Ebon. His ale arrived, and he took a deep gulp. "It seems there is a strong case to be made for Lilith's guilt."

"Mayhap," said Ebon, nodding slowly. "Yet we lost sight of her for only a moment."

"Much can be done in a moment. A moment is longer than I need to cut a man's throat, I promise you."

Ebon shuddered and looked into his wine cup. "You think she did it, then?"

"I think more and more signs point that way. If Lilith had a hand in the theft from the vaults, or in Credell's death, it seems the family Yerrin stands much to gain."

"The artifacts, you mean? That was Theren's guess."

"The family Yerrin thwarts us in many things, and seeks ever to expand their influence. If they had even a handful of the more powerful artifacts in the Academy's bowels, Drayden's star might wane. Do not shrug—you might not care for your father's ill fortune, but I would wager you care for Halab's."

Ebon flushed. "Of course I wish no harm upon her. And what is more, if it is true that Yerrin played a role in the attack upon the Seat, then I have no wish for their future success. They must be brought to justice."

Mako smirked. "How very noble of you. I think you will have ample opportunity to catch her and expose the truth."

"Why?"

"She has stolen from the vaults already, but now she has killed Credell before their doors. Why? Why would she have been there, if not to steal again? She was thwarted this time by Credell, but that does not mean she will give up. Keep following her, Ebon. Catch her in the act, and you shall have your justice. Mayhap you shall even have it before another corpse is on our hands."

Ebon frowned into his cup. "I hope so."

"We will speak more of this later. I have not only come to ask you about Credell's murder. I bring word from the family."

Ebon sighed. "What is it this time?"

"They will arrive to the Seat upon the morrow, and hope you will join them in the manor."

A shiver rippled through him, sliding down his back from the base of his skull. He tried to hide it, though Mako's glinting eyes said he had failed. "I will, of course. You may tell them."

"I shall. And that brings this conversation to an end—and just in time."

Before Ebon could ask what the bodyguard meant, the Academy's bells began to toll, signaling the end of morning classes and the serving of the midday meal. Ebon gaped. "How did you . . .?"

Mako pointed to the rear of the tavern. On a shelf behind the bar sat a large hourglass. The tavern's owner turned it over even as Ebon watched.

"I am no wizard, little Ebon, though the look on your face was a delight. Often simple observation serves better than magic. I wish you well in your quest for the truth—only take care, and do not place yourself in danger you cannot get back out of. It would have been a tremendous waste of my effort to save you from the attack on the Seat only for you to die now."

"I will keep that in mind," said Ebon, giving him a wry smile. "I would hate to see your effort wasted."

Mako laughed, tossed a gold weight on the table for the drinks, and slipped out the door.

NINE

Students were already pouring out into the streets by the time Ebon reached the Academy's wide front doors. He waited until a sizable crowd was pressing through and then slipped inside between them. Mellie was back on watch, and she fixed him with a suspicious glare as he passed by. But he escaped without incident, and she did not call after him. He rounded the corner of the first hallway and pressed himself against the stone, letting out a long sigh of relief.

"Ebon!"

He very nearly jumped out of his skin at the shout.

There was Perrin, her massive frame trundling down the hallway towards him, brows almost joined as she frowned.

"Instructor Perrin," stammered Ebon. "I—that is, I—"

"Stow it." She folded her arms and peered down at him through narrowed eyes. "Did you not think I would notice your absence? An empty seat is a tad conspicuous, especially so near the front."

Ebon bowed his head. In truth he had not thought overmuch about it—Credell had been too terrified to say anything of the many times Ebon had vanished from the classroom. "I am sorry, Instructor. I was only—"

A massive hand clapped down on his shoulder, squeezing tight—but not painfully. When he raised his eyes again, Ebon found Perrin looking back at him with soft concern.

"You do not need to tell me where you have been. Last night was a terrible tragedy, and none could fault you for needing to clear your mind after what you saw. Only next time, tell me."

He ducked his head again, but this time in shame. She thought he was upset over Credell's death. And Ebon supposed he was, but that was far overshadowed by his worries about Cyrus, and Lilith, and now his family's arrival upon the Seat. What did it say about him that he had so little concern for the death of his first instructor at the Academy?

But he could say none of this, of course, so he only mumbled, "I will remember, Instructor. Thank you. And again, I am sorry."

Perrin clapped his shoulder again—Ebon thought the spot might bruise—and left him. Ebon shuffled towards the dining hall, trying not to feel so wretched. The moment he stepped inside, Kalem and Theren leapt up from their seats and came to him.

"Where were you this morning?" hissed Kalem.

"I made a wager with him that you went to see your lover," said Theren with a grin. "Tell me I am a gold weight richer."

"You are." Ebon could not help matching her smile. But Kalem drew back, his eyes filled with reproach.

"Ebon, what possessed you? No one minds you having a lover. But leaving your classes to visit her?"

"My thoughts would give me no peace," said Ebon, frowning at him. "You cannot tell me your mind is inured to the sight of corpses, even after the attack on the Seat."

Kalem had no answer for that, and he lowered his eyes. But Theren took their arms and pulled them both towards the door. "Enough of that. Come to the library, Ebon, for we have something to show you."

"What is it?" said Ebon. "I have not even eaten."

"I took a roll for you." Theren produced the mangled, squished thing from her pocket and shoved it into his hand. Ebon grimaced. Soon they whisked him into the library and up the stairs, where they huddled in their third-floor corner. Kalem went to the wall and put forth his power, and the stone shifted to reveal his secret cubbyhole. He drew an old tome of plain brown leather, unadorned, with no title on the cover.

"I found this book," said Kalem.

"In the library?" said Ebon, raising his eyebrows. "Wonders may never cease."

"It was hidden," Kalem said, scowling. "It was covered in dark and dust behind a bookshelf."

"Most likely it fell," said Ebon. "What of it?"

Kalem looked at him, almost haughty. "Ebon, I know nearly every inch of this library. The shelf was flush to the wall until, at most, a week ago. Someone wanted to hide this book."

Theren took the book to show Ebon. "They wanted to hide it because it is from the vaults."

Ebon recoiled. "Do . . . do you mean it is enchanted?" He swallowed hard, wondering if he should run.

She rolled her eyes. "It is not from *within* the vaults, you craven. It is a logbook. A very *old* logbook."

Ebon relaxed and, after a moment, leaned forwards to look at the book with fresh interest. "But why would it be here?"

"Why, indeed? Especially one so ancient. It is centuries old, and at first I doubted it could have any unchanged entries."

"What do you mean?" said Ebon.

"When an item comes to the vaults, we enter it in a new page on a logbook, with the room's number noted here." Theren pointed to the top right corner of a page, where a number had been scrawled and then crossed through with a red X. "Once all the entries have been crossed out, the logbook is retired to the archives. This book is from hundreds of years ago. The entries should have been replaced with other artifacts. But one—"

Ebon pointed to the entry on the open page. It described a cloak of green cloth and the enchantment placed upon it. "A spell of warding? What is that?"

Theren glanced at it. "Look here—runes of silver sewn into the collar and imbued with mentalist spells. They infuse the cloth with power so that it protects the wearer with magic. Though the cloak would still be cloth, and therefore light, it would protect you like a shirt of mail. Although see here." She pointed to the bottom of the page, where a note had been added: *Verified to be drained upon the twelfth of Yunus, Year of Underrealm 823.*

"Drained?" said Ebon. "What does that mean?"

"Any wizard can put some of their magic into an object," Theren explained. "A sword imbued with elementalism may burn with fire at a word, or, as with this cloak, mentalism may make objects much stronger than normal. The magic will leach out with time, often in the course of a day or so. But if runes are carved or woven into the object, they can be made to hold the magic for longer—or, in the case of some mighty Wizard Kings, forever. That is why these artifacts are kept within the vaults and out of reach until their power fades. It was a command issued long ago, around the time of the Fearless Decree. The King's law says no wizard may sit a throne, and a king with enough enchanted objects is as good as a Wizard King."

"Enchanted objects are outlawed, then?"

"Yes and no," said Kalem. "Many can be found throughout Underrealm, and some wizards will make small enchantments for everyday use. The Mystics do not concern themselves with such trifles. Only objects of great power are controlled. The lord chancellor of the Mystics is the final authority on which artifacts must be kept within the vaults, and which are not worth the trouble."

"One entry in that logbook remains," said Theren. "One artifact that is still within the vaults—or was, until it was stolen."

Ebon flipped through the pages to find the entry, glancing at the other listings as he did. There was a sphere of gold, bearing runes like those on the Academy's front door. The text said that, with the right words, it could erupt into a giant ball of flame and consume everything nearby before returning to its original shape. The next page described a circlet that let the wearer vanish from sight. He turned page after page, reading about each artifact in turn. Some held power he could scarcely imagine, while others seemed only to have a practical, everyday sort of use. It seemed different lord chancellors of years past had had very different ideas of what sort of enchantments should be protected within the vaults.

But all the entries were crossed out with a red X—until at last he found the one that was not.

The Amulet of Kekhit
This amulet of crystal is bound in gold and depends from a chain of silver. Its dark powers were hers, and show no signs of decay despite the many centuries since it was pried from her long-rotting bones in the southern reaches of Idris.
Added to the vaults upon the 10th of Arilis, Year of Underrealm 194

The artifact's name had two lines drawn in red ink beneath it, but nothing more was said of its properties. There was a crude sketch of the amulet; the crystal was shaped like an arrowhead, pointing down and away from the wearer's throat. Ebon flipped to the next page, but it was only the logbook's next entry.

"This amulet—that is what was taken?" said Ebon.

"I am sure," said Theren. "See where they have drawn a line beneath it? They must have planned this for some time."

"I fear I do not understand what it does," said Ebon.

"Nor I," said Theren. "But it is crystal, and therefore it must be powerful. Nothing holds magic so well as crystal. This *is* the missing logbook. When I could not find the entry of what had been stolen, I thought it was a clerical error. But it was here, in this book, which someone stole. And there is something else. Keep turning the pages."

Ebon did, and soon came upon where some leaves had been torn from the book. One remnant had some smudged writing near its spine, but he could not make out what it said.

"Why are these pages torn?" said Ebon.

"More artifacts—likely more they plan to steal. Mayhap they tore the pages out to better keep the secret and then tried to hide the tome."

"Why not destroy the book, rather than hide it?" said Ebon. "It seems it would hardly have been missed if you did not know where it had gone."

Theren shrugged. "Mayhap the thief meant to take the amulet and then choose other artifacts to steal later. Or mayhap they meant to destroy it, but they were nearly discovered holding it and concealed it in haste. Who is to say?"

"Should we tell Jia? Or the dean?" said Kalem.

"No. I will arrange for it to be found in a way that leaves us all blameless. Hopefully they will read through the pages and realize what has been taken."

"But still we know nothing of the amulet's powers," said Ebon.

"We have a name," said Kalem. "Kekhit. We must discover who she was. She sounds familiar, but I cannot place her. Doubtless we will find something in *An Account of the Dark War and the Fearless Decree*. I will start searching at once."

"If only there were more than one copy," said Ebon, shaking his head. "I would like to help in the search."

"We know she lived in Idris and was long-dead by the year 194," said Kalem. "The two of you should search for more books from that time. Who knows but that you may find the truth before I do."

Theren gave a long-suffering sigh. "Does it matter if we know what Kekhit's amulet does? We know Lilith has stolen it and that we must reclaim it from her. The amulet's enchantments do not seem important."

Kalem frowned. "We still do not know for certain that Lilith stole the amulet."

Theren glanced over his shoulder, and her eyes hardened. "We could always ask her ourselves."

They followed her gaze. There was Lilith, a few dozen paces away and heading straight for them. Ebon tried to speak a word of restraint, but Theren leapt from her chair and strode forwards to meet her. Kalem and Ebon scrambled to follow, flanking her on either side as she and Lilith faced off. Ebon realized that he and Kalem probably looked a great deal like Oren and Nella when they stood like bodyguards by Lilith's side. That was not an entirely comfortable thought.

"Good day, Lilith," said Theren evenly. "How odd that you should seek us out, for I have had a mind to speak to you as well."

Lilith stared, blinked, and then turned her gaze to Ebon.

"Good day, Ebon. I hope you have been well.

Some friends and I have been congregating here in the library after the Academy's hours, and I was wondering if you might like to join us." Slowly she turned to Kalem. "You, too, would be most welcome, Kalem of the family Konnel."

Ebon blinked. He gave his friends a sharp look, but they both seemed equally mystified. He cleared his throat, drawing Lilith's attention back to him. "We have questions for you, Lilith, as Theren said."

Theren's eyes had grown dangerously narrow. "Where were you when the Seat was attacked?"

For a moment, Lilith said nothing. Then she shook her head, as though the thought were distressing, before finally turning to Theren. "What do you mean? I was home in Feldemar. You already knew that. All of you did." She gave three sharp blinks and returned her attention to Ebon. "What say you, son of Drayden? We would be most privileged by your presence—by both of you. We call ourselves the Goldbag Society, after all." Her lips twisted in a small, self-deprecating smile.

Theren's breath came quicker. She took a half-step forwards. Ebon wanted to place a hand on her elbow, but he was suddenly afraid she might strike him. "Your petty arrogance does you no favors, Lilith. Why did your family draw you home to Feldemar just as the Seat was attacked?"

Lilith focused on her again, brow furrowing as though it were a great inconvenience. "I . . ." She shook her head. "What are you saying? Do you mean to say I had something to do with the attack?"

"I said nothing of the sort." Theren's smile grew cruel. "But now that you mention it, is there any truth to such a thought?"

Again Lilith shook her head, her eyes growing sharp and focused. She took a step back, staring at Ebon and Kalem as though seeing them for the first time. "I cannot believe this. I do not know what foolishness made me invite you to our gatherings."

Theren stepped forwards as though she would catch Lilith by the hand and prevent her escape. "You did not answer me. Why did you mention yourself in connection to the attacks, Lilith? What are you hiding?"

Lilith was shaking with rage—but, too, her eyes were hurt as they stared into Theren's. "That you would think such a thing of me shows your ignorance. I was devastated when I learned of Dulmun's treachery. Until we learned what had happened, I wept every day for fear that my friends and classmates—and yes, even you—might have perished in the fighting."

"Sentiment is an ill look for you," spat Theren. "Like an adder wrapping itself in feathers and calling itself a songbird."

Again Lilith retreated—this time in earnest, turning away. But she stopped after a few steps and gave them a withering look over her shoulder. "Call me an adder, then. But call me also a fool for thinking your death a tragedy."

She swept off, and for a moment Ebon thought Theren would pursue her. He seized one elbow, and Kalem the other, and they half-dragged her to their chairs in the corner. But when he looked back over his shoulder, he saw Lilith was looking at them again. Fury twisted her face, and angry tears wet her cheeks. At last she turned and ran away, vanishing among the bookshelves.

By the time they returned to their chairs, Theren was shaking. She rounded on Ebon and Kalem. "That manipulative little sow. I know she had something to do with the theft, and there is a fast way to prove it. We must get into the vaults."

"Get *into* the vaults?" said Kalem, his eyes wide. "You are mad. We could be expelled."

"Not if they do not catch us. And if we visit the room where the amulet was stolen, I will know for certain whether it was Lilith who did the deed."

"How?" said Ebon, shrugging. "What do you hope to find?"

"Every wizard has a . . . a sort of signature," said Theren. "Think of it like handwriting. An imprint upon the spells they cast. One wizard who knows another well can read the signature. If I can investigate the vault where the artifact was taken, I can tell if it was Lilith who stole it."

"Spell-sight? That is a wildly inaccurate practice, and prone to errors," said Kalem. "Every instructor speaks of its unreliability. No king's court will accept such as testimony, except in some of the outland kingdoms."

Theren slapped her hand on the back of a chair. "I know Lilith's mark. I will know if it was her."

A moment passed. Ebon cleared his throat and then quietly said, "What do you propose to do?"

She gave a thin-lipped smile. "I can sneak into the vaults with Kalem. After I conduct my search, Kalem can shift stone and tunnel our way out."

"Only Kalem?" said Ebon. "What of me?"

Theren shook her head. "Forgive me for saying so, but you could do nothing to help. You do not yet command the magic required to aid our escape."

Ebon gave them both an uneasy look. Then he stepped away from the chairs, to the corner where the wall sat exposed between two shelves. He reached out and set his hand on the stone. Magic coursed through him. The stone melted and warped beneath his hand, folding away to reveal the hidden shelf where Kalem stowed books he wished to keep secret.

Theren's brows arched. "You have learned to shift stone?"

"Ever since the attack on the Seat," Ebon said, forcing his thoughts away from the sound of Cyrus' scream.

"That is often the way of it—once the first step is taken, the rest come easier," said Kalem brightly. "I knew nothing of this, Ebon. Congratulations—you are learning far more quickly than I did."

"Only because I am six years older," said Ebon. "And I cannot put the stone back, only push it away."

"I can replace it," said Kalem. "And this will make the tunneling faster."

"You are interested in the plan, then?" Theren grinned. "This may work after all. Two alchemists to aid our escape, instead of only one."

"You mean transmuters."

"I mean be silent, Kalem."

"When do you propose we act?" said Ebon.

Theren pursed her lips. "We can do nothing to-night. It would be best to avoid the vaults until Sunday. The Academy will be on holiday, and I will be performing my services. Lilith will not. The days between now and then will give me time to prepare."

Ebon sagged, for a thought had struck him. "Very well," he sighed. "If we must."

"What troubles you?" said Kalem.

"It is my family," said Ebon, lowering his gaze. "They arrive upon the Seat on the morrow."

"How could they interfere?" said Kalem. "There is no way they could know what we mean to do."

"Of course not," said Ebon. "But my father will no doubt have some torment for me, in one form or another."

With an encouraging smile, Theren clapped his shoulder. "Try not to worry overmuch. If you should be drawn away Sunday night, I believe Kalem and I can manage without you."

Kalem straightened and reached for his book. "And in the meantime, we still have work to do. Who knows what we might learn before then if we find out about this Kekhit?"

Theren sighed and stood. "Very well. We are bound for the bookshelves after all, Ebon, though it pains me as a woman of action."

Ebon joined her, and together they returned to the shelves, searching through spines in the library's quiet.

TEN

The next morning, Ebon sat in class with Perrin beside him. The poor bench groaned and creaked under the woman's mammoth weight, and Ebon held himself ready to leap out of the way should it snap to kindling beneath them. Perrin had already gone about the class and set the other students to their tasks before coming to him.

"We did not have time yesterday, but now you will learn your aim while under my tutelage," Perrin began. "You had one spell to master before you graduated your first class. Here, you will have three."

"Three?" said Ebon, dismayed. It had taken him two months to turn wood to stone and pass Credell's class. He did not relish the thought of taking more than half a year to graduate from this one.

"Three to pass, though I expect you to learn many more while you are here. The three tests are these: to turn your stone rod back into wood, which is harder than you might expect; to turn a flower to ice without changing its shape; and to turn obsidian white."

The last one made Ebon blink in surprise. "Changing a stone's color? That cannot be harder than turning stone to wood."

"It is far, far more difficult," said Perrin gruffly. "Matter has many properties. Some are simpler than others. Color is one of the strangest."

Ebon snickered, but stifled it quickly as Perrin's eyes narrowed. "My apologies, Instructor. It is only that I do not take your meaning. Color is color."

"Oh?" said Perrin. "Tell me, what is stone?"

He blinked. "It is . . . it is rock. The stuff of the earth. It comes from the ground and the mountains."

"And what is wood?"

"The stuff of trees. You cut them down and take them apart, and there is your wood."

"And what is green?"

Ebon blinked. "I . . . it is the color of grass, and leaves. It—"

"No. Those are things that have the color green. But what *is* green? A leaf may *look* green, but that does not mean it *is* green. What is color itself? You know, do you not, that there are those who cannot see colors, or to whom different colors look alike? People who see no difference between green and blue?"

"Yes," said Ebon, nodding slowly. "I know this."

"If they do not see the green in a leaf, does that mean the leaf is no longer green?"

"Of course not," Ebon said, irritated. "It is only something wrong with their eyes."

"Who is to say? Who is to say that we do not imagine the green in the leaf, and they see it for its truth? Who is to say that the color I see when I look at good tilled earth, is not the same color you see in a cup of wine?"

Ebon shook his head. "That is ridiculous. I know what I see. Anyone does, if they are not mad."

"Ridiculous, you say?" Perrin smiled grimly. "Mayhap you are right, mayhap not. But you are a student, and the purpose of the student is to ask questions—not assume you know the answers already. You say you know what you see? Let me show you something."

She placed her hand on the table. Light flooded the room as her eyes glowed with a furious luster, brighter than any Ebon had seen. He focused on the hand—and then, suddenly, it was not there. It did not fade, nor wisp away in smoke. It simply vanished. Ebon jumped up with a cry.

"What happened?" Perrin spoke through gritted

teeth, forcing each word from her mouth. "Why are you frightened?"

"Your hand!" said Ebon. "It . . . it is gone!"

"It is not," said Perrin. "It is there. I feel it. I am moving my fingers now."

"But I cannot see them!"

The glow died in her eyes, and her hand reappeared. She flexed her fingers, curling them into a fist before reaching towards Ebon. He withdrew, frightened. She only wiggled her meaty fingers. "Go on. Take my wrist."

Slowly, tentatively, Ebon did. Her hand enveloped his, gripping him firmly, solid, present—*real*. Ebon shuddered. As he looked about the room, he saw that the other students were looking at them both with awe. He turned back to Perrin. "How did you do it?"

"It is difficult to explain. Except that there is something—the air, is how I perceive it—that controls how you are able to see my hand. I can twist it so that it shows you nothing. And so my hand disappears." Perrin looked around the room. "That is a powerful spell of transmutation—rarely can a wizard master it. And before you go thinking wild thoughts of my strength, take note that even such a small illusion required all of my concentration. There are transmuters in Underrealm who can make their whole bodies vanish. But if you never reach such skill, do not count yourselves among the weak. It is a rare ability. Also, you should all be working."

The other students hurriedly dove back into their books and spells.

Perrin turned her gaze on Ebon again. "Color is not nearly so hard. Yet it is far, far more difficult than simply changing the substance a thing is made of. You have learned to turn wood into stone. But with color you must go deeper, smaller, until you can find the thing that makes a stone appear grey—or black, in the case of obsidian—and turn it white instead."

"I understand," said Ebon, slowly nodding.

"Of course you do not," said Perrin, smiling a little. "Not yet. That is why you are in my class. Though unless I miss my guess, you wish you had passed it already."

Ebon looked away. "Is it so obvious?"

"Do you think you are the first student to arrive late at the Academy? When I attended, our oldest student had seen more than twenty years. Though I would wager she faced less jibes than you, seeing as how she could tweak the ears of most children."

That thought made Ebon smile. "Thank you, Instructor."

"You are welcome. Now, fetch your book again. You will find many bits of wisdom that should help you master your first test."

Perrin rose, the bench screaming in relief, and moved on to the next student. Ebon went to the shelves to find his book. But once there, he looked over his shoulder at Perrin.

The instructor was a giant, and often impatient. Yet there was a deep-seated kindness in her heart that made Ebon feel safe in her care. And certainly she was a far sight better than Credell.

He felt a stab of guilt at that thought and turned back to the bookshelf.

Soon Ebon had found the book and returned to his seat. The spine cracked as he laid it out and began to read. He quickly lost himself in the words, spelled out in careful, tiny script by some transmuter of ages gone, which spoke of the properties of different types of matter. Many of the terms whisked around and about in his mind, spinning until he felt dizzy. But he squeezed his eyes shut briefly and pressed on, determined to learn what he could.

The time whisked away as he lost himself in his studies, hardly mindful of the students practicing their magic around him. But after a time his attention was dragged away from the pages as the door to the classroom clicked and swung open. Ebon looked up to see Dasko, one of the advanced weremage instructors, a man with grey-flecked black hair whose beard was trimmed close. When Ebon had fled Credell's class in the mornings, he had often seen Dasko teaching students upon the grounds. The instructor's gaze went to Perrin, to whom he beckoned.

Perrin frowned and excused herself from the student she was speaking to. When she reached the door, Dasko did not bother to lead her outside, but spoke quickly in whispers. Ebon dropped his gaze to the book so he did not appear to be eavesdropping, but he leaned as far forwards as he could, cupping his left hand across his cheek so he could surreptitiously plug one ear. Still he could hear little more than snatches. *". . . the artifact . . . pendant . . . another vault . . ."*

The whispers stopped abruptly. Ebon could not help himself; he looked up. Dasko's eyes were fixed upon him, and he quickly looked back down. But the instructors did not resume speaking. Ebon let his eyes wander, so it looked like an accident when he eyed the door again. But Dasko was still watching him, and now Perrin was, too.

"Ebon," said Perrin. "Come here, if you would."

The class went deathly silent. Ebon's ears burned, but he tried to feign indifference as he stood and approached the instructors.

"This is Instructor Dasko." Perrin's voice was low, betraying nothing. "He brings a message from Instructor Jia. She wishes to speak with you."

That took Ebon completely unawares. "Jia? What for?"

"I imagine she will tell you. Off you go—but once you are done, return without dallying."

"Of course." Ebon followed Dasko out into the hallway. The door closed behind them with a sharp *click.*

ELEVEN

DASKO LED HIM ONWARDS, THOUGH EBON WELL RE-
membered the way to Jia's study. What could this possibly be about? Dasko and Perrin had said something
about the vaults. But why should they think that had
anything to do with Ebon? It seemed impossible that
they could have discovered what he and his friends
planned for Sunday.

He thought of Jia and Dasko standing over Credell's body, and his stomach wrenched. They must be
investigating the murderer.

The day the Seat had been attacked, Jia had seen

him flee from the other students. That had been explained, with Adara's help, but mayhap she still regarded him with some suspicion.

But she could not possibly think he was involved with Credell's death. She had been one of the few people at the Academy, instructor or otherwise, who had been kind to Ebon from the moment he arrived.

Dasko spoke suddenly, surprising him. "You are Ebon, of the family Drayden, are you not?"

"Yes."

"I am Dasko. I have seen you about the Academy, of course, though it was not until recently that I learned your name."

"Ah," said Ebon uncomfortably, not sure what response was expected of him.

Dasko turned to regard him keenly. "Now is an ill time, for Jia awaits you. But I had wondered if, on some occasion, I might speak with you privately."

Ebon swallowed—he hardly thought that instructors needed permission for such a thing. "Of course. I am at your service."

"Excellent. Soon, then. Here we are."

And indeed they were. In his surprise, Ebon had lost track of their progress, but now they stood at the door that led to Jia's study. Ebon gave Dasko one last, awkward nod, which the man returned before striding away through the halls. Then Ebon lifted a hand and knocked.

"Come in," said Jia from the other side. Ebon

turned the latch and stepped within. "Ebon. Excellent. Please come and have a seat. Would you like a cup of water?"

"Now that you mention it," said Ebon, realizing that his throat was as dry as the deserts of home. "But I can pour it."

"Do not be silly. Sit." She rose and went to the side table, poured two wooden cups, and placed Ebon's in front of him before returning to her seat. But when she caught sight of his face, she must have seen how frightened he was. "Did Dasko not tell you why I wished to see you?"

The bluntness of the question took him by surprise. His skin crawled beneath his robes. "No, Instructor."

She looked skywards. "Blast that man. Doubtless he did not think of it, and has forgotten what it was like to be a student. You are not in trouble."

Ebon could not help it: he let out a loud bark of laughter, nearly choking on his water. He put the cup down and coughed, and then sank into the cushions while pounding on his chest.

Jia graced him with a small smile, though she hid it quickly. "I imagine you were worried."

"I may have been," said Ebon, his voice hoarse with choking.

Her smile died. "Well and good. But this is still a matter of gravest importance. I must ask you some questions, and it is imperative that you are absolutely honest."

Ebon sat up straighter. "Of course, Instructor."

"Tell me again what happened when you left us on the day the Seat was attacked."

His heart quailed. He had guessed wrong. This was to do with Cyrus, not Credell. She had said he was not in trouble, so she did not suspect him of anything. But still this seemed a dangerous line of questioning.

"I thought I had explained that already."

"Tell me again. The whole of the tale, from beginning to end."

Shifting in his seat, Ebon repeated the same lie he had told her before, when he and Adara had landed on the shores of Selvan and then made their way to the other refugees. It was a lie Adara had helped him craft. In his ear he heard her voice as though she were speaking to him now.

They must believe your reason for leaving them, and so it must be something you would do—good-hearted, if mayhap a bit foolish.

"After the blue-clad soldiers attacked us in the streets, I thought I saw someone running close by. They wore black robes, and so I thought a student had become separated from the group. I chased after them."

"Which was—"

"Foolish, I know," said Ebon, ducking his head. Hopefully she would think it was shame at her chastisement rather than at the lie he told. Again he heard Adara's soft words.

The best lie is rooted in truth, yet you can make no mention of me whatever. Therefore I shall be someone else—someone who will speak to the truth of your tale, if I ask them to.

"But still, I did it. And when finally I caught them, I found only a woman in a black dress who had fled the fighting. I tried to return with her to the other students, but you had already left through the wall. I followed the trail to the docks, from which you had already sailed. There was a small rowboat that had been cast off from its ship and was nearly too far from the docks to reach. I dove into the Bay, swam to it, and rowed back to her. Then we set out for Selvan."

"The woman's name?"

Mitra.

"Mitra. She told me she was a handmaiden from the palace."

Jia sighed and leaned back, steepling her fingers. "Very well. We have spoken with the woman, and she tells the same tale. I am sorry I had to ask again, but the dean insisted."

A wave of relief washed through him, though he tried to hide it.

Jia looked away for a moment and then leaned forwards again. "Ebon, tell me one thing—and no matter your answer, I vow to you that I will not be upset. Do you swear that you did not return to the Academy at any time during the attack?"

His heart skipped a beat. "No, Instructor. I mean,

yes, I do swear it. I did not return here." Then he hesitated. He had no wish to further this line of thinking—and yet, he had *not* returned to the Academy, and could hardly say anything to incriminate himself. So he pressed on: "Why do you ask?"

She regarded him carefully. "Have you heard any rumors floating about the halls of late?"

Ebon blushed. "Mayhap. Something to do with the vaults."

Carefully she folded her hands on the desk. "Yes. I would ask you *never* to repeat such rumors. They do no one any good, though of course all our attempts to quell them have only redoubled them. But yes, something was taken from the vaults. Already we sought the thief, of course, but Instructor Credell's death has given the search a fresh urgency. Whoever broke into the vaults may have had something to do with the murder. So I will ask you once more, and then leave it alone. Did you return to the Academy during the fighting? If you saw anything—anything at all—it could be the kernel of information that helps us discover the thief's identity—and mayhap the murderer's."

Ebon understood at last, and relaxed. They were questioning him not about Cyrus, but about the theft—and not because he was a Drayden, but because he had become separated from the group. He could answer honestly and with a clear conscience. "No, Instructor. I swear it—I left the Academy when you did, and returned with you. I know nothing of the vaults. I am only relieved you do not suspect me of the theft."

Jia smirked. "Oh, there was no question of that. The vaults are protected by incredibly powerful enchantments and—you will forgive my saying so—you were only a first-year transmuter. We know without doubt that you had no hand in the theft itself."

Ebon laughed wryly, and it earned him another smile. "Mayhap this is the first time I am gladdened by my own lack of power."

"Not for long, I think. Under Perrin's able tutelage, you should progress through your lessons most quickly."

He sat up. "I will return to class and attempt to prove you right."

"Not just yet," she said, holding up a finger. From a drawer in her desk she withdrew a slip of paper and handed it to him. "A missive, sent for you."

Ebon frowned—and then he recognized the Drayden family seal pressed into the wax that held the parchment closed. He blanched.

Jia's eyes hardened. "Is everything all right?"

He tried to force a smile. "Fine, Instructor." He took the letter and cracked the seal. There in his mother's thin handwriting was a simple note:

We have arrived, and await you in the manor.
—Hesta

Carefully he folded the letter and stowed it in a pocket. His throat was suddenly dry, and he took another sip of water.

"Ebon, you look troubled. Tell me what is wrong."

"It is my family," Ebon said reluctantly. "They have arrived upon the Seat."

Jia leaned back in her chair, letting a few heartbeats of silence stretch between them. "I see. Far be it from me to pry into your affairs, Ebon. But I hope you know that you need not visit them if you do not wish to."

Ebon gave a wry smile and shook his head. "If I did not, they would send someone to fetch me."

"The family Drayden is powerful indeed, but their reach does not penetrate the Academy's walls." Ebon heard steel hidden in her words—not anger at him, but an unyielding promise of strength. "Especially since Dean Cyrus was lost. Stay if you wish, and I vow that no one will drag you forth."

Her conviction, and the kindness that rested behind it, brought a lump to the back of his throat and made his eyes smart. But he wondered if she would speak so confidently if she knew of Mako, who seemed to appear and disappear from the library on a whim. "I thank you, Instructor. And if it were only my father who wished to see me, I might do as you say. But it is my mother as well—in fact, the note came from her— and my aunt Halab, who has always been kind to me. And most of all, my sister, Albi, who I have missed the longest. No. I will go to see them, though the good will be tarnished by the bad."

"As you wish. You may go now, if you like. I will send a note along to excuse you from the day's classes. As I said, discuss the vault with no one."

"I will not, Instructor."

She gave him a sharp look, eyes glinting. "Not even with Theren and young Kalem?"

Ebon swallowed and looked away. "I . . . of course not, Instructor."

Her pursed lips made him wonder if she believed him. "Hm. Well, if you should think of anything else that might help . . ."

"I will tell you at once, Instructor," said Ebon. "And . . . thank you."

He left her and made for the Academy's front door, shaking his arms as he went, for a thrill of fear still coursed through him.

TWELVE

EBON STOPPED IN THE FRONT HALL. HE HAD MEANT TO go straight into the street and make for the manor. But now he wondered if he should go up to his dormitory and change into fresh robes. His hands shook no matter how he tried to rid himself of his anxiety, and his breath came so shallow that it set his head to spinning.

He heard his father's voice in his mind. *Coward. Sniveling coward.* And indeed, he felt himself on the verge of tears. Self-loathing filled him at the fear that blossomed in his breast, and yet he could not dismiss it.

What did he think would happen? Did he think his

father would strike him? Harm him? Try to kill him, even? No, certainly not. Especially not if Halab were there, which she would be. Would Shay try to remove him from the Academy? Ebon doubted it, for he could have done that by letter—and again, there was Halab. She would object, and Shay would not gainsay her.

Mayhap Ebon only feared the look in his father's eyes—the hatred he knew he would find there, and the scorn.

He forced himself to square his shoulders. Never mind going upstairs to change. He had no other clothes—only his student's robes were allowed in the citadel. He could don a fresh set, but why? It would make no difference to his father. Let Shay see him with some of the day's dust upon him and with palms smudged with ink from his books. Ebon was a wizard now—or at least he was studying to be one. Shay could face that truth or fly into a rage at it, but it would change nothing.

He went to the Academy's wide front door. Mellie stood there, and Ebon made to stop and explain. But before he could, she reached over and opened the door without saying a word. He stared for a moment, confused, but then shook his head and left. He had long ago given up on trying to make sense of the mad woman's actions.

Winter had come at last to the High King's Seat, and snow fell gently from the grey above. Though clouds covered the sky, they were thin, and so the sun still shone through them, lighting the island in its glow. The snow muffled all sound, so that the clattering of construction and the rumbling of wagon wheels sounded distant, like a city observed from atop a mountain.

Ebon had retrieved his overcoat from where it hung outside Perrin's classroom, and he wrapped it tighter about himself. His hood helped keep his hair free of the falling snow. Quietly he murmured thanks that the streets were clear, for his shoes were not meant to wade through deep drifts. Servants of the High King had been about, their horses dragging great plows that pushed the snow off and into the gutters.

Back home in Idris, the cold had sometimes been worse than this. But Idris was a desert, and never saw snow. Some thought that meant the land was gentler, but in truth it was the opposite. Here in the green lands, the earth itself resisted any changes in weather. When the day was hot, the ground held that heat so that evening took longer to cool the air. And when the sun rose in the morning, the trees clutched at night's chill and sent it wafting along on dawn's breezes.

In the desert, change came fast and harsh. The sun's absence turned night into a frozen void where one could die from exposure in no time. And daylight's baking rays were reflected by the sand itself so that travelers were roasted from above and below. All life and society in Idris were tailored around the desert's merciless nature, from the homes to the horses.

Despite the snow that dusted him now, Ebon found this land far gentler, and felt grateful for it.

He had thought the road to the Drayden manor would seem longer, with the dread of his father looming over him. But in fact, it seemed far too short a time before he stood outside the gates, hands shoved under his arms to protect them from the chill. He hesitated before stepping forwards, keenly aware that he could still turn around and go back to the Academy. Certainly his family would fetch him, one way or another, but it would stall the reunion for at least another day.

But then he thought of his father the last time they had seen each other. It had been in the courtyard, the very one before which he now stood. And without saying farewell, his father had hidden within a carriage, concealing his face in the curtains, too ashamed to so much as glance at his only living son.

Ebon's heart burned. *He* was not the coward. That epithet belonged to his father.

He stepped forwards and pounded on the iron gate.

A hatch slid open, and a yeoman peered out. "Master Ebon," grunted the man. "You are expected. A moment, my lord."

The hatch screeched shut, and then the gate groaned as men dragged it open. A slight wind wafted out from the courtyard through the gap, making Ebon blink. When the gate was open, he saw the courtyard was filled with wagons. Trade goods to be sold upon the

Seat, Ebon guessed—spices, most likely. He trudged through the snow, for here there were no shovels or plows, and through the front door.

No one waited for him in the front hall, nor on the high landing that overlooked it. The staircases were empty, and no servants could be seen moving through the adjoining hallways. But Ebon heard voices from the upstairs common room, and then a light laugh that sent his heart racing: that was Albi for certain, though there was something different about her voice.

Excitement seized him and banished thoughts of his father. He leapt up the stairs two at a time, hand gliding on the rail as a smile forced itself across his face. Feet pounding on the stone, he ran like a child down the hallway and threw open the door.

There they sat—but not for long, for as soon as they saw him they all rose to greet him. Halab caught his eye first, her beaming smile warming him to the heart, and then his mother, who rushed forwards to embrace him. But she was overtaken, as a short plump figure threw itself past her and into Ebon's arms, clutching his neck and crying delight into his ear.

"Ebon, you useless, horrible, *horrible* . . ." Albi's words vanished, replaced by sharp sniffs as she choked back tears.

He held her, arms locked as though he might never release her—though he did, when Hesta arrived and demanded a free arm to hug her with as well.

Albi drew back a step, looking up at him with shining eyes.

"You have grown taller," she said.

"I? It is you I can hardly recognize." He laughed and hugged her close again.

But then a shadow darkened his mood, for a man stood up behind Halab. Ebon braced himself—but then he looked again, for it was not Shay who stood there, but a man he did not know. A man of the family Drayden, certainly—he had the eyes, the stolid brow. Doubtless some cousin or uncle of Ebon's. But another glance around the room confirmed it: Shay was nowhere to be seen. And then, in the room's deepest corner, Ebon saw Mako was here as well. The bodyguard leaned against the wall, a sarcastic smile playing across his lips as he watched Ebon.

Hesta must have seen the confusion in Ebon's expression, for her lips tightened. "Your father was caught up in business the very day we left Idris to come here. He was forced to stay home."

Ebon looked at Albi. "I . . . I thought from your letter that he would be here."

His mother looked as though she thought he had gone mad, but Albi gave a sad smile of recognition. Another would have thought Ebon was disappointed that Shay was missing, but Albi would know how overjoyed he was. "He, too, thought to visit. His decision to stay was made at the final hour."

"It was all quite sudden, but nothing to concern

ourselves with," said Halab, who had now approached to stand behind Hesta. Ebon's mother and sister drew aside in deference. "Well met again, my dearest nephew. My heart has been fairly sick in your absence."

Ebon kissed one cheek and then the other, gripping her shoulders tightly. "Dearest aunt. How I have missed you."

She turned and gestured to the couches surrounding the hearth, where the fire still burned. Together they crossed the room—but they halted before taking their seats, for the man still stood there, looking at Ebon with something very much like a glare.

"Doubtless you remember your uncle, Matami— brother to your father and I." Halab inclined her head. "He came in Shay's place."

At hearing the name, Ebon found that he *did* remember. He had met Matami once or twice, although the last time was quite some years ago. "Of course," said Ebon, bowing deep. "Well met, uncle. It has been a long time."

"Indeed it has." Matami gave a loud sniff and turned away, returning to his seat. Albi met Ebon's gaze and playfully rolled her eyes. Ebon barely managed not to laugh out loud.

He took an armchair between Halab and Hesta. Albi left her chair and sat on a rug at his feet, her head leaning on his knee. "So, Uncle Matami," said Ebon. "What business do you conduct for my father here upon the Seat?"

"Nothing you need concern yourself with," said Matami, each word terse and clipped. But when Halab gave him a sharp look, his jaw tensed, and he continued. "I mean only that you are a student of the Academy now, and doubtless the family's business would strike you as uncommonly dull."

In fact, Ebon thought he might be right—but he almost wanted to inquire anyway, only to prove Matami wrong, for he found himself with an immediate dislike for the man that only grew with every passing moment. But over Matami's shoulder, he saw Mako snickering while sipping his ale. Ebon's mood lightened at once, and he suppressed his own smile as he gratefully took an offered goblet of wine.

Evidently Halab was still dissatisfied with Matami's answer. "No need to be so brusque, brother. Matami is here to escort the wagons in the courtyard—doubtless you saw them when you arrived—as well as the goods inside. They are spices for the High King's palace."

"Spices?" said Ebon. "That many wagons full will surely fetch a fine price."

"They do not mean to sell them," said Albi, sounding annoyed. When Ebon looked down at her in surprise, she sighed and looked skywards as though searching for strength. "They bring them as a *gift*. Something to ease negotiations for a new trade route through Wadeland. I see only wasted riches. That many wagons would fill our coffers to bursting for a decade."

"And the new trade route will fill them for a century," Halab chided. "Dear niece, this is a lesson you must learn well: today's wealth is well spent if it earns tomorrow's fortune."

Again Albi looked at Ebon and shook her head, and again he had to stifle his laugh. Halab suppressed a smile.

"I see your secret, scornful looks, girl," she said, delight dancing behind her words. "I will attribute it to youth, rather than disrespect. You are wise beyond your years, but life will bring you more wisdom still."

"As you say, dear aunt," said Albi. "But now that Ebon has arrived, may we eat? I fear I will simply *starve.*"

"Of course." Halab motioned to the servants standing near the door. "We will take our supper now."

They rose and went to the dining table at the other end of the room. The last time Ebon had eaten here, they had sat at a high table and chairs, after the fashion of the Seat and most other kingdoms. Now the dining table had been replaced with one in the Idrisian design, a low table with cushions all around it upon which they could sit cross-legged. One by one they settled in. Halab gestured for Ebon to sit by her right hand at the head of the table, with Hesta to her left. Albi quickly seated herself beside Ebon while the servants brought dishes and trays of food. Matami did not look pleased to be shunted down near the other end of the table, but he took his seat beside Hesta without comment.

Ebon's mouth watered at the smell of roasted lamb. It was placed at the table's center, and before him were set small plates of figs, light crackers, and chickpea spread mixed with many fine spices. Liya, one of the household servants, leaned over him to fill his goblet with wine.

"Thank you." Ebon reached over to lift the goblet and make it easier for Liya to pour. But she recoiled with a sharp hiss of breath, and wine spilled from her pitcher. Ebon yanked his hand back before it got soaked, and the wine splashed on the table instead.

"Liya!" said Halab sharply. "What is the matter with you?"

Ebon looked up at her. The serving woman's face was filled with fright—far more than seemed appropriate in response to Halab's mild rebuke. "I am sorry, mistress. I will fetch him a new place mat immediately."

She ran from the room and soon returned, replacing Ebon's mat as quickly as she could. Hoping to dispel the awkwardness, Ebon met Albi's eyes and made a face. She giggled.

Soon the dinner had been served, and the servants withdrew. Ebon dug into his lamb, savoring the way the sweet, tender meat broke apart in his mouth. He was unable to help himself from letting out a small groan of delight. Albi nearly choked on her food as she giggled again.

"Do they starve you at the Academy, my son?" Hesta smiled from across the table. "You sound as though you have not eaten since we saw you last."

Ebon shook his head. "The Academy takes excellent care of us, Mother. Only, they must serve so many, you understand, and their cooks cannot hope to match the skill of ours."

"And do you find yourself missing all the trappings of home? Your family has never kept you wanting for luxury, dearest nephew." To Ebon the words sounded almost like an accusation, but Halab smiled to soften them.

"I have grown used to life within the Academy. It is only now that I realize how different things are from the way they were in Idris."

"And your studies?" said Hesta. "Are they going well?"

Ebon smiled, trying to make it look modest. "Well enough. I wish I were moving faster. But I did complete my first class in two months when it should have taken a year." A thought came to him, sudden and perhaps mad, but he went on with it. "I could show you a spell if you wished. A small one only."

Albi's eyes shone, and Halab gave an indulgent smile. But Mother's eyes widened, and for some reason she looked at Matami with what looked like fear.

"If you wish," said Halab. "Only do not put a hole in the table, please."

"Of course not," said Ebon, shaking off his worry at Mother's expression.

He picked up an empty wooden cup from the table. Focusing, he called forth his magic. The room seemed to grow brighter as his eyes glowed.

Stone rippled out around his fingers, turning the wood until the spell was finished. He placed the cup, now wholly stone, back on the table with a small *thunk*.

Albi squealed with delight. But Matami was glowering down at his food, and his cheeks grew darker by the moment.

Halab's eyebrows rose. "That is most impressive. I knew when I sent you there that my faith in your wits would not be misplaced."

"*My* instructors also say I am a quick student," said Albi, beaming. "Since you left, Ebon, I have been learning all sorts of new things, from accounting to history to everything in between."

"I have noted you show particular interest and skill in the courts of the nine lands," said Halab with a gentle smile. "That subject is complex and intricate, and ever-shifting, yet it is one of the most valuable things any merchant could know."

Ebon frowned slightly. His father had never permitted him to learn much about the other kingdoms. It seemed he was fearful that Ebon might seek a better life, mayhap someplace where he might be permitted to learn his magic.

Now Halab cast her bright smile to Albi, before turning to place her hand upon Hesta's. "Bright minds run in the family, it would seem. I can only imagine your pride."

"What mother could wish for more than to see her children succeed?" said Hesta. Yet it seemed to Ebon that some worry still hovered about her. Matami had stopped eating entirely.

It felt as though the wind had fled from Ebon's sails, though he knew that was foolish. He had thought Halab and his mother would wish to speak of him, not Albi. After all, they saw her far more often. And sky above, he had performed magic! Was that not more impressive than the knowledge of courtly graces?

He took another sip of wine, trying to dispel such thoughts, and replaced the goblet on the low table. He was reminded of the table that had been there before, and that cast his mind back to the night he and his friends went to the eastern docks, where they saw the manor's servants stealing away on a ship like thieves, taking the furniture with them.

Carefully he drummed his fingers on the wood, trying to appear nonchalant. "I notice many things in the manor have been replaced. The furniture, the tapestries and rugs. Even these dishes look new. Were things lost in the attack upon the Seat?"

Halab's happy smile dampened, and she glanced at Hesta for a moment before sliding her eyes quickly away. Hesta looked down into her lap, suddenly fidgeting with her napkin. But Matami had looked up at last, and now he fixed Ebon with a withering glare, so furious that his brows nearly joined to one above his eyes.

"I only learned of this after the assault," said Halab. "But Shay decided to redecorate. He had everything removed from the manor and brought back to our estates in Idris, to be replaced with new things. He said he wished to rid the manor of its western trappings and make a home in the proud tradition of Idris again."

Clearly Albi did not know the source of Halab's sudden anxiety, but she caught the room's mood. Her eyes roamed from one face to the next but found no explanation. For his part, Ebon felt a tingling on the back of his neck; a heightened sense of awareness seemed to have come over him, bringing a roiling in his gut and a light-headedness that sharpened his thoughts.

"It is very fortunate," he said carefully, "that my father did so just before the Seat was attacked. Imagine the damage if all our possessions had been here when Dulmun sacked the island."

Halab's worried frown deepened—and Ebon saw that she looked at Matami for a moment before averting her eyes.

"Most fortunate indeed," said Halab.

Matami had not taken his eyes from Ebon's for so much as a moment. "We should all be blessed with such fortune," he growled. "It is a sign of some higher favor. Not like the Yerrins, whose home was demolished in the attack. Pompous fools." He drank deep of his wine.

"We are fortunate," Halab repeated. "Indeed, when I heard of the attack—after I learned that you had survived, Ebon, for of course that was my greatest worry—I grew concerned that this manor might have fallen. Only then did Shay mention what he had done."

The table went quiet as she sipped gingerly at her wine. Ebon glanced across the room to where Mako still leaned against the corner wall. The bodyguard fixed him with a hard stare, and there was a glint in his eye that did not come only from the fireplace. Ebon wondered if Mako was thinking the same thing as him.

Just then, there was a soft knock at the door. "Enter," said Halab, and a courier strode in, wearing the white and gold of the High King. She dropped her missive into Halab's hand and withdrew without a word. Halab glanced at the paper before looking up and giving them all a smile.

"We have been summoned to the palace," she said. "They have offered us an audience faster than I thought."

She stood, and the rest of them hastened to join her. Hesta and Matami went to Halab's side. But before she left, Halab went first to Albi and then to Ebon, giving each child a long embrace.

"You will likely be gone before we return," she told Ebon. "You must visit us again while we are still here. And if you have friends at the Academy, you must bring them, for we would all like to meet them."

"Farewell, my son," said Hesta. "It has gladdened my heart to see you again."

"And you, Mother." Ebon hugged her tight, inhaling her sweet perfume. He had not known how badly he missed it. "I will see you again soon."

They left. The moment the door shut behind them, Albi whirled to Ebon and seized his hands.

"Finally!" she said, laughing. "I thought they would *never* leave. Come now, Ebon. I want to hear everything—and I want to tell you everything I have been up to, as well. But first, you must put on some *proper* clothes."

Ebon looked down at himself, feigning insult, though he could not hide his smile. "Proper clothes? What is wrong with my Academy robes?"

"Do not pretend to be simple," she said, pushing his shoulders. "Go! Fetch yourself something more fitting to your station, and then let us walk in the garden. It is beautiful, more so with the snow, and not so smoky as it is inside."

"As you wish, my lady." Ebon bowed low, which earned him another slap on the arm, and then he left to find himself some new clothes.

THIRTEEN

EBON CLIMBED TO THE SECOND FLOOR AND MADE FOR his room, but when he reached the door he paused. Its fresh-cut planks and shining varnish spoke of new carpentry. He looked across the hall. The opposite door was not so new, but it bore a small scorch mark near the stone floor.

So. The attackers had gone through the Drayden manor. And Shay's "fortunate" decision to empty the place of their possessions had likely saved the family much coin. The armies would have rushed through the rooms and found nothing to steal. Likely they had destroyed the door to Ebon's room out of spite, or mayhap frustration.

Then he opened the door and found that it did not lead to his room at all. Instead he found a sitting room. There was a bookshelf at one end, some tapestries on the other walls, and a single armchair beside the fireplace. His bed was gone, as were his bureaus and chests. The one mark he had left upon this house, scrubbed away like a recalcitrant stain.

Ebon swallowed past a suddenly dry throat and stepped back, closing the door softly. Quick footsteps down the hallway drew his attention. It was Liya, the servant who had spilled his wine at dinner. She looked up and saw him just as he saw her. Her steps faltered.

"Liya," he said, forcing his voice to be calm. "Do I still have any clothes here? Have they been put somewhere else?"

She looked back over her shoulder, shifting on her feet as though she might run. But then he saw her take a deep breath, composing herself by the time it escaped her lips. "Yes, milord," she said timidly. "This way, please."

He followed her down the hall and around the corner. There was another wooden door, just like the one that had once led to his room. She opened it to reveal a storeroom. Crates and barrels lined the walls, stacked in neat and orderly rows. Atop one stack was a chest with a lock, but he could see from the way the lid was ajar that it had not been secured.

"If milord will help . . .?" Liya took one end of the chest, and Ebon hastened to take the other, and together they brought it down to the floor. Ebon swung it open to find a familiar sight—the fine golden silks he had grown up wearing.

"Just what I wanted. Thank you, Liya."

"Of course, milord." But Liya would not meet his eyes, and it seemed she wanted to leave the room but was unsure how he might react.

"Liya," he said, frowning. "What is it?"

Her eyes widened, and she clutched at her dress with her hands. "Nothing, milord."

"You are afraid. Of what, I do not know, but of something, certainly."

She shook her head quickly, too quickly to make her words ring true. "I am not, milord. I swear it."

Ebon found himself growing exasperated. "Tell me the truth, at once. I may not rule this household, but I am nephew to the one who does. Out with it, or Halab will know the reason you withheld yourself."

Her olive skin went pale. "No, milord! Please, please not that. It is . . . it is only that . . . we are all grateful to see you alive, young master. And you must understand; we were ordered to leave the Seat. We never meant to leave you behind."

Ebon balked. The thought was so strange that for a moment he could not react. When he did, it was to laugh. "Liya, of course I know that. I never thought you meant to abandon me."

He stepped forwards, reaching out a comforting hand for her arm. That was a mistake. She shrieked and drew back. She hesitated, but then fear got the better part of decorum, and she fled through the door back into the hallway.

Staring at his hand, Ebon felt realization crash upon him like a wave from the Great Bay. His magic. She feared his magic, as though with a simple touch he might strike her dead. The thought was so simple-minded and foolish that he wanted to laugh. But the fear in her eyes had been real enough.

Was that what the servants of the Drayden household thought? That he had become some dark wizard of evil, and would return to them like some lesser Wizard King? A tyrant whose commands were to be obeyed without question?

Why should they think otherwise? You are your father's son, after all.

He forced such dark thoughts away. Darkness take her. He was scarcely even a member of this house any longer, and its servants could think of him whatever they wished.

The golden silks felt glorious, and Ebon worried that he might smudge them with his ink-stained fingers. But he had no time to bathe, so he closed the door and changed anyway. When he was done, he looked down on himself in wonder. Once, garments such as these had been part and parcel of his everyday existence. Now they seemed like the height of unnecessary opulence. His Academy robes were of cloth so rough it was almost burlap. But rather than feeling more comfortable, this outfit felt too smooth, like a slithering serpent sliding along all his skin.

He shook off the sensation and made his way downstairs. The back door stood open, letting the cold air flood through the bottom floor. Ebon closed it behind himself as he stepped into the gardens. There was Albi, waiting for him with her coat pulled tight about her and a fur hood covering her head. But there, too, was Mako, standing aloof a pace or two from the girl, arms folded and bright teeth bared in a grin.

Albi turned. "Ebon!" she said, relief plain in her tone. "How wonderful you look. Much better than those drab black rags. Come."

She took his arm and very nearly dragged him away through the gardens. Ebon got only a glance behind them at Mako. The bodyguard's grin widened, and he gave Ebon a mocking wave with two fingers before retreating into the manor.

"Thank goodness," said Albi in a hushed tone. "That man has always terrified me."

"Mako?" said Ebon, raising his eyebrows. "He used to make me uneasy, I will admit. But terrifying? I think you exaggerate."

He felt her shudder where their elbows were locked. "I mean it. He seems to view everyone as a meal about to be devoured. If I could do any more to avoid him without being rude, I would."

Ebon thought of the room upstairs, the terror in Liya's eyes when she looked at him. His mouth twisted. "Mayhap you do not give him enough credit."

She snorted, but said nothing more. Ebon turned his gaze away from her out to the garden. The manor had been built upon a sizable plot of land, as far as property went upon the Seat, though compared to the Academy it seemed a cramped patch of dirt. Many of the plants were dead to winter's cold, but plenty of evergreen trees had been put about, and their verdant branches showed stark against their light dusting of snow. The plants were strange to him, and familiarity had not lessened their oddity. What scrubs grew in Idris were thin, small, and hardy. They bore the night's cold as well as the day's heat, but that was because they were small and self-contained. These pines and the live oak at the garden's center were like grand old men who refused to cow before winter's stormy assault, and Ebon felt like a child in their shadow.

Albi gripped his arm tighter. "I have missed you so much, dear brother." Then she drew back her other hand and struck him in the chest as hard as she could.

"Ow!" he cried, rubbing at the spot. "You have a strange way of showing it."

"How could you fail to write me?" she said, pouting. "I did not receive so much as a hasty scribble until the Seat was attacked, and we all feared you might be dead."

"I doubt you *all* feared it," said Ebon, thinking of

his father. But her scowl deepened, and he spoke hastily to avoid another smack. "I am sorry. Of course I should have written you. But even before the island was attacked, my days were much occupied with fear and danger."

That earned him a snort. "You make it sound *quite* dramatic."

"In truth, it was," said Ebon. "Indeed, I almost died more than once."

He spoke in earnest, but Albi only laughed. "Oh, Ebon. Do not think to wheedle out of this with outlandish tales. Only promise to write me more often in the future, and we may leave it at that."

A part of him was irked, for he had thought he might confide in her, at least, the way he did with Kalem and Theren. But then again, there were things that had happened in the months before the attack that he wished to tell no other. So he simply said, "I promise."

"Good. Now, tell me of your magic! After so long, I can only imagine how pleased you must be to put it to use. I thought I would simply *die* of delight to see you cast a spell."

He smiled. "It is a greater pleasure than I can say. I am only a simple beginner yet. But still . . . the power . . . sometimes I cannot believe it."

"Show me again," she said, eyes dancing.

Ebon looked about them on the ground and found a small branch, about as long and thick as his index finger. He stooped to retrieve it, and then concentrated. His eyes brightened, and stone rippled along the branch until it was all grey. Releasing the hold on his magic, Ebon placed the branch in her trembling hand.

Albi did not speak for a long moment. Her mouth parted in a silent circle. Then she gripped the branch in both hands and tried to break it. She strained, but nothing happened.

"It is stone through!" she whispered, as though someone might be lurking around the corner to eavesdrop. "Did you turn it all the way? And the cup?"

"Every part of them both," said Ebon, not modest enough to hide his smile.

Albi clapped her hands once and laughed. She tucked the branch into a pocket in her cloak. "I will hold this always as a keepsake. And to think you learned this after only a few short months. As I said before, I have proven to be a quick study as well—and in more things than book learning." Her eyes danced, and she leaned in closer to speak in a false whisper. "I have had a romance, you know."

Ebon nearly froze, a flush creeping up from his collar and into his cheeks. "A . . . you what?"

"Oh yes, a very passionate one," she said, giggling as her blush matched his own. "Such a charming, handsome boy. We stole many kisses here and there, in dark corners while I was visiting his family with Mother. But sadly, he was royalty. After a time I felt I had to ignore him and rebuff further advances, because after all, his family would never allow us to be wed. Still. If I seem a bit womanlier to you, that is no doubt why."

She gave a self-satisfied little smile and smoothed the front of her dress, though Ebon saw no wrinkles. *Womanlier?* he thought. True, Albi had grown what seemed an incredible amount for the few short months since they had seen each other, and she carried herself with a more mature air than before. But Ebon thought of his own dalliances with Adara, and the crimson deepened in his cheeks.

"Why, Ebon!" she laughed, mistaking his look. "I do believe I have embarrassed you."

Should he tell her? Of course not. Albi might keep some of his secrets, but only when she thought they were important. She would see nothing wrong in his visits to Adara, and so she might make mention of them to Shay. That could be a disaster.

He forced a tight smile and said, "I did not know you had such a rebellious streak within you, dear sister."

Another flashing smile answered him. "I know. I feel so *scandalous.* And we had to keep ourselves so carefully hidden, for it was the first time I was permitted to join Mother and Father on a caravan excursion. First we traveled north to the capital, and then west to explore the new route we wish to . . ."

On she went, telling him about the trip, her first with their parents where she actually had a role to play. The story was all too familiar, for he had gone on a few such excursions himself. Now that he was no longer there to attend them and learn the family's trade, he supposed it was only natural that they would bring Albi along in his stead.

With a shock he realized that that life was slipping away from him, and he did not want it to. Mayhap he had never wanted to follow in his father's footsteps, transporting spices across Underrealm to fill the family's coffers. But long years had let him grow somewhat used to the idea, and now he realized it might never be. What would he do when he graduated from the Academy? He had asked Theren that question often enough, for she was on the cusp of having to make that decision. But he had rarely thought of the answer for himself.

And as his thoughts ran further, he realized suddenly that the answer did not concern Albi at all. She did not care if he finished his training and returned to the family's business, or went off into some other kingdom entirely—so long as he wrote her, most likely, and visited on occasion. He could hear it in the way she spoke of her exploits with the caravan, and as he thought back, in the way she had turned every conversation away from him and to herself instead.

Had she always been so vain? And, a far more perplexing thought: had Ebon been the same when he was in her position?

He thought of Liya's face in the storeroom earlier, and how it had filled him with annoyance rather than compassion. His mood darkened further.

"—and do not hate me for saying so, but Father's mood has been much gentler since you entered the Academy, and I think especially so since now I will be the head of the family."

Albi's words snapped his attention back to the present. He stared at her for a moment, letting the words play back in his mind so that he could understand them. And yet still they held no meaning. Albi seemed to recognize that she had said too much, for she looked at him wide-eyed, and her mouth worked as she fought for some explanation.

"What do you mean?" But he knew the answer even as he asked.

"I mean only . . . Ebon, please, do not be angry with me."

The pain in her eyes, the sorrow for him, sealed the knowledge in his mind. Shay did not only mean to remove Ebon from the family's business dealings. Ebon's inheritance, his role as the future head of the family, was now forgotten, like a nightmare fading in daylight.

Had Father made the decision the moment Ebon joined the Academy, out of spite for losing his son to the fate he had always hated? Or had he concocted the plan for other reasons? Had he removed Ebon from his inheritance in the same breath he had ordered the Draydens' possessions removed from their manor upon the Seat?

Did Shay remain home in Idris because business

held him? Or mayhap because he was ashamed to face the son he had left on the Seat to die?

From nowhere, a laugh bubbled up in Ebon's breast. It erupted before he could stop it, and he was glad to learn that it was hearty and cynical, rather than desperate.

"Ebon?" said Albi, still looking at him fearfully. "What is it?"

"Nothing," said Ebon. For truly, that was what he faced. His father's motivations did not matter, because Ebon never needed deal with him again. He was cast out from the family, from its business, and from his role as its future patriarch. Halab would always give him her favor, and that was more than enough.

How often had he wished, as a boy, that he did not bear the name Drayden? In effect, that was what he faced now.

"Nothing," he said again. "It is only that I made a wish when first I came to the Seat, and that wish has come true. Mayhap I should have been more careful in making it. But then again, mayhap this is all for the best."

She still looked at him askance, clearly unsure, and likely now worried that his thoughts were addled. He gave her the most reassuring smile he could muster, and once more took her arm. "Come," he said, pulling her along. "Tell me more of your trip. I want to hear everything."

FOURTEEN

They walked in the garden and spoke until Albi said she was too cold, and then they sat together and spoke near a hearth inside the manor. And as before, Albi spoke mostly of herself, and all that she had done since last she saw Ebon, and some things she had done before, and whenever Ebon spoke of himself she barely nodded before relating it to another of her stories. Soon he stopped trying, and simply listened. Despite the dark cloud that had been cast over his thoughts, it *was* good to hear what Albi had been up to in his absence.

At last Albi yawned and said she might nap, for they had traveled long to get here and had only arrived the night before. The afternoon was now winding on, and the faint glow of the sun through the clouds was edging towards the western horizon.

They stood together, and Ebon gave her one last hug. "I cannot tell you how glad my heart has been to see you again, dearest Albi."

"And you, Ebon." She gave him a gentle slap on the arm, not nearly so hard as before. "But if you ever forget to write me again, I will return to the Seat with an army of sellswords."

"I will remember."

She made for her bedchamber, and Ebon for the storeroom where his Academy robes waited. He found them neatly folded and stacked. Mayhap Liya had done it, in some sort of apology for her earlier conduct. Or mayhap it had been another passing servant. It did not much matter, he supposed.

His Academy robes felt much more comfortable, and he sighed with relief once changed. He had no wish to stay for another encounter with the servants, so he went downstairs and to the front door—but there he found Mako waiting, leaning on the wall and picking at his nails with his long, silver knife.

"Greetings, young lord," said Mako, with a curious amount of courtesy. "Might I walk you back to the Academy—at least for part of the way?"

"Certainly," said Ebon, and gestured for Mako to

join him. He said it lightly enough, but in truth his mind was already racing. Mako never spoke privately for idle purpose.

The streets were soft and muted about them, and there were no passersby. But still Mako waited until they were a long way removed from the Drayden manor before he spoke his mind. He looked both ways cautiously and stepped closer so that Ebon could hear his growling murmur. "Did you notice that your uncle did not seem pleased to see you?"

"I did. But if he is my father's brother, I count it as no great surprise."

"Yet his scorn for you was not the only strange thing. Did you note his response when you asked questions about the manor being redecorated?"

"I did, and I thought it odd," said Ebon carefully. "It does not seem my uncle has any great affection for me. What did you make of his mood?"

Mako did not answer directly, but chuckled and said, "His ire should strike you as nothing new, when your father has hated you all your life."

Despite himself, Ebon felt his ears burning. His jaw spasmed, but he forced himself to speak anyway. "Do you bring up his odd behavior for a reason, or not? You already told me that our family had nothing to do with the attack upon the Seat."

Mako seized Ebon's throat in an iron grip and dragged him from the street into an alleyway. There he shoved him against the stone wall of a building, bringing his own face to within an inch of Ebon's. His breath smelled of something rancid, though it was hidden by mint.

"Still your witless tongue in the streets, you gold-shitting little fool."

Ebon glared over Mako's hand. But he knew the bodyguard was right, and that he had been foolhardy to speak so openly. Anger had provoked him. And now it made him drag Mako's hand away so that he could whisper, "Mayhap if you ceased playing games and said what you meant to say in the first place, I would not be so tempted to speak out of turn."

Mako did not glare at him, but neither did he wear his usual self-effacing smirk. His eyes were pits of ice, and that ice penetrated Ebon's soul, such that fear seeped in at the frayed edges of his anger. Though he could not see it, he was well aware of Mako's hand hovering at the hilt of his long, cruel dagger. The white of his scars fairly glowed against his dark olive skin.

But when Mako spoke, it bore none of the frigid tone that his look promised. "I did not tell you the family was blameless in the attack on the Scat. I told you I did not *learn* of the attack from a Drayden."

His hand left Ebon's throat, and Ebon slumped back against the wall. Though he hated to look weak, he reached up and rubbed his neck ruefully, for he thought a bruise might form. "I do not understand the difference you mean to imply."

"Mayhap Matami indeed had something to do

with the attack, and your father as well. Mayhap they kept the truth from me. I assumed they would not—after all, they could hardly ask for a better agent to help with such a plan. But then, long has your father been uncomfortable with the favor I have shown you; and that favor comes because Halab does the same, which he also resents."

Ebon released a sigh, and it crystallized to mist in the frigid air. "You mean they may not have told you because they feared you would warn me."

Mako nodded. "Just as I did, the moment I learned."

A long silence followed. Ebon stared at his shoes and tried to wrestle the feelings battling in his breast. This day was one for hard truths, and each had struck him like a blow: first, that his father would not even come and see him on the Seat, so ashamed was he of Ebon's enrollment in the Academy; second, that he had been robbed of his inheritance, which would now pass to Albi; and finally, now, the possibility that his death had been planned by his father all along, mere collateral damage in the wake of some grand scheme that spanned all of Underrealm.

But one thing troubled him. Shay was not the master of the family Drayden. "Halab directs our family, not my father. She would never have had anything to do with the vile treason of Dulmun."

"Certainly not," said Mako. "That is plain, if for no other reason than that you were left here on the Seat. Halab has always loved you better than Shay has."

"And because it would be the very highest of crimes against the High King."

Mako raised one eyebrow and shrugged. "As you say. But if what we have begun to guess at is correct, I believe we are looking at a plot by Shay, and possibly Matami, operating without the knowledge of Halab."

Ebon quailed at the thought of him and his friends slipping through the Academy grounds at night, and what they had planned for this Sunday. "So Lilith is innocent?"

"Impossible." Mako shook his head and turned to pace back and forth. But he stopped himself almost immediately, and went to the mouth of the alley to lean against the brick wall opposite Ebon. "Yes, impossible. Or so I think. Shay and Matami could never concoct such a scheme on their own. They would need help within the Academy. They might have thought to use Cyrus, but he was always an untrustworthy sort."

That made Ebon's heart skip a beat. He licked his lips. "Was? You speak as though you are certain he is dead."

Slowly, Mako's eyes turned to him, and once more they were pits of ice. "Are you not certain yourself?"

Ebon was glad he had put his hands in his pockets, for they were shaking like an old man's. "He might have fled the Seat. That is what some say."

"Some say foolish things." Mako spat, the saliva sinking into a wet hole in the snow. "In any case, Shay and Matami would not have brought him into their conspiracy, for he would certainly have told Halab. They must have seduced Lilith instead—or, mayhap, they are working with higher contacts in Yerrin, and Lilith is in the employ of those contacts."

He pushed off from the brick wall. Again he paced, now holding a clenched fist to his chin, tugging on it as though he pulled an invisible beard. "Yes. Yes, that would make sense. They think to make a play for greater power. By this temporary alliance with Yerrin, they think to increase their own standing."

Ebon was still shaking from the dark truths Mako had hinted at before. Could the bodyguard possibly know what had transpired between Ebon and Cyrus when the Seat was attacked? It seemed impossible. But in any case, the best thing was to draw the man's mind elsewhere. "Why? For what ultimate end? We have never had love for Yerrin."

Mako met his gaze. "To take Halab's place at the head of the Drayden family. In exchange for Yerrin's help to get there, Shay and Matami will promise more favorable relations with Yerrin once in power."

"But . . ." Ebon shook his head, unwilling to believe it. "But what would happen to Halab?"

The bodyguard's nose flared slightly. "Nothing that I would allow, I promise you that."

Still Ebon did not want to think it could be true. "But this would not help the family. Already we are stronger than Yerrin. It would weaken us, and strengthen them."

"Yes, it would weaken Drayden—but it would strengthen Shay and Matami in the process," said Mako. "They would sacrifice the family's power to enhance their own. It is the opposite of what Halab would do. And that is why they think she must be removed."

His voice rang with finality. Ebon squared his shoulders. "You are certain of this, then?"

"Rarely am I certain of anything, nor should you be. Yet it seems the likeliest thing."

"We must catch them."

"I shall work on that. You must focus on Lilith." Mako put a firm hand on Ebon's shoulder. "Catch her in the act, Ebon. Have her dragged before the King's justice and put to the question. She will expose those in her family giving the orders. They in turn will expose Shay and Matami, if indeed they are involved in this plot."

"Then I will expose her," said Ebon.

"Good." And just like that, as though he were done casting a spell, the ice faded from Mako's face, and his sardonic smile flew in to replace it. "I think you and I shall form a fine team, little goldshitter."

Ebon smiled grimly. "I think I prefer goldbag."

"I knew you would say so. Until we meet again, then. Good fortune this Sunday."

He stepped around the alley's corner, and when Ebon stepped around to follow him, Mako was gone. But then Ebon heard a scrape from up above, and he looked up in time to see a leather boot vanish over the edge of the tile roof.

At last I have caught him in the act. Not a spell after all.

It was only then that he realized Mako had wished him good fortune on Sunday, though he had never mentioned the plan to break into the vaults. Ebon's gaze jerked back towards the sky, where the body-guard's boot had vanished.

FIFTEEN

Ebon returned to the Academy just before the end of the afternoon's study. Quickly he made his way to the third-floor alcove, where Kalem and Theren listened with rapt attention to his account of the afternoon's doings—including his conversation with Mako.

"You told him about our plan?" said Kalem, voice edging towards panic.

"I did not," said Ebon. "He has . . . ways of learning such things. I long ago gave up trying to understand it."

"I think you should try again," Kalem shrilled.

He must have realized how loud he sounded, for he looked anxiously over his shoulder before going on. "One whisper of our plot in the wrong ear, and we could all be thrown out of the Academy for good."

"He means us no ill will," said Ebon.

"Not that you know of."

"I know it."

Theren slapped her hand against the table. "Enough of this. There is nothing we can do about it now. But I have had an idea—one I think may be more import-ant, and a relief to you besides, Ebon."

He frowned. "What do you mean?"

"You think Shay and Matami may have had some-thing to do with Lilith's scheming because they stand before your naked eyes," she said, speaking quickly in her excitement. "Yet I have another idea. One that would make more sense, if you would rather not be-lieve your own father has turned kinslayer. What if the Drayden helping Lilith has been someone else entire-ly?"

Ebon and Kalem exchanged an uncertain glance. "Well, spit it out," said Ebon. "Though I do not see how you could know my family better than Mako and I."

Her grin widened. "You do not see it, do you? And that is why it is the perfect deception. It is not your father, or your uncle. It is Cyrus."

Kalem's eyes widened in recognition. But Ebon felt a void open in the pit of his stomach, a void that sucked in his fears and anxieties and anger and spit them back up as raw, red shame burning its way to his heart.

What could he say? How could he refute her idea, which he knew for a fact to be wrong, without confessing his crime? Ebon had had his doubts when Adara insisted that he must keep Cyrus' death a secret. But whether or not he could have told them before, he certainly could not do so now.

"I . . . I find that hard to believe."

"That is what makes it so perfect," said Theren, smiling in triumph. "We know he hated you. And we know that, at the end, he blamed your family for cutting him out of their plots and schemes. He fled the Academy in terror, and he knew that if he returned, he would be tried and found guilty under the King's law, then to die a slow death under the knives of Mystics. So instead, he thinks to amass power for himself by collecting artifacts from the vaults of the Academy. He knows them better than any. And he might have enlisted the help of the family Yerrin, for certainly he would not have gone to his kin, who he thinks betrayed him."

"This does make sense, Ebon," said Kalem. "I might never have thought of it, but Theren is right— that is what makes it such a devious scheme."

"He was scum, Ebon." Theren's cheeks spasmed as she bit them, her lip curling in a snarl. "You know that better than most."

At last Ebon saw why Theren had seized upon this idea and why she believed it so strongly. Cyrus had attacked Ebon upon the Academy's grounds, and she had watched, afraid to intervene. Still she blamed herself for the beating Ebon had taken, and now she thought she saw a chance, however small, at redemption.

"Tell me," she said. "I have given you several reasons it could be true. Tell me one piece of proof against it."

Ebon raised his hands, gesturing helplessly as he said the only thing he could. "I cannot. But even if it is true, still we must catch Lilith."

"You are right," said Theren, her savage grin widening. "Sunday night cannot come fast enough."

The next few days passed far too slowly, like leaves clinging stubborn to a tree, and with Ebon wishing all the while for Sunday night to be over and done with. Certainly sneaking into the vaults would terrify him, but it could not be worse than the waiting.

Sunday after dinner, Ebon met Kalem in the halls near the library. They stood awkwardly with their arms folded, leaning against walls and trying not to look suspicious. Finally Kalem threw his hands up in the air.

"Where is she? I am beginning to have doubts about this whole thing."

"Only now?" said Ebon. "I thought you doubted it from the first."

Kalem only glowered, and when he spoke it was not

to answer. "What if we cannot escape as she planned? She says enchantments keep us from tunneling in, not out. How would she know? She is no transmuter."

"You mean alchemist."

"I mean alchem—" Kalem stopped short, his eyes narrowing.

Just then they heard the rumbling of iron wheels, and soon Theren appeared from around the corner, pushing a mammoth wooden cart that looked like it might fall over. It was swathed with many blankets.

"There you two are," she said. "Well, here it is. Our manner of entering the vaults."

"Would you like to say it louder?" said Kalem, looking about nervously.

"Oh, calm yourself. And climb aboard." Peeling back a few of the blankets, Theren revealed a lower shelf of the cart, built just above the wheels so that, with the blankets laid down, no one could tell it was there at all.

"You mean to sneak us in on this thing?" said Ebon. "I feel as though I have taken splinters just from looking at it."

"I am sorry—did you expect a cushion?" said Theren. "Sit, little goldbag, and be grateful."

Ebon was not grateful, but he sat, and Kalem climbed in beside him. Theren threw the blanket back down so that they were hidden. Ebon and Kalem looked at each other nervously as the cart began to roll on.

They stopped after a few moments, and there came the creaking of a large door. There were two, Theren had told them, before they reached the administration room. Within it was a closet in which this cart and many others were kept, where she would stow them until she was ready to move on. At the creak of the second door, Ebon held his breath; now they were no longer alone.

"Good eve, Egil," said Theren brightly.

"Hello, my friend," came an ancient and creaking voice. "Stay awhile, and listen. I have found an account of something most interesting."

"I am afraid I cannot," said Theren. "I have yet to complete my entries for the day. Another time, mayhap."

"Ah. Very well, then. Another time."

There came the sound of another, much smaller door, and the cart rolled forwards again. The second door shut, and they found themselves in utter darkness.

"This must be the closet," whispered Kalem.

"I think so." Ebon risked peeling back one of the blankets and peeking out. Slowly his eyes adjusted to the scant light from under the door. They were indeed in a closet, filled with more carts like the one upon which they sat. He slid out and onto the floor as silent as a mouse, and Kalem quickly followed. Together they stole over to the door, where candlelight illuminated them from below and cast Kalem's eyes in shadow.

There was nothing to hear, other than the thin

scribbling of quills on parchment from Theren and Egil, and Egil's persistent cough. But Ebon knew there was another person in the room—a palace guard standing at the vault's main door. He wondered suddenly if they should stay in the cart. What if the guard thought to investigate the closet?

He was just about to reach for Kalem's shoulder and say as much, but then in the room beyond, Egil dissolved into a fit of hacking coughs. They went on and on, until Ebon could fairly hear the phlegm splashing out of the old man and onto the table. He cringed.

"Egil, are you all right?" Ebon heard swift footsteps as Theren went to his side. "Quick, run and get him some water."

"You get it," came the voice of the guard.

"I cannot—I am in the middle of my forms, and if I stop now I shall have to start over. Run to the kitchens. It will not take you a moment."

There was silence as the guard hesitated. But then they heard hasty footsteps as she left, and then a few sharp slaps as Theren pounded Egil on the back. Soon the coughing died away, and with effort he spoke in a rasp.

"I am all right. I am all right. Thank you, Theren. Drat these fits. They are coming more and more often. Not long now."

"Do not be so morbid, old man."

He chuckled. "You are a good child, Theren. Thank you. You should get back to your forms."

"They can wait a moment. And besides, *you* should be going to bed. It is late, after all."

"Mayhap you are right. But I have not finished this page—"

"The page can wait. You need your rest. Come on, off you go."

Another croaking chuckle. "Very well. You will make a fine mother one day, if you wish it—or you can simply continue to baby me."

"As long as you will let me. Good night."

"Good night."

Slow, shuffling footsteps receded. Then Theren ran to the closet and threw it open.

"We must hurry. That took far longer than I thought, and we have little time."

Ebon and Kalem leapt up and followed her to a wide, iron door on their left. Theren threw the latch and flung it open, ushering them inside before closing it once more. Immediately she set off at a run down the hall, torches flickering to either side at the wind of her passing.

They had no time to gather their bearings, but as they ran, Ebon noted their surroundings: thick wooden doors in rows to either side, each set in a stone arch with a pointed peak. Torches lit the place well, but left every corner flickering in shadow. The ceiling was oppressively low compared to the Academy's usual spaciousness, and he found himself ducking with every other step. And something else was odd. His skin had begun to crawl from the moment he set foot in the vaults, hair rising on the back of his neck as though some danger pursued him.

"This place gives me an ill feeling," he said as they ran.

"It is the enchantments," said Theren. "They are worked into every door, but only wizards can sense them. They are the artifacts' greatest protection."

"Not very good protection if we strode in so boldly," Kalem pointed out.

"They are for the rooms, not the halls themselves," said Theren. "The rooms are where the darkest secrets are kept."

They turned a corner, and then another. The itching under Ebon's skin increased until he wished to stop and claw at himself. Then Theren skidded to a stop, so quickly that Kalem and Ebon slammed into her from behind. There before them was a door—or rather, a frame, for the door was gone.

"Here it is," said Theren. "This is the room from which the artifact was taken."

"Well then, search for Lilith's spell-sight," said Kalem.

"I will," said Theren, glaring at him. "You go to the corner and keep a lookout."

Kalem ran off, grumbling. Ebon lingered as Theren fell to one knee and ran her hands along the edges of the doorframe, eyes glowing.

Curious, he leaned over to look past her and into

the room. It was a plain space, no more than four paces to a side, made of the same black granite as the rest of the Academy. But the floor was polished white marble, and in the center of the room sat a table of silver that stood on a single leg. The table lay bare. Looking still closer, he could see all sorts of designs traced into it. They looked familiar, but he could not place them—until he remembered the same sort of designs worked into the Academy's front door.

Theren looked up for a moment, following his gaze. "They are sigils of enchantment," she said. She turned back to the door, but kept speaking. The soft glow of her eyes lit the iron framing under her fingers. "Meant to protect Kekhit's amulet from thieves, but in some cases they protect anyone present from the power of the artifact."

"I should like to learn enchantment, if I can," said Ebon.

"I wish you good fortune," said Theren. "There are few who teach it. Fewer still among alchemists." Then her hands fell, and the glow faded from her eyes as she hung her head. "Damn it. Darkness damn it all."

"What?" said Ebon, stepping forwards quickly. "Is it her?"

"No. I was certain it would be, but it is not." Theren looked up in regret. "I am sorry."

Ebon muttered a curse. "And you do not recognize it as anyone else?"

"No one that I know of. It is partially obscured,

though done in haste. I only know that it is not Lilith, and that I know for certain."

Just then, Kalem came running down the hall towards them. "Someone is coming! We must flee!"

"Who is it?" said Ebon.

Theren gripped them both by the arm. "Never mind that—*run!*"

She took her own advice, and they were quick to follow. Turn after turn she led them down, until Ebon was lost. Every hallway looked the same. Once he was sure they passed the same open door where they had started, but that was impossible. At last they found a place with a sort of alcove, in which rested a small iron bench.

"Here," she said. "Under the bench. It is the most likely place to be overlooked. And they will no doubt have lost us by now."

Kalem fell to his knees, and the hallway flashed white with the glow in his eyes. Stone melted away beneath his fingertips. Ebon knelt beside him and did his best to help. "Who was it?" he said through panting breaths.

"I could not see," said Kalem. "As soon as I heard their footsteps, I ran as quickly as I could."

SNAP!

The air crackled with power. The stone, which only a moment before had been flowing like water, snapped back into place. In an instant, the wall was just as it had always been. Ebon and Kalem looked at each other in confusion—but then Ebon felt Theren's hand tugging him up by the shoulder, and he rose to stand beside her. Before them stood Xain, eyes dark with fury, and Jia, with a white glow fading from her eyes.

SIXTEEN

JIA MARCHED THEM THROUGH THE HALLS TOWARDS THE dean's office, one hand on Theren's shoulder and the other on Ebon's. Kalem followed meekly to the side like a beaten dog. Xain was just beside them, his footsteps silent.

When they reached the door, Jia released Ebon's shoulder to open it. Ebon began to step in, but she jerked him back. Xain hesitated half a moment before entering first, as though he had not expected such deference. He swept over to his desk and sat in the wide, plush chair. Jia nudged them forwards before taking her place at Xain's side. Ebon approached the desk meekly, eyes on his feet, and Kalem beside him; but Theren carelessly threw herself in one of the chairs.

"Stand, Theren," snapped Jia. "This is not some casual visit."

Theren obeyed without question, her expression calm. Standing beside Ebon, hands clasped behind her back, she spoke first. "You should let the two of them go. All of this was my idea."

Jia scoffed. "Even if that were true—and I have my doubts—they would be guilty for following you. We do not teach our pupils to blindly follow every mad suggestion that comes their way."

"I forced them to do it," said Theren. "I said I would spread their darkest secrets through the school if they did not do as I asked." Ebon risked a glance in her direction, but she kept her eyes on Jia.

"Oh?" Jia arched an eyebrow. "And what dark secrets are those?"

Theren spread her hands. "They did as I asked."

Xain had stayed silent and moved not a muscle. His hands gripped the arms of his chair, and Ebon might have thought the dean was not even listening to the exchange—and mayhap that was true, for his eyes never left Ebon's face.

But Theren's casual indifference had struck a nerve in Jia, and she slapped her hand on the desk. "This is not some jest, Theren. You know the vaults are forbidden to students except in performance of their servitude, and you know *why*, better than most who study here. And as an aside, you have utterly disregarded the entire point of your services, and from this point on, you will help clean the privies instead."

Theren did not even blink. "That seems fair, Instructor."

Jia's nostrils flared. "There will be more punishment than that, I can assure you." She turned to Ebon and Kalem. "And the two of you. What were you thinking? Theren has some history of getting into trouble, but both of you are from proud families. I had hoped you might have some positive influence on her, not the other way around."

"I have told you it was my idea," said Theren, speaking before Ebon could reply. "I have learned to read the signs of other wizards. I noticed while filling out my logs that something had been taken from the vaults, and I thought I might be able to discover who."

"Spell-sight," Jia said with a snort. But then her eyes sharpened. "You did not sense anything, did you?"

Ebon thought he saw the corner of Theren's mouth twitch. "No, Instructor."

"And the two of you? What was your role in this foolery?" Theren opened her mouth again, but Jia raised a single finger and silenced her. "I have heard quite enough from you. I have directed my question at Ebon and Kalem."

Kalem looked uncertainly at Ebon. Ebon squared his shoulders. "Theren said she could use our help after she had searched for the . . . the signs of the other wizard's power, or what have you. We were meant to use our transmutation to leave the vaults."

"So that you would not be detected. How fortunate for us, then, that someone had already warned us you might be trying to sneak inside. Students always seem to think that rumors only fly into their cars and not into ours."

At first Ebon was confused, but then he realized: *Lilith.* In anger at their argument, Theren had said she would prove that Lilith was the thief. Lilith must have guessed at their intent to sneak into the vaults and gone running to Xain or Jia. That explained how they had been found so quickly. Theren's cheeks flushed red, and she ducked her head to hide the fury in her eyes.

Xain moved for the first time, pushing back his chair and then standing to lean over his desk. Still his gaze was fixed on Ebon, who looked at the floor again.

"I do not believe you," said Xain softly. "I think this was a plot by the Drayden boy."

Ebon felt the blood drain from his face.

Theren opened her mouth again, but Xain spoke first, and sharply. "Be silent. I speak not to you, but to him. What say you, Drayden? Do you deny it?"

He could not raise his eyes. He did not know what to say. If he denied it, he condemned Theren. If he admitted it, though it was false, he would take the blame upon himself.

But then Theren scraped her shoe upon the floor and cleared her throat. She had taken the blame from the first. Hopefully she had some sort of plan. So Ebon raised his head and met Xain's eye. "The truth is as Theren told you."

"You lie. It is plain to read in your voice, as well as your eyes. Gather your possessions. You are banished from the Academy."

The world spun beneath his feet. A high whine sounded at the edge of Ebon's hearing. His hand shot out to grip Theren's arm, a desperate attempt to steady himself. But then Jia cleared her throat.

"Dean," she said quietly. "The Academy's rules do not provide for such a punishment. Not unless you believe their intent was to use the vault's artifacts to wreak havoc upon their fellow students—and then you would have to expel all three of them."

At that, Xain hesitated. He straightened slightly, sweeping his gaze to Theren, and then to Kalem. His jaw worked, muscles spasming under the skin. But at last he sat, leaning back in his chair and propping his chin upon his fist. "I have half a mind to," he said, but the fire was gone from his tone.

"Consider yourselves lucky we did not flood the hallways with flame, as is our right," said Jia. "And consider yourselves on notice, as well. You will *all* receive punishments for this, and if you should do anything so idiotic ever again, I shall banish you myself. Do you understand?"

"Yes, Instructor," they mumbled in unison.

"Very well. Come."

They left the room on Jia's heels. Once in the hall, they all turned their steps towards the dormitories—but Jia snapped her fingers and pointed. They paused, but when she did not move, they quickly followed her directions. She took them down the hall around the corner, where she stopped and glowered at them with arms folded.

"What in the darkness below possessed you?" Her voice was now filled with a much greater fury than she had shown in Xain's office. "That was by far the most foolish thing I have seen any student do in all my days here."

Ebon's face burned. Xain's hatred was easy to bear, for he knew it was rooted in a falsehood. But Jia's fury was righteous, and he knew it. "We are sorry, Instructor. It will not happen—"

"Again? It certainly will not. If it does, I promise that expulsion will be the *least* of your worries. How could you do this, Ebon, after we spoke in my office? And you, Theren." She rounded on the girl. "Do not think I am unsympathetic to your situation. But also, do not think I would hesitate to throw you out of this place on your ear, no matter where you must go afterwards."

At last Theren showed her shame, cheeks darkening as she averted her eyes. Ebon stared at her in wonder. So Jia, too, knew the tale of Theren's life outside the Academy, and the home to which she loathed the thought of returning. But he had little time to think on it, for Jia turned to him and Kalem.

"I spoke no falsehood concerning your families. Your lineage has its share of stains, Ebon, but I thought you might wish to cleanse them. This is not how you go about it. And Kalem—you are *royalty.* Did you spare a single thought for how you would shame your king, if I were to send him word of his cousin behaving like a common thief?"

To Ebon's shock, Kalem burst out crying and hid his face in his hands. Jia stopped her tirade at once, and though she tried to keep her stern demeanor, her eyes softened. Tears spilled freely between Kalem's fingers to drip on the stone floor, and he scrubbed at his nose with the back of his sleeve.

"I did!" he sobbed. "I did think of it. But . . . it is only that I cannot stand it anymore. The sights we saw out on the streets. The instructors who were killed, and the students as well. And now Credell, who taught me only a few years ago. I see his face. I see *all* their faces, in my dreams, and sometimes with my waking eyes. I only . . . I only wanted to *do* something. Something to help. What if they come back for us?"

Jia's face transformed to a vision of perfect shock, but no more so than Ebon. He realized his mouth was hanging open, and he closed it with a snap. Then he elbowed Theren so that she did the same. Jia turned to them.

"Is this true? Is that why you embarked upon this mad scheme?"

"Yes," said Theren. "I told you I wanted to see if I could learn who had broken into the vaults. I suppose that was only half the truth. I thought . . . I thought that mayhap it might help defend the Academy. Somehow. It was a foolish thought, I know. If only there were something I could do . . . that *we* could do." She raised her eyes to the sky, blinking hard as though fighting back tears. Ebon bit down on his tongue to keep from laughing, and kept his eyes on the floor to hide the smile.

Kalem's sobs redoubled, and he lurched towards Jia, wrapping his arms around her waist. She started, hands drawing back. But after a moment she lowered one to his hair and patted his shoulder awkwardly with the other.

"Will Dulmun come back, Instructor?" said Kalem.

"They will not," she said softly. "They know that if they should try, the High King has now gathered much strength upon the Seat to repel them. And the instructors will keep you safe, besides. Now stop crying. It is unseemly for a son of royalty."

Kalem nodded and sniffed hard, stepping back and swiping at his nose again. Ebon reached out and draped his arm across the boy's shoulders. He looked plaintively at Jia. "He has been inconsolable since the attack, Instructor. We have tried our best to comfort each other, but we all bear the same scars. We only thought that taking action—*any* action—might do us all some good."

Jia sighed. "I suppose I understand, at least in part. But you must never do anything like this again. If you find your thoughts so occupied, you may always come and talk to me, or whichever Instructor you prefer. We are here to help you, and to protect you. You must let us do both, or we shall indeed be in far greater danger."

Ebon nodded quickly. "Of course, Instructor. I understand. And we will not try anything of the sort again."

"Promise me."

"We promise," said Theren vehemently.

Jia waved her hands quickly. "Then be off with you. It is nearly time for bed."

They turned and made off down the hallway. As soon as they had rounded the corner, they broke into a jog, and then a run once out of earshot. They did not stop until they reached the foot of the stairs leading to the dormitories.

"That was a brilliant performance," said Theren.

Kalem looked at them both. His eyes were still tearstained, but he wore a broad grin. "It was, was it not?"

Ebon shook his head. "I wish you had done it in front of Xain. His judgement is far harsher."

"Did you see the hate in his eyes? He would have shown no pity. Not like I knew Jia would."

Theren snorted. "Remind me never to believe a word that comes out of your mouth, Kalem."

They all burst out laughing.

SEVENTEEN

The moment Ebon entered the dining hall the next morning, he felt many eyes upon him. He stopped in the doorway, looking at the other students in confusion—but the moment he looked at the students watching him, they quickly turned away. Some whispered to their friends behind their hands and turned back when they thought he might no longer be looking.

He moved forwards again, frowning—and then it dawned on him. Word must already have spread of their exploits in the vaults. These were not looks of fear, or scorn—most were curious, and mayhap some even admired what he had done. A grin tugged at the corner of his mouth, which he quickly tried to suppress.

Ebon reached the line of students who awaited their meal. There, just two students ahead of him, was little Astrea. Her frizzed hair stuck out even more than normal, as though she had not taken much care to brush it that morning.

"Astrea," said Ebon. She did not move. He tried again, louder. "Astrea!"

She turned to look at him, and a chill struck his heart. Great bags hung beneath her eyes, which were bloodshot, and her skin was paler than could be explained by long hours of study. It did not seem she knew who he was at first, for she had to blink twice before recognition dawned in her eyes.

"Ebon," she said, trying to smile. She stepped out of line to join him. Her thin arms wrapped him in a hug, but it was a half-hearted thing.

Credell's death must have struck her far harder than he had thought. Guilt coursed through him, for he had not once gone to check on her since they saw the body. She was only a child. He opened his mouth to ask her how she fared, but then thought better of it. Instead he patted her hair and said softly, "I have greatly missed seeing you."

"I have missed you, too. But I will soon graduate into your class."

"Thank the sky," said Ebon, giving an exaggerated sigh. "I need you to teach me. Perrin is a fine woman, but she does not understand the intricacies of my mind as you do."

That earned him a small smile, which warmed his heart to see. "I do not think your mind is very intricate."

Ebon clutched at his chest. "You wound me." She giggled, and his smile broadened. "I hope you have been spending time with your other friends. I know they are not so entertaining as I am, nor as clever, nor handsome. But none of us should spend our days alone, especially now."

It seemed she understood his true meaning, for her eyes clouded. "I have been spending time with my sister," she said softly. "She has been a great comfort to me."

He frowned. Then he remembered the night they had found Credell—the older student, Isra, kneeling beside Astrea and holding her away from the sight of the corpse. "Isra? She is your sister?"

Astrea shrugged. "In a way. We both come from an orphanage in Feldemar. Or we did, until our sponsor found us. I suppose we should say we are part of her household, now."

"I did not know," Ebon said quietly. The thought that Astrea was an orphan, bright-eyed and kind as she was, saddened him greatly. He tried to imagine himself in her place. She must have loved Credell very much, for he was always kind to the other students, and never feared them as he had Ebon. And now he was gone. No wonder Astrea looked so worn. Ebon wondered if he could even keep attending class every day, were their roles reversed.

Astrea looked down at her shoes now, and her chin had begun to tremble as though she might cry. Quickly Ebon put a hand to her shoulder and smiled. "I cannot wait to study with you in Perrin's class. There are three spells to learn before you can pass the second year. One is to change obsidian's color to white. I have never heard of such a thing."

She blinked, banishing tears as he drew her interest once more. "I know," she said, and then leaned in to whisper. "I have even been trying to practice the spell. Let me see if I can . . ."

Her brow furrowed, and she put one of her fingers to the edge of the wooden bowl. For a heartbeat, light flashed into her eyes and then faded. When she withdrew her finger, the spot was a shade lighter.

Ebon gawked. "That is incredible, Astrea. But how can you be so far advanced, and still not perform the passing spell for the first-year class?"

Astrea shrugged with a self-conscious smile. "Some wizards take more easily to one spell than another. But I am almost done with the testing spell, too. I meant it when I said I would join your class soon."

They had reached the table at last. Attendants scooped porridge into their bowls, and they made their way through the dining hall towards their friends. When they reached the center of the room, Astrea gave Ebon a final smile.

"I will see you soon," he promised.

"And I you," she said, wandering off.

Kalem was waiting at their table when Ebon sat down. "Good morn," he said, speaking around cheeks filled with food.

"Good morn," said Ebon. "Did you have as much trouble sleeping as I did?"

"I cannot know, for I was not there. But most likely, yes. I kept starting awake with thoughts that Dean Forredar might change his mind and expel us after all."

"I thought he might abduct us in our sleep, and have us thrown into the Bay," muttered Ebon. That, indeed, had plagued his nightmares. He had seen it, like the day he had fought Cyrus on the cliffs, except that he was Cyrus and Xain was the one on the ground. The dean gripped Ebon's ankles and turned them to stone, and then he was falling, falling into the ocean, where dark waters swirled around him and crawled down his throat.

"But morning has come, and still we reside within these walls," said Kalem. "I, for one, am grateful."

"And I," said Ebon. "But we must decide what to do next."

Kalem fixed him with a glare. "Ebon."

"Come now, Kalem. A thief is still on the loose,

and a murderer. And we know Lilith must have been the one to tell the instructors what we were up to. It is another sign of her guilt."

Leaning forwards, Kalem spoke in a harsh whisper. "And what do you mean to do about it? I mean to do exactly what we should have done from the first: *nothing*."

"You were eager enough to pursue Lilith before. What of her guilt? What of the family Yerrin's treason against the High King?"

Kalem shook his head. "I was a fool before, and so were you, for agreeing to Theren's scheme. We are Academy pupils, Ebon, and hardly advanced in our training. We only barely escaped with our skins intact. We have landed ourselves in as much trouble as I have ever been, and I will not do anything to make it worse."

Ebon opened his mouth to answer, but then he heard raised voices a few tables away. He turned and saw Astrea standing beside the table where she had been eating, facing another student her age. Ebon recognized him as a boy named Vali, a weremage, and one of Astrea's friends. But now the boy stared at Astrea with cold eyes while her face contorted with tears. It was her voice Ebon had heard.

"What do you mean?" said Astrea, shaking. "You are not making any sense."

"I am not your friend." Vali's voice was odd, monotonous. "I do not wish to see you."

"We are in the library together every day, you idiot," said Astrea, her voice cracking.

"I am not your friend," Vali said again, and then turned to leave her. Astrea burst into tears and slumped back down to her bench.

Something was wrong. Ebon frowned, trying to place it. He took a step forwards—but before he could go to Astrea and comfort her, the dining hall door burst open.

Theren flew by him in a rush, her face twisted in rage. Ebon and Kalem glanced at each other and then scrambled to follow. Soon they were a half-step behind her. Finally Ebon saw where they were headed: Lilith, sitting with some other seventh-years. Her back was to them, so that she was unaware of Theren approaching from behind. Too late, her cousin Oren looked up and saw them. He tapped Lilith on the shoulder to warn her. But Theren was already there, snatching Lilith by the back of her robe and dragging the girl to her feet.

"You flap-mouthed sow!" she cried, shoving Lilith back so that she nearly fell across the table.

Oren leapt forwards, trying to shove Theren away. She caught one of his wrists and twisted it, kicking his leg as he recoiled in pain. He fell back, his rear striking the bench hard. Lilith's friend Nella stood to the other side, but she seemed reluctant to enter the fray. Ebon realized her gaze was on him. When the Seat had been attacked, she and Ebon had stood together against the Shade soldiers. Now they looked at each other uncertainly, neither willing to leap in on behalf of Lilith and Theren.

But the girls did not need the help. Lilith had found her feet, and she stared daggers into Theren's eyes. Theren's nose was less than a finger's breadth from Lilith's, and she matched the girl's stare with equal hatred.

"You were a fool to go along with the Drayden boy," said Lilith.

"Do not dare to point fingers." Theren shoved her again. Oren shot to his feet, but he seemed reluctant to take another trouncing from Theren. "No one would have known if you had kept your fat lips together. Have you forgotten all the things I might tell them about *you?* One stray whisper—"

"You should be thanking me. Now you have been kept out of his schemes—whatever they might be." Lilith looked past Theren to glare at Ebon. He tried not to shudder. "You have called me an adder, but you ignore the snake in your own pocket."

The students all around were on the edge of their seats, some with their mouths hanging open, as though they could not wait for the argument to burst into a fight, mayhap one of spells. Cautiously Ebon reached out and took Theren's arm.

"Come, Theren. Leave her be, and get some food in you."

"Yes, heed the words of a sniveling Drayden," sneered Lilith. "Only do not be surprised or come running to me when you find his knife between your shoulder blades."

Theren had drawn back a step, and though her fists were shaking at her side, her face was an impassive mask. "You are the one who has shown herself faithless, and not for the first time."

To Ebon's shock, Lilith grimaced in obvious pain. Her eyes glistened, though he could not believe there might be tears in them. "You have tried endlessly to paint me as an agent of evil. It will never work, and that infuriates you. One day you will see how wrong you are. I only hope it will not be too late."

She turned sharply, robes flapping out like a cloak, and resumed her seat. Oren still gave them a sullen look, while Nella breathed an audible sigh. Theren looked as though she might push the matter, but Ebon and Kalem took her arms and turned her gently away. They made their way back to the table and sat, while nearby students discreetly averted their eyes.

"Here," said Ebon, pushing his plate in front of her. "I was finished anyway."

Theren stabbed the gruel with her spoon but did not scoop any to eat. Kalem was staring down at his hands, mouth working as though searching for words to say.

"We might have gotten away with it," said Theren. "Damn her."

"All ended well enough," said Ebon. "It is done."

"So I should forget it?" said Theren. "I will not.

She must have had something to do with the theft. Why else would she have warned Xain?"

"To spite you, or mayhap for pure mischief," said Kalem. "You said yourself that you could not sense her power in the vaults."

"Mayhap she learned to hide it." But even Theren did not sound convinced by her own words.

"You spoke of things that you know about her." said Ebon. "Why do the two of you hate each other so? Her loathing of me, I understand. My family and hers have—"

Theren shot to her feet and stalked away from the table, leaving Kalem and Ebon to eat their breakfast alone.

EIGHTEEN

FOR MANY DAYS AFTERWARDS, THEY HAD TO REMAIN on their best behavior. Jia, or mayhap Xain, must have passed word to their instructors. Ebon found that Perrin now watched him closely, and was reluctant to let him leave class for any reason, even to visit the privy. When they met and studied each day in the library, Kalem and Theren told him that their classes were much the same. Under such careful watch, it was impossible to continue searching for the thief who had broken into the vaults.

Since Shay had not come with the rest of his family, Ebon did not fear to see Adara, and so he visited her every other day or so. Upon one such visit he at last arranged for her to meet Kalem and Theren for dinner. They decided to see each other upon the last day of Febris, the eve of Yearsend.

Astrea soon graduated into the second-years' class with Ebon, performing the same graduation ceremony as he had. Ebon was surprised to find her presence a great comfort, for he had not had any luck making friends among his new classmates. Though he was unable to speak with her often, or for very long, she would always smile at him as they passed each other in the classroom—though he could see how tired her smile had become, for she went about her days haggard and careworn, showing a glimmer of life only in his presence or Isra's.

After sneaking into the vaults, Ebon often felt that the eyes of all the faculty were upon him, especially Xain's. But in a way that was a blessing, for it made him focus upon his studies, and under Perrin's tutelage he found a renewed passion for learning that he had not felt since before the Academy. Credell's sniveling had made him doubt he would ever become a true wizard. But now his childhood dreams were rekindled, and they burned twice as bright. Often he would study halfway through the midday meal, poring over a tome until his groaning stomach forced him to leave.

In addition to studying books, he was thrilled to be practicing his spells. Now that he could shift stone,

Perrin encouraged him to do it a bit every day. Shortly after the incident in the vaults, Perrin presented a small wooden box and set it on the desk. It was less than a handbreadth wide, and hollow, yet it had been filled with stone in some manner Ebon did not understand. That is, until Perrin placed her fingers upon it, and the stone began to shift and ripple like water. "Practice moving the stone out of the box. That should be easy enough. But then—and this shall be the hard part, at first—put the stone back in."

Ebon soon learned the truth of her words. Shifting stone away from him was simple: he touched it, and it radiated from his fingers like brushing away dust. Yet whenever he tried to put it back into place, the stone rippled away from him and around his skin. He could not try for long without growing frustrated.

"This is often the way of it for transmuters," said Perrin. "When first we learn to shift stone, or anything at all, we can only push it away like an infant batting at a coin held before its face. Eventually they learn to take hold of things and move them where they will."

Ebon glared when she said that, not sure he enjoyed being compared to an infant. Fortunately for him, there was much else to learn.

Before the attack on the Seat, Kalem had taught him to spin mist from the air. Now Perrin let him practice it in the classroom. The first barrier, and the greatest, was learning to spin it more than a few inches from his body. Theren and Kalem had laughed when he first cast the spell, for the mists clung to him and made him look like a man made of smoke. Try as he might, Ebon could not seem to push the mists farther out. When he attempted it, they simply vanished to nothing.

"You are thinking with your skin," Perrin told him. "Your own magic is a conduit. You cannot turn all the air in a room to mist just by touching it—that would require you to be as large as the room. You must learn to see the mists you have created as an extension of *you*. Follow it out from yourself in your mind's eye, and turn the air it touches into still more mist."

Ebon felt his head spinning, but he tried it anyway. Mist clung to his hand, and he focused until he could *see* the mist, hovering in the air, clinging to his skin. Then he tried to feel the air beyond it, but he saw only darkness. He grit his teeth and thought harder. The mist vanished.

"No, *use* the mist. It is not your tool; it is a part of you."

"I am trying," said Ebon.

Perrin sighed and stood. "Practice will help. You remember how much easier your testing spell became after you cast it for the first time. They will all be like that, for a long while at least. And then, one day, your mind grows used to the process, and learning new spells is no longer so taxing."

Ebon crossed his arms on the table and rested his chin upon them. "And when will that happen? After my fortieth year?"

Perrin slammed her meaty hand on the table. Ebon jumped and sat straight on his bench. "None of that," said Perrin. "You will learn nothing by moping. You will learn only through effort. Now try it again."

Day after day Ebon struggled with his mists. Perrin spent more and more time watching him, lips pursed and brow furrowed beneath her massive shag of hair. Each time he became aware of Perrin's gaze, Ebon's concentration began to waver. Soon the thin fog he had managed to wrap around his arm would vanish entirely. Then he would groan with frustration and fight a mighty urge to flip his table over.

"Mayhap it would be good to distract yourself with another lesson," said Perrin one day.

Ebon frowned. "Another one? I have not mastered the mists yet, nor shifting stone. Would it not be better to focus on them rather than take on another spell?"

"Some instructors might say so, but I call them fools. Sometimes it is better to pursue many things at once. With each spell we flex a different part of our mind. Each may teach us something of the other. Yes, if you sit there and try endlessly to spin your mists, you may learn it faster than if you practice other spells in between—yet I think you will learn all of them faster if you practice all of them in turn, and change between them to freshen your mind."

Ebon had never heard of learning this way, but he was willing to try; he thought he might scream if he had to spin mists even one more time. "Very well. What am I to learn?"

"What do you know of defensive magic?"

Ebon's eyes widened. He remembered the day he toured the Academy. Upon the training grounds, he had seen students of all the four branches practicing their craft. And where the transmuters had been practicing . . . "I have seen alchemi—that is, transmuters, turn arrows to dust in mid-flight."

Perrin chuckled. "You are a long way from that, I am afraid. Indeed, that spell is like invisibility—only a handful of transmuters are capable of learning it. But the simplest magical defense is stopping another wizard's spells. That is far easier than halting a physical attack—and far safer to practice, as well. What have you learned of the four branches and their relationship to each other?"

"Not as much as might be hoped, I am sure."

"Each branch has its mirror," said Perrin. "Mentalism to elementalism, transmutation to therianthropy. A wizard may dispel magic of their own branch, or of its mirror."

Ebon shook his head. "What do you mean, dispel? All of this is strange to me."

Perrin smiled. "Spin your mists."

Ebon frowned and reached out a hand. His eyes glowed, and a thin fog sprang to life to wrap around his arm. But then Perrin's eyes glowed in answer, and there was a *snap* on the air. Ebon felt his connection severed, and the mist vanished. He gawked at his arm, now laid bare.

"That is what I mean," said Perrin. "You can stop the spells of another wizard if you learn to sense them being cast."

"I can stop other alchemists from using their magic?"

"And weremages as well." Perrin leaned forwards with a smile, her eyes alight with interest. Ebon noticed that she had said *weremages,* not *therianthropes,* and had not corrected his use of *alchemists.* "Weremagic is our mirror branch, and our spells are intricately tied to theirs."

Ebon did not say it aloud, but he thought of when he had snuck into the vaults. He and Kalem had been burrowing through the stone to escape, when there was a snap, and the stone had reverted back to its true form. When they had turned, they had seen Jia with her eyes glowing. Now he realized that she had dispelled their magic.

"I see," he said, nodding slowly. "That makes sense to me. Alchemy and weremagic are of a kind. They both turn things into something else—a weremage changes their own body, and we change that which we touch. Firemagic and mindmagic are similar in that they both exert power outside of the wizard."

Perrin grimaced. "That is too simple a way of putting it, but you have the idea. And that is why you should be wary of battling a mindmage or firemage.

Anyone with a degree of skill could strike you down before you could get close, where you would be able to defend yourself."

With a sick lurch in his gut, Ebon thought of Cyrus atop the cliff overlooking the Great Bay. "I will keep that in mind," he muttered.

Perrin must have noted Ebon's somber tone; she frowned, but she let it pass. "Well, to practice a counterspell, you shall need a spell to counter. Astrea, come here, if you please."

Ebon looked up with delight as Astrea rose from her desk and came to join them. She frowned as Perrin directed her to sit on the bench beside Ebon. The instructor then produced a wooden rod and placed it in the girl's hand.

"Take the other end of the rod, please, Ebon," said Perrin.

He did, though he felt just as confused as Astrea.

"Good. Now, Astrea, I want you to change the rod to stone, just as you did for your testing spell. Ebon, you must feel her magic as she casts it, and try to stop her. Now, begin."

Astrea looked at Ebon, and he back at her, and he knew that neither of them had the faintest idea what Perrin was talking about. They shrugged at the same time and giggled. Then Astrea began to concentrate. Her eyes glowed, and Ebon felt a familiar prickling along his spine—the sense that another transmuter was using their magic in his presence.

Slowly, stone rippled along the wooden rod towards Ebon's fingers. He narrowed his eyes, trying to sense the stone as it turned. But he could only see the material itself, and not the magic acting upon it. In a few moments it was done; the rod had turned to stone, and Ebon released his grip with a sigh.

"Let me turn it back," said Perrin, reaching for the rod. But Astrea withheld it from her.

"I can do it, Instructor," she said meekly. Her eyes glowed once more, and the rod rippled back into wood. Perrin gave an appreciative smile, and Ebon sat gaping.

"I did not know you could turn the rod back into wood, child," said Perrin. "That is most impressive."

Astrea only shrugged. "I learned that spell before I could do it the right way. Everyone says I was supposed to learn wood to stone first."

Perrin shook her head. "That is the way of magic. Some wizards take to some spells more easily than others, and in truth there is no 'right' way to learn. You should take pride, for that is one of the testing spells to graduate this class."

"Even I have not learned it yet," said Ebon, giving her an encouraging smile.

Astrea smirked at him, though it was half-hearted. "That is not a surprise. You are brand-new to the Academy."

Perrin's laugh rang through the room, making the other students pause at their desks. "I will leave the pair of you to practice. Remember, Ebon: search for her magic, and stop it with your own."

She went off to the next student whose hand was raised. Astrea turned the rod to stone again, while Ebon tried in vain to keep the wood in place. After a few attempts, he still sensed nothing. He dropped his hand from the rod with a frustrated growl.

"I am sorry," Astrea said quietly. "I will try to slow my spell."

"No, it is certainly not your fault," said Ebon. "It is mine. Perrin gave me this spell because I had grown frustrated with the others, and yet it turns out I am no better at this one."

Astrea gave him a small smile. "I have enjoyed my other spells. Have you learned to shift stone yet? I cannot seem to do it."

"Yes," said Ebon, not without some small degree of pride. Then, thinking that might have sounded boastful, he added, "Of course, I can only shift it away from myself. I cannot control it enough to put it back inside the box."

"Nor can I," said Astrea. Then her mood dampened, and a shadow seemed to swallow her features. "My friend Vali told me his second-year lessons were beastly. Though he is a weremage, and I know our spells are not the same."

Vali was the boy she had had the row with in the dining hall. Ebon forced a smile, hoping to turn her mind away. "I am certain you will pass this class before

I will—likely before the year is behind us. No doubt I will be an old man, my beard hanging to the floor, before I finish, and you will come back to the Academy to visit me."

She tried to smile, but her chin trembled as tears filled her eyes. "I do not understand him. Vali, I mean. First he told me he wanted nothing to do with me. But just this morning he came to me and said he did not know what he was thinking, and that of course he has always been my friend. I cannot make sense of it. I saw the look in his eyes then—it was as if he did not know me."

Ebon sighed. He should have known it would be foolish to try and distract her. First the death of her instructor, and now this—not to mention the attack upon the High King's Seat. She was only a child, and it made him heartsick that she had suffered so much in so short a time. Gently he put a hand on her shoulder.

"Sometimes people grow apart, Astrea. It cannot always be helped. And you should not try too hard to remain close to someone who does not see your worth."

His soft tone broke her; she sniffed hard and swiped at the tears that leaked from the corners of her eyes. "Too many have gone and will never return. I do not want to lose anyone else."

"I am here, and you will not lose me," promised Ebon. "Indeed, you would be hard pressed to get rid of me. And you have Isra. I do not know her well, but from what I have seen, I do not think she plans to leave you any time soon."

Astrea scooted forwards and hugged him. Ebon held her tight, patting her hair as tears soaked his robes. Over her head, he saw Perrin watching the two of them. For an instant he feared she might rebuke them for talking when they should be studying. But instead, she nodded and gave him a sad little smile.

These days we must all take care of each other, Ebon thought.

When Astrea had composed herself, she shifted away and retrieved the wooden rod. Ebon took the other end with a smile. "Come, wizardling," he said. "Do your worst."

She did, now with the hint of a grin.

NINETEEN

The next day was the last of Febris, and the eve of Yearsend.

It was the day Ebon would take Kalem and Theren to sup with Adara, and his nerves tormented him throughout his morning classes. His distraction must have shown, for Perrin barked at him more than once, telling him to keep his mind on his spells. The moment the midday bell rang, Ebon made for the dining hall, gobbled his meal, and then spent the rest of his spare time out upon the grounds. He shook his hands often as he walked, letting them chill in the freezing air, hoping to untie the knots his stomach seemed determined to twist itself into.

While he paced, he saw a curious thing: the boy Vali, Astrea's former friend, was out walking alone. His arms were crossed over his chest, and he shivered, but it seemed to Ebon that it came from more than the cold. Too, the boy's face was haggard and careworn, his cheeks gaunt, eyes darting in every direction. Ebon felt a twinge of pity. Mayhap the boy was consumed with guilt for the way he had treated Astrea. These days were dark, and worked in strange ways upon the mind. He hoped the two of them could find a way to reconcile.

But then Vali passed, and Ebon thought of his dinner with Adara. Again he grew anxious, and Vali was quickly forgotten.

Free study in the library was no better. Ebon sat staring at the pages of his book, his eyes unfocused and unseeing. Every so often he would shake his head as he came out of it, but then a moment later his thoughts returned to wandering. After a time, Theren leaned back in her chair with an exasperated sigh.

"Sky above, Ebon. Why are you so troubled by tonight's meal? You have *lain* with the woman. A meal with her cannot be this terrifying to you."

Ebon started at Theren's frankness and looked over his shoulder, but they were alone. Kalem was off somewhere among the bookshelves, searching for a mention of Kekhit. He frowned at her.

"I am not 'terrified.' I am only a bit nervous. Mayhap I am afraid you and Kalem will embarrass me."

Theren arched an eyebrow. "You forget I know Adara already, Ebon. If she did not wish to see me again, she would not have accepted your invitation."

He glowered at that. Then a thought struck him. He spoke carefully, trying to appear nonchalant. "Theren . . . when you say you know Adara . . . how did the two of you—"

She silenced him with a sharp look. "I know what you are asking at, Ebon. And you ought to know better. If Adara and I met as lover and guest before you knew her—or even after—that is none of your business."

Ebon swallowed. "That *is* how you know each other, then?"

Her eyes hardened. "I have said neither yes, nor no. I have said it is none of your business, and you do yourself no favors with such thoughts. She is a lover, Ebon. She may have known me, or any other here in the Academy, or upon the Seat. It is none of your concern."

"I know that," said Ebon hastily. "I do, it is only . . ." He hesitated, searching for the right words. He looked around the edge of his armchair to ensure Kalem was still safely stowed among the shelves. When he spoke, he could not meet her eye, but stared at his fidgeting hands. "I know it is foolish of me, Theren—trust me, I know it. Yet . . . I catch myself wishing I were more than her guest. Certainly I feel as though she is more than my lover. And sometimes I see in her eyes . . . I do not know, for I *have* heard many things about lovers' words. But I think she may feel the same about me, or at least something similar."

Theren did not answer for a long moment, and as Ebon raised his embarrassed gaze, he saw something horrible: not anger, nor even irritation, but pity. She shook her head and closed the book in her lap, which she had only been half-glancing through anyway. Then she leaned forwards until their faces were level and gently placed one of her hands on his.

"Ebon," she said carefully. "Your thoughts wander a road that will only end in heartsickness. A guest's dealings with a lover can be many things, and all of them wonderful. But it is never anything more than it is, if you take my meaning. And if there is no honesty between you and her, then your time together will end in darkness, and sooner rather than later."

He shook his head quickly, smiling even though he did not feel like it. "Of course I understand that. It was foolish of me to speak. Forget I said anything."

"Do not be dishonest, Ebon. With me, or with her. Speak to Adara. She must hear your thoughts, and you must hear her answer. Dancing around it will only make things worse."

"Of course," Ebon repeated, and forced himself to chuckle. "Forgive me. I was foolish to trouble you."

Theren looked as though she was about to say

more. But her gaze drifted over his shoulder. Ebon followed it to Kalem, nearly running as he came towards them, hoisting a book like a trophy over his head.

"I have found her!" he said in a shouted whisper, as though he wanted to crow but was afraid to disturb the library's peace. "I have found Kekhit!"

"Be silent!" said Theren sharply. Though no one was close enough to hear, Ebon understood her caution. The last thing they needed was for some instructor to hear them discussing the Wizard King whose amulet had been stolen from the vaults. "Sit down and tell us what you have found, but keep your voice hushed."

Kalem nearly leapt into his armchair between them, flipping the book open to a page he had held with his thumb. "Here she is. I had been searching in ancient histories of Idris, but none bore mention of her. At last I realized that many tomes from before the Dark War had been lost, and such histories would not help us. Then I thought to look in accounts of the Dark War itself. By the account of that logbook page we already found, Kekhit died long before that time, but if she was as powerful as she seems, I thought there might be mention of her—like an echo of her power reverberating down through the centuries, having finally faded away before we were born."

"Very poetic," said Ebon, arching an eyebrow. "Now, stop regaling us with your brilliance, and tell us what you have learned."

Theren hid a smirk as Kalem scowled. But the boy lowered his eyes to the page and held his finger against a passage. "Here it is. This says she was an ancient Wizard King of Idris, and a being of unstoppable power. She could hide the glow in her eyes when she cast her spells, so that her foes had no warning of her attacks. Her magic could strike whole armies dead, and she once captured a dragon and forced it to serve as her steed, when wyrms were not so uncommon in Underrealm."

Ebon's eyes widened at the thought: a wizard riding through the sky upon a dragon's back, raining death and fire from above. But Theren snorted and rolled her eyes. "Nearly every ancient Wizard King has some such tale. By the time of the Dark War, men were wiser, and history better kept. Then there were no more such tales. The thought of riding a dragon is a flight of fancy and nothing more."

Kalem shrugged. "You may be right. There are more accounts of her strength, though I will not trouble you with them now. But one thing is interesting; some say she was Elf-touched, for it is said she lived for four hundreds of years."

Theren laughed out loud. "Four centuries? Nonsense."

Ebon might have believed the dragon, but now even he had to shake his head. "That is impossible, Kalem. There are Elf-touched who walk the nine lands even today. But they live their spans and then fade like all the rest. Elves do not grant everlasting life—that gift is theirs alone."

Kalem gave them both an exasperated look. "I am not vouching for the author's integrity," he snapped. "I am only relaying her words. Now, do you wish to hear about Kekhit's amulet, or not?"

Theren and Ebon leaned forwards together. "The book speaks of it?"

"In fair detail," said Kalem. "It seems Kekhit enchanted many objects with dark and eternal magic. Of all the artifacts she imbued with power, none have lost the strength of their spells. Chief among them was her amulet, which she wore always, and never let another lay a hand upon it. It allowed her to transcend all other Wizard Kings of her time, giving her the strength to cast darkfire without the use of magestones."

Theren's face blanched, and she drew back in her seat. But Ebon looked between them without understanding. "What is darkfire? I have never heard of this."

Kalem's face grew solemn, and he leaned in to speak quietly. "You remember when I told you of the power of magestones? And how a transmuter who consumed them could cast a spell called blackstone?"

"I do," said Ebon. "It is a sort of corruption, is it not?"

"One that destroys anything it touches," said Kalem, nodding. "Darkfire is similar. It is a flame, blacker than the darkest night, and it will burn steel and flesh like parchment. It cannot be put out once it is started. Water cannot douse it, nor can it be suffocated. It burns until it peters out, utterly consuming everything in its path."

Ebon felt a tingle creeping along his skin. His mind's eye filled with visions of melting flesh and bone, and he thought he might be ill. "That is horrible," he said, and the words cracked. He cleared his throat to strengthen his voice. "Can magestones grant no powers but those for evil?"

"None," said Theren, shaking her head firmly. "It is the same for all the four branches. To mindmages, magestones give the strength of mindwyrd. It gives us a voice of command, so that we may order anyone to do what we wish, and they have no choice but to obey, even once they are out of our sight. It is a perversion of our natural power; with my magic, I can move your body easily enough. With magestones, I can take command of your mind, so that your body enforces my will."

The library seemed to have darkened around them. Ebon shook the feeling off. "And weremages?" he said, fearing the answer. "What does it do to them?"

"It is called hellskin," said Kalem softly. "They become twisted monsters, like demons of the darkness below. Their shape depends on the weremage and their strength, but their skin is always covered with jutting horns and barbs, and their strength is unmatched by any natural creature. In their hellskin form, weremages are impervious to magic, and the greatest among them can tear armies apart with their bare claws."

Ebon felt the blood drain from his face. Theren saw it and smirked. "Now do you understand why the Academy so stringently bans any discussion of magestones? Many of us react as you do now, terrified and afraid for our very souls. But some students hear such tales and can only think of the power magestones would grant them."

"I want nothing of such power," said Ebon quickly.

"Then you are surprisingly wise. But what else does the book say of Kekhit, Kalem?"

"That is all. But still, that is a great deal more than we knew before."

"So the thief's plot may have something to do with darkfire," said Theren, eyes sharp. "And we know they are a firemage as well."

"Like Lilith," muttered Ebon.

"Exactly."

By unspoken agreement, they rose from their chairs. "Where did you find that book, Kalem?" said Ebon. "It seems we have much more to learn, if we mean to save the Academy."

TWENTY

DESPITE THEIR EARNEST SEARCH, THEY FOUND NOTHING the rest of the day. Ebon half wanted to spend the evening in the libraries to continue the hunt, but at the same time, he had no desire to miss their dinner with Adara. And so, reluctantly, they left the library and made ready for an evening upon the Seat.

Some days ago, Ebon had asked Theren to recommend a fine tavern for their meal, and she had spoken of a place called the Sterling Stag. She had only been there once, but it had served the finest food she had ever tasted. When Ebon asked her how she had afforded such a meal, she glowered and told him to mind his own business.

Before they left, Ebon bathed and dabbed on a bit of perfume he had bought some time ago and kept hidden in the chest at the foot of his bed. Finally he met his friends in the hall and set out with them into the streets. Kalem had washed as well, and had even combed his hair. To Ebon's great surprise, even Theren had prettied herself up for the occasion, with two thin braids running back along her temples to join a tail into which she had woven back her hair. When she caught him staring, she gave him a pointed look, and he quickly turned.

Snow had at last come to the Seat, and now it drifted down gentle and lazy upon the air, dusting across their skin and catching in their eyelashes before melting. They had to draw their hoods up against the chill, and each wore the simple black coats given to students in wintertime. Kalem kept looking at all of them nervously, lips twisting one way and then another.

"Our student robes look a bit . . . plain, do they not?" he said, brushing at his legs as though they were dirty.

"It is a great honor to study at the Academy—or so I have been told," said Theren.

"We look presentable enough. Do not worry." In truth, Ebon's words were for him as much as for the boy, for he found himself more nervous than he had thought he would be. Theren saw it, and she frowned.

"Ebon, you should not be this anxious."

He scowled. "I am not anxious. I only wish for the evening to go well."

"I know it. I will be on my best behavior."

"And I," said Kalem, but his voice cracked.

Ebon's favorite haunts were all to the west of the Academy, and the Drayden family manor was due east, but the Silver Stag was to the southeast, and so he was walking along unfamiliar streets. But Theren knew her way, and she led them without pause. As they neared the High King's palace, buildings grew ever finer. More were made of stone, and so bore less damage from the attack upon the Seat. Second floors, and even third, became more common, and the walls were often painted in bright colors. One place looked familiar, and Ebon realized his aunt Halab had taken him there when the High King's armies marched forth from the palace. But Theren turned away, and after only a few more blocks, they stood before a grand two-story building with a stag painted in silver upon the door.

"Here we are."

"Well, let us not stop," said Ebon. "Most likely she has arrived already." But he did not take the first step.

"Indeed. We should not keep her waiting." But Kalem, too, remained frozen.

Theren smirked and shook her head. "You are hopeless, the both of you." She seized their arms and pulled them forwards, nudging the door open with her foot before half-tossing them both within.

At once Ebon thought it must be the friendliest tavern he had seen on the Seat. A bright buzz of conversation hung in the room, and no one spared them more than a curious glance before returning to their meals. A crackling fire burned in the hearth and flooded the room with warmth, which was strengthened by the many lanterns that hung low on the walls, so that the place was as well-lit as though it were daylight. Ebon saw no others in Academy robes, not even instructors. Instead there were many people with fine clothing, dresses and tunics and pants all woven with the most expensive silks. A dozen perfumes wove a wreath of heady odor, and he drank it in with a long breath. They scanned the room, searching for an empty table, but before they found one, the tavern's matron approached.

"The grandest of evenings to you, young ones. I am Canda, and master of the Stag." She was a burly woman, and tall, and gave them a look that was both polite and appraising. "I hope I give no offense, but I must tell you that the price of board here is more than you might be used to. Have you the coin to pay for it?"

"We have," said Ebon proudly. "But there is a fourth in our party who may have arrived already. A woman of Idris?"

"You mean Adara?" Canda beamed a sudden smile. "Forgive me, young masters. She did not tell me you were Academy students, or I would have brought you to her at once. She waits at your table. Let me show you the way."

Canda set off through the room, leaning back and forth as she wove through the tables, and Ebon followed with Kalem and Theren close behind. A moment later he saw Adara. Tucked in behind a table in the corner, she was resplendent in yellow silk trimmed with gold. With a start he realized she had worn the gold for him, for it was the color of the family Drayden. He flushed, even as she caught his eye and they traded a grin. She rose at once and came around the table to greet them.

"Adara, it is my pleasure to introduce you to Kalem of the family Konnel," said Ebon. "You already know Theren."

"Indeed. Well met." Adara leaned over to kiss Theren's cheeks.

"Idrisians," said Theren, rolling her eyes. Ebon elbowed her. "And well met, of course."

Adara smiled and then turned to Kalem. "And it is my pleasure to make your acquaintance, young lord."

She made as if to give him the same greeting as Theren, but Kalem drew back, shifting on his feet. "Er . . . ah . . . I am sorry," he mumbled. "In Hedgemond, it is . . . that is, such a greeting . . ."

Adara nodded at once. "I am unfamiliar with Hedgemond's customs," she said easily. "My apologies if I was unseemly."

"Not at all," he said, shaking his head.

Ebon stifled a grin as Adara turned to her chair. He

took his seat beside her, with Kalem at his other hand and Theren to Adara's right.

Canda smiled. "Tonight's meal is a fine roast of beef, and a salad prepared in the manner of Idris, with vinegar at Adara's request. I also have some figs, if you would like them."

Ebon smiled at Adara, and her eyes glinted with delight. "That sounds wonderful," he said. "And wine as well, please, for all of us."

Adara raised a finger. "Mead for me."

Canda nodded and drew away. Ebon looked to Adara with surprise. "Mead? I thought you took wine."

"I do, when I am with the guild, for they choose what drinks to provide. When it is not my coin, I am not choosy. But wait a moment—you have hardly given me a proper greeting."

She slid her hand across his cheek to the back of his head and pulled him in for a deep kiss. When finally he drew back, Theren was looking discreetly away; but Kalem was staring with eyes wide and mouth open. It was a moment before he came to his senses and blushed. Adara cast her gaze upon him with a smile.

"I apologize again, young lord, if we have given you further cause for embarrassment."

"I should be the one to apologize," mumbled Kalem. "I am your guest. It is only that I am unused to such things. Forgive me."

"Think nothing of it."

Just then, a girl came by with their wine. Kalem

drained one cup quickly and then refilled it from the flagon. Theren raised her eyes at him. Adara sipped at her mead.

"Very fine," she said, licking her lips in satisfaction. "You made a fine choice in this place, Ebon."

"You may thank Theren. It was at her advice. Where did you learn to drink mead? It is not common in either Idris or Feldemar."

"But I have not been to only those kingdoms. I left Feldemar in my youth and dwelt for a time in Dulmun."

That darkened their mood, and they fell silent. Ebon and Kalem looked down at the tabletop, and even Theren picked with her fingernail at the edge of her cup.

"My apologies," Adara said softly. "I spoke without thinking. I did not mean to silence a pleasant conversation."

"It is nothing," said Theren. "You cannot be blamed for the war Dulmun chose to wage upon us."

"They have always been a proud people," said Adara. "Though I am as shocked as anyone at their revolt, they are mayhap the least surprising kingdom in which to find such treachery—for they are, after all, descendants of Renna Blackheart herself. I am only glad no others have joined them."

"Not yet," said Theren. "But few are willing to wage war against them, either."

"Hedgemond is willing," said Kalem.

Ebon was scarcely paying attention to the conversation, for he was deep in thought as he looked upon Adara. It surprised him, though he knew it should not have, that he had never learned of her time in Dulmun. There was still much of her past he did not know. It bothered him, though he knew it should not.

Adara caught him staring. She gave him a small smile and a peck on the cheek. "Enough of darkness. Let us speak of something more pleasant. What have the three of you been up to? It has been some days since Ebon and I spoke."

Theren's mouth twisted. "That subject is not much brighter than the other. We have found nothing of use, only dark words of peril."

Kalem looked wide-eyed at Ebon. "She knows of the theft from the vaults?"

Ebon nodded. "Of course. That is the least of the secrets she carries."

"Indeed, I had heard before Ebon told me. The Academy is a wonderful place for many things, but keeping secrets is not one of them." Adara smiled and placed a hand over Ebon's. "But what are these dark words you spoke of?"

"We think we may have found what was stolen from the vaults," said Ebon. "An amulet. One of immense power, though we know not what it does."

Theren leaned in and lowered her voice. "It belonged to some Wizard King of ages gone by. One named Kekhit."

Adara shook her head. "I have never heard of her."

"She is a thing of ancient times. She may even predate the years of Underrealm," said Ebon. "Now we are searching for any tale of her, some history that might help us understand what the amulet might do."

"I have been doing some searching of my own," said Adara. "I will spread word of this and see what may be learned from those who help me."

Ebon frowned. "What searching?"

Theren gave him a crafty smile. "Do you know nothing of the guild of lovers? They are a meddlesome lot."

Adara gave her an admonishing look before turning back to Ebon. "Different houses and members within the guild maintain close contact with each other. Our clients' secrets are never shared, but some information may be passed along, if it does not violate trust. Since you first told me of the theft from the vaults, and then of that ghastly murder, I have had friends searching for any sign of the culprit."

Ebon's stomach lurched, and he spoke soft but urgent. "Adara, that may be folly. If anyone were to learn of your prying . . ."

"They will not," she said, raising an eyebrow and smirking, as though Ebon were both very sweet and very foolish. "The guild looks after its own. In any case, I have learned nothing certain about the theft. Though I have heard many other whispers. It seems there is a girl skulking about the Seat. She wears black robes, like a student of the Academy."

Theren looked at Ebon. "A girl? What did she look like?"

Adara shrugged. "No one has gotten close enough to see. But she has spent much time around the northern end of the Seat, and after curfew."

Ebon raised an eyebrow at Theren. "That sounds like something you might do, Theren."

She frowned. "Since the attack I have been unable to sneak out. The sheds to help me are gone, and the instructors have placed new enchantments upon the walls, and reinforce them often. And besides, I have no business in the north. It could be Lilith."

Kalem sighed. Ebon shook his head. "But for what purpose, Theren? If you think she is the thief, why would she spend time in the city?"

Theren glared, but she had no answer. Adara quickly went on to fill the silence. "Whoever she might be, she is only one of the figures now skulking in shadows. Ebon, your family's man, Mako, has been poking his nose all about the island."

Ebon shrugged. "That is nothing unusual for him."

"His activities have greatly increased," said Adara. "That man's heart is as dark as a sky without moons. Do not trust him."

"Mako warned me the day the Seat was attacked, and that saved our lives," said Ebon, somewhat surprised to find himself defending the bodyguard. "If he is crafty, and somewhat caustic-tongued, that does not mean he is rotten through."

"The deepest rot is the hardest to see," said Adara. "I do not mean to tell you what you should do—only that you should be careful."

Gently she touched his cheek, and his irritation faded. Theren smirked and shook her head, but Kalem lowered his eyes and flushed with embarrassment. Ebon gave him a pat on the shoulder. "There there, little lordling. You will soon be a man grown, and may yet become used to those who do not hide their affections."

"I did not think my presence would cause you such discomfort, Kalem." Though she had been easy enough twice before, now it seemed to Ebon that he heard annoyance in Adara's tone. "I know Hedgemond is no place like the Seat, or Idris where Ebon and I hail from—yet I had not thought it so bashful a kingdom as you make it out to be."

"It is not that," mumbled Kalem. "It is . . . it is only that . . . well, you are very pretty, and . . . womanly."

Adara's irritation vanished at once. She laughed lightly, spurring Ebon to chuckle. "I shall take that as a high compliment, good sir, since I know that many fair ladies must have visited the courts of your family. Have I mayhap taken for discomfort what was, in fact, curiosity? If you should ever wish to step beyond the blue door, I am well familiar with the lovers in the various houses upon the Seat. I assure you I could find a suitable partner from among them for you."

Kalem's face went beet-red. "I . . . I thank you for

the offer, but no. I do not think I would enjoy such a thing."

"I must heartily disagree," said Ebon. "I myself found it most enjoyable." Adara smiled and placed her hand on his thigh beneath the table.

"Oh, I am certain it would be a pleasure," said Kalem. The red of his face deepened as he heard his own double meaning. "But . . . I have a hope that one day I will find one whom I love, and that my first tryst might be with her. I do not wish the one without the other, if you understand me."

"I do indeed," said Adara softly. "And I praise you for knowing your own mind so well. It is not common, especially among men so young, if you will forgive me for saying so. Many never think upon what they truly want, and such a thing always leads to tears. For many, love is a necessary part of intimacy. For others, the two are close friends, often present together, but not always. It is better to know which is true for you before engaging in either."

Kalem bowed his head and said nothing. Theren leaned away in her chair, throwing an arm over its back. "I myself have always known which was which. To my mind, anyone who thinks they are one and the same is a fool." She gave Ebon a hard look, and he glared back.

But Adara only cocked her head. "I do not know if that is true."

As if to prove Theren wrong, Ebon reached down

to where Adara's hand rested in his lap, and scooped it up in his own. Without thinking, she laced her fingers through his, and he kissed the back of her palm. "I think that a night in bed may not always be a night in love," he said softly. "And yet, sometimes, one may lead to the other, so that love springs forth unbidden."

The words sounded foolish in his own ears as he said them, and he half expected to receive one of Adara's sharp, exasperated looks. But she smiled instead, a soft and gentle smile, hinting at nothing, promising so much. He had never known how much hidden meaning was in her eyes until then, when all pretense seemed removed, and he could peer deep into her heart for the first time: pure and unadorned and revealed at last.

She leaned in close, and in a murmur so low only he could hear it, said, "Sometimes love springs forth indeed."

Lover's words, came the whisper in his mind. But he could not stop the thrill in his heart.

TWENTY-ONE

THE REST OF THEIR DINNER PASSED LIGHT AND FAIR, and after they finished eating Kalem returned to the Academy with Theren. But Ebon and Adara stepped beyond the blue door, and he lingered there longer than he should have, so that by the time he returned to the streets he had to hurry home for fear of missing curfew. Upon a time that would not have troubled him, but now the Academy was strict about such things, and besides, he was still closely watched after his adventure in the vaults.

He was only a few streets away when the sun vanished behind the western buildings. He picked up his pace, intent on reaching the Academy before dark. But as he cut through an alley between two busy thoroughfares, a hand swept from the shadows and dragged him towards the wall.

The hand clamped over his mouth, silencing his sharp and sudden cry. His every muscle tensed as he readied himself to fight, to cast a spell, to do something—but then he recognized Mako and scrabbled to drag the bodyguard's hand away from his mouth.

"There are other ways to get my attention," he groused. "You frightened me half to death."

But then he paused, for Mako was looking all about him, peering over both shoulders as though expecting to see someone lurking, waiting to strike at them both. A *crack* around the corner made the man jump, though Ebon recognized it as the sound of a barrel falling from a cart. This was so unlike Mako's usual conduct that Ebon was shocked into silence.

"I have found something most interesting, little goldshitter. But we must act quickly if we are to take advantage of it."

Ebon frowned. "What is it? What did you find?"

"You know I have my ways in and out of the Academy—ways that allow me to pass through the citadel unseen, to visit you, and to see what may be transpiring within its walls."

"I do, though I know not how, exactly."

"Nor should you." Mako smiled for the first time,

and Ebon found that strangely comforting. "Some knowledge is dangerous for others to have. Suffice it to say my pathways take me through nooks of the Academy that are seldom seen. Yet it seems one such nook has been visited by another."

His fingers fished in a pocket on his black leather vest, and from it he drew a piece of parchment. This he unfolded and held before Ebon.

"Do you recognize this?"

Ebon frowned—but only for a moment before his eyes shot wide with shock. It was a page torn from a vault logbook. From the yellowed edges, and the fact that the paper had been torn out, Ebon would have wagered it came from the same logbook they had found in the library, where they had learned of Kekhit's amulet.

"Where did you get this?"

Mako cuffed his ear and snarled, "I told you, in one of the Academy's hidden passages. You are not seeing what is important. Look again."

Ebon scanned the page and read:

This globe's origins are unknown, though it has passed from hand to hand through the centuries, and many Wizard Kings used it. Likely one of them created it. A mentalist or elementalist who speaks the word—then there was a word that was all inked over, as though some later cleric had sought to obscure it—*shall cause the globe to erupt with terrible energy, killing all nearby, but sparing the caster. This is a mentalist enchantment, and summons no fire or thunder.*

The learned scholar will recognize this as a common enchantment in elder days of both mentalism and elementalism, but this is one of the more powerful examples found to date.

Ebon shuddered at the thought of what such an artifact could do in a crowded room. Unbidden, his mind showed him an explosion in a classroom, and he pictured the broken bodies left in the aftermath. But then he saw what had caused Mako such distress: words in red ink, drawn near the bottom of the page and underlined twice.

30 Febris

He stared at it for a moment. "The Eve of Yearsend. What do you mean for me to see about it? It is today's—"

Realization struck him like a hammer blow, and his knees went weak. Mako saw it. His grin widened and turned cruel.

"You see it now, do you not, goldshitter?"

Ebon snatched the page and threw the bodyguard's hand from his shoulder. He began to sprint from the alley towards the Academy, but Mako seized him and dragged him back around.

"Let me go! I must warn them!"

"Warn who? Think, boy. What do you mean to do with what we know?"

Ebon blinked at him. "Catch Lilith, of course."

"But catch her doing what, exactly? Show your instructors now, and doubtless they will post guards around the vault. Lilith's name is not on that page. As it stands, she is blameless. You will not prove her guilt unless you find her with this orb afterwards, for now you know what you are seeking."

Ebon shook his head at once. "No. I will not let her steal it. I must catch her in the act. Last time, an instructor lost his life, and there is every reason to believe that may happen again."

Mako frowned, but he must have seen the resolution in Ebon's eyes. "Very well. Hurry then, goldbag, and pray you are not too late. I have heard no tumult in the Academy yet, so there may still be hope. But where will you say you found this page?"

"I do not know," said Ebon, wanting to run. Even now he was wasting precious time. "Where did *you* find it?"

Mako shook his head. "A fine attempt, but I am not so easily fooled. Say you found it under a hedge in the garden. Here." He took the page, dropped it under his boot, and mushed it about with his heel. It came up grimy and torn in the corner. "That will help the lie. Now go!"

Ebon turned and sprinted for the Academy's front door.

His shoes pounded on the stone floors of the hallways, and the slapping sound ran on ahead of him, echoing all around so that it sounded as though an army ran beside him.

But no. No army. Only me, and mayhap too late.

At first he thought to make for the vaults, to catch Lilith on his own, but almost at once he realized the folly of such a plan. She might have Kekhit's amulet, and therefore power beyond reckoning—but even at her weakest, she was far more than Ebon's match. So he ran instead for the instructors' offices.

Halfway there, he rounded a corner and nearly ran into Theren. Eyes wide, she opened her mouth to ask him a question. "No time!" he cried, wheezing and short of breath, and ran on. She caught up a moment later, running by his side.

"Where are you going?"

"Jia. Lilith is about to strike."

Her eyes narrowed as she doubled her pace. She reached Jia's office before he did and threw open the door for him. They practically fell in across the door-step. He thanked the sky above, for Jia was there at her desk with Dasko. Both instructors looked at them wide-eyed in shock.

"What is the matter?" said Jia.

"Instructor," said Ebon, wheezing as he thrust forth the logbook page. A fit of coughing claimed him, but he choked out his words. "I found this. The vault thief—they mean to strike again. Tonight."

He thought she might look alarmed, or mayhap frightened, but she glared at him instead. "Ebon, you were specifically warned to stay out of—"

"No!" cried Ebon. "I found this in the gardens by chance, I swear it. Just look, Instructor!"

Dasko had taken the page from Ebon, his eyes scanning the text. He took Jia's arm, and she met his eyes. For half a moment they stared at each other. Ebon held his breath.

THOOM

A blast rocked the Academy, thundering through the halls. A chorus of screams followed it.

Jia and Dasko fled the room, forgetting all about Ebon, who followed at once. On he ran, though Jia screamed at them to stay back, to return to their dormitories. On, past the students who stood mute and terrified, torn between curiosity at the commotion and fear of another attack, and mayhap a corpse awaiting them all. On, with Theren beside him saying "Not again, not again, sky above, please," a terrible whimper made all the worse coming from her.

Another boom rocked the hallways, and more screams told them which way to go—though of course they did not need guidance, for they knew it came from the vaults.

Just before they rounded the corner and reached the entrance, Jia and Dasko's eyes glowed white, and the two wizards transformed. Jia's robes sank into her flesh, and hair sprouted all over her body as she turned into a massive bear, its head nearly striking the ceiling. Dasko had become a beast of the far northern jungles, a catlike creature with a huge mane of golden fur.

Together they roared, loud and terrifying enough to make Ebon's heart skip a beat. Almost he stopped in his tracks, for his limbs had seized up, but he forced himself onwards. Theren had not abandoned the chase, and her eyes glowed as she reached for her magic. He would not abandon his friend, nor his instructors, though he did not know what he might do to help.

They crashed through the first door and into the vault's office. The last time Ebon had passed through it quickly. He remembered the two high, tall windows in the walls. They were open now, their shutters flapping. He remembered the wide wooden desk where Egil worked, and the several smaller desks around the room's edges.

But now his eyes were drawn to the student hovering in the air ten feet off the floor. A maelstrom poured through the windows, becoming a funnel of destruction that whipped him about. A lanky towheaded boy, eyes wide with pain and fright. Astrea's friend, Vali.

And Vali screamed as magic crushed the life from him.

Horror-struck, Ebon was so focused on Vali that at first he missed Lilith. Then he saw her standing near the vault's entry. The door listed open. Lilith's eyes glowed as she held her hands high, commanding the squall. She grimaced as she shouted at Vali: "Stop it! Stop it!"

Theren gave a wordless cry as her eyes sprang to light, and she leapt forwards to fight Lilith's magic. Jia and Dasko stormed ahead, one of Jia's massive paws catching Lilith in the chest and flinging her to the ground. Dasko planted a clawed foot on her abdomen. But Lilith managed to keep an arm raised, and the glow in her eyes did not die. Her lips quivered with words of power.

Ebon searched the room for something, anything to do. He saw a number of other students who had gathered at the commotion—Lilith's friends Oren and Nella were there, and some other members of the Goldbag Society. Isra was there, her dark brown eyes wide and staring, horror-struck, at Vali suspended in midair.

Ebon leapt forwards and pushed the three of them to draw their attention. "Use your power! Stop her!"

Oren blinked without understanding, and Isra did not even look away from where Vali hung in the air.

Ebon shoved Oren harder. "Stop her!" he cried again, pleading.

As though waking from a dream, Oren shook his head. He nudged Ebon aside as light sprang into his eyes. Nella, too, shook off her horror, and her eyes glowed.

But it was too late. With a cry, Lilith's arm fell to

the stone floor. Vali screamed as the wind blasted him towards the wall. He struck the stones with the force of a thunderbolt.

A wet *snap* filled the air.

He crashed to the ground, head lolling to the side at a hideous angle.

The room fell silent for a long moment. Then a piercing scream stabbed the quiet behind Ebon.

He turned, and his heart broke.

There, in the vault's outer doorway, stood Astrea, clawing at her cheeks and neck as her wail rose higher and higher, until it seemed to be the only thing in the world.

"Get her out of here!" Jia had taken human form again, and she waved a sharp hand at Ebon as she spoke. Shaken from his inaction, he went forwards to take Astrea's arm and pull her from the room. Isra darted to his side and reached down, sweeping Astrea up into her arms.

As he stepped out through the door, he took a final glance back. Lilith had been seized by the instructors and several students. Someone had made a gag from a torn piece of robe and wrapped it around her mouth. She stood staring after Astrea with wild, sightless eyes. Theren stood to the side, stricken with horror.

Then the door closed behind him, and there was only Astrea's scream. He tried to put a comforting hand on the girl's arm, tried to speak words of peace. But Isra had very nearly enshrouded the girl, and her eyes filled with raw fury whenever Ebon tried to reach out.

"Astrea," he said, trying to avoid Isra's hateful glare. "Astrea, it is all right. It is all right."

"It is not all right!" Astrea screamed, slapping at his hand. "He is dead!"

"Go away," Isra hissed. She turned back to Astrea, holding her closer, murmuring to her. Ebon barely made out the words. "Be calm. Be calm. Breathe deeply, and put Vali from your mind."

Astrea's breath came ragged, sucked in and pushed out between her teeth. Her hands shook where they clutched at Isra's robes. But slowly the tears stopped pouring from her eyes. Slowly her look grew far away as she focused on Isra's words. Her breaths grew deeper. Calmer.

"There," said Ebon quietly. "Good. Well done."

"I told you to leave us," said Isra. She released Astrea and stepped towards him, pushing him hard in the chest. "You filthy goldbags. Can you not leave us alone? Can you create nothing but blood and suffering?"

Ebon blinked at her. "I . . . I had nothing to do—"

"Be silent!" Isra cried.

Her eyes blazed with light. Fear seized Ebon's heart as an unseen force hoisted him a foot above the stone floor, and he knew it was her magic.

"You never fail to find ways to kill us without blame. How many died in the attack on the Seat? Who started this war? Who will die on its battlefields? Not you, goldbag."

He tried to speak but could not. Some students stood within sight of them, but they were frozen in horror. Ebon swallowed hard and tried again.

"I want nothing of this war," he said, every word quivering. "I am sorry. I know not what madness seized Lilith, I swear it."

For a moment she only stood there, chest heaving with her breath. But then she let the glow slip from her eyes, and Ebon fell to the floor, only just managing to keep his feet.

"Leave," she rasped, and then turned to Astrea, who clung to her once more. "Leave, goldbag. You can do nothing to help. You can only hurt."

Ebon wanted to answer, but had no words to do so. Instead he turned and moved off down the hallway.

TWENTY-TWO

EBON WOKE TO A DARK DAY AT THE ACADEMY.

It was the first day of Yearsend, but there was no celebration. Ebon was grateful that classes were suspended for the holiday, for he could not imagine trying to sit in Perrin's classroom and read tomes of magic.

Instead he, Kalem, and Theren went out into the gardens. Many students had chosen to remain inside, for it was now the dead of winter, and so they were alone among the hedges and bare rosebushes. For a while they said nothing, listening only to the crunch of their shoes in the snow, watching only the mist of their breath upon the air. Ebon had his hood up against the weather, as did his friends, and so they rarely even looked at each other.

"She stole more artifacts from the vaults," Theren said at last. "From what I can tell, the count is more than half a dozen. I no longer serve in the vaults, but I spoke with Egil, and he let it slip. She must have gone back and forth a few times, emptying rooms until Vali . . ." Her words tapered off.

Ebon shrugged his shoulders, hunching them as though against a bitter wind. He could scarcely close his eyes without seeing the boy's head twisting to the side and hearing the snap of a neck. Credell's death, at least, had happened out of sight. And he was an instructor. To murder a child so young . . . it made him heartsick to imagine the letter that must have been sent home to Vali's family.

Lilith had been dragged off and delivered to the Mystics. They would not kill her at once, though the penalty of death was certain. First they would try to learn where the stolen artifacts had gone. He had been there when they took her away. Before they managed to gag her, she had muttered, "He was supposed to join us," over and over again. As she passed him in the hall, she had still been trying to repeat it around the cloth that gagged her.

"Credell was a tragedy," said Theren, the words quivering. "But had I ever imagined she might kill a boy so young, I would have stopped her. I would have snapped her neck mys—" Her voice shattered at last, and she hid her face behind her hood, her shoulders shaking with sobs. Ebon had only seen Theren weep once before, and like then, it was an unnerving sight. He and Kalem looked away, feeling suddenly awkward.

Footsteps crunched across the snow towards them, and they looked up, grateful for the distraction. To Ebon's surprise, it was Dasko. The instructor came forwards with his hood up and hands tucked into sleeves, shielding them from winter's chill. He stopped a few feet away and nodded to each of them in turn.

"Well met," he said softly. "I had hoped . . . I am sorry I could not come and see you earlier, Ebon. But I wondered if I might still speak with you, as I requested some time ago? I would not think to trouble you now. But mayhap after the Yearsend feast?"

Ebon glanced at Kalem and Theren. "Of course, Instructor."

"Very good." But Dasko remained, fidgeting with his hands and tugging on his thumbs. Then his head jerked up, and he winced.

"That is only part of the reason I have come. I must discuss an unpleasant bit of Academy business. Might I . . .?"

He waved a hand. Ebon glanced at Kalem and Theren, and then stepped away with Dasko. The instructor's grey eyes wandered for a moment before he spoke to Ebon in a low murmur.

"Last night . . . I know that after you left the vault's office, you and Isra had words."

Ebon's ears flushed with shame. "We did," he muttered.

Dasko's frown deepened. "We know she struck at you. With her magic."

"I cannot blame her for that," said Ebon. "What we had all seen . . . and then, I would not leave her and Astrea be when she asked me to."

A sigh slipped from Dasko. "Then you do not wish to punish her?"

Ebon blinked, looking at him with wide eyes. "Punish her? No, of course not. Sky above, how could I think to do so?"

The instructor's shoulders sagged, and he ran a hand through his hair. "Thank goodness. She broke the Academy's rules. If you wished it, you could ask for punishment to be meted out. But I am greatly relieved you have no such wish. You are right that last night would have put a terrible strain on anyone, and for Isra in particular." He shook his head.

Curiosity poked at Ebon despite himself. "What of her? I have never thought she viewed me very highly."

"Indeed not," said Dasko. "It is not a happy tale, and mayhap it is not mine to tell. But it might shed some light on her actions, and since you have shown her mercy, I see no reason not to tell you. Isra was sent here an orphan, as was Astrea."

"I heard something of that from Astrea herself."

Dasko grimaced. "She likely did not tell you—mayhap she does not even know—why Isra came to that orphanage in the first place. But her parents were killed by the royalty of Wadeland."

A chill crept up Ebon's spine. "What? Murdered?"

The instructor looked away. "As with many things, the truth is not so simple. Her father was crushed under the prince's carriage. When her mother sought recompense, the king tired of her pleading and had her executed."

Ebon stared at him. "But that is monstrous. The King's law—"

"Provides for no such thing, I know," said Dasko. "The king of Wadeland is foul indeed, but the High King cannot interfere with every injustice across Underrealm. Especially when no witness remained to bring word of this misdeed to her."

"I cannot believe . . ." Ebon shook his head, afraid he might be sick. The way Isra spat every time she said the word *goldbag*—at last he felt he understood.

"I told you it was no happy tale," Dasko said quietly. "But I have taken enough of your time. Be with your friends, and be grateful you are all whole. Also, I have this for you."

From an inner pocket of his robes Dasko produced a letter and placed it in Ebon's hands. Ebon broke the Drayden family seal and unfolded a letter from Halab, inviting him to the manor for lunch to celebrate the holiday.

Hot fire burned in his veins, and he could not stop his hands from shaking. Lunch with his family would mean he would have to see his uncle, Matami, and Matami might have been involved in Lilith's crimes. That truth might come out as the Mystics questioned Lilith, but then again it might not. From what Ebon knew, the Mystics were not seeking accomplices, but only where she had taken the artifacts. The thought of sitting across from Matami's haughty, smirking face for an entire meal made him want to melt a stone and throw it in the man's eyes.

He forced himself to stay calm. Matami's presence might be unbearable, but it would be good to see Halab and his mother, and especially Albi. "Thank you, Instructor. May I send a reply?"

"Of course." From a pocket, Dasko produced a bit of charcoal and gave it to him.

Ebon walked back to Kalem and Theren. "I am invited to a meal with my aunt. When last I saw her, she invited me to bring any friends from the Academy I might wish. What say you? Will you come with me?"

They both nodded, so Ebon scrawled his answer on the parchment and handed it to Dasko.

"Very good, Ebon. We shall speak on the morrow." He gave Kalem and Theren a small nod before leaving.

"What did he have to say to you?" said Theren. "You spoke longer than I thought you might."

But Ebon had no wish to speak of Isra's story, which still turned his stomach. He only said, "In her anger,

Isra used her magic upon me last night. It was a small thing, and no harm came of it. But Dasko wished to make sure I did not want to see her punished. I told him of course I did not. It is Yearsend, after all. A time for forgiveness."

"Yearsend," said Kalem with a sigh. "It seems such a hollow thing. Who can care for a holiday now?"

"Mayhap we need it," said Ebon. "Something to take our minds from the darkness we have borne witness to. What better for the purpose than a celebration?"

"Midday meal in a goldbag's manor, and the Yearsend feast for supper," said Theren. "Fine distractions indeed. Yet I do not think they will rid me of the darkness."

"Try to let them," said Kalem. "It is not as though we can blame ourselves for what happened."

Theren chewed at her cheek. "We knew what she was up to. We might have done more to stop her."

"You did all you could—we all did," said Ebon. "We were very nearly expelled because of it."

But Theren only shook her head and looked away.

An hour before midday, they went to their dormitories. Now that Ebon knew Shay would not be in the Drayden manor to see him, he took a bit more care to wash away the stains of the Academy. He bathed, donned fresh robes, and dabbed on a bit of perfume.

The hourglass in the common room told him he was running late, so he hurried to the front hall. Theren was already waiting, and it seemed that she had done nothing special with her appearance. Kalem joined them soon after, scuttling down the stairs and still trying to fix his mussed hair with his fingers.

The streets did much to lift their spirits, for they bustled with Yearsend celebrations. Those outside the Academy cared little for what took place within its walls. They caught many friendly smiles, and soon Ebon found himself returning them. Some vendors gave away little sweetmeats without asking for coin in observance of the holiday, and horses and carriages were a bit more considerate of passersby on foot. Many musicians played as they walked, singing fine songs while they strummed at lutes and small handharps. Soon Ebon and Kalem were laughing as though it were a day like any other. But Theren's mood only darkened the further they went, and after a time she rounded on the others with a snarl.

"How can you giggle to each other so? As though you are little children."

Kalem stopped in his tracks, frowning. "We are only trying not to dwell in darkness, Theren."

"Look around you. Darkness is everywhere, and we cannot help ourselves but dwell in it." She folded and then unfolded her arms, fists bunching as though she wanted to strike at the air itself. "I hope they drag the truth from Lilith on the tips of sharp knives. May she lead them straight to her accomplices—and for my own satisfaction, I hope it *is* that worthless ferret Cyrus. Nothing could make me happier than to see that dung heap die the slowest of deaths."

Ebon lowered his gaze to his shoes so Theren could not see his sudden discomfort.

Kalem shook his head. "Mayhap she will. Mayhap not. In any case, whoever her accomplice is, they have lost their way into the Academy. They have no choice now but to slink away into the darkness, never to return."

"You may believe that," said Theren, scowling. "I am not so sure. Cyrus may try to strike again."

"Mayhap."

They reached the Drayden manor soon after, much to Ebon's relief. They stopped before the wide front gates as Ebon knocked. As they waited for a guard to open the way, Ebon glanced back at his friends. Kalem inspected the place appraisingly, but Theren stared wide-eyed. Ebon smirked.

"Are you overawed, Theren? This is not so great a building as you seem to think. After all, you dwell within the Academy."

Theren jerked her gaze from the manor to glare at him. "You think rather highly of yourself for one born into such wealth through no fault of your own."

Ebon chuckled. Just then, a guard opened the hatch and saw him, and soon the gate swung open. They stepped through the gap as soon as it was wide enough, and Ebon led them through the courtyard towards the manor's front door.

"What is in these wagons?" said Kalem, pointing at Matami's trade wagons, which were still out in the open.

"Spices and other trade goods for the High King," said Ebon.

"That many wagons filled with spices?" said Theren, gawking again. "But that would be worth a fortune."

"And now you know why our coin purses are so deep. Here we are."

Ebon opened the front door and led them inside. The entry hall was bright with many candles and torches lining the walls. Someone must have notified Ebon's family of their arrival, for they found a reception waiting: Halab, Hesta, and Albi.

"Dearest nephew," said Halab, coming forwards to give Ebon a tight hug.

"Dearest aunt," said Ebon, kissing her cheeks. "Allow me the pleasure of introducing my friends."

But she interrupted him, smiling at them each in turn. "There is no need. I know their names already. Welcome, Kalem of the family Konnel. The honor of your house is well-known throughout the nine lands. I have had many favorable encounters with your kin, and I look forward to many more in the future."

Kalem's mouth opened slightly, though it seemed he was lost for words. Theren rolled her eyes and folded her arms. But then Halab turned to her and gave a deep bow.

"Well met, Theren. Tales of your prowess as a mentalist have reached me even here in my manor. I am graced by your presence, and ever grateful for the friendship and kindness you have shown my nephew. I worried greatly for Ebon when he stayed here upon the Seat, for he had neither family nor friends to look after him. You have my thanks for being part of the remedy."

Theren seemed as flustered as Kalem. She cleared her throat and looked about uncomfortably, before trying to mimic Halab's bow. "It was . . . it *is* my pleasure, I suppose, milady. Though friendship might be a strong word, for sometimes it seems I only get him into trouble, and he only gets me out."

Halab laughed, so warm and hearty that every face in the room burst into a smile. "What else are friends for, dear girl?" She stepped forwards to embrace Theren, and then Kalem. But when she drew back from the boy, he flushed and, stepping forwards, kissed her first on one cheek, and then the other. Halab went stock still in shock, and Ebon's eyes widened.

"I have heard that that is the proper greeting in Idris," said Kalem, mumbling and keeping his eyes lowered.

A slight flush crept into Halab's cheeks, but her tone maintained nothing but grace. "It is, son of Konnel—though, normally, it is reserved for family greeting family, or for very close friends indeed."

Ebon tried desperately not to burst into laughter,

for Kalem's face went so red it was nearly purple. He jerked and twisted, trying to stammer out an apology, but his voice shook so hard he could not get out so much as a word. But Halab only laughed again, and this time they joined her.

"Worry not, my friend." Ebon put a comforting hand on Kalem's shoulder. "Your intent is welcome, even if your knowledge is lacking."

Halab then waved an arm to beckon Hesta and Albi forwards. "Allow me to introduce my sister by law, Hesta, Ebon's mother, and Albi, her daughter, Ebon's sister."

"Well met," said Hesta, bowing. Albi joined her a half-moment later, for she was giving Theren an appraising look. But when she rose from her bow, she gave Kalem a wink. "Will you try to kiss my cheeks, Kalem? We shall have to see if I try to stop you."

Kalem's blush deepened. Halab arched an eyebrow, while Hesta slapped her daughter's wrist. "Albi! That was ill said. It is not seemly to embarrass a guest in our home."

"I did not mean to embarrass him, mother," said Albi, and this time her wink to Kalem was broader. "Who says I spoke in jest?"

"Albi! If you cannot compose yourself, you may take your supper alone," said Hesta.

"Forgive my niece," said Halab, giving her a steely look. "She nears womanhood but does not yet know what to do about it. In time she may yet learn to behave as befits her station."

Finally Albi wilted. "I meant no offense," she said, lowering her gaze. "Forgive me."

"Think nothing of it," said Kalem. "After all, I have embarrassed myself far worse already."

"That you have, my friend." Ebon laid his arm across the boy's shoulder. "But the day is yet young, with much time to redeem yourself. And I smell lamb."

Lamb it was. Halab led them to the dining room, where the meal had already been laid. There, waiting for them in an armchair, was Matami. He rose as they entered, giving Ebon a curt nod.

"Nephew."

"Uncle. My friends, Theren, and Kalem of the family Konnel."

He nodded without speaking, looking at them as though they were pieces of dung he had just noted on the bottom of his shoe. Then they sat to eat.

Again Ebon thought he might melt from the fine taste of the food, with each bite seeming more delicious than the last. Beside him, Kalem closed his eyes often, rolling the food around on his tongue.

Theren showed no decorum whatsoever. She moaned anew with every bite, and her lips smacked loudly, for she chewed with her mouth open. Ebon had never noticed it before; in the Academy's dining hall, there was so much bustle amid the hum of conversation that such a thing could go unremarked. He wondered if she had eaten this way in the Sterling Stag, and how he could have missed it. It made him more and more uneasy, and he kept trying to nudge her under the table, but she ignored him. Across the table, Albi stared at Theren with wide eyes, utterly scandalized. But Matami's scowl grew with every wet smack of Theren's lips.

To their credit, Halab and Hesta were the picture of decorum. They ate primly and quietly, and if they noticed Theren's atrocious manners, they gave no sign. Once she had eaten her fill, Halab dabbed at her lips with her napkin and turned to Ebon. "Troubling news has reached me, nephew. It seems that tragedy has struck the Academy again."

The room's mood darkened at once. Even Theren ceased her loud chewing. "It has, Halab," he said quietly.

"What happened, exactly? Word does not reach my ears so quickly without being twisted in the mouths of those who bring it."

"There is a student—or there *was*, I suppose I should say. It seems she was stealing things from the vaults beneath the Academy."

"Vaults?" said Albi, perking up.

"Rooms in the basement, protected by magical enchantments," said Kalem. "Inside there are powerful artifacts that grant the owner abilities akin to wizards, or else strengthen the magic of wizards who hold them."

"How fascinating," said Albi in a voice of silk. "Thank you, Kalem." She smiled sweetly, and Kalem gulped.

"Her name was Lilith, of the family Yerrin," said Ebon. "Last night, she was caught in the act of her theft. The student who caught her was . . . that is, she . . ." He could not go on, and let the words subside.

"She killed him," said Theren, voice clotted with fury. "Just a boy. Younger even than Kalem."

"Such a tragedy," said Albi. "But what more can one expect from a Yerrin? They have always been a treacherous clan."

Ebon fixed her with a look. "Her cousin, Oren, fought to stop her. He pitted his power against hers, and though he failed, that does not lessen the effort."

"Were you there, my son?" Beside him, Hesta's eyes shone as she regarded him.

Ebon frowned. "Yes, Mother. But I was unharmed. She struck only at Vali."

"How horrible that must have been," she said, shaking her head. "I am so sorry you had to witness it."

Her hand held his tightly, thumb caressing his palm. A sudden lump formed in his throat, and he blinked back the smarting in his eyes. He could not remember the last time his mother had touched him so, for he never saw her without his father, and Hesta knew well that Shay would scorn them both if ever he found his wife coddling their son, as he saw it.

"We are whole," he said, placing his other hand over hers. "That is all that can be asked. Others are not so fortunate."

"And may you ever remain so, now that the criminal faces the King's law." Halab raised her goblet. "To those in the darkness."

"To those in the darkness." Around the table they raised their cups and drank deep.

TWENTY-THREE

TALK SOON TURNED TO LIGHTER MATTERS, AND IT WAS not long before the meal was done. Halab excused herself. She and Hesta had some business in the city, but she promised she would return before long. Matami vanished without a word. Ebon wondered whether he ought to leave the manor with his friends, but before he could, Albi bounced to his side and seized his arm tight.

"Well, brother, what say you? Shall we walk in the garden again? This time there are more of us, and mayhap this company is more interesting as well." She fixed Kalem with a coquettish smile. The boy blushed and stared at his shoes.

Ebon tried to hide a frown, but did not entirely succeed. "I suppose so. But let us show my friends the manor first."

"Oh, what greater pleasure could there be?" said Theren, rolling her eyes. "I have often longed to explore the dwelling of wealthy goldbags."

Albi gasped. But Ebon shook his head ruefully. "Try not to mind her. I have had to grow used to it. There are many in the Academy who resent us for our coin. Some of the other merchant's children, or children of nobility, wear the term 'goldbag' like a badge of honor."

"Well," said Albi, looking at Theren askance. "I do not know that I wish to get used to it. But come. Let us show them about."

And so she and Ebon took them room to room, showing them the fine craftsmanship of the furniture and the artistry of the tapestries and paintings. Kalem was most interested. Ebon knew the boy's family had fallen upon hard times, and likely he now walked among more wealth than he had ever seen. What was more, Albi would often take his hand briefly as she pulled him from room to room, or press up against his arm as she pointed out a particular detail in a painting, so that Kalem grew ever more flustered as they went, and tried with increasing difficulty to keep his eyes on the manor itself. Ebon soon found himself frustrated with Albi's obvious flirting, but worried that if he mentioned it, it would only get worse. She had always loved to tease him.

Theren seemed impressed at first, but quickly became bored. Soon Ebon practically had to drag her from room to room, following behind Albi as she grew ever more relentless in her advances towards Kalem. At last he felt he had to end it. He interrupted her just as she was explaining the history of a painting hanging in the main hall.

"It has grown too warm and stuffy in here," said Ebon, fixing her with a sharp look. "Why do we not step out into the courtyard to cool ourselves?"

Albi glowered. "I suppose, if my brother is uncomfortable."

"He is," said Ebon. "Come."

Outside, the frosty air was indeed a welcome relief from the heat of the manor's fireplaces and torches. Ebon sighed, watching his breath waft up into the grey sky. Before them lay the wagons, arranged in neat rows, canvas roofs covered with a light dusting of snow.

"When does Matami mean to bring the wagons back home?" said Ebon.

Albi turned from Kalem, whose eye she had been trying to catch, to stare daggers at him. "Who knows, or cares? He will take them home when he leaves the Seat. I have heard it will be soon, but nothing more exact."

Ebon frowned. A thought tickled the back of his

mind—something important that he could not place. Something about the wagons, full of spices for the High King, soon returning home to Idris. All under Matami's command . . .

It came in a flash. If he and Mako had been right in their suspicions, Lilith might have been in league with Matami and Shay. Now she writhed under the knives of Mystics who sought to learn where the artifacts had gone.

But what if they lay before Ebon's very eyes?

Albi was caught up in some whispered conversation with Kalem. Ebon snatched Theren's elbow and drew her aside.

"What has gotten into you?" she said, shaking her arm from his grip.

"The artifacts. What if I was right before, and Lilith was in league with my uncle? If she stole the artifacts and brought them to him, and he means to take them back to Idris . . ."

Ebon trailed off, letting his eyes rest upon the wagons. Theren followed his gaze, and then gave a start. "You think they are here?"

"They could be. Who would think to look for them? He could have done it under my aunt's very nose, planning to bring them home to my father."

"There is only one way to find out for sure." Theren gripped his arm, dragged him towards the wagons, and opened one of the back flaps. But the wagon held nothing.

"Search the others," said Ebon. They split up and went wagon to wagon down the line. But one after the other was empty.

"What are you doing?" Albi appeared at his elbow, and was now looking at him as if he were mad.

"Where are the spices?" said Ebon. "All the goods you brought from Idris? They are not here."

"Of *course* not," said Albi, rolling her eyes. "We have delivered them already and are waiting for the wagons to be refilled before leaving."

"Are they *all* empty?" said Ebon. "Has anything come in, mayhap, to bring back to Idris? Anything recent?"

Albi looked skyward in thought, and then opened her mouth to reply.

"What in the darkness below do you wretches think you are doing?"

Matami pounded through the snow, approaching them with fury blazing in his eyes. He seized Ebon's shoulder and shoved him away from the wagons.

"Leave off!" cried Theren, going to Ebon's side. She scowled up at Matami, who tried to loom over her, though he was only two fingers taller. He raised a hand to strike her, but that was a mistake. Theren's eyes flashed with light, and she put forth a hand. Matami reeled suddenly, struck by an invisible force. Albi screamed.

"Guards!" cried Matami. "Take her!"

Drayden men in chain shirts, holding spears and

with swords on their belts, streamed into the courtyard from the manor and the gatehouses. But they balked upon seeing Ebon there with his friends.

Matami seized one of the guards by the arm and shoved him towards the children. "I told you to take her! Vile little witch—you shall be flogged for this, and the boy as well." His sharp, dark eyes fixed on Ebon. "And you would be wise never to return, nor should you have come today. Spare the family further disappointment from any association with your feckless, worthless self."

Still the guards seemed reluctant to move. Theren's hands remained raised, and her eyes held their powerful glow. "I see only one worthless wretch here. Why do you not try to take me yourself? You call Ebon a disappointment, but at least he is no coward."

Matami bared his teeth, and he turned to the guard beside him, grasping for the man's sword.

"Stop this madness!"

Halab's shout pierced the courtyard, ringing in Ebon's ears. He turned to see her behind them, standing in the gateway leading to the street. But she did not meet his eyes, for she never removed her furious gaze from Matami.

Ebon's uncle blinked, and his hands froze halfway to the sword. "Sister," he rasped. "These three—"

"Silence your weeping sore of a mouth." Halab came forwards, pushing the children firmly aside to stand before them. A finger pointed at the guard beside Matami, who straightened to attention at once. "You there. Jarrah, is it not?"

The man bowed at once. "Yes, my lady."

"Strike my brother in the stomach, and do not be gentle."

Matami's mouth gaped in protest. Jarrah hesitated only a moment, but then he saw the resolve in Halab's eye. He turned, driving his mail-covered fist into Matami's gut. Matami gasped, his breath leaving him, and fell to his knees in the snow.

"Get him up," said Halab. Jarrah dragged Matami back to standing. "And now put him back down."

Again Jarrah punched Matami, and this time the man whimpered as he fell to all fours in the snow. Ebon winced, averting his gaze. But beside him, he saw Albi watching their uncle with her chin held high, eyes bright, a grim smile playing at her lips.

Halab stepped forwards and seized Matami's collar, dragging him back to his feet and staring into his eyes. He could not meet her gaze, but turned every which way to avoid her.

"Sister," he said, still gasping from Jarrah's blows. "I only—"

"You are only a sniveling, spineless wretch," said Halab. "You dare to call my dearest nephew worthless? Know this: I value his life more than yours by a wide, wide margin. His friends are my guests—*my* guests, *Matamiya,* and yet you dared to order violence against them. Thank the sky my guards are wise and did not follow your madness. Even our servants prove they are worthier than you."

She released his collar, folding one hand into the other and twisting the ring on the middle finger of her left hand. Matami sagged in relief, probing at his tender stomach. But then Halab removed the ring, and struck him in the eye with her own balled fist. He cried out and fell again, clutching at his face.

"I have always been able to tumble you, and I see nothing has changed," said Halab, her voice dripping with scorn. "Were you anyone but my brother, I would throw you to the King's law, or mayhap mete out her justice myself. Never lay eyes upon my nephew again. Now begone."

Matami reached up towards the guards, seeking their help to stand. But Jarrah and the others stepped away, lifting their gazes from him in contempt. So he scrabbled on the ground until he could stand and then, without a backwards glance, slunk away between the wagons. But from the moment she banished him, Halab turned away, ignoring him, and she looked upon the children with sorrow. Absentmindedly, she shook out the fist with which she had struck Matami.

"Dearest nephew, and you, my guests. I thank the sky above that I returned when I did. This was unforgivable."

"Matami's conduct, mayhap, but not yours, dear aunt," said Ebon.

"He is right," said Kalem. "Think nothing of it, I beg you."

There was a moment of silence. Then Ebon drove a sharp elbow into Theren's ribs. "Ow! Oh, er . . . it is no great worry. I could easily have bested him in a fight."

"You should never have needed to," said Halab, shaking her head. "This is my household, and his dishonor falls upon my own head."

"You cannot be responsible for Matami, Halab," said Albi, smirking. "He has always been such, or at least as long as I have known him."

Halab sighed. "He has never enjoyed being the youngest of us. It clouds his thoughts, leading them to anger more easily than is desirable. I assure you, his intentions are not so bad as they seem—though of course, intent matters little when one's conduct is so wretched."

Kalem stepped forwards and gave her a bow. "I hope I do not speak out of turn, madam—but for me, he is more than overshadowed by you, in whom intent and conduct are united in honor, and both warm the heart."

From the corner of his eye, Ebon saw Theren roll her eyes. But Halab put a hand to her breast, cocking a head as she smiled down at Kalem.

"Now here is one whose courtesy cannot be held in too high of esteem, and whose silver words could charm the heart of a carrock. I thank you, Kalem of the family Konnel, and am reminded of my own words, when I looked forwards to more favorable meetings with your family. From this day forwards, I shall call no meeting more favorable than ours."

The boy flushed and retreated behind Theren's shoulder. Ebon smiled at Halab. "Now we must be going, dearest aunt. The day wears on, and the Academy holds a Yearsend feast."

"You cannot leave after this," said Halab. "I had meant to attend business in the palace, but I will postpone it. We can hold our own feast to atone for today's unpleasantness, though it will be on short notice."

"Please, do not trouble yourself," said Ebon. "Dark times have fallen upon us all, and nowhere more so than in the Academy. But now that they have passed, it would do us well to draw together and spend this Yearsend in each other's company, so that the healing of our hearts may begin."

Halab inclined her head. "Your words are wise, dearest nephew. Already you have learned much at the Academy, and you do our family a great service. I hope we may see each other again soon."

"Of course we will." Ebon stepped forwards to kiss her cheeks. "Farewell."

Kalem held forth a hand. But Halab used it to pull him close into an embrace, and then did the same with Theren. "Visit whenever you wish. I am at your service, and the manor is yours."

Theren raised an eyebrow. "And what of the goblets

and silverware within the manor?" Ebon snatched her sleeve and dragged her away.

Albi said her farewells last, primly shaking Theren's hand and giving Ebon a hug. But Kalem she kissed on the cheek, much to his embarrassment. "I hope to see you all again soon," she said, though she never took her eyes from Kalem's.

They left at last, setting out into the streets and winding their way back towards the Academy. As the manor vanished from sight behind them, Theren was first to break the silence.

"Your aunt was a kind and honorable woman. I have heard very different things about the Draydens. If they were all like her, I imagine your family's name would be no terrible thing."

"You are right," said Ebon. "I have been disliked all my life because of my family name. Halab has been my only consolation. I think she tries to guide my kin in the right direction. But they resist her, as Matami clearly shows."

"She is not the only one," said Kalem. "Your mother also was very gracious, and your sister most polite." His cheeks reddened again, and he avoided their eyes.

"Polite indeed," said Theren, smirking as she pushed his shoulder. "And you were most charming in turn. See to it that you do not charm yourself into her bed."

"*Theren!*" cried Kalem, looking as though he might be ill. "She is a child."

"She is nearly a year older than you."

"*I* am a child!"

But Ebon ignored them both, for his thoughts were preoccupied by what Kalem had said. Yes, his mother had been kind to his friends. Yet throughout his life, she had never been kind enough to protect him from his father. Never did she participate in Shay's cruelty, but she never spoke against it, either. Today she had been concerned at the thought of Ebon witnessing Vali's death. Did she not realize that that had disturbed Ebon nowhere near as much as the hatred and scorn of his father?

Theren seized his sleeve, startling him from his thoughts. He blinked as he looked at her. "What?"

She pointed past him. "There. Look at that cart."

Ebon followed her finger to a wooden cart down the street, loaded with several crates. Beside it walked a man in dark grey instructor's robes, while two of the High King's guard flanked the cart on either side. And looking closer, Ebon could see that the instructor was Dasko.

TWENTY-FOUR

"That is Dasko," said Kalem.

"Hush!" said Theren. "We can see that. Get out of sight."

"Why?" asked Ebon. But she and Kalem were already scampering behind the edge of a nearby shop, and so he followed. The alley they ducked into stank, and Ebon covered his nose with a sleeve, reluctant to touch anything.

"Theren, what are you doing?"

"Are you not curious what Dasko is doing out here, or what is in the cart beside him?"

"Curious? Certainly," said Ebon. "But not enough to skulk about like some thief."

"I want to follow him," said Theren. "It is the first day of Yearsend. Why is he not on holiday?"

"A student died only yesterday, Theren," said Kalem quietly. "No doubt the faculty have much to look after."

"This far into the city? No, there are too many questions. Come, and let us have answers."

Theren darted out from the alley, for Dasko and the cart had turned down a side street. Ebon and Kalem hastened to follow. From building to building they scuttled, keeping always in the shadows, though in truth Dasko and the High King's guard did not seem overly cautious. They never looked about—and why should they? They were in the middle of the street. It was not as though they moved in secrecy.

Soon Kalem grew impatient. "This is folly. Clearly they are up to nothing nefarious, and the Yearsend feast will be starting soon."

"Leave if you wish," said Theren. "I mean to see where they are going."

Kalem clearly considered it, and Ebon was almost tempted. But just as he had resolved to leave, the cart pulled to a stop, and the guards took position at its rear. It had halted in front of a modest stone dwelling, two stories like the Drayden manor, but nowhere near as lavish. But Ebon noted that none of the other buildings on this street had doors accessible from this side—their front entrances were all on other sides, other streets. It gave the home a sense of isolation, and there were few passersby.

Theren drew them farther out of sight into the alley. "Sky above," she breathed. "Why are there so many guards?"

Ebon blinked, for at first he could not see what she was talking about. But then he looked again. There were two more guards from the High King's palace, one at each of the building's front corners. Near the home's front door stood two figures in regular clothing—yet when Ebon looked closer, he recognized two instructors from the Academy, neither wearing their traditional dark grey robes. Then Theren pointed to the roof, and Ebon saw two red hoods silhouetted against the sky. Mystics, standing guard from on high. Bows were slung on their backs.

"What is Dasko doing?" said Ebon. "What could possibly justify this many guards?"

"Never mind their number," said Kalem. "Why three different groups? What would the High King, the Academy, and the Mystics all wish to guard?"

"What indeed?" grated a harsh voice just behind them.

Ebon jumped and turned around, heart in his throat. There behind them stood Dean Forredar. Kalem gave a little squeak, and Theren's face grew stony. But Xain ignored them both, instead casting all of his ire upon Ebon. Ebon, for his part, tried to match the wizard's gaze.

"Why are you skulking about here, Drayden?"

"We are on our way to the Academy from my family's manor."

"Yes, your manor," Xain sneered. "I know it is close by. That is why I chose this place for my home. How do you like it?"

Ebon glanced over his shoulder, at a loss for words. "Your . . . home? This is where you live?"

"I am only recently returned to the Seat, and have been searching for a suitable dwelling. When I found this one, I knew I had to have it—so close to the Drayden manor, where I can keep an eye upon the scheming of your kin. Keep foes closer than friends, as they say."

"It seems a sturdy house," said Kalem, his voice cracking.

Xain ignored that. "I have a warning for your family, Ebon. Tell them to be on watch, for they are being observed. Too long did they plague me when last I dwelt on the Seat, and too long did they keep me gone after they drove me out. Now I have returned, and I have the High King's favor. The days of their power in Underrealm are numbered."

"I had nothing to do with whatever quarrels you had with my family," said Ebon. "I mean you no ill will."

"Ill will? What does your will matter? You have been raised as one of them. Doubtless you have joined their schemes without even realizing it. So whoever your master may be, tell them what I have told you."

"I have no master." But even as Ebon said it, he thought of the task Mako had given him, the counterfeit uniform he had delivered in the dead of night. He shook the thought away. "Nearly all of my kin hate me anyway."

Xain looked to Theren and Kalem then. "As for the two of you—you would do well to quit this boy's company. No matter what he has told you, you cannot trust a Drayden. Walk by his side, and one day you will find yourselves alone and friendless, betrayed in pursuit of some long-festering scheme."

"I can choose my friends for myself," Theren snapped.

Kalem raised his hands, palms outward. "I think tempers have run high. Certainly there is some sort of common ground—"

Light snapped into Xain's eyes, and he raised a hand. "Begone," he growled. "And if I catch you skulking about again, I will not be so lenient."

Theren raised her own hands in response, but Ebon seized her arm even as her eyes glowed to meet Xain's. "No, Theren."

He pulled her towards the mouth of the alley, refusing to meet the dean's eye. At first Theren resisted, but in the end she let herself be pulled along. Once around the corner, they broke into a jog, and then a sprint once out of sight of Xain's home.

After a few streets Ebon felt safe enough to stop. He bent double, hands on his knees, while Kalem sank to the ground, his back against a stone wall. Theren scarcely seemed winded, and she glared back the way they had come, fists on her hips.

"Why was Dasko there?"

"Did you not understand even that much?" said Kalem. "He was helping Xain move into his new home."

"I know that is what they were doing," said Theren. "But why *Dasko?* He is an instructor at the Academy. Any number of day laborers could be hired, if Xain needed to move a few crates."

"It is likely they are friends," said Kalem. "I know Xain and that new instructor, Perrin, attended the Academy together. Dasko seems of an age with them. It is not Dasko's presence that intrigues me, but that of the other guards."

"I think I know something of that," said Ebon, for he had just remembered his conversation with Mako. "Xain performed some great service for the High King, for which she honored him greatly. It is why he was allowed to return to the Seat after my family drove him out, as you heard him say. The guards must have been posted by the High King."

"She could command the Mystics *and* instructors from the Academy to join her own guards," said Theren, nodding. "That makes sense. But what threat does she think Xain faces? What threat does *he* think he faces? Surely he is not afraid of Ebon's paltry might—though I mean no offense by that."

Ebon raised his eyebrows. "No, clearly not."

Kalem pushed himself up from the ground. "Well, we will do ourselves no good sitting here wondering about it. And now my robes are soaked by the snow. Come, let us return home, before I catch my death of cold."

"Xain is a firemage," said Theren, laying her arm across Kalem's shoulders as they set off together. "You could return and ask him to dry you out with his flames."

Ebon shook his head and went after his friends.

TWENTY-FIVE

THEY GATHERED IN THE DINING HALL FOR THE YEARSEND feast some time later. The food had been laid out and hidden beneath white sheets held up on wooden frames, concealing the meal from view. But the sheets could not mask the smell, which wafted through the hall and set every mouth to watering.

The instructors' table stood at the head of the hall. Xain sat in the place of honor with his son Erin beside him. Once the hour struck, Xain stood and raised a goblet of wine. Everyone quieted, and he waited a moment in silence. When at last he spoke, his thick voice filled the room's every corner, thrumming in Ebon's breast.

"Since the time before time, Yearsend has been an occasion for joy. We herald the passing of another year of our lives, and the sky's bounty that has allowed our survival. But that celebration is always tempered by mourning, for we acknowledge those who have gone to the darkness below, and thank them for their gifts in life. This year has given us more cause for mourning than most. Many have been lost, and some greater than others."

His next word cut short in a choking sound, and he bowed his head. The hall was deathly still. Ebon, Theren, and Kalem looked to each other uncertainly. The silence lasted only a moment, but when Xain raised his head, his cheeks were wet.

"Some give their lives that we might go on. Others give their lives that we might find redemption—they bring us back from the darkness, though we stand on its brink. Still others give their lives to time's natural sway, and then our mourning is not so bitter. But worst of all are those who are taken without reason, claimed by the madness of a sick mind, or by the treachery of a kingdom breaking its vows. Often we seek explanation. It is rarely to be found. We can only honor the dead, who we shall never see again."

Another pause. Ebon heard many students in the hall hiding their sniffles, while others sobbed openly. Xain raised his goblet higher.

"To those in the darkness."

Every cup lifted. "To those in the darkness."

They drank, and then the first course was brought round the tables.

That evening's Yearsend feast left nothing to be desired, fulfilling every wildest tale Ebon had ever heard of the celebration's splendor upon the Seat. Throughout each year, the Academy had to serve hundreds of students three times a day. While the food was wholesome and hearty, it was rarely delicious. During Yearsend, it seemed, the cooks aimed to make up for all the rest of the year's plain fare. There were fine roasts of meat, of boar and beef and lamb, flavored with wonderful spices, served tender enough to fall off the bone. They were joined by crops from all across the nine lands, so that the students had chickpea spread and figs from Idris, and then at the next table, buttered yams and yellow rice from Calentin. In the center of the spread was a table filled to bursting with desserts, where honeyed confections of every type were piled high, and students were free to take what they wished. Wine was also served, although this was held by the cooks, and only given to students who were old enough, and even then withheld if they thought a student had had too much. The last thing the Academy needed was a drunken brawl with hundreds of young wizards who had yet to fully command their powers.

Again and again Ebon went to the serving table to load his plate with more food, again and again leaning back on his bench and clutching at his belly, afraid it would burst. At last he gave up, leaning heavily on the table, sipping lightly at the last of his wine. Kalem's head was nodding beside him, and across the table Theren was licking honey from her fingers.

"A particularly fine feast this year," she said, and gave a loud belch.

"I will not say it is the finest food I have ever eaten, yet I would count this as my favorite meal," said Ebon. "Rarely in my life have I been able to take such a meal with friends, rather than a father who made my life a torment."

"Hmmm?" said Kalem, looking at them sleepily. "Ah, yes. A fine feast indeed."

Theren chuckled and shook her head. But then Ebon felt a hand on his shoulder and looked up to find Dasko standing over him.

"Good eve, Ebon. Have you enjoyed your feast?"

Ebon nodded. "Very much so, Instructor. I hope you have as well."

"Indeed. Might we still take that walk, as I requested?"

"Of course." Ebon stood, but then he looked to his friends.

Theren waved him off. "Go. I should get this one to bed." She pointed to Kalem, who seemed in danger of falling asleep and drowning in buttered yams.

"Good night, then," said Ebon. "I will see you upon the morrow." And he set off through the dining hall after Dasko.

Dasko led him through the hallways and out a white cedar door into the training grounds. The moons lit the night well, and torches mounted along the citadel's walls helped them pick their way forth on the garden path. The instructor did not speak immediately, but let the night's silence rest, occasionally looking up at the stars as they shone bright in the sky.

"I have only been an instructor here for a few years," Dasko said at last. "I studied here in my youth, of course, but that was long ago. I feel as though I have been rediscovering the place anew. It is certainly a different experience, being an instructor."

Ebon blinked and then frowned. "I imagine it would be."

Dasko sighed. "My apologies. I am not certain how to say what I mean, and so I prattle about inconsequential things. That, and not my preoccupation with Lilith's crimes, is what kept me from speaking with you before today."

He stopped, and Ebon halted beside him. Again Dasko looked up at the stars, his jaw working.

"Before I returned to the Academy, I was a mercenary," he finally said, his voice so soft that Ebon leaned closer to hear it. "I fought for a sellsword army that marched across the nine lands. We served with many great families, both merchant and noble. And in one campaign, I served your family. The Draydens. That is when I met your brother."

Ebon felt as though someone had struck him in the

gut. He had scarcely thought of Momen since first he came to the Academy. Indeed, ever since his brother's death years ago, Ebon had tried to avoid thinking of it at all. He felt suddenly light-headed.

"Momen and I became fast friends after our first battle together," Dasko went on. "When you came to the Academy, I hardly noticed you, though sometimes a thought tickled my mind. Then, after the attack on the Seat, Jia was frantic, because you had been separated from the rest of the students. Though we eventually found you, her mention of your name was what let the pieces fall into place—Ebon of the family Drayden, younger brother of my friend Momen. During all the time we served together, he would speak of you more often than anything else."

A gasp escaped before Ebon could stop it. His eyes burned, and he turned away, swiping at them with the back of his sleeve. The air felt suddenly frozen, and he raised his hood against it. Dasko took his shoulder gently and guided him towards a stone bench. Ebon sank onto it, hiding his face in his hands and trying to master himself.

"I am sorry to resurrect grief," murmured Dasko. "I did not mean to bring sadness, but advice."

"What advice?" said Ebon, no longer caring at how his voice broke. He found himself growing angry with Dasko—angry that the man would presume to speak of his brother, who he could not have known half so well as Ebon.

"Before Dean Cyrus fled the Academy, it seems that you and he had little love for each other," Dasko said carefully.

Through his grief, Ebon's heart skipped a beat. What did Cyrus have to do with anything? "He was not overfond of me, no."

Dasko looked him in the eye. "Was that because of some personal disagreement between the two of you, or because of some more general schism between you and the family Drayden?"

Ebon shrugged and looked away. "I know not what you speak of."

"I think you do," said Dasko. "Momen often felt the same way—never comfortable in the company of his family, and always burdened by their reputation, which as you know is fearsome. Always he wanted to cast off their name, and something tells me that you may be similar."

Though he would have been loath to admit it, a thrill trickled through Ebon's heart. He never knew Momen had felt the same way about their family. "Even if that were true, what do you expect me to do? I was born a Drayden. I will die a Drayden."

"Yet you need not live your life under the suspicion of others. You must know that Dean Xain thinks ill of you for no other reason than your family's name. I know it cannot be easy to shed that shadow when everyone you meet can see only the darkness it wraps around you."

"And what can I do about that? In truth, I am used to it. I have little choice but to duck my head and hope to go unnoticed."

"But you have been noticed, Ebon," said Dasko, leaning forwards. "Xain does not wish to admit it, but the other faculty know you suspected Lilith from the first. And you may have helped expose her earlier than she would have been otherwise. Soon the Mystics will have wheedled the artifacts out of her. Because of you, the Academy now takes steps to ensure the artifacts will be safer in the future. You should be proud of that, at least. And you owe nothing of that to your family."

"Pride in myself helps nothing. Certainly not Xain's view of me."

"That is what I mean to say. You have helped, whether he sees it or not. Continue to do right, but not in the hope that Xain will love you. Your kin have wounded him, and that wound may never heal. But do it because of the people you may help along the way. That, I think, is what Momen would do."

Ebon stood from the bench, glaring at him. "That is too far."

"I am sorry," said Dasko, standing and bowing his head. "You are right, I presumed too much. Yet I only say what Momen told me on occasion: that he wished to return home and help you, for he knew life with your father would be harder once he had gone."

Though he held his scowl, Ebon felt some of his anger dampen. Momen could not have known just how true his words would prove. He turned away from Dasko, loosing a breath into mist upon the frigid air, and steered the conversation in another direction, hoping to ease the burning in his heart.

"You said they have not yet drawn the truth from Lilith? I had not thought it would take this long to find the artifacts she stole—especially the second time, for she did not have long to hide them."

Dasko shrugged. "She must have worked quickly. It will not be long. The Mystics are . . . very persuasive when they wish to be."

"Will they kill her?"

"Not the Mystics, no," said Dasko softly. "But once they have recovered the artifacts, they will turn her over to the constables, who will put her to death under the King's law."

And there might vanish any hope of learning Lilith's link to Matami or Shay. Ebon ground his teeth in frustration. It seemed that she would suffer for her crimes, but that the conspirators behind her—and he was sure such conspirators existed—would escape, for no one seemed to be looking for them.

Yet, mayhap if Ebon could speak to her . . .

His heart raced. What excuse could he invent? No one would believe he and Lilith had ever been friends. But there was Nella. Ever since the attack on the Seat, she and Ebon had been . . . if not friendly, at least cordial. Yes. It might work.

He turned back to Dasko. "I wonder . . . I know

her crimes were terrible. And Lilith and I had a grudge from the moment I arrived here. Yet there are those who never had the chance to say farewell, and if Lilith will never return, it seems cruel to deny them that opportunity. I am close to one who is dear to her."

Dasko nodded, cutting him off. "Theren. I know."

Ebon balked. Theren? How could Dasko ever think Theren and Lilith were friends? Yet the certainty in the instructor's eyes was unmistakable. Ebon nodded and quickly continued. "Just so. Could it be arranged, do you think, for us to visit Lilith? I wish for my own sort of peace with her, and I know Theren desires the same."

The instructor frowned. "I do not know if that would be wise, Ebon. For one thing, she will not be the same as when last you saw her. The Mystics are never kind to their prisoners. And they will likely be reluctant to have her speak with any outsider. *I* know your character, but they will not."

"Please, Dasko," Ebon begged. "Help me with this, so that this chapter of our lives may be left behind us. I promise we will urge Lilith to tell them what she knows. And the sight of a friendly face may pry loose what the blades of the Mystics cannot."

Dasko's frown deepened. But he looked away in thought before nodding. "Very well. I will see if I can arrange something with Jia, if it is that important to you—and, mayhap, as some token of payment for the ill will borne against you here at the Academy, which you did not deserve."

"Thank you, Instructor. If given the chance, I promise I shall not waste it."

"I believe you," said Dasko, shivering suddenly. "And now let us return to the citadel. I am not yet an old man, yet I find myself less resistant to the chill than I was in my youth."

They made their way back to the Academy and parted once within, heading off to their beds. But Ebon lay awake for a long while, thinking of Momen and Lilith and Theren.

TWENTY-SIX

THE NEXT DAY, EBON WANTED TO TELL THEREN WHAT he had asked Dasko about their visiting Lilith. But his courage failed him every time he sought to speak, and so the day passed without her knowing. The second day was the same, and the third. At last he decided to tell her when the moment seemed right, and not before. After all, there was every chance that the Mystics would not allow Lilith to see them at all. What good could come, if that were the case, from telling Theren?

So they spent the first three days of Yearsend in calm and rest. All day Ebon was with Kalem and

Theren, either in the Academy or out upon the Seat. Though studies were suspended for the holiday, they spent a few hours each day in the library. Kalem still searched for more lore concerning Kekhit, and Ebon helped, but it was a half-hearted quest now. Lilith had been caught, and whatever mischief she had plotted with Kekhit's amulet, she could not hope to accomplish it now.

They spent their evenings in the dining hall or out upon the Seat, telling each other tales or listening to musicians fill inns with their splendor. Ebon felt a sense of peace he had not felt in a very long time. True, there were rumblings that the High King was readying her armies to make war on Dulmun at last, and whispers about the nine kingdoms—how some were on the cusp of joining the war, while others were on the cusp of joining it on the wrong side. But all was peaceful on the Seat. Even war rested during Yearsend.

It was a leap year, and so they had a fourth day of holiday to enjoy. The dawn came bright and cold, and they lounged in the library for most of it. Ebon had received word that his family would be hosting some royals. Halab had given him the opportunity to visit the manor, but had not required it, and so he had declined. He had attended such dinners before, and knew he would be bored to tears. So in the morning he sent word to Adara asking if she wished to meet in the evening, and by the midday meal she had replied that she would be delighted. She had even painted her lips and pressed them to her letter, which Ebon laughed to see.

As the sun began its long march towards the horizon, they left the Academy and made for the western end of the Seat. Kalem hummed aimlessly as they went, and Ebon drank deep of the crisp air. But Theren scowled as she walked, and after a while gave Kalem an irritated look.

"Cease that humming. Soon studies will resume. Let us have a proper period of mourning, at least."

Ebon stifled a grin. "All good things end, Theren."

She pushed him, nearly making him stumble into the snow. "Yet you need not remind me. Do you know how my mind grows numb, studying my lessons when my skills are so far advanced?"

"And doubtless your humility troubles you greatly, as well," said Kalem, wide-eyed and innocent. Quickly he ducked Theren's swinging fist.

They made for Leven's tavern, the place where they had first met, and one of their favorite haunts on the island. It was far enough removed that there were rarely other students about—but this time Ebon ran into Isra at the door. He did not see her coming out as he entered, and their shoulders struck each other. She glared at him, and he ducked to avoid her dark, intense eyes.

"My apologies," he said.

She did not answer him for a moment. Then at last she said, "Well? May I pass?"

Ebon blushed, for he had not realized he was still blocking the door. "Of course, of course," he said, stepping aside. She made to move past him, but he spoke quickly before she could go. "How is Astrea?"

Isra met his gaze, now with softer eyes. "Well enough. I am taking care of her."

"Thank you," said Ebon. "I will try to spend more time with her once classes resume, to help ease her mind."

To his surprise, Isra's face hardened. "I hardly think that would help."

Ebon frowned. "What? I—"

"Everyone knows you have been meddling about the Academy. Who is to say you did not provoke Lilith? She is another goldbag, after all, just like you."

"You speak strong words about something you do not understand," said Theren, giving the girl a scowl. "Ebon is nothing like Lilith."

Isra snorted. "Easy words for you, who may dip your hand into his pocket to pay for fine food and drink. A goldbag's friends defending a goldbag. Yet you, too, will suffer in their war."

She turned and left them. Theren made to follow, but Ebon seized her arm. "Let her be. We are all distraught after events of late. Some show it differently than others."

"I would like to show her something, certainly," Theren growled. But she let Ebon bring her inside.

Leven hailed them the moment they entered the

bar, and they waved back from the doorway. Their table was empty, and they made their way towards it. But then Ebon noticed that at one table sat Oren and Nella, Lilith's companions. They were together in a corner, shoulders hunched over their drinks, neither of them speaking. Their eyes wandered, and Ebon could not help feeling that they looked somewhat lost.

"Give me a moment," he said, letting Theren and Kalem go on without him. He crossed the room until he stood by Oren and Nella's table. Nella gave him a courteous nod, but Oren only glowered up at him.

"My condolences for what happened to Lilith," Ebon said softly. "That cannot be easy."

Oren's brow furrowed deeper. "Get away from us, you sniveling little—"

"Oren!" Nella cut him off. They matched glares until Oren relented, taking a sip from his cup. Nella looked back up to Ebon. "Thank you. But I do not believe Lilith could do this."

"Times are strange indeed," said Ebon. "Many have revealed in themselves things we can scarce imagine."

"You mistake me," said Nella, frowning. "I mean I *do not* believe Lilith could do it. She is no monster. I know it. I—" Her voice broke, and she looked away.

Ebon stood uncomfortably for a moment. Then he tossed a gold weight upon the table. "Have yourselves a fine bottle tonight."

Oren glared. "We do not need your coin, Drayden."

"I know you do not need it. But I wish to give it. You may choose not to believe me, but her fate brought me no joy. Good evening."

He backed away. For a moment he thought Oren would throw the coin at his face. But Nella picked it up, nodding her thanks, and then waved down a barman. Ebon crossed the room and joined his friends at their table.

"And why did you feel the need to take your life into your hands?" said Kalem, looking across the room in fear.

"They have lost a friend," said Ebon quietly. "If you think they do not feel the pain of that, just as we would, you misunderstand them."

"Their friend is a murderer," said Theren, glaring into her cup of wine.

"I think there is more to it than that," said Ebon. "That is why I want to talk to her."

He spoke the words without thinking, and caught himself too late. His eyes widened. Theren's look sharpened at once, though it took her a moment to understand. When she did, she leaned in to whisper.

"You mean to speak to Lilith? What madness has taken you, Ebon?"

"I need *both* of us to speak to her. We know, though no one else wants to admit it, that Lilith could not have worked alone. I could still have traitors in my family, and they must be exposed."

"You want *me* to come with you?" Theren leaned

back and folded her arms. "Never. Not though my life depended on it. I have no wish to lay eyes upon her again."

"Not even if it might save more lives? Even now the artifacts may be on their way across Underrealm. The criminals behind the theft are at large, and no one is yet safe."

Theren glared, but Ebon met her gaze and did not waver. Kalem looked uncomfortably between them. "Theren, it could help," he said. "And besides, if you are so angry with her, you will never get a better opportunity to say so."

"You will never have another opportunity at all," said Ebon. "Once they find the artifacts, Lilith will be put to death."

Theren blinked and looked away. "Very well. If only to help you, and because of my failures to do so in the past."

"Thank you." Ebon put a hand on Theren's. "I will not forget this."

"You had better not," she said, sighing. Then her eyes slid past him, and brightened. "But forget all of that now. Someone has arrived."

Ebon looked over his shoulder to see Adara stepping through the front door. She wore new clothes, or at least ones he had not yet seen, colored violet and trimmed in black. Ebon and Kalem stood to greet her, Kalem blushing furiously.

"Good evening, Theren, and to you, Kalem," said

Adara. She smiled, and then drew Ebon in for a kiss. "And good evening to you, my love."

He grinned back at her. "A good evening it is, now. Please, sit. We have ordered a fine bottle for ourselves, and Leven knows to bring you some mead."

"Thank you," she said, sliding down the bench. He took his place beside her. Leven soon came with the mead, and together they raised a glass.

"To Yearsend," said Ebon. "A more eventful year I have never seen."

"To Yearsend," they said, and drank. Kalem's eyes kept darting to Adara and then away again, his fingers fidgeting with his cup.

Theren raised an eyebrow. "What has you so anxious?"

Adara laughed lightly. "It seems I have made the son of Konnel uncomfortable again. I chose to wear his family's colors tonight."

"Aha," said Ebon. "Kalem, you did not tell me."

"It is only that I was surprised," said Kalem, his eyes on the table. "And it has . . . er . . . well, it has made me think of someone else."

"Oh?" said Adara. "Has the young lord at last found a spark to ignite a flame within his heart?"

"Nothing so grand," said Kalem, but his cheeks had gone bright red.

Ebon frowned, but Theren laughed. "We visited Ebon's family only a few days ago. His sister Albi took quite a liking to our little noble-born friend."

Adara looked to Ebon, and when she saw the look of annoyance on his face, she giggled. "Look at the dutiful brother, holding back such stern words."

"I have no words," said Ebon, hiding his face behind his goblet. "Albi's doings are none of my concern."

Theren snorted, while Adara hid a smile. But then she leaned forwards, and in a low voice said, "When you sent your letter this morning, Ebon, I was most glad. I have heard something more from the other lovers. It seems many Academy instructors and other faculty have been seen along the east end of the Seat, though no one knows quite what they are doing."

Ebon nodded slowly. "We saw something of this already. The new dean, Xain, has moved into a dwelling there, and it seems the High King has placed a guard around his house—though I know not why."

Adara frowned. "That hardly seems to account for it. There have been many goings-on—far more than could be explained by one man taking residence in a new home."

"We were there," said Theren, shrugging. "We saw them bringing in his possessions."

"Well, that is not all," Adara went on. "That Academy student has been seen about again, the one I spoke of before. Only this time they were spotted to the east, in the same area as the dwelling you speak of."

Ebon shook his head. "That does not matter now. Lilith has been caught, and is in the care of the Mystics. You will not see her skulking around again."

"The student was seen only last night."

They all went very still. Ebon, Kalem, and Adara shared a look. "Last night?" said Ebon. "But Lilith was captured four days ago."

"Then it is not Lilith lurking about," said Adara.

Theren stared down at her hands. But Kalem shook his head. "And we never had any reason to believe it was, if you think about it. Likely it is someone causing harmless mischief—mayhap going to see a lover, as you do, Ebon."

"Yet I always return before curfew," Ebon muttered. All this talk of Xain's home and the skulking student had brought it back: the itch in his mind he had felt in his family's courtyard, like something heard and then forgotten. And now the image of Xain's home joined his scattered thoughts.

He started in his seat as he suddenly felt someone at his elbow. Looking up, he found Oren standing over their table. The boy's dour expression had gone, and he smiled down at them magnanimously.

"Greetings, Ebon and Kalem. Ebon, I am sorry for speaking angrily before. My mind is much preoccupied these days."

Ebon looked to Theren uncertainly. She broke off from glaring at Oren just long enough to give Ebon a steely look. "Worry not overmuch," said Ebon carefully. "These are strange times."

"Indeed. That is why I have come. I thought you and Kalem might wish to join me in the library. A number of us gather there in the evenings to share wine and conversation. We call ourselves the Gold-bag Society." He chuckled and shook his head. "Every merchant's child. Every son and daughter of royalty."

A chill crept down Ebon's spine. He looked past Oren for Nella, but the girl was nowhere to be seen. "That . . . that was Lilith's gathering," he stammered. "But she is gone."

Oren shook his head. "I have taken her duties in running the group. Your company would be most welcome—as would yours, son of Konnel."

Ebon could see that Theren was about to do something foolish, so he quickly cut her off. "I thank you, Oren, but I will decline. I have friends to spend my evenings with already."

But Oren frowned at Theren. "She is no merchant's child. No son or daughter of royalty."

Theren shot to her feet. "I have had enough of this, and more besides. Leave us. You were not invited here, and they have already said they do not want to join your goldshitter club."

Oren did not move. Instead he glared at her, planting both fists on the table. "They *must* join."

"We *must* do nothing," said Ebon, growing irritated. "Leave us be, or—"

Light flooded Oren's eyes as he reached for his magic. But Theren struck first, not with a spell but with her fists. One hand chopped hard at Oren's throat, and the other struck him between the eyes. He fell back with a cry, his head striking a table on the way to the floor. He rolled over onto his stomach, groaning, while Kalem shouted and gripped Theren's arm to keep her from going after him.

Ebon was standing, unsure of what to do. But when Oren turned back to them, the glow had gone from his eyes. Instead they were wild and wide, turning in all directions. At last he focused on Ebon, mouth twisting in hate.

"I know not what I was thinking," he spat. "To have you and this whelp of a boy would shame us all."

"I am glad you have seen reason," said Theren, her voice filled with steel. "Now begone, or next I will use my spells."

Oren fought to his feet and swept away, weaving between tables and bursting through the tavern's door. What few curious eyes had found them slowly drifted away. Ebon took his seat, as did Theren, who was still fuming.

"That was most odd," said Adara, still looking in the direction Oren had gone.

"Mayhap you can tell your lover friends about it," said Theren. "More whispers to slither across the Seat."

"Theren," said Ebon, frowning.

"It is all right, Ebon." Adara put a calming hand on his arm. "He was beastly. I am sorry it tarnished what was a most pleasant evening."

Ebon smiled at her. But Theren snorted and stood from the table. "The night is still young. I shall see you back at the Academy. Just now I find I need something more than wine to soothe me."

She flung the tavern's door open and left. Kalem frowned. "Do you think she will seek Oren, and try to finish their fight?"

Ebon shook his head. "Theren is hot-headed, but even she is not so foolish. I believe she makes for a house of lovers."

Kalem blinked and sank back on his bench. "Ah. I see."

"Speaking of which," said Adara, her hand sliding onto Ebon's leg. "Theren was right about one thing: the night is yet young."

Ebon smiled, but then he paused. He looked at Kalem, raising his eyebrows. Kalem rolled his eyes.

"Oh, go on. It is the eve of the new year, after all. I shall go spend mine alone, in the library. Only do not leave me to pay for the drinks. My allowance is late, and it has been scant besides."

Ebon threw a gold weight onto the table, and then he and Adara stole off into the night, making for the blue door to the west.

TWENTY-SEVEN

Class began the next day, and it seemed everyone in the Academy was all too eager to throw themselves into the business of learning once again. Ebon hoped that Yearsend had been a healing time for them all: a time to reflect upon their tragedy, to wrestle with their feelings, and then to put sorrow behind them. Now life could go on as it had before, and everyone seemed eager to embrace it.

But three days later, Ebon received a sobering reminder of the Academy's losses, though he did not recognize it when first it came. A messenger in dark grey robes came to the door—one of the Academy faculty, bearing a scrap of parchment that bore only a few words:

Please come and speak with me. You are still not in trouble.
Jia

That made him smile. He showed the note to Perrin, and she waved him off before resuming her lessons with Astrea, who these days barely looked up from her desk.

When he reached Jia's study, Ebon was confused to find Theren already waiting. Jia waved him towards an empty chair, and he sat.

"I have spoken with Dasko since you made your request, and also with an old friend in the Mystics. She has secured their agreement to let the two of you see Lilith."

Theren had been scowling since before Jia began speaking. Now she opened her mouth to speak, but Ebon saw the fury in her eyes, and interrupted her.

"Thank you, Instructor. It will do us good, I think, to see her."

Jia looked bemused, knowing something of his feud with Lilith. And she was no fool—she likely knew something of Theren's feelings towards Lilith as well. Yet for some reason, she had arranged the meeting anyway. He would not squander this chance, for he might never have another opportunity to learn the truth of Lilith's motives.

But before she answered him, Jia grew solemn once more. "You must understand something before you go to see her. Lilith has been put to the question since she left us—more than half a week ago, now. Do you understand what that means?"

Ebon understood only too well. He swallowed hard. "Yes, Instructor." Theren nodded grimly.

"She will look much the worse for wear, to say the least, for still she withholds the location of the artifacts she stole. You have been allowed to see her on one condition: you must make an attempt, at least, to draw that information out of her. Those artifacts cannot remain outside the Academy's control."

"We understand, Instructor."

She softened. "And one more thing. When you see her . . . you must understand that the Mystics' questioners take no pleasure in what they have put Lilith through, nor in the further action they must take if you fail. It is their duty. And it is in the service of the Academy's safety—as well as the safety of all the nine lands."

Ebon bowed. "Yes, Instructor." From the corner of his eye, he saw Theren hesitate.

"Lilith will die, then? It is certain?"

Jia's lips twitched, and for a moment it seemed to Ebon that her eyes shone. But she blinked, and the moment was gone. "Yes," she said flatly. "She killed another student. We all witnessed it."

Theren's throat worked, eyes wandering as though she had not heard Jia's words. She nodded, but would not meet the instructor's gaze.

Jia stood to lead them out of the Academy and into the streets, making her way towards a tall stone building a few blocks distant. Ebon had passed the building a few times, but had never learned its purpose. As they came to a stop before its doors, he realized it must be a station for constables, for two of them stood in their red leather armor before the door.

Inside, the broad front room held more of the lawmen. But in the back corner were a pair of Mystics, both of their cloaks drawn about them. One, the taller of the two, had his hood down. The other had their hood raised, covering their eyes, and what little Ebon could see of the face was covered by still more red cloth, like a mask drawn over their features. He felt a little thrill of fear as Jia led them forwards.

"These are the students," she said gently. "The ones to see Lilith."

The taller Mystic said nothing, but only looked down at his companion. The shorter one spoke, and the voice, though raspy and harsh, revealed its owner to be a woman. Still he could not see her eyes. "You mean to see the murderer, Jia."

"Yes," said Jia softly. "The murderer."

The Mystic's head jerked towards the door behind her. "She is in there. We will be just outside, ready to act if she should try to harm you."

"Lilith will not be able to harm me," said Theren, eyes flashing.

"Can you now?" The Mystic erupted in a hideous, bubbling laugh. "Somehow the spirit in your words tells me you are no liar. Are you a firemage, then, the same as she?"

Theren frowned. "A mindmage."

"Still better, or so I have always said." Again came that laugh, sending shivers along Ebon's arms. "Well, you have come for a purpose. See to it."

The Mystic pushed open the door. Theren did not hesitate, and pushed in at once. But Ebon looked at Jia uncertainly until she ushered him on with a wave of her hand.

There, sitting and chained to a table in the room's center, was Lilith. Ebon did not recognize her at first, and thought they must be in the wrong room. The girl's hair had been cropped close to her head. Her limbs were pale and gaunt, and though she still wore the black Academy robes they had brought her here in, now they were covered with filth and matted with blood. Blood, Ebon guessed, from the cuts that covered her body. They were on her fingers and her hands, her ankles and feet. They had left her face free from cuts, but not from bruises, which welled up her cheeks and eyelids until she looked a different person.

Ebon threw a hand to his mouth, suddenly nauseated. But almost worse than her wounds was the look in her eyes. They were wide beneath the swelling, roving wildly in every direction. They must have been starving her, or else she would not eat, for her body had wasted away. She murmured and whimpered and grunted in an unending stream of unintelligible words as though she were half-mad.

The sight of her froze Ebon in his tracks. Beside him, Theren looked just as horror-struck. But Lilith did not even appear to see them.

Theren started when Ebon at last put a hand on her arm. He led her forwards, and they took their seats across the table from Lilith. Ebon leaned over, trying to put himself in the girl's line of sight. But her eyes moved with him, and away, so that he could not meet her gaze. He wanted to speak, but knew not what to say. To his shock, Theren was shaking beside him.

"Lilith?" Ebon said softly. "It is Ebon and Theren."

"Why?" said Lilith, the word snapping like a whip from amid her mutterings.

Ebon looked at Theren, and she back at him. Then he leaned forwards. At least she knew they were here. "Lilith . . . we have come to speak with you. We want to know why . . . why you killed Vali. And Credell."

She slapped her palms on the table and then winced at the sound of it. *"I did not kill Credell!"* she rasped, looking him in the eyes for the first time. But then she looked away again, eyes roving across the walls. "I did not kill Vali either. I do not think I did. I wanted to help him. To save him. He was supposed to join us. The goldbags. I asked him."

Theren sat up straight, sudden anger flashing in her eyes. "You asked him to join your little club, and killed him when he refused?"

But at Theren's cry, Lilith retreated into herself. Her wrists were chained, but she pulled them as far back as she could, and drew her knees into her chest, whimpering.

Ebon placed a hand on Theren's arm. "I do not know that that is what she is saying," he whispered. "Or that she truly understands what we are asking."

"I do," insisted Lilith, whispering without looking up from beneath her close-cropped hair. "I do."

He leaned in across the table, keenly aware that the Mystics were just outside and could likely hear every word. "Lilith. Were there others involved?"

Lilith chewed at her nail. She had already bitten it away, and blood sprouted from her skin beneath her teeth. "I did not kill any others. *I did not kill Credell.* I did not kill . . . I hope I did not kill Vali."

"What do you mean you *hope* you did not," said Theren. "We were there, Lilith. We saw you."

Ebon waved her to silence. "I do not mean more victims, Lilith. We know there were no more. I mean others you were working with. Other conspirators. Can you name them?"

Lilith shuddered in her chair. "I . . . there was another. Another. I cannot say."

"Please," said Ebon. "Please, Lilith, tell us. If we find them, we can find what was stolen."

She stopped moving, and when her eyes met his, they were clear as fresh water. "And what will happen to me then?"

The room went still. Theren looked away. Ebon shook his head. "Then, at least, the pain will end."

Lilith burst into tears, burying her face in her arms on the table. "It is not fair. Not fair, not fair. I do not want to die. Do not want to die. I cannot remember the face of the other. And I do not want to die."

"I doubt Vali wanted to die," spat Theren. But it seemed to Ebon that some of the venom had seeped from her tone.

That only made Lilith recoil further. Ebon could feel her slipping away. He scooted forwards in his chair. "Is it worth it, Lilith? Staying alive, only to suffer more of this pain?"

She curled up in her chair again, rocking back and forth. "I do not want to die. I cannot remember. I did not kill Credell. I do not want to die."

"Please, Lilith. Where did you take the artifacts? Tell us that, at least."

There was no answer, and from her fevered mutterings, he knew none would come. Ebon sighed and stood, pushing his chair back. Together, mute, he and Theren left the room. The Mystics stood solemn outside, heads bowed. Jia must have seen failure in their expressions, for she looked at them with sad eyes.

"It was good of you to try," she said softly. "We should be going."

She took them outside the constables' station. But Theren's legs shook beneath her, and she gripped Ebon's arm for support. When Jia turned to see what was the matter, Theren forced a smile. Ebon could see the tears shining in her eye, threatening to spill forth.

"I wonder if I might walk back alone, Instructor? I need more air to clear my head."

Jia frowned. But Ebon met her gaze. "I can remain with her. I, too, would not mind some time out of my classroom."

"Of course," said Jia, nodding. She gave Theren a final, mournful look, and then slipped away through the city streets.

At once Theren staggered off, away from the street and down an alley between two buildings. Once in the shadows she began breathing hard, her shoulders heaving, little screams of frustration bursting forth every few moments. She turned to the brick wall beside her and struck it with her fist.

"Theren!" cried Ebon. "Theren, stop it!"

She ignored him and struck again. Her eyes burst into white light, and her magic spilled forth. A chunk erupted from the wall with a *crash,* and a shard of stone grazed Ebon's cheek, flinging him to the ground.

"Stop it!" he screamed.

At first he thought she did not hear him, for again she punched the wall. But then she stopped and turned, leaning back against the brick with her eyes closed as she faced the grey sky.

"What is the matter with you?" said Ebon. "You act as though you have been seized by madness."

Theren shook her head, eyes still closed. "I suppose I have, after a fashion. You have asked me often before why Lilith and I hate each other so. Or I suppose I should say, why I hate Lilith, for she has never returned the courtesy. It might have been easier if she had."

Ebon pushed himself up from the ground, trying to dust the mud from his sleeves. With a finger he gently probed his cheek, and it came away with a small streak of blood. He pressed the cut hard with his palm. "Speak plainly, Theren."

"We were lovers once."

That was somewhat more plain than Ebon had intended. The air went very still. She gave a deep sigh and then at last opened her eyes to meet his gaze.

"Lilith and I. For almost three years, before the two of us knew much of what we were doing."

Ebon blinked, shaking his head. "You . . . you and Lilith? But you have hated goldbags since even before we met. It is . . . I do not understand."

"I hated them, it is true. Yet you and Kalem have earned my trust, for you are not like most of them. Neither was Lilith, once. She was only a child, or scarcely more than one. And of course we were not in class together, but we studied together in the library, and we spent time together in other places. I learned another side of her, and it was one I came to love dearly. She felt the same. But then, as we both grew into adulthood, she began to act more like the rest of her kin. The family Yerrin is not so dark as your own, but neither are they gentle folk. And Lilith was a favored scion of their house, unlike you, who have long had cause to take issue with the evils of your clan. Lilith embraced them instead. And so I knew I could be with her no longer. She never forgave me for leaving—but I think her feelings for me never faded, as mine did for her."

"But . . . but you were so eager to prove her guilt," said Ebon, shaking his head. "How could you . . .?"

Theren blinked hard, fighting to hold back her weeping. "I thought her family was behind it. I thought to prove it, and thus to show her—to show Lilith—that they had no love for her in their hearts. At last I thought she might see the folly of her ways. I did not know she had been seized by this madness. And now Vali . . . that poor boy . . ."

She turned away.

So much seemed clear to Ebon now that had been strange before. The way Theren had always hated Lilith, beyond logic or reason. The way Lilith would never fight back, no matter what Theren did to her.

"It must have been terrible for you. Seeing her do that."

Theren choked on a sob and tried in vain to turn it to a barking laugh. "It was. For many, love is a cruel and unkind mistress, and never more so than with Lilith and I."

"Love, you say. Do you love her?"

She shrugged. "Who knows? I think it is better I do not, for her time in this world will soon be ending."

"Yet often love springs forth unbidden."

Even through her tears, Theren smirked. "This is not some Elf-tale between you and Adara, Ebon. This is life, and life is cruel. Lilith embraced its cruelty, and now she will pay the price."

Once, Ebon might have been secretly pleased at the thought of Lilith's death—not that he wished her such harm, but that she would no longer torment him. But now, its inevitability only made him feel hollow.

He reached out a hand for his friend.

"Come, Theren. It is cold out, and the day is only just beginning. Let us leave the streets, and try to leave our troubles as well."

"I do not think it shall be as easy as that." But she took his hand and let him draw her away from the wall, and together they made their way back to the Academy.

TWENTY-EIGHT

THE MEMORY OF LILITH IN THE CONSTABLES' STATION haunted Ebon for the next few days. Often he would catch himself thinking of her in class, when Perrin's sharp rebuke would bring him back to his spells. Or he would sit in the library, staring at the same page for nearly an hour. At last he would realize that he was not seeing the words on the page at all, but Lilith's wild, darting eyes.

Her madness struck him as odd. He knew that torture could do strange things to a mind. Lilith's frantic muttering and wordless rocking in her chair seemed like something more than that. But he had no idea just what it might be.

Fingers snapped before his eyes, bringing him back to the dining hall where he ate with Kalem and Theren.

"Ebon," said Kalem. "What is the matter with you? You have not spoken since we sat down to eat, nor have you touched your food."

"I am sorry. My thoughts these days are troubled. What were you saying?"

Kalem sighed and turned away. "Oh, nothing of great import. But *you* had better treat your classes with better attention. I hear Perrin has half a mind to kick you back to the first-years' class."

Ebon chuckled. "She did, until yesterday when I managed to shift stone back into the box." It had almost been an accident, but still he had done it; after shifting the stone from the little wooden cube, he had managed to scoop it all back in. When he tried repeating the spell, of course, the stone had splattered all over the place, but at least he had done it the once.

Theren was silent beside them, glaring down into her oatmeal, sullen as she had been since their visit to Lilith. Ebon had come to regret bringing her along. He was glad to know the truth of her relationship to Lilith, but it was obvious she had been greatly disturbed by what they had seen.

When their meal was over with, they made for the hallways. Theren struck off on her own without a word, while Kalem ruefully shook his head and bid

Ebon farewell. He headed for Perrin's class, but soon a sharp whisper stopped him. He rounded and saw Oren lurking in an alcove.

Ebon glanced up and down the hallway in both directions, suddenly unsure. He wondered if this might be some trick—especially since he did not see Nella, who he trusted more.

With a frustrated growl, Oren seized his sleeve and dragged him down the hallway, ducking out the first white door they found and emerging onto the Academy's grounds. Quickly he hauled Ebon to the great outer wall, stepping into a hedge where no one could see them.

"What is this about, Oren?"

The boy's eyes were wild. "I have heard you saw Lilith."

Relief flooded Ebon, and he loosed a sigh. "Oh. Yes, I did. But you could have asked me that in the hallway."

Oren ignored him, seizing the front of his robes. "How is she? Are they treating her well?"

Ebon gave him a quizzical frown. "No, Oren. They are not. She is a murderer, and being put to the question for . . ."

He stopped, for he could not tell Oren about the artifacts. Then he took another look at the boy and realized there was something odd about him. His hands spasmed where they held Ebon's lapels, and every muscle in his face was twitching. His eyes darted every which way, not seeming to search for anyone coming near, but simply out of an inability to sit still. Gaunt was his face, drawn thin as though he was starving. It had only been four days since Ebon had seen him last, but the change in his features was startling.

"Are *you* all right, Oren?"

"Of course I am," Oren snapped. "I am not the one under the knives of the Mystics."

"You do not look well."

"*I am fine!*" cried Oren, shaking him. Ebon seized his wrists and tried throwing him off, but Oren had the grip of a madman.

"Fine, then," said Ebon through gritted teeth. "Let me go. I have told you what I saw."

"Lilith could not have done it, Ebon. She *would* not. And *could* not. I know her. She is my cousin. We have spent all our lives together. She is no murderer, I tell you."

Ebon felt himself soften. He put a hand on Oren's shoulder. "I was there, Oren. You and Nella tried to stop her. And we all saw what she did to Vali."

"She did not," said Oren, shaking his head. "She was . . . that was . . ."

"I am sorry," said Ebon. "But at least it is over."

"*She did not!*" Oren shoved Ebon away, and light sprang into his eyes. He held out both palms, and flames erupted in the center of each. Ebon raised his hands to shield his face, terrified.

But then the flames winked out as quickly as they had come. Oren stared at his palms, horrified.

"I did not mean . . . I would never . . ."

Ebon tried to answer, but Oren ignored it, turning away. He wandered slowly off, still staring at his hands, muttering *I would never, I would never.*

A thrill of fear coursed through Ebon, and he made his shaky way back to Perrin's class.

The next day, Ebon was practicing his counter-magic again. He sat opposite Astrea on the bench, each of them holding one end of the wooden rod. He could tell her heart was not in it, and yet still he could do nothing to stop her.

"Try again," he said. "I think I am ready."

Astrea sighed. Her eyes filled with light, and she pushed stone up along the wooden rod. Ebon's own eyes glowed in response. He sought for the stone, try-ing to stop it. He could *almost* see it, *almost* glimpse the particles of stone sliding along the wood. But they were surrounded by some sort of glow, and he could not see through it to the stone beneath.

Soon it was done, and Astrea held up the stone rod with a sigh. Ebon growled in frustration. But then he thought again about what he had seen. He squinted at the rod, and a careful smile stole across his face.

"Try it again."

"Ebon, I am weary of this."

"Please, Astrea. I have just thought of something that may work."

She sighed, changing the rod back to wood, and then placed the other end in his palm. Once more her eyes glowed, and stone rippled along the rod.

Ebon focused on the glow. He saw it sliding along the wood, transforming it piece by piece. But now, rather than trying to stop the stone, he seized the glow, and . . . *squeezed.*

Snap

The magic winked out of existence. The light vanished from Astrea's eyes, which widened as she looked down at the rod. Ebon laughed and held it aloft. It was made of wood, with not a spot of stone to be seen.

Across the room, Perrin straightened from where she was teaching another student. "Have you done it at last, Ebon?"

"I have, Instructor!" Then he heard his own crowing and cleared his throat. "That is, with Astrea's help, I believe I have learned my first bit of counter-magic."

Perrin thundered to the front of the room and then waved Ebon to join her. "Ebon, tell the class what you have learned."

Ebon held up the rod. "When Astrea first turned the rod, I could see only the stone turning the wood. But I could not stop it, and so she always bested me. But at last I learned to look for the magic itself. It appeared as a glow, surrounding the stone as it moved along the rod. When I focused on the glow rather than the stone, and stopped it, her magic failed."

"And that is the answer," said Perrin. "Only

through practice and concentration can we see magic clearly, and that is what lets us defend ourselves against it. Magic appears differently to some—many see it as a glow, the way Ebon does. Others see it as a rippling in the air, or a fine dust swirling about. However we see it, it is not *until* we see it that we can learn to control it. The heart of transmutation is to see the *thing* for what it is, and change it. In counter-magic, you must see the magic itself. Though this is not one of your passing lessons for the class, it is nevertheless an important one. Take pride that you have learned it."

Ebon beamed. The other students wore expressions ranging from interested to disgruntled. Back on the bench, Astrea seemed numb, and had not lifted her gaze from the desk. The sight dampened Ebon's spirits.

The bell rang for the midday meal. Ebon looked uncomfortably away and made for the door. But outside it, to his surprise, was Dasko. The Instructor pushed himself away from the wall with a nod.

"Ebon. I had wondered if we might walk together before lunch?"

"Certainly, Instructor." Ebon bowed.

Dasko nodded again and waved Ebon down the hallway, towards a white cedar door leading back out to the gardens. For a moment, he was reminded of his encounter with Oren. But the warm sun outside dispelled such uncomfortable thoughts, though it fell on a world still covered with snow.

"I heard through the door that you have learned

your counter-magic. That is a fundamental of magic that some wizards do not grasp until years later in their educations."

Ebon shrugged. "I have the advantage of being older than most of my peers."

Dasko shook his head. "It is not only that. Magic is something ethereal and ephemeral. It is change itself. That is why so many wizards struggle to move from their testing spell to other spells, but learn much faster once they have passed that first step. Too many wizards focus on the thing before them: the wooden rod, or for therianthropes, the color of our skin; the stone the mentalist tries to lift, or the spark the elementalist seeks to summon. They do not learn to see the magic itself, the pure force of alteration that influences all the world."

Though he nodded, in truth Ebon's head had begun to spin. Dasko laughed and clapped his shoulder.

"Momen used to wear the same expression when I spoke to him of magic. A man of action, your brother was. Do not trouble yourself with my words. They are certainly too heady for a student in a second-year class. They will make more sense in time."

"Of course, Instructor. But none of this is why you came to see me, unless I miss my guess. What can I do for you?"

Dasko held his smile, though it lost some of its spark. He looked ahead at the path as they walked. "I thought to ask about your visit with Lilith."

Ebon studied the ground. Oren's interest made

some sense to him, but now Dasko? It seemed Ebon and his friends were not the only ones who wished for more of an explanation of the recent tragedies. "Did Jia tell you nothing?"

"Nothing much. She was not in the room, or so she said, and so details were hard to come by."

"It was . . . terrible. She seemed mad, as though her deeds had driven her mind to ruin. Or mayhap it was the torture. She recoiled at the slightest sound, and her body was an awful mass of bruises and wounds."

"You say she acted mad?" Dasko's eyes lit with interest. "How, exactly?"

Ebon frowned. "I . . . her eyes darted all about, and her fingers would not stop twitching. She chewed at them, though they bled and must have pained her greatly. She reminded me of a trapped animal—desperate to escape, but only hurting herself more."

Dasko frowned, stroking his close-trimmed beard with one hand while slowly nodding. "I see. That is interesting, to be sure."

"I do not understand, Instructor. Can you not go see her yourself? Surely you do not require permission, as Theren and I did."

"My duties here have prevented me," said Dasko, looking away. "As well as certain other duties I have been asked to perform, outside the Academy's normal hours."

Ebon remembered him unloading crates from the cart into Xain's home. But surely the dean must have moved in by now. Mayhap Dasko was one of the instructors required to stand guard. "I see. Then, may I ask why this interests you so?"

Dasko quickly shook his head. "Do not trouble yourself over it. It is only that I have been wondering something. I knew Lilith, you see. She attended the Academy before I came here as an instructor, and we had more than one occasion to share time. She could be . . . very difficult as a student. Yet I would never have taken her for a killer."

That reminded Ebon of what Oren had said the day before, and what Nella told him in the tavern on the final day of Yearsend. He frowned.

Crunching footsteps approached, and Ebon looked up to see Jia strolling towards them as though by happenstance. But from the careful look in her eye, and the slight flush in her cheeks as Ebon saw her, it took but a moment to realize she sought them. When Dasko turned back, the smile tugging at the corner of his mouth confirmed it.

"I . . . hope you will excuse me, Ebon. Instructor Jia and I had meant to meet each other over the midday meal."

Ebon nodded quickly—too quickly, and he felt foolish. "Of course, Instructor. Do not let me intrude, or keep you from your duties."

Jia took Dasko's arm, and he led her off through the garden. Ebon made for the dining hall, unable to banish a secret smile.

TWENTY-NINE

LATER, IN THE LIBRARY, EBON SAT WITH KALEM IN their alcove. Theren had not joined them for the midday meal. Now it was some time into the afternoon's study period, and still she was not with them. They read together for some time, until at last Kalem looked up from his book.

"Do you think she is all right?"

Ebon shrugged. "Why should she not be?"

Kalem frowned and returned to his book. But only for a moment, for they both heard pounding footsteps moving along the library's third floor in approach, and looked up to find Theren running full tilt towards them.

In a flash they were on their feet. But looking behind her, Ebon saw nothing wrong. She was not being chased, other than by the curious looks of other students disturbed by her flight. And the look on her face was not one of terror, nor anger, but of fierce joy. She seized the front of Ebon's robes and shook him, her voice quivering in excitement.

"I do not think Lilith did it," she said, speaking fast. "I know who it was."

Ebon blinked, trying to pry her hands from his body. "Calm yourself, Theren. Everyone is watching."

"Who cares? Lilith is innocent."

Finally he removed her hands from his lapels. "Come, Theren, sit, and tell us what you mean, from the beginning."

She growled, but she took her seat between them. Ebon took one last look over his shoulder. The few curious onlookers turned back to their books.

"Now, what do you mean by this, Theren? You were there, as I was, when Lilith killed Vali. We both saw it, as did many others besides."

"No," said Theren, vehemently shaking her head. Then she paused. "Well, yes. We did see that. But I have thought much, and have had an idea: *mindwyrd*."

Kalem's eyes widened. But Ebon frowned. "I do not understand."

"Mindwyrd," said Kalem. "Do you remember? It is

the power mentalists gain when they consume mage-stones—the power of command, so that anyone who hears their voice must obey."

"Exactly," said Theren. "If someone had Lilith under the control of mindwyrd, they could have forced her to do what she did. Lilith would have obeyed without question, for she would have had no choice."

But now Kalem shook his head. "That may be possible, Theren. But do you honestly believe someone in the Academy could be using magestones? Surely someone would have noticed by now. The wizard's eyes turn black instead of white for more than a day after the stones are consumed. Lilith killed Vali nearly a week ago. If she was involved in Credell's death, it is many weeks. How could black eyes have gone unnoticed for so long?"

"What if the wizard is not in the Academy?" crowed Theren, far too loud. Ebon shushed her, and she glared at him, but still she lowered her voice to a whisper. "It could be someone beyond the citadel walls. Someone who sent Lilith in to do their dirty work each day, and then made her return to keep the mindwyrd strong, for it will fade if the victim's contact grows stale."

"It is possible," said Kalem. "But even if we acknowledge that, what then? Again, we have an idea that something *may* be true, but no evidence to prove it."

"But we may," said Theren. "I have heard tales of the effect mindwyrd has on its victims. They say it drives them half-mad, as Lilith was when we saw her in prison. She was haggard, her face gaunt and her eyes filled with insanity. These are only rumors, though— that is why I need your help. If we can find proof here, in the library, that these are symptoms of magestones, we can prove her innocence—or at least cast doubt's strong shadow upon her guilt. And once we have done that, I believe we can work towards proving who held her under mindwyrd while she committed her crimes: Cyrus."

Ebon froze. His mouth opened, but he could not summon words. *No. No, no, no, Theren.*

Kalem arched a brow. Theren leaned towards him, speaking faster. "Think. He fled in terror from the attack on the Seat, and he knows that if he returns, he will be branded a traitor and a coward. Doubtless he could have kept running, to find some hovel in an outland kingdom where he might spend the rest of his days. But Cyrus was always a greedy steer. I think he returned and worked his mindwyrd upon Lilith to steal the artifacts for him. Then he could retreat to some outland kingdom to live his days in wealth and power. Mayhap he might even try to take a throne, establishing himself as a new Wizard King."

"That would be foolish," said Kalem, shaking his head. "No one would stand for it. The High King would cast him down at once."

"He could take a new name, so that no one would even know he was a wizard," Theren argued. "And the High King is embroiled in a civil war. What attention could she spare for some usurper on the other end of Underrealm? It is the best possible time for such a scheme."

Ebon had to speak, but he shook with fear at the knowledge of what he must say. "Theren," he began. "This is . . . I am sorry, but this is not—"

She scowled at him, jaw working. "Ebon, I know I have given Lilith no end of grief while you have known me. But I have mocked and derided you and Kalem as well, and yet I know you are not murderers. Lilith is the same. She is vain and small-minded, but she is *not* a killer. Since Credell's death, I have told you how I could not believe Lilith was capable of such an act. Mayhap some part of me—some hidden part I did not wish to acknowledge—saw the truth, even when my eyes could not. I am certain of this, Ebon. Cyrus *must* have done it. He has been influencing her with—"

"I killed Cyrus."

Her words snapped to a halt. She and Kalem went still as statues. The boy jerked in his seat—back, as though he meant to stand, and then forwards again.

"What . . . what did you say, Ebon?"

Ebon could not lift his gaze from his lap. In a whisper he said, "It was the day the Seat was attacked. You remember when I ran off from the group. I told you, and everyone else, that I thought I saw an Academy student fleeing the battle. In truth, I saw Cyrus, and Adara was by his side."

Kalem frowned. "Adara? Why would she . . .?" But

Theren looked at Ebon with pity, and Kalem's words faded to nothing.

His cheeks burned, but he forced himself to speak on. "I caught them upon the southern cliffs of the Seat. There, where that little cove had been marked on the map we found, was a boat that Cyrus meant to escape in. I confronted him, for I thought he was kidnapping Adara. It turned out I was wrong, but he grew wroth and attacked us both. He nearly killed me, and with his magic he throttled Adara as well. In my desperation, I found my magic. I turned his feet to stone, and then Adara cast him into the Great Bay, where he sank and drowned."

Theren sagged in her seat, placing one hand to her forehead. Kalem stood, hands twisting at his sides. He turned as if to walk away but paced behind his armchair instead. Ebon felt wretched.

"Darkness take it all," Theren murmured.

"I am sorry," said Ebon. "I should have—"

She shook her head. "No, Ebon. I do not blame you. I even see why you did not tell us. It is only . . . it means Cyrus is not behind this."

"It could be someone else," Ebon said. "Some other wizard manipulating her—"

"They would have to know the Academy."

"What if it was someone in the family Yerrin? Someone who first gleaned information about the vaults from Lilith, and then held her in mindwyrd when she refused to help them on her own?"

"The family Yerrin deal in magestones, or so it is said by many," said Theren. "But they never consume the stones themselves. Magestones are a slow poison of the mind. Yerrin knows this better than anyone. No agent of that house would risk themselves. Cyrus was the only person who made sense."

Ebon stared at his shoes again. "Still. There could be someone," he murmured.

"I suppose there could," said Theren. But she sounded utterly defeated.

Kalem had gone still behind his armchair, head bowed. Ebon looked up at him. "What are you thinking?"

The boy shrugged. "What is there to think, Ebon? I know not what to say."

"I imagine you are angry."

"Angry? I . . . I do not know. We are friends. But this . . . this is wrong."

Theren sat forwards. "It was in defense of his own life, Kalem. You knew Cyrus—"

Kalem gave her a hard look. "If that is true, he could have told the story. The King's law would have protected him."

"The King's law, mayhap," said Ebon quietly. "But my family? Never. You know the King's law matters little to them. Mayhap Halab would have forgiven me. And I can never guess at Mako. But my father . . . my father would never have stood by. It would have been the excuse he long hoped for. He would have killed me."

"Mayhap. Mayhap not," said Kalem. "You could have figured out some way. Something. *Anything*, rather than keeping this deed in the dark. Sky above, Ebon, you could have told *us*. We could have thought of something—or agreed to keep it secret. Together. But this? I cannot abide by it."

He stepped out from behind the chair and made to leave. Ebon stood. But Kalem only gave him a sad little smile.

"I will not tell anyone what you did, Ebon. You need not fear that. But in the last few months I have grown to love you, mayhap more dearly than my own brothers at home. I thought we had grown to trust each other."

"We do," said Ebon. "I do."

"How can you say that? Were our positions reversed, what do you think I would have done?"

Ebon found it suddenly hard to speak. But he forced the words out, hearing the tears lurking within them. "You would have told me."

Kalem left. Ebon watched until he was out of sight among the shelves and then sank back into his chair, head in his hands.

THIRTY

KALEM DID NOT EAT WITH THEM THAT NIGHT OR THE next day. During breakfast and the midday meal he sat pointedly at a table far away, and did not so much as glance in Ebon's direction. When it came time to study in the library that afternoon, he was nowhere to be found.

Ebon thought of finding another place in the library to study so that Kalem could have his nook. After all, he had been there long before Ebon, and had shared it when Ebon came to the Academy. But Ebon still held some hope that Kalem might forgive him, and if that happened, he wanted to be where the boy could find him easily.

But the afternoon's free study passed, and there was no sign of Kalem. When Ebon and Theren went to the dining hall and fetched their suppers, they saw him sitting many tables away. Still he would not look in their direction.

So they ate, neither of them speaking. Now that he had told his friends, Ebon felt terrible that he had kept the secret from them for so long. But also, the weight of Cyrus' death seemed to have mostly fled. When alone, or in a quiet place, or trying to drift off to sleep, he no longer saw the scene playing out in his mind.

That was little comfort, though, when he had to bear Kalem's hatred instead. And he was not the only one who harbored a strong resentment for Ebon. Whenever he chanced to look at the head of the dining hall, Ebon saw Xain staring daggers his way. That was nothing unusual, mayhap, but today his anger seemed to have gained a particular intensity.

"Mayhap he heard about our visit to Lilith," said Theren, after Ebon mentioned it. "I have noticed him giving me a dark glare as well. I do not think he appreciates our meddling, as he no doubt thinks of it."

"At least with her capture, I no longer have to worry about him thinking I am the killer."

Theren shrugged. "Do not worry about that. I am certain it is only a matter of time before he finds something else to blame you for."

That forced a chuckle from him, though his smile quickly vanished. "Even though the threat is over, I still feel its shadow hanging over the Academy. I thought it would have dissipated by now. No one seems fearful. Only sad."

"Of course they are," muttered Theren. "We have all suffered loss. I only wonder if the pain will ever fade."

Ebon saw Astrea sitting at a table with others, yet still seeming so alone as she stared at her food. Isra was beside her, but even that could not bring her any cheer. Likely this darkness would accompany the rest of her life. For how could it ever be healed? Who could explain to a child so young why Lilith had done what she did? Especially when no one knew her ultimate aim?

"For some, I doubt it," he said sadly.

Theren must have misunderstood, for she patted his arm to comfort him and said, "Kalem will forgive you. He only needs time."

Ebon looked back at his food. "I do not know about that. He holds honor highest of all virtues. More so than you, and certainly more so than me."

"Do not be so certain. He values friendship greatly, as well. And you must remember, Ebon: before meeting us, Kalem had only a few friends. He gave himself to us fully, for we went through much together in the days before the attack. After that, to learn you did not trust him . . . but give him time, and I think he will understand why."

"It is not that I did not trust him! I only . . ." But he stopped and hung his head. How could he defend himself? If he had trusted them, he *would* have said something.

The doors of the dining hall flew open, slamming into the walls on either side. Ebon turned his head to look, and his eyes shot wide.

There in the doorway stood Oren, chest heaving, shoulders hunched together, hands formed to claws. His eyes were wild, scattered, searching everywhere. He was muttering something Ebon could not hear, growing ever louder until they could finally make out the words.

"In my head, in my head. Cannot get her out. Always there, in my head. Always *whispering.*"

At the head of the hall, the Instructors shot to their feet. Some began to come forwards. But Oren's eyes finally fixed on Ebon, and he pointed with a shrill scream that stopped everyone cold.

"You! You know! You know she did not do it!"

Ebon's mouth worked, but he could say nothing. Theren stepped around the table to stand beside him, her lips set in a grim line.

"You know! You know she is in my head! *Whispering!"* Oren screamed.

Then he flew into the air.

Ebon flinched, for he thought Oren was leaping for him. But the boy had been hoisted up by his neck. He froze ten feet up, feet thrashing for purchase. A gurgling burst from his throat as he struggled for breath. For a horrible moment Ebon thought it was Theren acting in his defense. But her eyes were not glowing, and she looked just as frightened as he was.

He seized her robes. "Look for the caster!" he hissed.

She understood, and together they turned in a circle, searching for glowing eyes in the hall. But the press of students was too tight, and now they were milling about, some trying to get farther from Oren, others pressing closer in fascination. There was Nella, pushing forwards, trying to help her friend. Kalem stood frozen in horror. Isra could not take her eyes from Oren even as she dragged Astrea away—Astrea who wept silently, still numb, her face a dead mask. But nowhere could Ebon see the glow of magic in anyone's eyes.

But then came the instructors, now forcing their way through the crowd. They leapt forwards, hands high, and Xain was at their fore. He gritted his teeth, muttering words of power through them, fingers twitching as he sought to bring Oren down from the air. Instructors of mentalism and elementalism stood beside him, trying to dispel the force that held Oren aloft. Those instructors who could not help tried to control the students instead, some of whom had begun to panic. They were guided away from Oren's swinging form, to the edges of the room and out of reach.

"Get him down," growled Xain. His blazing eyes swelled until they lit the space all around him like a burning sun. "Damn it, get him *down!*" Theren leapt to his side, unleashing her power to help.

Oren jerked, moving towards the floor in fits and starts. But too late. All around the dining hall, cutlery flew into the air—knives and forks, all spinning in languid circles.

Suddenly they tore through the room like a cloud of wasps. In a storm they struck Oren, impaling him in a thousand places. Some struck the students behind him who had tried to flee the hall.

Then the magic ceased, and Oren slammed to the ground, his eyes staring sightless.

Everyone began screaming at once—the students who had been struck, now lying on the floor with steel protruding from their skin, and all who had witnessed it, who now pressed for the dining hall's door like a panicked mass of beasts. Perrin bellowed, trying to restore order and direct the flow of bodies by placing her massive frame in the way. Jia stared horror-struck at Oren's corpse on the stone floor, but soon shook herself to awareness and helped the other instructors manage the frenzy.

A hand seized Ebon's collar and threw him back. It was Xain, eyes filled with malice.

"He said you knew. What did he mean? Speak, or I will roast you."

"I know nothing," Ebon choked. "I swear it!"

Light blazed in Xain's eyes, and blue fire sprang up around his palm. "Why did he name you?" he snarled.

"The magic that killed him had the strength of mage-stones behind it. Where are they?"

The dean was crazed. Blood filled the corners of his eyes, mayhap from the effort of trying to save Oren, or mayhap from pure rage. But then something struck Xain from nowhere, and he flew away. Ebon jumped, backing into a table. Theren stepped in front of him, eyes still glowing from the spell that had batted the dean away.

Xain shot to his feet, eyes blazing with light. A gust of wind blasted from his hand—but Theren raised her hands to meet it. The spell stopped cold.

She struck, and Xain was forced to take a step back. Gritting his teeth, he countered with a stronger gale. Again Theren batted him aside, the wave of her hand almost flippant.

Then a brown shape seized the dean, and Ebon recognized it as Jia's bear form. She turned partway back to human, but she kept her size, so that she stood many hands taller than him. Her body bulged with muscle, and she was taller and broader even than Perrin. She dragged Xain up until he was forced to stand on his toes, and when she spoke, her voice was a raging growl.

"Master yourself, Dean. Ebon had nothing to do with this. Mentalism killed Oren. You must have felt that when you tried to stop it."

Xain's breath heaved in ragged gasps. He stared her in the eyes before his gaze slid past her to Ebon. Even as he watched, the rage in the dean's eyes cooled to ice—though that made it no less terrible, and in fact Ebon found himself more afraid than before. With a jerk, Xain threw off Jia's hand and stalked from the dining hall.

Most of the students were gone by now. Someone had fetched a tablecloth and covered Oren's body. Slowly Jia resumed her natural form. She stared at the bloodied cloth on the ground for a moment before going to Ebon. He met her eyes and saw sympathy within them.

"Are you all right, Ebon?"

He nodded weakly. "He did not harm me. Not in truth."

She shook her head slowly. "You did not deserve that. But in addition to his . . . relationship with your family, the dean has a particular distaste for those who would use magestones. It does not excuse his conduct, though it may help you to understand it."

Ebon's eyes were fixed on the cloth covering Oren's body. "What happened to him?"

Jia only shook her head. But Theren spoke softly. "It was mindmagic. I could sense it, but I could do nothing to stop it. It was power like I have never felt— not only strong, but somehow corrupt. If it is true what Xain said, that that was the strength of magestones, then I now know why they are such a great evil."

"I searched for the black-glowing eyes," said Ebon. "But I could not see them. No one was casting a spell upon him, save you and the others who tried to save him. Certainly I saw no black magelight. The murderer must have been skulking out of sight. Mayhap they were outside in the hallway, or in a nearby room."

Scowling, Theren shook her head. "That is not how mentalism works. It needs line of sight. The murderer was in the room. You must have missed them in the crowd."

Jia looked just as frustrated. But then she froze, and a look of horror fell across her face.

"Instructor? What is wrong?" She did not answer, and terror bloomed in Ebon's breast. "Jia?"

At last her eyes found him. He saw her tears welling forth.

"Lilith," she whispered, and then turned to bolt for the door.

Ebon and Theren looked at each other for half a heartbeat, and then ran after Jia as fast as their legs could carry them.

THIRTY-ONE

It took some time to secure Lilith's release. Jia's friend was not there, and at first the other Mystics would not take her word. They said that Lilith was held on the command of the dean, and only his command could release her. She had to send a messenger to get a letter from Xain. At first she wanted to send Theren, but the girl refused to leave the prison until Lilith left it as well. Then she wanted to send Ebon, but quickly thought better of that.

At last a street messenger was sent, and one as well to the family Yerrin. Lilith's parents arrived first—both of them merchants in fine green cloth trimmed with silver, whose faces were a heartbreaking blend of sorrow and relief. Theren greeted them awkwardly, and introduced Ebon—but they had little attention for anything other than the door leading to the jail cells. So Ebon and Theren stood off to the side, trying not to look at the Yerrins.

"I forgot to thank you for helping me in the dining hall," Ebon muttered after a while.

"Think nothing of it," said Theren. "Xain was wrong to act as he did."

"Wrong or not, you were glorious," said Ebon, shaking his head. "I knew something of your strength. But to defeat the dean himself so easily . . ."

She shrugged. "Likely he withheld his strength. He did not wish to harm me, but only to get through me so he could reach you. He did not even unleash flame."

Ebon gripped her shoulders and turned her to face him. "You are a boastful person by nature, Theren, and only modest when you know you have no reason to be. It does not suit you. You may have saved my life, and we both know it. Accept my thanks."

Her jaw tightened as she fought a smile. "Still your flapping lips, Ebon. You are so dramatic."

He sighed and shook his head before pulling her into an embrace. She did not return it, but neither did she push him away.

When Xain's decree finally arrived, it was delivered by none other than Nella, who greeted Ebon with a stiff nod.

"I heard what was happening and insisted on bringing this myself," she said.

"We came as quick as we realized the truth." Ebon looked away, for he felt too ashamed to meet her eyes. "It was our fault this happened to her in the first place."

Nella did not seem to want to look at him, either. "This is the second time you have proven yourself to be not entirely a bastard." He gave her a quick look, but saw her wearing a small smile, which he easily returned.

After reading the letter, the Mystics sent two constables into the prison to fetch Lilith from her cell. They all had to wait far longer than made sense to Ebon—surely the prison could not be so vast that it took this long to fetch her.

But when Lilith finally arrived, he thought he understood better. She could barely walk, and was mostly carried by the constables who held her arms. She looked far worse than the last time he had seen her—the swelling in her face had receded, but black bruises remained, splotching her already-dark features like grisly birthmarks. The cuts on her hands and limbs had multiplied, and her lips were bone-dry and cracked. The fireplace lighting the station's front room cast her face in hideous shadows and made her look like a demon of the darkness below.

Jia and Lilith's parents moved to help. But Theren was faster. She seized Lilith with a piteous cry, wrapping her arms around the girl in a tight embrace.

Lilith's arms fumbled and grasped, as though she could not see Theren and was trying to feel for her presence. But once her arms were draped over Theren's shoulders, she held her tight as she could, and tears leaked from her wild, wandering eyes.

"Forgive me," Theren murmured into her shoulder. "Forgive me, please, for I will never forgive myself." Lilith's eyes still stared into an unknowing distance, but her fists tightened on Theren's cloak.

Then Lilith's parents were there, and they helped the girls hobble awkwardly towards the door. Jia stood back so as not to intrude. As they passed Nella, Lilith reached out a tentative hand, and her friend gripped it tight. But Lilith would not release her hold on Theren.

Before they stepped out into the cold, Lilith's parents helped her into a cloak, lined with fur to protect against the chill. It seemed Lilith hardly noticed them as they put it on. But just before they led her outside, she blinked and looked around. Her eyes rested first on Theren, and then on Nella.

"Where . . . where is Oren?" she croaked.

Everyone was deathly silent. Tears streamed from Jia's eyes, though her face did not twitch.

Ebon stepped forwards, unable to meet Lilith's gaze. "Oren fought for you," he murmured. "He never believed—not for one second—that you were guilty. He gave his life trying to make the rest of us see it. I wish I had listened sooner."

Lilith's eyes filled with tears. Her hands twitched, as

though she were grasping for something that was not there. Her parents bowed their heads and then went to help her outside. But she seized at Theren all the more tightly. "No," she whimpered. "No, no, no. Do not make her leave me. Do not make her leave me alone."

Theren met their stares. One after the other, they nodded. And so Theren was the one to help Lilith out to the street where a carriage waited for them. She climbed in with Lilith, soon followed by her parents. As the driver readied the horses, Theren thrust her head out the carriage window.

"I will return soon." She held out a hand, and Ebon gripped it tightly. "Keep yourself whole."

"I will," said Ebon. "See to her."

Theren nodded. The driver switched the horses, and the carriage set off down the street, leaving Jia, Nella, and Ebon to watch it go. Once it was out of sight, Jia turned to them.

"Now we should return, for there are many in the Academy who still need our help."

Nella nodded and set off down the street. But Ebon stayed where he was, staring at his feet. Jia cocked her head at him, waiting until he met her eyes.

"If it is all right, Instructor, I would rather not return just yet. I feel the need to stay in the open air a bit longer. To clear my head."

She studied him long enough to make him wonder if she knew the truth of his mind. At last she nodded. "Very well. Only do not stay out past your curfew."

"Thank you, Instructor."

She gave a final nod, and then went off to follow Nella back to the Academy.

Ebon turned his steps west, seeking the blue door.

Though she greeted him with startled delight, Adara could see at once that something was wrong. She drew him to her room as quickly as she could. He tried to give her a smile, but it was a broken thing. She sat him at the edge of her bed and held his hand.

"What is it? What is wrong?"

"There has been another murder," Ebon managed to whisper.

Her brow furrowed. "I thought Lilith had been caught."

"Lilith was not the murderer."

"Oh." It was a tiny sound, full of understanding. "Do you wish to speak of it?"

"Yes." But then he said nothing.

She waited a moment before tracing a finger along his neck. "Do you wish to do something other than speak?"

That made him smirk. "Not just now."

"Refusing me again? You might as well save your coin, for I fear you waste it by visiting me here."

He lifted her fingers to his lips, planting a tiny kiss on each in turn. "I never waste my time when I spend it with you," he murmured. She smiled and leaned over to kiss his cheek.

"Come, then. Lovers know many arts." She had him slide down to the floor, resting on the soft rug, and then sat on the bed behind him. With her fingers she kneaded at the muscles of his shoulders and neck, working out the knots. He moaned at the skill of her hands, rolling his head back and forth in pleasure.

For some time they sat like that, Ebon enjoying her ministrations. With each kink smoothed, he felt his worries lessen in strength. Yet they would not vanish entirely.

The Academy must be a madhouse now, he thought. When he realized the truth, freeing Lilith had seemed the only important thing in all the nine lands. But now the Academy had a murderer on the loose yet again. He could not stop seeing Oren's body sprawled on the dining hall floor beneath a blood-spattered cloth.

"Lilith's cousin. A boy named Oren. He nearly scuffled with us in the tavern. Do you remember?"

"I do."

"It was he who was killed. He was hoisted in the air before the entire Academy and nearly throttled to death. Then the killer struck him with a flurry of knives."

Her hands stilled for a moment, and he heard her gasp. "That is awful. But that means you must have caught the murderer, have you not? Everyone would have seen the culprit."

Ebon shook his head. "They remained hidden. How, we do not know. And now Lilith weighs like an anvil on my conscience."

Adara lifted a hand from his shoulder to stroke his hair. "You did what you thought was right, Ebon. You were not the only one who thought you saw her kill a child."

He shook his head. "She was put to the question. I saw what the Mystics have done to her. It may have driven her mad. Yet this whole time, she was never to blame."

"Nor were you. Your friends acted the same. Do you blame them?"

Ebon barked a sharp, bitter laugh. "I could not if I wanted to."

She scooted over and leaned down to look at him. "What do you mean?"

"I told them, Adara. Of Cyrus, and the truth of what happened when the Seat was attacked. Kalem has not spoken to me since."

Fear shone in her eyes. "Ebon, that may not have been—"

He shook his head. "He will not tell anyone. And Theren does not think I did anything wrong."

Adara snorted. "That sounds like Theren. But Kalem is royalty."

"He will not tell anyone. You may trust me."

She kissed his cheek and leaned back to keep rubbing his shoulders. "Then I will. In all things."

"The worst of it is that I cannot deny Kalem is right. He says I should have trusted him and told him what happened from the first. I think he is right. I *should* have. He would have believed in me—indeed, he *has* believed in me, but I have not returned the courtesy. And now I know not if he will ever place his faith in me again."

"You might be right. And I wish I had not advised you otherwise. It seems I was wrong about Kalem."

He reached back and took her hand. "It was not your fault. I did the deed, and so the blame is mine."

She squeezed his fingers. "We did it together. We share all consequence. But from what I have seen of Kalem, I think his mind will change. Your friendship will be stronger for it. No longer will you have to keep everything to yourself—and to me, of course."

He pushed himself up from the floor, taking his place on the bed beside her. His heartbeat thundered in his ears, and spots danced at the edge of his vision as he clutched her hands. "There is one thing I have kept to myself all my life," he whispered, afraid to meet her eyes, "but I gave it to you the moment I saw you. My heart."

For a moment she did not answer, and her hands went still. Inside, he winced, certain he had made a mistake. They had spoken easily of love for some time, but it had been a game to her, as it should have been to him. His cheeks burned, and now the thunder of his heart was a roar, savage and angry as an ocean storm.

Their eyes met, and hers were shining. She lifted a hand to his cheek. "I have discovered myself feeling the same way," she whispered. "And it is as surprising to me as anything ever has been in this life. Sometimes love springs forth unbidden, you said, and it has for me."

His hand covered hers on his cheek. "Adara . . ."

Her mouth worked, the muscles in her jaw spasming. Then her words spilled in a rush, as though she wished to rid them from her mind. "Ebon, you may come to see me here behind the blue door—always, every day, if I had my way. Or we could see each other . . . elsewhere."

Ebon frowned. "In taverns and the like? I . . . I should love to do that again, if that is your wish."

Quickly she shook her head. "Not in taverns, Ebon. In my home. I do not mean . . . I do not mean as your lover, and you my client. I mean together. A binding of the heart, and not of coin."

The world froze about him. A voice in the back of his mind screamed *lover's words, lover's words,* and it sounded terribly like his father's. But from the depths of his heart poured unadulterated joy, and it cast aside the shadows of Oren's death and Lilith's torment like the sun burning through the clouds.

He fought for words. But he had been silent for too long, and Adara's cheeks flooded with color. She rose from the bed and walked to the side table where a pitcher of wine waited, her hands shaking. "Forgive me," she said, her words quivering and threatening to break. "It was a foolish jest—something I thought you wanted to hear. I know this is all a game, of course. I do. I—"

Ebon went to her and, turning her by the shoulders, covered her mouth with his. They melted into each other, her fingers buried in his hair, and his arm pressing her tight against him. A long while that kiss lasted, an eternity, and when it ended it left them breathless.

"It was not a game, Adara. It has never been, and it is not now. If I hid my words behind smiles and laughter, it was not because I thought them jests. I have been told of lover's words, and felt sure you were only saying what I wished to hear. I did not mind—I never could, for you are a lover, and that is what I came for. But always I wished it could be real, though I felt sure it never would be."

She seized his robes, her grip fierce, a fire burning in her eyes. "It was. It is."

Then she pushed him back upon the bed, and no more words were spoken.

It was a long while later before Ebon was ready to leave. He had certainly missed his curfew, but he would take any penalty gladly. As he cinched his belt over his robes, Adara gave him a final kiss. Ebon smiled as he looked over the room.

"It is a strange thought that I will not see this room again—or at least, not so often."

"Mayhap I will bring you back here on occasion, for the memories if nothing else."

"I will send word when I can see you next."

"And I will tell you where to find me." She smiled,

a bit nervous, and clearly embarrassed. "It is strange, but I am anxious about showing you my home. It is senseless, considering how well we know each other in . . . other ways."

He chuckled and kissed the top of her brow. "I think I understand."

But then her eyes went wide, and she placed a hand on his chest. "I nearly forgot, for you were so solemn when you first arrived. Though I no longer know if it will be important. It concerned Lilith. Or rather, her family."

Ebon frowned. "The family Yerrin? What of them?"

"Her kin were under investigation by the High King herself. It seems they were already under suspicion. Apparently some scion of the house was found to be in league with the Shades—a distant aunt of Lilith's, I think. But Lilith's actions worsened their standing further, and the clan meant to disown her parents. After what you have told me, it seems likely that is no longer the case, but still I meant to tell you."

"Thank you, but I suspect you are right. Now that Lilith has been proven innocent, the family Yerrin will doubtless be . . ."

Ebon trailed off, for his mind had begun to race, and the nagging thought at the back of his mind had finally burst to the fore. Yerrin. *Yerrin.* He ran to the chair where he had put his shoes and pulled them on as fast as he could.

"I must go at once. The lovers you speak with—

they have seen Mako poking about the Seat, have they not?"

"They have," said Adara, frowning.

"Please, please tell them—if they see him again, they must tell him to come visit me at the earliest opportunity. Tomorrow, if he can manage it. Tell him the usual place. He will know it."

"But—"

"Do you understand?"

"I do, my love. But why? What do you know?"

Ebon leapt up and ran for the door. But just before leaving, he stopped to kiss her again. "Nothing yet. But with Mako's help, mayhap everything."

Then he flew out the door and into the street, sprinting for the Academy.

THIRTY-TWO

WHEN HE RETURNED TO THE ACADEMY, EBON WAS grateful that Mellie did not seem inclined to report his staying out past curfew. He supposed another murder lent perspective to what was truly important in the school.

He went to seek Theren and Kalem. But Theren was still at the Yerrin manor, and Ebon guessed she would spend the night. Someone in the common room said Kalem had gone to bed. For a moment Ebon considered waking the boy, but at last decided against it. Kalem was already angry, and he would surely resent being roused.

So he returned to his dormitory, but he found it impossible to sleep. Eventually he gave it up and went to the common room, where he sat by the fireplace and allowed his thoughts to spiral through his mind. Piece by piece he assembled a theory that explained all that had happened in the school thus far. Before he knew it, the blush of dawn seeped in through the common room's high windows. He yawned and stretched, suddenly feeling the sleepless hours he had spent there. But sleep could wait.

He sought Kalem in the dining hall and soon spied him among the press of students. When Kalem saw Ebon approaching, he turned the other way. But Ebon caught up and put a hand on his shoulder.

"Kalem. I must speak with you."

"I have no wish to do that, Ebon."

Ebon leaned in close. Kalem began to draw away, until Ebon whispered, "It is to find the murderer."

For a moment Kalem stood stock still. Then he looked into Ebon's eyes. "Have you discovered who it is?"

"I may have, but I will need your help to be sure."

Kalem looked back and forth, clearly uncomfortable. "What do you need my help for?"

"Not here. Will you meet me in the library this afternoon?"

Again Kalem was still. Finally he nodded wordlessly, and then made off to eat breakfast alone.

During his morning class, Ebon was a squirming

ball of energy. He practiced shifting stone, and his counter-magic with Astrea. She was even more withdrawn and quiet than she had been before, but when Ebon saw it, he only gave a grim smile.

Soon this will all be over, he promised her in his mind. *Soon your nightmare will be behind you, and all of ours as well.*

He snatched a roll of bread during the midday meal, for he did not think his stomach would let him have anything more. After eating the roll, he made his way to the library and went straight to the third floor. First he went to the bookshelves and lingered there, hoping for Mako to arrive. But there was no sign of the bodyguard by the time the study period started. Ebon returned to his nook, where he found Kalem waiting.

The boy sat with arms folded, and he looked at Ebon with suspicion. Ebon sat in an armchair and leaned forwards, clasping his hands between his knees. They looked at each other a long moment before Kalem sighed and turned his gaze.

"You said you needed my help. Here I am. What is it?"

"Who stands to gain from painting Lilith as a killer?"

Kalem blinked, frowning. "What do you mean?"

"It hurts the reputation of the family Yerrin," said Ebon. "And who is Yerrin's greatest rival?"

"The family Drayden. Your kin."

"Exactly." Ebon scooted still farther forwards in his chair. "It must have been them. We know it was not—" He had been about to say *Cyrus*, but Kalem's eyes hardened, and he skipped the word. "Well, we know it was not a wizard in the Academy, and we know it was not the family Yerrin. That seems plain, now that one child of Yerrin has been killed, and the other tortured into madness. Who is left?"

Kalem shook his head. "We have already suspected this for some time. Nothing has changed."

Ebon raised a finger. "But something has. Theren had a piece of the truth, though she did not know it, nor did we. She believed Lilith was working under the control of mindwyrd. That, I think, is how my father and uncle did it. They fed a mentalist magestones and then used their mindwyrd upon Lilith, forcing her to steal artifacts and further increase their power. And by pinning the blame on her, they further weakened our rivals, the family Yerrin, and pointed all eyes upon them."

At first Kalem only pursed his lips, staring into the distance as he pondered Ebon's words, until at last he gave a reluctant nod. "That seems possible. Entirely possible. Only, wait—with Lilith in jail, how did they arrange for Oren to be killed?"

Ebon sighed. "That is the one piece I have not been able to put into place. A mentalist *must* have line of sight. That means they were in the room."

Kalem's eyes widened. "Or in the hallway just outside. They would have been behind Oren after he entered, but we would not have seen them."

"Of course!" Ebon reeled in his seat. "That is the only thing that makes sense."

Kalem smiled, but his expression soon darkened, and he stared back into his lap. "Still, I do not think this knowledge will help. We will never be able to prove it."

But Ebon only smiled. "But *that* is just what is so urgent. Now that we have guessed at the only possible truth, I have a man who can help us prove it. Wait here."

He stood. Kalem looked at him quizzically, but Ebon waved a hand. "Please, I beg of you—stay seated until I summon you. I was wrong not to have faith, for you deserved all my trust and more. But now I mean to rectify the mistake."

Kalem settled back into his armchair, though he still looked suspicious. Ebon set off towards the shelves again and ducked between two so that Kalem was lost from sight. He waited, aimlessly scanning the shelves.

"You are a brave boy, or a foolish one, to summon me as you did."

Ebon smiled and turned—but his smile faltered, for the bodyguard was uncomfortably close.

"Thank you for coming." Ebon took a half-step backwards. Thankfully, Mako did not follow.

"What do you want? Be quick, for as it turns out, I am in the family's employ, and that means I have real work that must be done."

"Yet what I have to tell you falls in with your duties," said Ebon. "I believe it concerns Halab's safety."

Mako straightened, one hand drifting to his dagger's hilt. "That is a bold statement."

"It is one I make with every confidence. But you must wait here a moment, so I can bring my friend."

"No." The word held a grim finality, and Mako's nostrils flared. "That is not how I work—nor should you. Family matters remain in the family. To do anything else is folly."

"This is not only a family matter, for many Academy students lie dead. And he is my closest friend. I trust him with my life."

Mako sneered. "I might trust him with your life as well, but not with mine."

Ebon met his gaze without flinching. "I trust him with Halab's life."

There was a long moment of silence, and then Mako rolled his shoulders. "Very well," he growled. "Bring him."

Ebon went quickly to fetch Kalem, before Mako could change his mind. But when Kalem rounded the corner with Ebon and found Mako there, he balked and tried to run.

"Kalem! Be still. He is one of my kin, and serves my family well. This is Mako—the one who warned me of the Seat's attack."

That made Kalem pause, and he swallowed hard while eyeing Mako. The bodyguard, much to Ebon's consternation, did nothing to ease the boy's mind, looking him up and down like a wolf inspecting a rabbit.

"Mako," said Ebon, pressing on before either of them could say or do anything regrettable. "I think I have at last found a link between Shay and Matami and the Academy thefts. We now know that Lilith was blameless—she killed Vali only under another's control, and may not have killed Credell at all. She stole the artifacts, but that was under mindwyrd as well."

"You speak with great certainty," said Mako. "How do you know?"

Ebon turned to Kalem. "Tell him the symptoms of mindwyrd."

The boy shrugged. "You know as well as I do, for Theren told us both."

Ebon shook his head. "I know nothing of magic. Not like you, Kalem. Please, tell him."

Kalem sighed. "Mindwyrd controls the body and the mind. As long as the mentalist maintains their control, by reestablishing it over the victim every day or so, no ill effects can be seen. But if that control slips, the victim will begin to show signs of madness. They will grow increasingly anxious, their eyes will show their insanity, and they often cannot sit still."

"That sounds very like Ebon," said Mako, baring his teeth in a feral grin. "Are you recovering from mindwyrd, boy?"

"Lilith showed these signs in the constables' station," Ebon said, ignoring the jest. "Oren showed them before he died. I even saw them in Credell. Kalem, do you remember how he came to Theren and asked her for the key to the vaults? That must have been under mindwyrd. I think Matami and my father did this, not to *build* an alliance with Yerrin, but to weaken them as rivals to our family. But they would need a mindmage. So I ask you, Mako: are there any mindmages in the family Drayden?"

The bodyguard's eyes had narrowed while listening to Ebon's theory, but at the last question they shot wide. "There is," he said slowly. "I spoke of him before: Drystan, a distant cousin of yours, who I have had no reason to suspect in any of this. Yet now that you bring him to mind, I recall something interesting: it seems he disappeared some months ago, off on some mysterious business for the family—or so Shay told me."

Ebon felt a thrill in his chest. "And where was he last seen?"

"Hedgemond." Beside Ebon, Kalem gave a start, and Mako fixed him with a look. "Yes, little goldshitter. Your homeland. My work for our kin never carries me there, and so I had not paid much attention to this cousin's disappearance."

"So?" said Ebon, trying not to look too eager. "You cannot deny that this rings with truth."

Mako's frown deepened, and he stroked his chin with a thumb. "It may be something," he said at last.

Ebon broke into a grin, but he quickly composed

himself. "What can we do? Can Halab intervene? Should we bring it to the constables?"

"No," Mako said. "Not that. Never. Halab may be able to act. But this is not enough evidence. We must find something irrefutable—something we can bring to her that will allow her to act without question. I know what will do the trick—but I shall need your help."

Ebon frowned. "What could you need *my* help with?"

"We will need to sneak into a place without anyone knowing we were there. You can shift stone now, can you not?"

Ebon shrugged. "I can shift it aside, but not put it back. Certainly I could not cover our tracks."

Mako moved so fast that Ebon's mind took a moment to see it. By the time he knew what had happened, he was face down on the floor with Mako's knee in his back. The man's silver dagger was pressed to his neck, the tip tickling his jugular. Kalem opened his mouth to cry out, but Mako gave him a look of steel.

"Breathe a word, and he dies," he hissed.

Kalem's mouth shut with a *snap*.

"What is this?" said Ebon, gasping from the pressure on his spine.

"Shift the stone," Mako growled.

"What?" The dagger tickled harder. "What stone?" he cried.

"The floor. Shift it. And I would advise you to be quick."

Ebon reached for his power, and the library grew lighter as his eyes began to glow. The floor rippled and twisted under his palm. The stone flew out from around his hand, creating an indent.

"Now," said Mako. "Put it back."

"I have told you, I cannot," said Ebon. Mako's grip tightened on his hair. "I swear! I have not learned it yet!" He was whimpering, but did not care.

"I can shift it!" said Kalem. "I can put it back. I will do what you want—only let Ebon go."

"No royalty," said Mako. "You have done your part, goldshitter. This is a Drayden matter, and a Drayden will solve it. Or—"

Ebon felt the dagger's tip nick his skin. At the edge of his vision, a red droplet splashed onto the stone.

"All right!" He tried to still his mind—not an easy thing with Mako's dagger so close—and focused on the stone. He gestured, trying to move it. But it only flew away from his hand, not under his control.

"Not good enough, boy," Mako sneered. Ebon heard his fingers tighten on the dagger's leather handle.

Ebon tried to focus. And as he did, he saw something . . . a sort of glow, surrounding the stone as it flooded like water.

The magic. *His* magic. The magic he used to shift the stone.

He focused, gripping it in his mind. The stone went rigid, molded like clay at his thought.

A long sigh escaped him. He scooped the magic

back into the hole, and the stone went with it. In a moment it was done, and the hole was gone. Ebon released his magic, and the glow faded. The stone looked terrible, like a hole in a wall poorly plastered over. But it was back in its place.

"Well done, little Ebon," said Mako softly. "That will do well enough. I will come for you tonight. Be ready."

The pressure vanished from Ebon's back all at once, and he gasped. Kalem seized his arm and helped him to his feet. By the time they stood, Mako was gone.

THIRTY-THREE

AFTER MAKO'S THREATS, KALEM STRONGLY URGED Ebon to reconsider working with the man, and Ebon could hardly blame him. He tried to defend the bodyguard, though he thought his arguments were made less effective by the hand he pressed to his neck, staunching the nick in his throat.

"It was only a bit of motivation," said Ebon, trying to smile. "And it worked, did it not?"

"He is a madman. I do not know what he has planned for the two of you, but I do not like it."

Ebon shrugged. "Remember, he has already saved

our lives once—and mayhap the Academy. He is a hard man because he must be, but Mako means us no harm." But Ebon wondered if even he believed the words. He had heard the malice in Mako's voice.

At last Kalem gave up trying to convince him, though Ebon was certain the boy still had his doubts. He wished Theren were there. If she had been present, he doubted Mako would have made his threats. She was powerful in her magic, and could have sent Mako flying with a flick of her wrist. But also, Theren could now help him reassure Kalem that working with Mako was the only way forwards.

And it *was* the only way forwards. Ebon was certain.

The rest of their study period passed quickly, if uncomfortably. It felt odd to Ebon, sitting there and trying to read, pretending that nothing untoward was occurring. How could he read tales of history, even those of the Wizard Kings, when his life promised such danger in the here and now?

As the final bell rang, they made their way out of the library. By unspoken agreement, they passed the dining hall. Ebon had no appetite, and doubted Kalem did either. Instead they made their way into the garden, where the sun had just begun to kiss the top of the Academy's outer wall. Cool air seeped into their bodies as they walked the grounds. There was no one to be seen; everyone was inside having supper.

When the sun's final sliver vanished from sight,

Ebon felt a presence and turned to see Mako lurking in the garden a few paces away. The bodyguard waved them forwards, and Ebon led Kalem into the shadows.

"Scuttle off now, royal boy. It is bad enough Ebon must see where we are going. No one else can know."

"Where *are* you going, exactly?" asked Kalem, folding his arms.

"Look at the spine this one shows," said Mako, arching an eyebrow at Ebon. "Mayhap I should rip it out, that we might see it more plainly."

"He means to lead me out of the Academy," said Ebon. "Is that right? You mean to take whatever path lets you get in and out without anyone seeing."

"Very clever, Ebon. Now tell your lover to leave us, lest I make him vanish permanently."

Kalem did not seem eager to budge, but Ebon gave him a nod. With a final reluctant look, the boy left. Mako gave him a little wave, twiddling his fingers in the air just before he was out of sight.

"Now then," said Mako. "Come and learn something you should not."

To Ebon's surprise, Mako did not lead him deeper into the garden, but instead towards the citadel. The bodyguard ran quickly from bush to bush, each time looking in every direction to ensure that no one could see.

Near the front of the Academy, the citadel joined the outer wall. There Mako went to a particular section of black granite, though Ebon saw nothing remarkable about it. He had to wait as his eyes adjusted to the shadows. In that moment, Mako did *something* that Ebon could not see. But when he was done, a section of the wall turned inwards to reveal a hidden door, so narrow that Mako could barely fit his broad shoulders inside it. But Ebon followed him in, and then Mako swung it closed behind them.

Utter darkness lay beyond. Ebon could see nothing, and could hear only his own ragged breathing. When Mako spoke, his mouth only a finger's breadth away, Ebon jumped. "Come along, little Ebon," the bodyguard whispered. "Not too far to go."

After a moment, Ebon could feel that he was alone in the passageway. But there were no footsteps, no faintest sound to follow. He was forced to put his hand on the wall and use it to guide himself along. A sudden, terrible memory gripped him: the passage beneath the watchtower on the south of the Seat, where he had followed Cyrus and Adara during the attack. It had been very much like this tunnel, and then, as now, he had been unable to see where he was going.

A slight grinding sounded from ahead, making him jump. Then Mako's hand clamped firmly over his shoulder to drag him forwards. Now, at last, there was some tiny shaft of light, and his eyes drank it in. They were in some sort of shed, with stone walls and a wooden roof. There were all manner of tools hanging on the walls—rakes, brooms, and shovels. Ebon thought they looked vaguely familiar. Then in a flash he recognized where they were.

"This is one of the outer sheds."

"Indeed," said Mako, who Ebon now saw stood just beside him.

Ebon spun to look the way he had come, but the wall was solid. "Where is the door? How did we get here?"

Mako's grin spread wider. "There are still some secrets I deem you unworthy of."

Ebon shook his head. "It is not only that. If I cannot find the door, I cannot come back to the Academy this way."

"Imagine the depths of my dismay." Mako's face was a mask of stone.

"Very well," said Ebon, glaring. "Let us get on with it."

Mako took him out of the shed and into the streets. The moons had not yet risen, but dusk's fading light let Ebon see well enough. Yet that was little help, for their route was so wild and winding that he was soon hopelessly lost. He searched for a landmark, such as the High King's palace towering over the buildings, but saw nothing. It seemed almost as though Mako was taking him down the narrowest streets, the tightest alleys, so that he could not hold his bearings for even a moment. And the pace soon had Ebon heaving and sweating in his robes.

"Where are we going, Mako?" he wheezed between breaths. "I cannot remain out all night. There is a curfew."

"I doubt we will be that long," said Mako, who of course was not winded. "And if we are, you can simply tunnel in through the Academy's outer wall, little alchemist."

"It does not work like that. The walls are enchanted."

Mako shrugged. "I fail to see how this is my concern."

Ebon stopped and glared. "If we do anything questionable tonight, and it is noted that I returned to the Academy past curfew, will that not level suspicion at me? And might that not be traced back to you and the family?"

He was gratified to see Mako pause before turning back to him with an appraising look. "Clever, little Ebon. Very clever indeed. Have this vow, then: if we are out past your curfew, I will see you safe inside the Academy walls. Agreed?"

"Thank you," said Ebon.

So they kept on, until stars shone bright in the sky and the faint glow of the moons at last shone from the east. Though Ebon was lost, he would have guessed they were somewhere in the city's northeastern reaches. Mako turned down a final alley to a dead end. Ebon was about to ask if they had taken a wrong turn, when the bodyguard pointed to the cobblestones.

"Now. Use your magic. Open a way through the street into the sewers below."

Ebon looked all around. "Here? Where are we?"

Mako cuffed him on the side of the head. Ebon doubted the blow had all the strength held in those brawny arms, but it still stung terribly. "I have no time for questions. Do as I say."

Glaring (and trying not to look as though it were a pout), Ebon reached for his magic. He knelt, placing his hands to the street, and soon the stone rippled away from his fingers. It piled up in little ridges around the edge of a hole that grew ever deeper. At last he reached the open space beneath, and an uneven circle of darkness gaped up from below.

"Well enough done," Mako said, and then leapt inside.

Ebon swallowed before gingerly lowering himself down. He clung to the hole's edge with his fingertips, hoping his feet would reach the bottom. Of course they did not, and he was forced to let go. He landed with a splash and a curse, before gagging as the smell of the place wafted to him out of the darkness.

"I think you should have worn more perfume, little Ebon," Mako chuckled. "Now close the way behind us."

"It is too high," said Ebon. "I need to touch it."

Mako growled, and then Ebon felt himself hoisted up by the waist. He stretched for the sewer's ceiling and put forth his power again. He remembered the way he had done it in the library, and controlled the magic itself rather than the stone. Soon the hole was sealed, and though it looked a terrible job, one would have to look closely to notice. Mako dropped him without ceremony, and Ebon splashed noisily back into the sewer water.

"Come now," said Mako. "Only a little way farther."

He set off, the muck slurping and sucking at his shoes with every step. Ebon cursed inwardly as he realized Mako had known they would go this way, but had not warned Ebon or had him bring better footwear. The bodyguard's boots kept his feet clear of the mess and the stink, but Ebon could feel the filth soaking into his shoes and staining his skin. Again he tried not to retch, and forced his mind to other matters.

The sewer itself was a grander space than Ebon had thought it would be. It was a true tunnel, round on all sides rather than the walls meeting the floor in corners. Holes in the ceiling occasionally led to gutters above, and splashing moonslight seeped through to guide the way. There were no platforms for them to walk, as in Idrisian sewers, and the walls were cut stone instead of brick. It had an ancient and unattended feel, as though forebears had laid these tunnels here in days before history, and had then abandoned them, so that now no one on the Seat even remembered they existed.

Ebon did not have long to reflect, for soon Mako stopped him. It had been some time since they had seen a gutter-hole, and only the faintest glow of moon-slight allowed them to see. Mako pointed at the ceiling. "Here. Open the way for us."

"Where are we?" said Ebon.

"What have I told you about questions? Do what I brought you here to do."

Again Mako hoisted him up, and again Ebon put forth his power. When he broke through the stones into the space above, he saw the faint glow of candles. A smell burst forth into the sewer, pleasant and familiar: perfumes of all the nine lands, in a heady mix that set his mind at ease.

Then Mako shoved him up through the hole into the space above, and Ebon realized he was in a house of lovers. For a moment, panic seized him, thinking this had something to do with Adara. But he forced himself to remain calm. He might not know what part of the island they were on, but he was certain it was nowhere near Adara's blue door. However, there were two sleeping forms on the bed, and Ebon dared not come any closer to see them.

He did not have to. Mako followed him up through the hole, and in an instant the bodyguard crept towards the bed. Ebon wanted to follow, but he was deathly afraid; the fear was nameless, baseless, for he knew not what to expect, only something told him he would not like it.

Stop being a coward, he told himself. He pushed up into a crouch and crept behind Mako. One of the figures on the bed—a man—was snoring, face down, his rear end exposed. Beside him lay another, younger man, smooth chest glowing in candlelight. From the beauty of the younger man's face, Ebon guessed he was the lover.

From a pocket in his vest, Mako drew forth a piece of black cloth. This he drew over his face, covering him from nose to chin so that only his eyes could be seen. From another pocket he produced a small vial. This he unstopped, and tipped its contents into his other hand. Ebon could see it was a powder of burnt orange.

Mako threw the powder into the lover's face. The man's eyes flew open in shock, but at once he slumped back, senseless.

Quick as a shadow, Mako stole around to the other side of the bed and reached for his dagger. Ebon's heart raced as Mako snatched the other man's shoulder and threw him over so he lay on his back.

Matami started awake, blinking hard as he tried to get his bearings. Mako brought the pommel of his dagger crashing down, knocking Ebon's uncle back to unconsciousness.

Ebon clamped a hand over his own mouth to stifle a cry. Mako took no notice, hoisting Matami over his shoulder and carrying him to the hole in the floor. Only then did he look at Ebon.

"I will go down first. Shove him in after me. I will catch him and make sure he does not break his neck."

Mako vanished into the tunnel before Ebon could

nod. Terror seized his muscles, and he knew not what to do. He could only look at Matami's nude form, lying with his arm twisted beneath him.

"Ebon!" rasped Mako from below. "If I have to come back up there, I will cut off one of your ears!"

That made Ebon crawl forwards quickly. First he tried to push his uncle's shoulders, but that only made him lurch slightly to the side. Grimacing, Ebon stood, hooked his hands beneath the man's flabby stomach, and rolled him over. Matami's head sank into the hole, followed by the rest of his body. Ebon was afraid he would tumble down into the darkness. But the fall stopped abruptly as Mako caught him. Slowly the rest of Matami slithered into the darkness to join his head.

Ebon hesitated for half a moment, staring at the door of the room. He could slip outside, leave through the blue door and make his way into the streets of the city, finding his way back to the Academy. Someone might see him, but what of it? It must be better than following Mako into the dark and the stink, to who knew what end.

"Come, little goldbag." Mako's voice floated up to him out of the abyss. "If you wish to save your Academy and all your little friends, there is work still to be done."

Ebon warred with himself a moment longer. Then he sat on the edge of the hole and dropped down into the sewer.

THIRTY-FOUR

AFTER EBON HASTILY CLOSED THE HOLE BEHIND THEM, Mako took him down the sewer—but they did not go back the way they came. Instead Mako led him farther onwards, with Matami hoisted over his shoulder like a sack of flour.

More twists and turns passed, but Ebon had given up trying to determine where they were. Instead he stared at his feet while they walked, and wondered just what mess he had stepped into. When he had determined to prove Matami's guilt, and therefore the guilt of his father, he had not imagined kidnapping Matami himself. He only hoped it would not get worse—yet something inside him promised that it would.

They had been walking on a downwards slope for some time, but now the sewer opened, causing Ebon to stop in his tracks. The ceiling rose abruptly to form a chamber many paces high. The sewer's filthy, watery channel disappeared into the floor, and there was a sort of raised central platform in the center of the chamber. On that platform was an iron chair, and Ebon could see that it had been bolted to the stone floor with great spikes. Chains were nailed into the chair, and there Mako brought Matami, lashing him into place tightly so that he could not move. Around the edge of the chamber were other doorways, leading to more passageways like the one they had come from. All led upwards, and where they entered the room, their sewage flow vanished into a grate under the central platform, where Ebon could hear the sound of rushing water.

"It is the central drainage chamber," said Mako. "Or at least, it is one of them. There are several such across the Seat—though this is the most removed from the city above, and therefore the best in which to hide things."

Ebon tried to keep his voice steady. "And what are we hiding, Mako?"

The bodyguard looked at him but did not answer. Instead he went to one of the other doorways, where a torch rested in a sconce on the wall. This he took down and lit, before carrying it to the center of the room. He placed it on the floor less than a pace from Matami's bare feet. They were lashed to the chair like the rest of him and now twitched from the heat of the flame. Finally Matami woke with a jerk, eyes wild as they had been in the lover's room above. Immediately he winced at the lump blooming above his temple where Mako had struck him. He tried to raise his hand to the lump, but found that Mako had lashed his wrists behind the chair.

"Mako? What is this? What happened to—"

He stopped, eyes roving the chamber, and then down at his own naked form. His face grew a bit paler in the torchlight.

"How dare you?" he growled. "Do you have any idea of the punishment that awaits you for this? You shall be flayed, Mako. I will see the skin peeled from your—"

Mako wore leather gloves. Now he removed one, and with his bare hand, he slapped Matami across the face with an open palm. He did not put much force in the blow—Ebon could see that from where he stood— but Matami's head jerked back. It barely stopped him speaking. He looked past Mako to see Ebon lurking at the edge of the room.

"Ebon?" he sneered. "You are part of this, are you, boy? Know this, then: you are as good as dead. Your father will doubtless wish to draw the knife across your throat himself, but I fear he will not have the pleasure. I will—"

But while he spoke, Mako had sauntered around behind him and drawn his blade. He snatched one of Matami's fingers, and the man's words cut off abruptly.

Ebon watched as Mako slipped the point of the knife beneath Matami's fingernail and twisted.

Matami screamed, his voice echoing from every surface and rejoining itself in chorus, so it sounded as though an army were screeching in pain. Mako held the knife there for a moment before withdrawing it, and then stood to lean over Matami's shoulder from behind.

"Now then. We will hear no more vague, pointless threats from your fat, sniveling lips, will we?"

Matami only glared at him, pushing breath between gritted teeth. Mako waited a moment and then shrugged. He knelt and plunged the knife under a fingernail on the other hand. Fresh screams rang in Ebon's ears, and he turned his face away.

"You will not! You will not! I swear it!" Matami shrieked.

"Good," said Mako, withdrawing the blade at once. He stepped out from behind the chair and went to the torch. From his boot he produced another dagger—shorter and less ornate than the one at his belt—and left it leaning on the torch that still sputtered on the ground. Then he stepped just inside one of the passages that led out of the chamber. When he came back into view, he held another chair—this one smaller, and wooden, with thin leather upholstery on the seat. He placed it before Matami, facing the man, and then looked to Ebon. "You can find another chair there, if you wish, little Ebon. You need not remain on your feet."

Ebon only stared at him. "This is wrong, Mako. We cannot do this."

He expected Mako to sneer. Instead, sympathy filled the bodyguard's eyes. "Dear little Ebon," he said quietly. "Halab's love for you is well-placed. You have a good heart, and she treasures it. But Matami must be put to the question, or truth will never out."

"Then let him be put to the question," said Ebon. "But by the constables. The King's law. Else we are as guilty in the law's eyes as he is."

Mako cocked his head. "You know that is impossible, do you not? I am a bodyguard, Ebon, and I serve Halab. A bodyguard's first task is not to keep their master safe from a drawn dagger. Do you know what it is?"

Ebon shook his head.

"It is to keep their master from being near a drawn dagger in the first place. Now Halab is in a situation where more than daggers may be drawn against her, and Matami is at least part of the cause. To keep her safe, I must remove the danger before it grows. Do you want Halab to be safe?"

That made Ebon balk. How could he say no? Mako must have taken his silence for assent, because he turned back to Matami. The man had not stopped scowling, and now he sneered in Mako's face.

"What are you prattling about, Mako? I am no danger, and you know it."

"What have you been doing in the Academy, Matami? What have you been seeking?"

Matami's frown deepened. "You speak nonsense. I have had nothing to do with the Academy."

Mako sighed, shaking his head. He stood and circled behind Matami once more.

"I have done nothing!" Matami screamed. "I swear it! I do not know what you are talking about!"

As though he had not heard, Mako lifted a hand and plunged his dagger into the skin. He slid it sideways, across the palm just below the surface, so that Ebon could see the lump of it sliding along beneath the palm's lines. His stomach lurched, and he turned his eyes. Matami's cries were bestial, animal, horrifying things.

When Mako was done, he went to the torch, and to the dagger he had left sitting atop it. The blade was glowing red hot. He went back behind Matami, and pressed the blade to the incision where he had slipped the dagger inside. The air filled with the hiss of sizzling flesh, and Matami's screams turned into screeches and shrieks. Slowly, casually, Mako made his way back to the wooden chair and sat before Matami.

"If you waste my time, you will regret it," said Mako. "You sent a child named Lilith into the Academy's vaults to steal artifacts. Tell me why, and tell me how."

Matami had surrendered all pretense of bluster or threat. "I swear to you Mako, I have done nothing of the sort," he said, voice shaking. "I know nothing of the thefts in the Academy or the murders they say have been committed there."

Mako's hand flicked. The dagger flew from his fingers and plunged into Matami's ankle. Mako kicked out with a boot, skewing the hilt to the side and prying the flesh open. Matami wailed and tried to move his foot, but the chains held him in place.

"Claiming ignorance helps no one, Matami," said Mako, wiggling his foot casually about in a small circle, widening the gap in the man's flesh. Blood poured from the wound to pool on the ground. "Telling me you know nothing only makes me angry. Telling me you *do* know something might improve my mood."

He finally stopped kicking the dagger about and bent down to withdraw it. Again he fetched the red-hot knife from the torch and pressed it to the gaping hole. Matami screamed again, finally subsiding as Mako replaced the dagger in the fire.

"I will tell you anything," said Matami. "Anything, I swear it. But I cannot tell you what I do not know."

"Why do you persist, Matami?" Mako sadly drew out the name, the way Halab had done when she trounced him. "Why do you persist? Do you think you will get out of this by speaking your lies? I know you had something to do with the attack on the Seat."

Matami's eyes flashed, and he fell still.

Mako pointed with his dagger, making the man flinch. "There it is. What did you do?"

"Nothing," said Matami, shaking his head. "I would never participate in treason."

A moment's long silence stretched. Then Mako looked sadly over his shoulder. "Ebon, you will want to avert your eyes."

"Please!" screamed Matami. "Please, I beg of you, I knew—"

Ebon turned away quickly as Mako lunged. There was a wet, slurping, grinding noise, and Matami's throat broke as he screamed himself raw. Then came the hissing sound of cauterized flesh. When Ebon at last turned back, there was a gaping, bloody, charred hole where Matami's right eye had been.

"The attack on the Seat," said Mako. "Say on, or lose what sight you have left."

"I did not know it had anything to do with the attack. I promise you. I would never have done it. But I received messages, orders. I was the one who sent the parcel, the one the boy delivered."

Mako seized a foot and slashed his blade across the bottom. "Which boy? Say his name, wretch."

"Ebon!" screamed Matami, his raw throat breaking further. "Ebon! I sent the parcel for Ebon! The one he brought to our man. Then I gave him his orders in the castle."

"And those orders were?"

"There was someone—a guest of the High King. I

did not know it at the time, but it was that man Xain, the one who is now dean of the Academy. The High King had him well guarded. Our man was meant to take the place of one of those guards, to be ready when we made a move on Xain."

Mako cocked his head. "On Xain? Why him?"

Matami shook his head. "Shay's orders did not say." Mako shifted in his seat. Matami screamed and thrashed against his chains. *"I swear they did not say! I swear it! I was only doing what I was told.* Then I received a map, showing landing points on the Seat, though I knew not what they were for, and I sent that to our agent. It was stolen from him, but I did not tell Shay, for I feared his wrath if he knew. I am sorry. I am so sorry, I should have told him. Please, please let me live. I should have told him, I see that now."

For a moment all was still. Ebon released a breath he had not known he was holding. Mako reached out and put a hand on Matami's shoulder. The man burst into racking, sobbing breaths, his chest and shoulders heaving.

"Your error was not in keeping the truth from Shay," said Mako gently. "It was in following his orders in the first place. For they have endangered all our family, and that means they have endangered Halab."

Beneath the blood from his ruined eye that covered his face, Matami grew pale. "I thought the orders were from Halab. I never thought Shay would act without her blessing."

Mako leaned in to embrace the man, an arm wrapped about his neck. He spoke so softly that Ebon could scarcely hear him. "If Halab knew about your scheming, would I be here now?"

Then he rose and went behind Matami again. Matami thrashed against the chains. "No! No, please! I have told you everything!"

"Not everything," said Mako. "What have you and Shay planned with the artifacts you stole from the Academy?"

"Nothing!" cried Matami.

Snik

Mako sliced off one of Matami's fingers. The dagger cut through the flesh and tendons like butter, and the finger fell to the floor with a wet *splat.*

"Eeaaah!" screamed Matami. *"Nothing! Nothing, I swear it!"*

Snik

Splat

Snik

Splat

One by one Mako took them, and one by one they fell, until Matami's screams were no longer of denial, but only of wordless agony. Between each, Mako repeated the question. "What have you planned with the artifacts?" But it seemed he no longer even cared to hear the answer.

Ebon's pulse thundered in his ears, and his fists shook at his side. Mako finished with one hand and lifted the next. But then something snapped. Ebon ran forwards, reaching for his power, his eyes blazing with light.

"No!" he cried. "Mako, stop it! Stop it at—"

Faster than the eye could see, Mako drove a fist into Ebon's chest just below the ribs. Ebon's air left him in a rush, and he crashed to the stone floor, unable to breathe or move.

As though he had not even noticed Ebon's presence, Mako stepped behind Matami again. The man's screams rang out twice as loud. How could the whole Seat not hear him? Ebon felt sure that constables and Mystics and the High King's guard would all come rushing down at any moment. But no one came, and Mako kept cutting.

The last finger fell. Matami kept screaming while Mako stepped back around in front of him. But he did not sit in his wooden chair. Instead, he straddled Matami, one hand cupping the man's cheek affectionately, the other still holding the dagger.

When at last Matami's screams subsided, he tried to speak again. At first he almost choked on the spittle and phlegm that had filled his mouth. From his one remaining eye, he gazed up at Mako in pain and terror.

"I do not know," he whimpered. "I do not know what you are asking me. *Please*."

"I know you do not," said Mako softly. "No one lasts through all ten fingers."

Then he dragged his blade across Matami's throat.

Ebon had only just begun to get back his breath. Now he flipped over and crawled to the edge of the platform. He did not make it before he retched, and his vomit splashed out across his hands. He forced his head over the brim, watching his sick pour forth into the thick, disgusting filth that seeped through the iron grate below. The smell of it made him retch again, twice as hard, and then again, until it seemed there could be nothing left inside him, and he was only a hollow shell.

Finally he pushed himself back from the edge and rolled onto his back. Flecks of vomit speckled the front of his robes, but he could not force himself to care.

He refused to look at Mako. But from the corner of his eye he was aware of the bodyguard unchaining Matami's corpse from the chair, and then dragging it towards one of the other passageways. There he dropped the body over the edge. Ebon heard it splash, and then a wet slithering as it was carried away down the channel, which must not have been covered by an iron grate like the rest. Then Mako came to stand above Ebon. He looked down for a moment, eyes sad, and then finally lowered a hand.

"Come, little goldbag," he said quietly. "It is over now. The sewer will carry him to the Great Bay, and he will not suffer any more. But we ourselves are still alive, and must go on."

Ebon stared at the hand, wondering if Mako really

expected him to take it. But then he took stock of himself, and realized he was far too weak to stand on his own. So he raised his hand, and he and Mako clasped wrists, and the bodyguard lifted him to his feet.

"Let us go now. I will get you back to your Academy, and safely within the walls. But there is something we must tend to first, for killing requires drinking afterwards."

With an arm around Ebon's shoulder he set off. And Ebon hated to admit, even to himself, how heavily he leaned on the bodyguard, without whom he might have sunk into the filth and the muck to join Matami's corpse on its way to the Great Bay.

THIRTY-FIVE

THEY LEFT THE SEWERS, AND MAKO LED HIM TO A tavern. Ebon stopped at the door, for he wanted nothing less in the world than to spend time with the bodyguard. But Mako put a hand on his back and pushed him—not unkindly—into the tavern.

As they entered, Ebon thought of how much he and Mako must stink. But though they walked among tables filled with the tavern's patrons, no one raised an eyebrow. Ebon wondered if, were he able to smell anything beyond his own stench, he might find the room's reek even worse. Certainly the tavern seemed suspect;

Ebon thought it the sort of room where no one asked questions if they were not ready to die for the answer.

Mako led him to a back corner, settled him in a chair, and took a seat himself. Ebon noted that his own back was to the door, while Mako faced it. The bodyguard waved down a stout barmaid and ordered some spirit Ebon did not recognize. They waited for the drinks in silence. Mako studied him, seeming to expect something—a question, mayhap, or an accusation. But when none seemed forthcoming, the bodyguard finally spoke.

"I think that through the years, you have wondered exactly what I do for the family Drayden. Do you know now?"

Ebon shook his head. He had thought of nothing since the sewer, nothing but Matami's ruined face, and he did not care to guess just now.

Silence stretched until the barmaid returned. She did not bring them cups of wood, but two small glasses—something that seemed an uncommon luxury in a place such as this. In the glasses was an amber liquid that curled Ebon's nose when he took a sniff.

"Brandy," said Mako. "Fine stuff. Finer than they usually serve here, but they keep a stock on hand for me. I visit often. Drink."

Ebon took a sip and nearly choked. Mako downed his glass in a single gulp and then held it up towards the barmaid. She hastened to fetch another. When she came back it was not only with another glass, but with a bottle. After she had gone, Mako leaned forwards, and though no one was close enough to hear, still he dropped his voice to a whisper.

"It happens that in the course of ensuring the family's safety and prosperity, a life must sometimes be taken. When that is the case, I am the one who goes knocking on doors and tickling with my knife."

Ebon's stomach did a flip-flop. "You are an assassin," he whispered.

Mako did not flinch. "Just so. Have you never wondered how Drayden reaches such favorable trade agreements and holds such power across Underrealm when we hail from the land of Idris?"

"What does Idris have to do with it?"

"It is Idris." Mako waved a hand in the general direction of the door. "Our home, yes, and a piece of my heart will always dwell there. But it is a dry and barren landscape, and boasts few resources. Yet we have turned what little we are given into the greatest collection of wealth that the nine lands have ever seen."

"We have spices."

Mako snorted and leaned across the table once more. "Do you think we could sustain our empire on spices? No. There are not goods enough within the King's law to earn the wealth we have built. Do you think the family Yerrin could rival us, if they only sold those bolts of colored silk they pretend to fill their wagons with?"

Ebon almost asked him what they sold instead, but

then he remembered what Kalem and Theren had told him: it was Yerrin who commanded the magestone trade. He turned away, and tried another sip of the brandy. It was not so distasteful as the first had been.

"Through the centuries, when some fool has stood in the way of the family, someone like me has appeared in their home at night and removed the obstacle," said Mako. "Many suspect it. None may ever prove it. I, and those few who serve me, are especially skilled."

"I want nothing to do with this arrangement. I would never ask anyone to kill for me."

Mako smiled. "You protest far too late, Ebon. All your life you have lived fat on the riches I have brought you. Your father's coin made you everything you are; it paid for your tutors, who made you wise; it placed you in noble circles, where you learned compassion and virtue; and even now it pays your way at the Academy, where you have learned your spellcraft." Mako studied him carefully over the top of his glass. "Unless I am very mistaken, it even pays for the lover who sometimes warms your bed."

Ebon slapped his hand on the table. "But I did not *ask for it!* Who knows of this? Did Matami, and my father?" A horrible thought struck him. "Does Halab?"

"Halab is the only one whose orders I obey," Mako said softly.

It was like a slap in the face. The room seemed to spin around Ebon, though that might have been the brandy. Always Halab had struck him as his family's rare exception, one bright light in the family Drayden that he might look to, when all his lineage seemed shrouded in darkness. Yet now he learned that she was the source of the shadow itself.

"Are you hurt?" To Ebon's surprise, he did not hear sarcasm or malice in the bodyguard's tone. "I can see that you are. You trusted Halab, for she has always been kind to you. And you may not trust me after tonight, but know this: you were not wrong to believe in her. I serve Halab willingly, and even with love, for I also served her father. He was the dark of a cave's deepest shadow, and she is the sun. She may be the gentlest master of the family Drayden in decades. Mayhap centuries. The number of us—we assassins—has dwindled since she took power, but we do not complain, for we have never enjoyed our work."

"You seemed to enjoy it well enough tonight," spat Ebon, and drained his brandy in one savage pull. But it was a petulant thing to say, and he knew it, for he could hear some sense in Mako's words. And it spoke to a truth he had begun to suspect: that though Halab was as kind as he had always thought her, at her core there was inflexible steel. He had seen it when Matami had tried to have him and his friends beaten, when Halab herself had struck him down.

But he could not forgive Mako so easily. He had not asked to be dragged into the sewer to witness a murder. So he reached across the table and took Mako's glass, and drained what remained of his drink.

Then he held both glasses high, dangling them loosely between thumb and forefinger. "Do you mean to fill these again?"

He half hoped the bodyguard would answer in anger or accusation. Instead Mako silently refilled both glasses from the bottle. It was half empty now. "Halab is no wanton killer. Rather than order an obstacle removed by violence, she will exhaust every other possible solution. And no one is put to death unless she knows something dark about them, something the constables have never caught wind of, or at least have never proven. In the circles of power where we walk, such darkness can be found more often than not."

"And Matami?" said Ebon. "What was his darkness?"

The bodyguard lowered his gaze. "When you and I first began to suspect him, I wondered that same thing. So I had him watched, to see what might be seen. But I found nothing, and yet I was certain he had something to do with the attack upon the Seat. And so I brought my suspicions to Halab. With tears in her eyes she told me the truth—something she had kept hidden for many long years. Once, almost a decade ago, he took a man without leave."

Ebon froze in his seat. His fingers shook on the glass. "That cannot be. Halab knew of this? And did nothing?"

"He was her brother, Ebon," said Mako softly. "You can blame her if you wish. But you know better than most the bonds that can exist between siblings, no matter the circumstance. The man was well paid, and remains so to this day, tucked in a corner of Idris and supported by our coin. This Halab did in some token of repayment—and to pay for his silence, in hopes that Matami would be safe from the constables' blades."

To learn that Halab knew of such evil, and had then gone to such length to hide it . . . Ebon's heart twisted in sickness and impotent anger. Was the Drayden name so cursed that even she, his favorite, must deal in darkness and vile misdeeds?

But then his thought turned in another direction. Albi came to his mind, and then Momen. Could he have turned them over to constables, even after such a heinous crime? He wondered. And wondering, he turned his eyes back to his glass.

"So you see," said Mako, "she sat with that shame—his shame—for so long. But when she learned he and your father may have had something to do with the attack . . . it only proved to her that he was rotten through, and had suffered no momentary lapse in judgement."

"And so she ordered you to kill him."

"No," said Mako. "That was my choice. She will wonder where he has gone, of course. She may ask me, and if she does, I will not lie. But she may not. Sometimes it is easier that way—she knows, and I know, and we both stay silent in our knowledge."

"What of my father? Will you kill him, too?" Even

as he asked, Ebon wondered how he would feel if the answer was yes.

But Mako shook his head. "Your father is different. He is dearer to Halab. And he is *your* father. I have no wish to cause you grief, Ebon."

"Do you think that would grieve me? To see him killed?"

Mako stared into his glass. "No child loses their father without tears. Not even the worst child. Not even the worst father."

Ebon sighed, rubbing the heels of his palms into his eyes. "I am exhausted, Mako. None of your words have changed my mind. I want nothing to do with any of this. My father has cast me out of my inheritance. I cannot say I am glad for it, but I thought I was free of his legacy forever."

"And you can be, if you wish. Yet still I must do my duty. And that means protecting Halab. Just now, it seems I am protecting her from Shay himself. Can you withhold your hand from that cause?"

For that, Ebon had no easy answer.

"As I thought. Now, we must find proof of Shay's involvement in the attack upon the Seat. And to do that, we must find the murderer in the Academy."

"How can we do that now? It seems the only one who knew anything was Matami, and he is now in the Great Bay."

"Matami knew nothing. Shay was too smart for that. He used Matami for messages, small tasks, but kept the more important ones from him. He must be using someone else—someone like your cousin, the mindmage—for the murders. He uses many hands, and none of them know the parts the others play, so that none may reveal the whole scheme. Indeed, he was foolish to let Matami know where his orders came from. But your uncle was foolish, and mayhap would not have otherwise obeyed."

"Then we are no closer to catching the murderer." Again Ebon rubbed at his eyes. "You have done nothing to make me less tired."

"That is the brandy. You must have patience. We will discover the truth. We have done much already, whether you think so or not. And you have proven your mettle, far beyond what could have been expected." Ebon scowled, but Mako raised his hands. "I speak the truth. And this, too, is true: never will I make you part of something like that again. I only thought it was time you knew the truth so that you could face it with both eyes open. Can you forgive me?"

Ebon held his scowl, but felt some of the fire die in his heart. "It is a bit early to speak of forgiveness," he muttered. "But mayhap I can understand you."

Mako smiled, and Ebon thought he looked genuinely pleased. "Good. Then let us get you back to your Academy. Curfew, I am afraid, is a long-forgotten memory."

THIRTY-SIX

THE NEXT MORNING, THEREN AND KALEM FOUND Ebon in the dining hall. Kalem was glad to see him safely returned. It took Ebon a moment to notice Theren—he had forgotten she had gone with Lilith. As she told him of Lilith's recovery, he gave a weak smile.

"What is wrong, Ebon?" said Kalem. "What happened last night?"

"Last night? What about last night?" said Theren.

Ebon shook his head. "I cannot speak of it now. Not here, at least."

They tried to press him at first, but he waved them

off, and at last they left him alone. But as he ate his breakfast, he decided to confess that afternoon in the library. He owed them that much, at least. He would not deceive his friends again.

His morning class was torturous. Now that he had learned counter-magic, Perrin wished for him to focus on the other spells. Mists seemed simplest, and he did not have to interact with any other students, or with Perrin herself. So he sat there, spinning his mists, trying to push them farther and farther from his skin. But in fact he found his spell weaker than the last time he had practiced. It was as though he had forgotten a piece of his magic—or mayhap it was only the distraction of the night before, the way he could not stop hearing Matami's screams.

THOOM

An explosion rocked the classroom, and Ebon fell to the floor in terror. Then he realized the blast had not come from within the classroom, but from beyond the door.

He scrambled to his feet and fled the room, a dozen other students on his heels despite Perrin's shouted orders to stay. Other classes joined them in the hall, running for the entryway where the explosion had come from. Ebon wondered what they were all doing. Hearing a blast or scream in the Academy had become almost commonplace by now. Surely they all knew to run, to flee the other way. Why, then, was he racing towards the sound? Why were the others?

Then he realized—he was going to help. He was sick of the attacks, sick of the wanton death that had plagued the school for months. If the murderer was there, and wanted to strike again, let them try. Ebon was not alone: an army of students stood behind him.

Together they flooded into the front hall, and dozens of eyes blazed with magelight as students reached for their spells.

But no one stood in the hallway. There were only the forms of students and instructors, lying on the floor as they twisted and moaned in pain. They all pointed outwards from the room's center, as though a blast had thrown them towards its edges. But where the blast had come from, there was no sign, for no one was burned or singed.

Near the front, one seemed worse off than the rest—and Ebon recognized the creaking old form of Cratchett, the instructor who held the front door whenever Mellie slept.

"Help him!" said Ebon, running forwards to follow his own advice. Half a dozen others rushed forwards to do the same. The rest fanned out, helping students to their feet. The fallen students were older, all in later-year classes. He saw Nella, eyes lolling in her head as she tried to gather her bearings, and Isra, groaning on all fours. They and their classmates fought to regain their feet, helped up by the younger students who had come flooding out from the Academy.

Ebon reached Cratchett and tried to help the old

man up. But Cratchett cried out in pain the moment they tried to move him, and screamed louder when they tried again. He was old; Ebon guessed his bones were brittle, and some might have broken when he fell.

The old man's eyes fixed on his, and he tried to speak. "She . . . tried to leave," he croaked. "But when I stopped her—"

His eyes bulged in their sockets, and his body jerked like a marionette's. Cratchett flew into the air, arms twisting horribly. But he uttered no sound—even when his bones began to snap, even when an unseen hand clamped hard on his neck, crushing it to a pulp. Blood spattered Ebon's cheeks, making him flinch. The corpse tumbled back to the ground amid the students' screams.

"Back!" cried a commanding voice. "Back into the citadel!"

Ebon turned and groaned. It was Dean Forredar, ushering the students out of the front room and back into the Academy's hallways. He helped the last few of the older students to their feet one by one.

That half-heard voice screamed in the back of Ebon's mind again, warning him of something. He looked at the students who had been struck in the attack. He recognized them all—not their names, or their faces, but one place he had seen them all before. The Goldbag Society Lilith had started. Not a student present now had been absent from that assembly.

Yet someone *was* missing.

But then Xain saw him, and Ebon's attention was drawn back to the present. The dean's eyes blazed with fury, and he pushed through the teeming crowd towards Ebon.

"Drayden! Standing in the midst of another attack? This time—"

But then Perrin was there, stepping up by Xain's elbow. "I was teaching my class when we heard the explosion, Dean. Ebon was at his desk."

"Ebon!" He turned to see Kalem and Theren running out of the hallways towards him. He gave them each a swift embrace, but then turned his attention back to Xain, who still looked darkly upon him.

"What happened?" said Perrin, seizing one of the students who had regained her feet. "Who did this?"

"I do not know," she said, shaking her head. "Our instructor was bringing us for some excursion out upon the Seat."

"Upon the Seat?" said Perrin. "That is not done."

The girl frowned. "It seemed odd to me. But she was our instructor. So we made for the front hall, but Cratchett tried to stop us. He and one of the students began to argue, but then—" She shook her head. "I barely saw what happened."

"You say Cratchett argued with a student?" said Ebon. "Who?"

The girl stared vacantly, as though searching for a long-distant memory, instead of something that had happened only moments ago. "I . . . I cannot remember," she murmured, and then eyed them all in terror. "Why can I not remember?"

But Ebon scarcely heard her. For the whisper in his mind now screamed, its words ringing with clarity for the first time. He stepped back, hoping not to be noticed, and took the sleeves of Theren and Kalem, drawing them close as they turned.

"The front door," he whispered. "It is open."

"What of it?" said Theren.

"The murderer escaped."

Kalem looked uneasy. "You cannot know that. They could have remained inside."

"I know it," said Ebon. "Because I know who it was."

Theren jerked in surprise. "You do? Who?"

"In a moment. We must go after them."

Kalem groaned. "Ebon . . ."

"They are not watching us. Go . . . *now.*"

He ran for the door, and his friends came behind him. No one saw them, no one shouted, and then they were in the city, fleeing through snow to the east of the Seat.

"We will most likely be expelled now," Kalem panted at Ebon's side. "So will you please tell me, Ebon, what we are doing?"

"All this time, we have been searching for the power behind Lilith. We wondered who held her under mindwyrd—and she *was* under mindwyrd, but other times, she was not, though we believed that she was."

"What?" said Theren. "Your words are senseless. Were you struck in the head?"

"A moment."

Ebon stopped at the corner of a building and looked back, to where he could just see the Academy entrance many streets away. But no one had pursued them. The street was empty, and the doorway remained clear.

"They are not coming after us," he said. "That is good. I think. Come."

And Ebon ran on. They followed him, east through the streets, through alleys and busy marketplaces. At last he skidded to a stop, doubled over with his hands on his knees, breathing hard.

"Where are we?" said Theren. "Why have you stopped here?"

"To rest. But only for a moment," said Ebon. "We will not want to be winded when we round the next corner."

Theren stood before him, hands at her hips. "Enough, Ebon. What is going on?"

He grimaced. "We have no time."

She gave him a harsh look. "After we spent weeks pursuing Lilith, only to falsely accuse her, I think this time I would rather be sure before I follow you blindly."

Ebon gave a frustrated growl. "Very well. Last night, Mako took me out into the city. He said he needed my help, for he suspected my uncle Matami had a hand in Lilith's deeds. But Matami knew nothing of Lilith."

"Are you certain?" said Kalem. "What if he lied?"

"He did not," said Ebon, his voice flat. "Mako put him to the question, and in the end, he slit his throat."

Theren's face hardened. Kalem gasped and put a hand on the wall beside him to steady himself. But Ebon only shook his head.

"I know your horror," he said. "Know that I did not wish it, and tried to stop him. I will live with what I saw for the rest of my days. But that is a matter for another time. Mako thought Matami was ignorant of Lilith because my father, Shay, kept the truth from him. But Shay is not guilty of this—it was another student at the Academy."

"How?" said Theren. "We know Lilith was under mindwyrd, and so were several others. What student could have had access to magestones—except for Lilith and Oren themselves, who we know were not the culprits?"

"Not magestones. Kekhit's amulet. The book said it gave her the power to cast darkfire *without* magestones. What if that was not all it did—what if it acted as magestones for any wizard, not just a firemage?"

Theren's eyes widened. "A mindmage. They would have mindwyrd, with no need to consume the stones, and none of the evils such consumption would bring upon them."

"And their eyes would not glow when casting their

spells," Ebon said softly. "For that, too, was the power of Kekhit. Do you remember what the book said? She could hide the glow in her eyes when she cast her spells. And the logbook said that the amulet's powers were hers. The wizard could have been right before our eyes, and we would never have known."

That sent them reeling. Theren paced, and then balled a fist to slam it into the home's wall. A smattering of snow slid from the roof onto their heads.

"But who?" said Kalem. "You said you knew who it was."

"Adara said the lovers have seen a girl skulking about the Seat," said Ebon. "And only one girl was there during every attack."

Theren rounded on him. "Nella. Lilith's so-called friend."

Ebon shook his head. "No. Her friendship is true. She could have done it—killing Credell after trying to breach the vaults, and then Oren once he realized what was going on. But Vali, too, was killed. And that was not part of stealing the artifacts from the vaults. That was because he was Astrea's friend, and a goldbag."

"Astrea's friend?" Kalem's eyes went wide. "Sky above. Isra."

"Yes," said Ebon. "Isra. She was there every time. I thought it odd that every death was so horrifying for Astrea, and that she was there for each of them. But she was only there because Isra brought her, so that she would have an excuse for being present."

"The conniving sow," Theren whispered. "I will kill her."

"No," said Ebon. "We must capture her and deliver her to the King's justice."

"She deserves death."

Ebon lifted his chin, heart blazing with fury. "And she will find it—by the King's law."

Kalem stepped between them to interrupt. "But Ebon, I still do not understand. Why are we here, and not in the Academy trying to find her? We should help."

"Because she is not in the Academy. I was a fool, and believed what Xain wanted me to. Dasko was not helping Xain move into his new home. He was helping Xain move artifacts out of the Academy."

Kalem gawked. "Into his house?"

"Where no doubt he has all manner of magical defenses," said Ebon. "They hoped to keep them safe, mayhap thinking the thief would not know where they had been moved. But do you remember what Adara told us, about the student who had been seen lurking about the city? I think that was Isra. If I am right, she makes for Xain's house even now, to take as many artifacts as she can lay her hands on."

"That is a mighty leap of thought," said Theren.

Ebon spread his hands. "Once I realized it had to be her, I knew there must be a reason for her outburst in the front hall. She was leaving the Academy because she knew the artifacts she desired were no longer there."

"But if you are right, why did we not tell the others?" said Kalem. "The instructors, the faculty? They should be here now to help us defeat her."

"Do you think Xain would have believed me?" said Ebon, scowling. "Who knows how much time we would have wasted trying to convince him, and then Isra would have escaped. And too many have suffered because of my mistakes already. I will not drag them along with me now."

Mako's voice came from the sky. "Ebon has always been such a noble boy." Then he dropped from the roof above them, landing catlike in the street.

In an instant Theren had raised her hands, and her eyes blazed with magelight. "Who are you?"

Ebon put a hand on her arm. "This is Mako. He works for my family. How did you know to find us here?"

Mako shrugged. "I did not. I was watching the home of the Academy's new dean when I saw a girl arrive. She slew the guards as fast as blinking and entered the house, but I could not follow her, for she erected a barrier of spells. I meant to fetch you from the Academy, and yet here I find you ready to serve."

"You think we will serve you?" said Theren. "I do not know you, save that Ebon tells us he saw you murder a man last night."

Ebon quailed as Mako gave him a withering glare. "Ebon is more flap-lipped than might be wished, it seems."

"There is no time for this," said Ebon. "Even now

Isra is in Xain's home, mayhap stealing artifacts as we speak. We must stop her. Mako, will you help us?"

The bodyguard shrugged. "Why not? I had nothing else to do today."

"Thank you," Ebon said earnestly. "Now come."

He stole around the corner, and the others followed. There was Xain's house—and there, as Mako had said, were the bodies of the guards Isra had slain. It had been the Mystics and High King's guard on the street, and in death they embraced one another in pairs, each with a sword buried in the other's belly. Kalem's face went Elf-white as he beheld them.

"Mindwyrd," said Ebon. "She must have made them kill each other. Mako, do not let her speak to you, or she will—"

"I know mindwyrd, boy," Mako snarled. "See to your own safety, and I will see to mine."

They reached the door. Theren rolled her shoulders. "I feel her spell. She put a barrier upon the door to keep it shut."

"Then we must find another way in," said Kalem. "If she has the amulet, her magic is backed by the strength of magestones. You cannot hope to break the enchantment."

Theren's eyes glowed. "We shall see. I think she made this barrier in haste."

She held forth a hand, reaching out with her power. Ebon saw a sort of shimmering in the air before the door, like waves of heat escaping a fire. But nothing else happened, and after a long moment, Ebon felt his sense of urgency growing.

"Theren," he muttered. "There must be a back door."

"Who is to say she did not bar it as well?" said Theren through gritted teeth. "Besides, I am almost through."

"You said she cast this spell in haste," growled Mako.

"Ebon, silence your hound."

To Ebon's immense relief, Mako actually smiled at that.

Then there was a quiet *snap,* and the glow faded from Theren's eyes.

"It is done," she said, voice weak. She cleared her throat and spoke with more force. "But it was powerful indeed. The amulet is nothing to be trifled with. Take care within."

Ebon looked at Kalem and Theren, and then at Mako. The bodyguard gave a mocking smile followed by a bow, and waved his hand towards the door. "I would not presume, little lord. After you."

"You are too kind," said Ebon, trying to sound braver than he felt. He put his hand on the doorknob and turned it. With a soft *click,* the door swung open into darkness.

THIRTY-SEVEN

BEYOND THE FRONT DOOR WAS A MASSIVE ENTRYWAY
that stretched nearly to the back of the house, a great
hall where tables could be set to hold feasts of mod-
erate size. To the left a staircase led up to the second
floor, while doors split off from the main hall to either side—two to the left, and two to the right. The
floor was polished wood, while the walls were plaster
between bare, raw beams that held the ceiling seven
paces high. Over the wood floor were laid two plush
carpets of Feldemarian make, if Ebon guessed right.
Broad windows were placed near the ceiling and in

carefully-laid alcoves, and if their shutters had not been drawn, they would doubtless have lit the hall with the morning's warm glow. Ebon had a brief thought that if he were not so terrified, the place would have seemed warm and welcoming.

But terrified he was, and in his mind every shadow held menace. All candles and lanterns had been snuffed out, and with the windows blinded, the place was filled with darkness. They studied their surroundings in silence, Ebon trying to guess where the artifacts might be hidden.

"It is a large building," said Mako, "and we must find her quickly. Split up."

"What?" Kalem said. "No. I will not. I do not want to be here in the first place, and certainly I do not wish to wander on my own, searching for a madwoman!"

"Do you wish to stop her, or not?" growled Mako.

"Not as much as I wish to survive!"

Ebon put a calming hand on his shoulder and met Mako's eyes. "It is folly for any of us to leave Theren. Only she can hope to defend us against Isra's magic."

"I can look after myself," said Mako, sneering. "But if you three are frightened, then stay together. Look for her upstairs, and I will search this floor. If she should kill you, try to scream as loud as you may. That way I shall know I am on my own."

"Thank you for your concern," spat Theren.

Mako nodded and ducked into the first room, dagger drawn and held by his side.

Theren led them up the stairs. Ebon whispered silent thanks with every step, for not one creaked beneath his foot. On the second floor they found another hall like the one below, but narrower, with many doors, and then a pair of double doors at one end of the hallway. Ebon guessed that led to Xain's bedchamber.

"Start there," whispered Ebon, pointing. Theren nodded and sneaked in that direction.

"How are we supposed to fight her if she has mindwyrd?" asked Kalem.

"If you stay out of her sight, she will not be able to cast it," said Theren. "All mindmagic requires line of sight."

"That holds true for regular mentalists," said Kalem. "How can you know it is the same for a wizard with the power of magestones?"

Theren was silent for far, far too long a moment before she muttered, "It is an educated guess."

They opened the master bedroom's wide doors with nary a creak. Ebon tensed, ready to leap upon Isra if she was within. But he saw nothing—only a bed, more modest than he would have imagined, and two simple bureaus along the walls. A door tucked into the room's corner spoke of a large closet, while another door at the other end led to a balcony. Ebon stole across to look outside. But the balcony was empty, and he stepped back in with a sigh.

"Let us go to the next room," he said.

Then the closet door opened, and Isra emerged into view.

For a moment, they all froze in shock. Then Ebon shouted, Kalem shrieked, and Theren's eyes glowed as she struck Isra in the chest with her magic. Isra flew back through the open closet door, lank hair and dark robes fluttering about her. Ebon jumped across the bed and rolled off the other end to the floor, while Kalem ran from the room like a rat on fire. Isra reemerged a moment later, and Theren's eyes blazed as she struggled to contain the girl's magic.

Ebon sprang up and ran for the door, snatching Theren's wrist as he passed. "She has the amulet! You cannot best her!" he cried.

Theren struggled for a moment, but then relented, and made to run with him. But Isra's spell struck her, flinging her through another door into an adjoining room. Ebon went to follow, but the wall before him crumpled as Isra battered it, and he turned tail to flee the other way. He ducked into the first door he saw, slamming it shut behind him and praying Isra had not seen which way he went.

He found himself in a small antechamber, with a large wooden chest, a single bureau, and two couches of muted green and blue. He threw himself under one of the couches—or started to, but recoiled as he heard a yelp.

There, his face pressed to the floor, was Xain's son, Erin. The poor child was terrified, his eyes wide and his fingers scrabbling at the wooden floor in hopes of escape. He opened his mouth to scream, but Ebon clapped a hand across it.

"Shhh! Shush, shush," he murmured. "I mean you no harm. I am not the one who attacked your home, I am . . ." He gulped at the lie. "I am a friend of your father's. You must hide yourself."

Erin looked as though he would not scream, so Ebon carefully removed his hand. "Where can I hide?" he whimpered.

Ebon looked around the room. The couch would not hide the boy from even a cursory search, but the bureau might do the trick. "There," said Ebon, pointing. "Here, come quickly."

He helped Erin to his feet, then opened the bureau and gave his hand to help the boy in. But no sooner had he shut the bureau than he heard the latch click, and the room's door began to swing open. In a panic, he threw himself to the ground and slid beneath the couch, clamping a hand over his mouth to muffle his breathing.

The door's wooden timbers swung past, revealing simple brown leather shoes beneath black robes. The shoes took one careful step into the room, and then another. The door swung shut silently, trapping them in the room together.

"Ebon?" whispered Kalem.

A rush of air escaped him, and he pressed his face against the wood floor. "I am here, Kalem."

"Thank the sky," Kalem hissed. Ebon slid out, and Kalem helped him to his feet. "I think I heard her make for the stairs, so I came to find you and Theren."

"We are not the only ones here." Ebon stole across to the bureau and cracked open the door. "Erin. Listen carefully. You must remain here. Do not open this door for anyone, not even me. If you stay where you are, you will be safe. Do you understand?"

"Yes," came Erin's terrified whisper.

"If I open the door myself, you will know you are safe," said Ebon. "But if you hear me calling out for you, asking where you are, then I am not myself, and you must not listen to me. Tell me you will not listen."

"I will not."

"Good lad." Ebon swung the bureau door shut again. To Kalem's questioning look, he whispered, "Xain's son."

"Sky above," said Kalem, eyeing the bureau in horror.

"He will be fine if he remains," said Ebon. "Come. If Isra has gone downstairs, she may be trying to escape."

They cracked the door and peered out. The hall appeared to be empty, and so they gingerly stepped into it. But as they did, the door beside the stairs creaked open, and they froze—until Theren stepped out from the room, and they both sighed with relief.

"Thank the sky," said Kalem. "Theren, have you seen her? She—"

Theren's eyes blazed with light, and she struck at them with her magic. A spell blasted them through the air, slamming them both into the doors of the master bedroom, which buckled under their weight. They landed hard on the floor.

"What is she—" Kalem groaned.

"Mindwyrd," said Ebon, gasping as he fought for his feet. He seized Kalem's elbow and dragged him up. Another spell narrowly missed them, shattering a piece of one of the doors and sending wooden splinters through the air. They dove beneath the bed, but then it flipped up, crashing into the opposite wall. Ebon rose, only to have Theren lift him up, her eyes blazing as she pressed him against the wall.

Kalem had gained his feet. He hesitated for a long moment, unsure of what to do, before leaping towards Theren with a cry. She raised her other hand, throwing him against a dresser, where he collapsed. Ebon looked down at her in terror, gasping for breath as he felt invisible fingers closing around his throat.

"Where is the boy?" she said, her voice a flat monotone. "Xain's son?"

"Theren," he wheezed. "Theren, she is controlling you. Fight her!"

She did not so much as blink. But then Mako stepped out of the hallway behind her, and his dagger's pommel came crashing down on the back of her head.

The magic holding Ebon vanished, and he fell to the ground. At once he leapt to his feet and ran to Theren, rolling her onto her back. He felt for her heartbeat—it was there, and strong, and he could see the rise and fall of her chest.

"Come now, Ebon," said Mako, grinning. "You did not think I would kill one of your little friends, did you?"

Kalem joined them. "She has left this floor. Mayhap she fled. We might think of doing the same."

"No," said Mako. "I do not think she would leave without the artifacts. I saw a basement entry on the ground floor. I meant to investigate, but heard the fighting here."

"Then let us go there," said Ebon. "If she escapes with the artifacts, there is no telling what havoc she could unleash."

Mako motioned towards the steps. "Once more I defer to your courage."

Ebon glared at him and, after a final glance at Theren to make sure she was well, he made for the stairs.

THIRTY-EIGHT

On the ground floor, Mako took them to the door leading to the basement steps. Ebon paused on the threshold and drew a deep breath. There were lanterns below, so that the darkness was not complete. But he could feel the empty space pulling at him, siphoning his courage like an insatiable void.

"How can we beat her?" Kalem whispered. "She has the amulet, Ebon. Only Theren could have hoped to stop her, and we no longer have her. We should flee."

"What is this amulet?" said Mako. "How does it work?"

"You know magestones," said Ebon. "The amulet gives her strength as though she had eaten them. And she may cast her spells without her eyes glowing, so that we will have little warning."

Mako frowned. "That will make her harder to kill."

Ebon held his gaze. "There will be no killing. She will be thrown before the King's justice."

"She is dangerous."

"So are you. Do you deserve death?"

Mako grinned. "Undoubtedly. But who is strong enough to deliver it?"

"Isra, if you underestimate her," said Kalem.

"That I very much doubt."

"Enough," said Ebon. He set his foot upon the first step leading down. After that, it was easier to take the next, and then the one after that. The stair only turned once, but as he rounded that corner, Ebon felt nothing in his life had ever been so hard as moving his foot. Had Kalem and Mako not been beside him, he would surely have wept like a child and fled. Instead, he forced himself to keep going.

At the base of the stairs was a wooden doorway with no knob or latch. Mako waved them back, pressing his ear to the wood. He listened, frowning.

"I can hear her. But she is far away. If I had to guess, I would say there is another hallway like the ones above. I think she is at the other end."

"How can we possibly defeat her?" said Kalem. "She will certainly see us coming."

"The hinges look well-oiled, as they are in the rest of the house," said Mako. "And the rooms are all interconnected. If we can move silently into the hallway, I think we can steal into the first rooms to the side and then get closer without attracting her attention. The two of you will go to the left, and I will go to the right. Once you reach the other end of the basement, find some way to distract her. When you do, I will—"

Ebon gave him a sharp look.

Mako grimaced. "I will *subdue* her."

"Good," said Ebon. "In that case, waiting does us no favors."

He opened the door. Just as Mako had guessed, it swung open in silence. They slipped through and ducked left, where an open doorway waited. Ebon glanced down the hall before they entered and saw Isra at the other end, kneeling before a huge iron door set into the wall. He could see the glow of her eyes, which she had not bothered to hide as she cast some spell—or, he guessed, worked to dispel some enchantment that held the door closed. But, too, he could see another glow coming from her—black and centered around her neck. It was the amulet, he realized, lending her the power of magestones.

Then they were in the room, and Isra was gone from view. On the other side of the hallway, Mako vanished behind the opposite door. Ebon and Kalem found themselves in a small storage room, with barrels and sacks stacked against the walls. Sure enough, a door led to another room closer to Isra, and then to another that was just beside her. Ebon stooped behind a barrel, with Kalem just behind. Together, they leaned over slightly to peer out.

Isra was still focused on the door, her hands working as she focused on breaking its enchantments. And then, just as Ebon was about to bob out of sight, he heard a *snap* as the enchantment was broken. A savage grin crossed her features. She stood, reached out with a spell once more, and used her magic to drag the door open. Ebon could only catch a glimpse inside, where many crates were stacked against one of the walls—the same sort of crates he had seen in the cart, the day they found Dasko loading them into the house.

From the doorway, Isra's eyes glowed as she raised a hand. She swiped through the air, and Ebon heard a sharp *crack* as every crate in the vault shattered. There came many crashes and tinkling as countless artifacts scattered across the ground.

"It is time," said Ebon.

"How are we supposed to stop her?" said Kalem.

"We are not. We are only supposed to distract her."

"How are we supposed to do *that?*"

Ebon shrugged and whispered, "When you do not know what to do, do what you know."

Then he leapt out from behind the barrel, waving his hands in the air and screaming wordlessly.

Kalem was a half-second behind him, shouting incoherent gibberish. Isra spun at once, eyes flashing as she struck with magic. Ebon only just dove out of the way in time. A barrel splintered where he had been standing. She turned to Kalem next, but he got behind one of the basement's stone pillars. Its edge shattered under Isra's spell.

"Thrice-damned little goldshitters!" roared Isra. "Can you not leave well enough alone?"

"I do not know that anything is well enough as it is," Ebon called out from his hiding place. "You have left too many corpses for that."

"*I* have left corpses?" Isra gave a horrible laugh as she stalked forwards. "How many corpses did the goldbags leave upon the Seat? And who among you faced the King's justice?"

She was far too close now, and Kalem jumped up to run. But she seized him with her power and hoisted him into the air. His eyes bugged out in terror—but she did not kill him. Instead her smile turned cruel, and power reverberated in her voice.

"Kill your goldshitting friend," she hissed.

She dropped him. At once, Kalem turned, his eyes glazed, and stumped towards Ebon's hiding place. Ebon was forced to run through one storeroom and into the next. A spell from Isra shattered the wall where his head had been just a moment ago.

"Kalem!" he cried. "Kalem, stop! You can resist her!"

Isra's voice was cruel. "You know nothing of the power of mindwyrd. Now the two of you may reenact the war your kin wage across Underrealm even now."

As if to prove her words, Kalem reached for a hammer that lay on a nearby barrel. His eyes glowed, and in his hands it twisted to a spiked orb of wood and metal. He flung this at Ebon as hard as he could, and then did the same with a metal spike. Ebon ducked behind a pillar. He grimaced at the sound of Kalem's footsteps just around the side.

"Kalem, forgive me."

He stepped out and seized Kalem's arm, even as the boy reached for Ebon with glowing eyes. He dragged Kalem in by the wrist, clenched his other hand, and drove the fist into the boy's chin. Kalem collapsed like a sack of beans, out cold before he struck the stone floor.

Before the vault, Isra snarled. "Do you think that will save you? It only means I will have you kill yoursel—"

Mako appeared behind her, silent as a shadow. He held his dagger high, and in his eyes was a killing light. He stepped towards her. But Ebon saw him, and his eyes widened. Isra saw it, and she turned at the last second. The dagger, which should have severed her spine, struck her shoulder instead, and she cried out in pain.

Ebon ran forwards to help, for Isra's eyes glowed as she looked up at the bodyguard. She lifted a hand—but nothing happened. For a heartbeat that image froze itself into Ebon's mind: Isra striking with magic, and Mako standing there unaffected.

Mako grinned as he reached down, seizing the front of her robes and dragging her up. Again he raised the dagger, already slick with her blood.

But then, in his mind's eye, Ebon saw Matami. He saw the ruined eye and the severed fingers. He saw old Cratchett, and Oren and Vali and poor, poor Credell, all of them the same—lifeless eyes staring at nothing. And he saw Cyrus, the old dean's flesh turning to stone beneath Ebon's fingers before he plunged screaming into the Great Bay.

"No!" he cried, and shoved Mako with all of his might.

The bodyguard hardly stumbled. His eyes flashed, and he struck Ebon a backhanded blow that sent him crashing to the ground.

But it was just long enough of a pause for Isra to recover. She seized a barrel and cast it through the air. It struck Mako hard, sending him flying into the next room. Ebon lay there, half-stunned, as Isra scrambled to her feet and dove into the vault. Hardly looking at what she was doing, she fell to her knees and scraped at the floor with both hands. She rose again with two armfuls of artifacts and broke into a run for the door.

"No," Ebon gasped. He struggled to stand, unable to manage it by the time she reached him. At the last moment he lunged, scrabbling to seize her arm, her robes, anything to hold her back. He missed her robes, but his fingers closed around a fine chain of silver, and as she ran it snapped off in his hand.

Ebon fell to the floor hard, grunting from the impact. But as he rolled over, he looked into his hand to see Kekhit's amulet, glinting up at him as though giving him a secretive wink. Isra reached the basement's far end, stepped through the door, and vanished up the stairs.

Mako had recovered, though his clothes were torn and ripped, and there was an ugly gash on his forehead. He made for the staircase, but he stopped for just a moment, looming over Ebon with a sneer twisting his lips. "You are a greater fool than I realized," he growled. "She will kill again. When she does, remember that those deaths are upon your head."

Then he turned and was gone.

Ebon groaned as he gained his feet. He stumbled over to Kalem, who was shaking his head as he lay on the floor. Ebon reached down a hand for the boy, pulling him up. Kalem blinked as he looked around.

"What happened? Where is Isra?"

"She caught you in her mindwyrd," said Ebon. "And now she has escaped with many artifacts. Come. We must try to catch her, if we can."

They ran up the stairs together, taking the steps two at a time, and then burst into the entry hall—and there they stopped. Mako was nowhere to be seen; but Isra stood just inside the front door. Over one shoulder she held a satchel, clanking with what were surely the artifacts. Her other arm circled Erin's neck. The poor boy's eyes were wide and frightened, and his legs shook so badly he looked as though he might topple at any moment.

"Erin, stay calm," said Ebon. "You will be all right."

"You make idle promises, goldshitter," Isra hissed. "You cannot promise the boy will emerge unscathed when you cannot even protect yourself."

Her eyes lit with magelight. Ebon braced himself, and Kalem raised his hands as though to ward off the spell. But then there was a loud *SNAP* upon the air, and Ebon heard a faltering step behind him. He turned to see Theren halfway up the staircase, leaning heavily on the bannister, her eyes glowing brighter than the moons. Her hand swung forth, trying to blast Isra. But Isra countered the spell with a strangled cry.

"Why do you throw your lot in with these pampered wretches?" she said. "They are the reason folk like you and I suffer."

Theren only glared. "The only thing I suffer from at present is the grating, hideous sound of your voice."

She blasted Isra with a spell that sent the girl staggering back. But she kept her grip on Erin's neck, and the boy yelped as he was dragged. With a frustrated shout, Isra fled through the front door and threw it shut behind her. Theren leapt down the final few steps, and Ebon made ready to run through the front door alongside her. But Theren stumbled when she reached the floor and fell to all fours on the ground.

"Theren!" cried Kalem, kneeling at her side.

Ebon reached down to help her up. Theren tried

to wave him off, but it was a weak gesture. "I am still dazed," she mumbled, shaking her head as if to clear it, and then wincing as though that had worsened the pain. "Blast that man of yours, Ebon. He strikes like a mule's back hoof."

For a moment Ebon was torn. Theren could not chase Isra, that seemed certain. And without Theren, he and Kalem had no chance against her. But if they let her go . . . his mind filled with the sight of Erin, and the boy's terrified cries as he was dragged away.

Erin. Sky above, the poor boy.

They all started in surprise at the click of the front door's latch. It swung open, whisper quiet. Standing in the frame with a look of wonder was Instructor Dasko.

THIRTY-NINE

WE ARE DOOMED, THOUGHT EBON.

How could he explain this? What possible excuse could there be? The vault was breached, all of the guards were dead, and Isra was nowhere to be found, nowhere to have the blame laid rightly on her head.

And Erin. Poor Erin.

Dasko's brow furrowed. "Ebon. What in all the world are you doing here?"

"I . . ." Ebon's throat was bone-dry, and he swallowed before trying again. "I . . . I guessed that the artifacts were here," he stammered. No, that was wrong,

wrong, *wrong.* "We knew the attack at the Academy was a distraction so that the murderer could steal the artifacts unimpeded. The guards were dead when we arrived. It was Isra from the very beginning—ever since Credell."

"Isra?" Dasko blinked. "The mentalism student? How?" But quickly he shook his head. "No matter. We can sort this out. I will help you, if I can, but you must come with me now. Xain and some other of the faculty are on their way here, along with many constables, and all of this can be laid before them."

Ebon felt the blood drain from his face. Over Kalem's head, Theren met his eyes. *Xain.* Xain, whose son had just been dragged into the streets as Isra's hostage. And constables, who would arrive to find three students in a destroyed home, with every inhabitant murdered.

Suddenly Dasko's eyes narrowed. Ebon looked down to follow his gaze. There in his hand was Kekhit's amulet. He almost dropped it in shock, for he had forgotten he held it.

Dasko stepped back, magelight springing into his eyes. Magic rippled along his limbs, increasing their size, and his skin hardened.

"Where did you get that?" he said, his voice deep and menacing.

"No!" cried Ebon. "I took it from Isra when we fought her. I did not take it from the vault!"

"Drop it," said Dasko in a bestial snarl.

Theren caught Ebon's eye again. She jerked her head. Ebon frowned. Then he caught a frantic motion at the bottom of his vision. Behind Kalem's back, Theren held out her hand.

Ebon swallowed and dropped the amulet into Theren's palm.

"Stop!" cried Dasko, leaping towards them.

"Be still," said Theren.

Dasko froze where he stood.

Theren stepped forwards, licking her lips. "You arrived to find the house empty, but you saw Isra running away through the streets, with Erin in tow. No one was here in the house when you investigated. You never saw us. That is what you will tell Xain and the constables when they arrive. Do you understand?"

"Yes," said Dasko, his voice utterly flat.

"Darkness below, *what are you doing?*" Kalem tried to drag the amulet from Theren's grasp, but she withheld it from him.

"The only thing we can, Kalem." But despite the determined glint in Theren's eye, Ebon could hear the quiver in her voice. "You know we would be blamed for all of this."

"We would not!" cried Kalem. He wrung his hands, pacing. "We could explain. They would believe us. They would *have* to believe us."

Theren gritted her teeth. "The only one who has to believe us is Dasko. And that is because I hold this." She lifted the amulet.

Kalem turned on Ebon. "You cannot agree. You cannot think this is the right course."

"The *right* course, Kalem? There is no right course now. This is the only way forwards that does not end in our torture and death."

They heard shouts from outside, followed by the sound of many boots tramping in the street. Theren blanched.

"We must go," she said. "Out the back door. Run!"

"No," said Kalem. "We must stay."

Theren seized one of his arms, and Ebon took the other. Theren looked over her shoulder. "Leave now, Dasko," she said. "Tell them what I told you, and forget you saw us here."

Dasko nodded. "The house was empty. There was no one here. I saw Isra fleeing through the streets . . ."

They did not wait to hear more, but pulled Kalem out the back door and into the alley beyond. They ran, boots pounding in the mud and snow, churning tracks behind them.

But they were not out of earshot before Ebon heard Xain's keening, anguished wail behind them.

Erin. Sky above. Poor Erin.

They did not stop running.

FORTY

Ebon sat out on the Academy grounds.

It was some days later—days that had passed like a fog while he hardly noticed. Now he had found a private bench buried in some rosebushes, and there he sat, alone. The students and faculty were in the dining hall, eating a mournful supper.

Theren had hidden the amulet somewhere safe—exactly where, Ebon did not know, and did not care to find out.

He had heard nothing from Mako.

The Academy was in an uproar. Half its faculty were

on the hunt for Isra and Erin, as were the constables, and the Mystics, and the High King's guard. Yet the many hundreds of searchers had turned up nothing.

Ebon guessed they were gone. Isra had taken her ill-gotten gains from the Seat and now fled across Underrealm with Erin in tow, to bargain with if ever she was caught.

And it was his fault. At least in part. He knew Isra was mostly to blame for all that had transpired. Yet he had insisted on investigating, and had taken them into Xain's home without help. Mayhap Isra would have escaped with the artifacts, but she almost certainly would not have found Erin.

He buried his face in his hands, rubbing at his eyes. He had hardly slept since that day, for he kept seeing Erin's terrified face. Too, he saw the rage in Mako's eyes, and the unbridled hatred in Isra's. They plagued him worse than Cyrus' death ever had.

When he lifted his face from his hands, he found that he was no longer alone.

There stood Xain, framed in the arch of a hedge and blocking the rest of the grounds from view. That arch was Ebon's only escape, as he was keenly aware. His mind flashed back to last year, when Cyrus had found him in the gardens just like this. Cyrus had struck him, battering him with mindmagic until Ebon thought his body would break. Now his hands balled to fists at his side. Another dean who hated him. And now, mayhap, another attack.

But no glow came to Xain's eyes. And when he lifted a hand, it was not to strike with magic. Instead he threw a piece of cloth upon the ground. The white snow made the cloth stand out in stark relief: it was dark grey, and made of a fine silk that only a wealthy merchant could afford. A shredded cuff from Mako's shirt, ripped free when Isra had flung the barrel at him.

"I know you had something to do with this," said Xain, his voice laced with poisoned steel. "I cannot prove it yet. But I *will*. And when I do, I will end you and all of your kin. I will scour the name of Drayden from Underrealm, and when I am done, only tomes of history will remember you: a footnote scrawled in blood, scorned and spat upon by all who read it."

This was not Cyrus' white-hot rage, nor the blind hatred of Isra. This was something worse, and Ebon found himself more frightened by it than he had ever been before.

Then Xain turned and walked away, vanishing into the citadel.

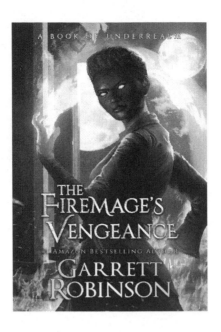

GET THE NEXT BOOK

Where has Isra taken Erin? What will Xain do, now that he thinks Ebon is to blame? Who is helping Isra in her madness?

Find out in *The Firemage's Vengeance,* the next book in the series. Get it here:

Underrealm.net/AJ3

ACKNOWLEDGEMENTS

I won't waste much of your time with this, but it's something I should have included for a long time now.

When I first began the books of Underrealm, it was truly a solo project. I had no beta readers. I didn't even have an editor or a cover designer.

All of that was a huge mistake, of course. And eventually I learned better. Now I produce each book with the assistance of an entire team, and the books are markedly better for it.

First and last, for everything—not just my books—I will always thank my wife Meghan. She went through years of hell so that we could get to where we are now. I owe her all of it, and only want to pamper her for the rest of her life.

My children make me who I am. If someone says that kids are the death knell of a career, you should know they're lying. I would not be writing if it weren't for my kids.

Amy is a somewhat recent friend, but one of the dearest. No one else I know can be so kind (and again, endlessly patient) while also tolerating exactly *none* of my crap. I am slowly learning how exhausting I must be to put up with, and no one impress me with their ability to do so more than Amy does.

On this book, for the first time, I was able to work with Karen Conlin. She has been my dream editor for years, and I could not be more pleased that the dream has finally come true.

My beta readers have saved numerous Underrealm books by this point (I will always tell the story of how *Darkfire* would have killed my career without them). Kristen and Karl in particular—thank you for your incredible feedback. My thanks as well to Dare and Matthew.

To the Vloganovel crew—too many to name them all, but you know who you are—this book would have taken even longer than it did without you. Thank you for being my constant companions on this journey through another world.

Finally—well, not *quite* finally—my readers. When I first started writing, it was hard to believe you existed. I am so grateful you found me. I am so grateful you have remained with me. I'll try to be worthy of you, always.

And now, *actually* finally—Meghan. You are always first. You are always last. And you are always everything in between.

Thank you all.
Garrett, 2016

CONNECT ONLINE

FACEBOOK

Want to hang out with other fans of the Underrealm books? There's a Facebook group where you can do just that. Join the Nine Lands group on Facebook and share your favorite moments and fan theories from the books. I also post regular behind-the-scenes content, including information about the world you can't find anywhere else. Visit the link to be taken to the Facebook group:

Underrealm.net/nine-lands

YOUTUBE

Catch up with me daily (when I'm not directing a film or having a baby). You can watch my daily YouTube channel where I talk about art, science, life, my books, and the world.
But not cats.
Never cats.

GarrettBRobinson.com/yt

THE BOOKS OF UNDERREALM

THE NIGHTBLADE EPIC
NIGHTBLADE
MYSTIC
DARKFIRE
SHADEBORN
WEREMAGE
YERRIN

THE ACADEMY JOURNALS
THE ALCHEMIST'S TOUCH
THE MINDMAGE'S WRATH
THE FIREMAGE'S VENGEANCE

CHRONOLOGICAL ORDER
NIGHTBLADE
MYSTIC
DARKFIRE
SHADEBORN
THE ALCHEMIST'S TOUCH
WEREMAGE
THE MINDMAGE'S WRATH
THE FIREMAGE'S VENGEANCE
YERRIN

ABOUT THE AUTHOR

Garrett Robinson was born and raised in Los Angeles. The son of an author/painter father and a violinist/singer mother, no one was surprised when he grew up to be an artist.

After blooding himself in the independent film industry, he self-published his first book in 2012 and swiftly followed it with a stream of others, publishing more than two million words by 2014. Within months he topped numerous Amazon bestseller lists. Now he spends his time writing books and directing films.

A passionate fantasy author, his most popular books are the novels of Underrealm, including The Nightblade Epic and The Academy Journals series.

However, he has delved into many other genres. Some works are for adult audiences only, such as *Non Zombie* and *Hit Girls,* but he has also published popular books for younger readers, including The Realm Keepers series and *The Ninjabread Man,* co-authored with Z.C. Bolger.

Garrett lives in Oregon with his wife Meghan, his children Dawn, Luke, and Desmond, and his dog Chewbacca.

Garrett can be found on:

BLOG: garrettbrobinson.com/blog
EMAIL: garrett@garrettbrobinson.com
TWITTER: twitter.com/garrettauthor
FACEBOOK: facebook.com/garrettbrobinson

EPILOGUE

ISRA CINCHED THE GAG TIGHTER AND THEN CHECKED the rope binding the boy to the wall. He winced with each tug on the cloth. She ignored it. He was a gold-shitter like the rest of them. Let him suffer. Let him suffer the way his father and the rest of them had made *everyone* suffer.

She raised her cowl and left the room.

The stone hallways stank and made her skin prickle with nerves, and she hated them. She briskly pushed through the stench to the tunnel that led out. This was far too perilous, and she would never have taken the risk. But she must see her patron. Another outcast, like Isra herself. And the only woman who could help, now that the goldshitter Ebon had spoiled her plan.

Soon she stood before an inn. The doorman must have been warned of her arrival, for he gave no second glance despite her shabby clothes. Not Academy clothing—no, she had rid herself of that at the first opportunity. Now she had a plain cloak of brown, and nondescript clothes like any peasant. It let her go unnoticed, and it felt like a return to her roots besides.

But that brought thoughts of Astrea. She shuddered, bowing as she blinked back tears.

Poor Astrea. All alone now.

Not for long. Not if her patron had any help to offer—and she would.

Stairs at the back of the inn's common room led upstairs to rooms for rent. But Isra's patron would not be staying there. Instead Isra turned left, where a storeroom door stood slightly ajar. Inside, there was a carpet in the room's center. This she lifted, revealing a trapdoor that she opened with a flick of her wrist and a flash of magelight in her eyes. Shallow stone steps descended into the ground—but not into darkness, for the way was well-lit by many torches. Down she went, into the earth's bowels, another blast of magic swinging the trapdoor shut behind her.

A narrow corridor led to her patron's room, a guard barring the door. A mammoth man, his fists as big as her head. He had never beheld her with anything but a scowl. His skin, dark as night, only made his glaring eyes stand out the more.

"I must see her," said Isra.

The guard's nostrils flared. But from within the room came a voice. "Let her in."

A ham-sized fist reached out and opened the door. Isra slipped inside, and it closed again behind her.

The room was nothing impressive—certainly far poorer than what her patron was used to. For her patron had once been a goldshitter, just like those who Isra hated. Those who had brought this *war*. But her patron had been cast out, and had learned what Isra had known her whole life: that the true evil in the world was not Drayden, not Yerrin, but all of them at once, and more besides. It was the merchants, the nobility, those who held themselves above their fellows by virtue of coin or a throne.

"I have heard no small amount of whispers." Her patron did not sound angry. If anything, she sounded amused. "It seems plans have gone . . . *most* awry, since last we spoke. You are lucky you came to me when you did. I have business I must attend to in Feldemar, and I leave upon the morrow."

Isra nearly growled. "I lost the amulet, but gained many more artifacts during my escape."

She held up her satchel for a moment before throwing it on the floor at her patron's feet. But she received no reply. Instead, her patron regarded her over steepled fingers.

"And the boy?"

"I took him, as you asked. When can I bring him to you? He whines."

"You will keep him. I cannot have him linked to me."

Isra scowled, but said nothing.

"I thank you for holding up your end of the bargain," her patron went on. "I am a fair woman, and will help you with your aims. You needed the amulet to achieve them, did you not?"

"I did," said Isra. "Without mindwyrd, the task is impossible."

"But would you take that power another way? From magestones?"

Isra paused. Magestones were another matter. She had heard dark tales whispered about the Academy halls since her arrival.

Her patron noticed the hesitation. "I will admit, it would be a . . . different path. Far more dangerous for you. Mayhap even fatal. But it would allow the plan to work. You would have what you desire. An end to this war, and to those who brought it upon your Academy."

"Then that is everything," Isra snarled, fury raging in her gut. "But magestones are worth a fortune, and you are no longer a goldshitter—if you have been telling me true."

Her patron smiled. Then the smile turned into a laugh, and she reached into her cloak, reemerging with a brown cloth packet which she threw at Isra's feet. Isra stooped to retrieve it. Inside, in two neat rows stacked atop each other, were long black gems that she could almost see through. She gazed in wonder.

"It is true I have little in the way of coin, nor the help of my kin who have abandoned me. But I am Damaris, once of the family Yerrin, and my greatest strength has never been the weight of my purse. It is the lengths I will go to achieve my aims. What of you, Isra? Do you have the same strength?"

With shaking fingers, Isra plucked a magestone from the packet and slipped it into her mouth. With a crunch and a swallow, it vanished down her throat.

She opened black eyes, and her lips parted in a rictus.